THE WITCH HOUSE

ANN RAWSON

RED DOG
UK

Published by RED DOG PRESS 2020

Copyright © Ann Rawson 2020

Ann Rawson has asserted her right under the Copyright, Designs and Patents Act, 1988 to be identified as the author of this work

This book is sold subject to the condition that it shall not by way of trade or otherwise, be lent, resold, hired out, or otherwise circulated without the publisher's prior consent in any form of binding or cover other than that in which it is published and without a similar condition including this condition being imposed on the subsequent purchaser

Paperback ISBN 978-1-913331-40-5

Ebook ISBN 978-1-913331-41-2

Hardback ISBN 978-1-913331-42-9

www.reddogpress.co.uk

For all witches and outcasts, everywhere and everywhen.

ONE

THE DAY I found Harry's body started well.

It was one of those bright, autumnal mornings that still feels like summer and I was happy. I had my life back. A different life, granted, but one in which I could do my own thing. I was determined to enjoy every moment.

Listen to me. I sound as if I've swallowed whole all the positive thinking tripe they shoved down our throats in group therapy. Kelly would take the piss if I told her. 'Positive self-talk!' she'd say, pointing and laughing. She'd tell me I'd been brainwashed into the psych ward cult and she'd cackle with delight – so long as she wasn't numbed by her meds already.

I'd promised to visit Kelly in the afternoon. She was back in Brookfields, poor cow. Ah, there it was. A momentary sense of unease, as I was reminded that my freedom might also be temporary.

I've never claimed to be clairvoyant. Grandma did, and she could be convincing. What else would you expect from the witch who lived in the Witch House? Not that I believed her. Whatever. It's not a hereditary trait – or if it is, it passed me by.

Meanwhile, the whole morning was my own. A picnic breakfast on the cliffs, and then to the shops, to find a treat for Kelly. I tossed a couple of cereal bars and an apple in my rucksack and filled up my water bottle.

I was on my way out when the phone rang. For a moment I lingered on the threshold, then stepped back inside and picked it up.

How I wish I hadn't. Good behaviour never turns out well for me.

It was my mother, of course. She was on her way to Cuckmere and she'd like to see me. I started to count to ten, then realised it wouldn't be enough.

"A bit more warning would have helped. I promised I'd visit Kelly today."

"I'm your mother, Alice. Do I have to make an appointment? You can put her off. You've put me off often enough."

The injustice was breath-taking. How many times had she visited me in hospital? Not many, except when she wanted something.

"She's relying on me," I said, through gritted teeth.

"As am I." Her tone was sharp.

I took a deep breath. "Visiting hours aren't until three," I said. "I'm off to the shops now, but I'll only be an hour or so."

"See you later, then," she said. "It's been far too long."

Funny how she made that sound like my fault.

In my childhood it had been a different story – then, I'd longed to see more of her. Much as I loved Grandma, I'd wanted my mother – the way we always want what we can't have.

I cast around for something to say that wouldn't start a row, but the silence lasted too long and she hung up.

I'm nothing at all like my mother.

Helen Hunter – how best to sum her up? Tall, elegant and always immaculately coiffured. Think Lauren Bacall. Dressed like she runs a boutique that sells vintage couture. As she does, in a rare fit of enthusiasm, or in the gap between assistant managers. My mother doesn't play nicely with others, or not for long. It's not just me.

When I was little, I adored her. I begged to be allowed to brush her thick, blonde hair. I thought one day I would grow out of my ugly duckling phase and turn into a swan.

Now, I'm perpetually in jeans and tee shirt, casual to the point of scruffy, topped off with tousled mousy hair. It's not much of a rebellion, but at twenty-two I'm mostly a disappointment. Even

Grandma, who loved me, called me a changeling. And still I can't help longing for Helen's approval, even though I know what I know. Enough of this self-indulgence. Helen was only checking up on me, making sure I was coping. At least she cared.

I caught the bus into town. I needed to buy some treats for Kelly, and I needed to ease myself back into the everyday world of busy streets and shops.

The shop was unlikely to be crowded so early, but I peered through the window to check. Then I took a deep breath and braced myself. Surely, I could hold the anxiety at bay long enough to pick out a few smellies? The automatic doors opened with exquisite slowness, taunting me. There was still time to funk it, turn tail and flee.

I grabbed a basket and held it in front of me, like a shield.

Choosing suitable gifts for Kelly was more challenging than I'd expected. I walked slowly through the perfumed fug, and checked out a few bottles, making sure there were no sharp edges, no breakable glass.

The noise level increased, and the aisle seemed narrower, as the shop filled up with a gaggle of schoolgirls.

Breathe in, count to four slowly, breathe out, count and relax.

They were all dressed in the familiar navy blazer with the Latin motto on the breast pocket. Laughing and joking, loud and shallow. That was me, three, no four years ago. I have to keep reminding myself I've lost a year.

One girl bumped into me, and I bit back the automatic impulse to apologise. I am allowed to take up space in the world.

Time to leave.

I took my place in the queue. The shop wasn't designed for the comfort and convenience of shoppers, but to maximise display space and profits. There simply wasn't enough room.

My skin prickled all over, I felt hot, crowded. I could sense the woman behind urging me forwards, even though there was nowhere to go.

"Wake up, you dozy muppet. That bugger pushed in."

I look round at the woman breathing down my neck – her face red, her voice becoming louder and more insistent.

She elbows me, pushing me forward. "Tell him to wait his turn," she says.

At the till, a man. Tall, well dressed – sharp suit, silk tie, impeccably polished shoes. Vaguely familiar. Definitely intimidating.

The woman behind pushes me. She actually pushes me. I consider pushing back, but I don't. I keep my eyes forward, looking down, trapped in between them.

It was too late anyway; he was already putting his card in the scanner. I watched the routine, waiting until it was my turn.

I lifted my basket – a box of tissues, some luxury bath oils, some pampering body lotion – on to the counter. The girl started to scan. Then she stopped, holding the tissues uselessly in the air. There was nowhere to put them. The man who pushed in hadn't moved his shopping out of the way. He was standing there, yapping away on his mobile phone, oblivious to the fact that he was holding everyone up. He didn't even know we existed. The girl on the till tried to catch his attention. He covered the mouthpiece and said, "Excuse me, can't you see I'm on the phone?"

I recognised him from somewhere. The dark floppy hair. The patrician face – sharp cheekbones, and one supercilious eyebrow raised.

Ah, yes. He was one of the Stockman clan. Mark. Property developer and recently elected MP for Cuckmere.

Grandma would have sighed for the old days – his father would never have been so badly behaved, nor his aunt. She taught them better than that, as she taught me.

I still miss her, difficult as she was.

The cashier shrugs. The woman behind taps her feet impatiently.

No. I can't do it. I can't breathe. It's all too much. My mother, the shop full of idiots, and now Mark Bloody Stockman.

"Sorry," I say, so quietly that I doubt anyone could hear. "Got to go."

I looked down, careful not to catch anyone's eye. If I couldn't see them...

As the door closed behind me, I could feel them all watching, hear them laughing. This time there was no room for doubt. They were laughing at me.

TWO

I'VE ALWAYS BEEN an introvert – or as Grandma would have it, shy – but this extreme social anxiety is new. Before her death, it never stopped me from doing anything I wanted. Now, navigating any crowded space is difficult, but shops are the worst. The rush of people overwhelms me, making it hard to find enough oxygen to breathe. I am trapped, my heart starts to beat faster, I feel my face glowing red heat and I know everyone is looking at me, watching and waiting for me to crack.

Breathe. Relax. Breathe. I counted the breaths in, and out again.

Thank the goddess and all that is sacred, I would get my time alone before my mother arrived. After enduring those months of being constantly monitored, I deserved some peaceful time on the cliffs to regain my equilibrium.

I walked down to the seafront. As I paused and gazed out to the horizon, I could feel my forehead relax and the tension dissolve. The sea was a dark grey-green slate; the sky slightly overcast. The moods of the sea change every day, but it is always there, deep and constant.

The white cliffs rise at the eastern end of the promenade and the road bends inland, taking an easy sweeping curve around the hill, the Beacon. On the other side, it's possible to walk the whole way under the cliffs, at low tide. The first part is concreted path, an extension of the promenade, but the rest requires scrabbling across stretches of pebbled beach and the occasional rock pool. In bad weather it can be dangerous, as chunks of chalk crumble away from the cliff, and smash on to the beach below.

I took the middle route, over the hill. The Roman way. Up the worn grassy path on the long slow incline of the cliff. After the initial gentle slope, the path became steeper. I pressed on, a little more slowly. I could feel the muscles in the back of my legs take the strain. I would have to rebuild the fitness I'd lost in hospital. There were rabbit holes around the path, and every so often I could see a rabbit thump off down the hill away from me.

I paused and turned back, to catch my breath and enjoy the view. I could see the streets of the old town laid out before me. In the far distance were the suburbs, the concentric semi-circles of bungalows and their green patchwork gardens that overflow the boundaries of old Cuckmere. To the north, the less salubrious part of town where a few old apartment buildings and red brick houses are squashed more closely together, with much less green to separate them. In the distance, the countryside was dotted with sheep.

The sun came out from behind the clouds, making everything clearer and brighter. I wished I had more time to stop, take my sketchbook out, and get in some drawing practice. Knowing the London train was bringing my impending doom closer and closer, I pressed on instead. Over the first hill, when the steep path levelled out again, I passed the first of the concrete gun emplacements, relics of the Second World War. Beyond, I could see a tall brick building with a glass enclosed top floor, the Coastguard lookout point.

Local historians tell us that there has been some kind of lookout on Cuckmere Beacon for a very long time. Neolithic, Iron Age, Roman. Now it's a nature reserve – purchased by the locals, a subscription raised from every household half a century ago to preserve it from the developers. People like Mark Stockman, for whom land was merely another resource to be squeezed for profit.

Kittiwakes nest in the cliffs below, warblers and woodpeckers in the woods on slopes falling away inland. Between the hawthorn, brambles and blackthorn, an orchid or two thrives, rarely noticed. There are lizards and grass snakes, and always rabbits, and more rabbits.

I've always been fascinated by the past, by the urge to reconstruct stories from the few pieces of the jigsaw that remain. It was an interest, an obsession even, that I shared with Grandma, ever since the day I found a Roman coin here on the hill behind our home. I reached up to check it was hanging round my neck on its gold chain – my talisman, something else I'd had to give up in hospital.

I ducked and made my way to the very spot I'd found it, through a tunnel of brambles and wild roses, sloes and stunted apple trees. In moments I came out into a huge, semi-circular clearing on the cliffs, illuminated by the clear autumn sunshine. A place where I spent so much time in my childhood – both alone and with Grandma.

I walked towards the large flat rock in the middle of the space. On a fine day like this, I would often sit on the grass in front of it, watching the sea and the sky, dozing and daydreaming.

Out of nowhere, my heart started beating faster. Something was deeply wrong. I sensed an otherworldly presence hanging in the air.

On the stone in front of me, a rabbit. Dead. Splayed open down its undercarriage, and spread eagled, staked through its heart with a sharp stick.

What monster did this? The sick, sick bastard. Defiling this sanctuary.

I was possessed by rage, then disgust.

Pulling myself together, I looked more closely. Wax residue, black, on the north side of the stone. All around the sides, fresh chalk markings, demonic looking sigils and pentagrams.

Not this again. After last time, I wanted nothing to do with it.

Channelling my rage, I forced myself to grab hold of the stick, firmly, but carefully keeping the rabbit attached. I threw the skewered rabbit away down the hill, down the cliff. It couldn't have been there long, blood dripped and sprayed on the grass. There was a stain too on the stone where it had lain.

I rummaged in my pockets, took out a wipe, and scrubbed away the black wax and most of the chalk markings. Too late, I realised I should have taken a photograph first.

If Grandma were alive, she would do some kind of cleansing ritual. I'd done what I could, but I checked my rucksack. As usual, Grandma's picnic set was at the bottom. I unzipped the leather case and took out the little silver salt shaker. Feeling a little self-conscious, I walked around the clearing sprinkling salt and vowing silently to deal with whoever was responsible.

I retraced my steps through the bushes and made my way to the next gun emplacement, a few hundred yards further on. There I sat down, and closed my eyes and repeated the breathing exercise until I had myself under control.

Ignoring the winding tarmac path down to the main road, the fastest route, I took the other path and walked past the signs that warned of danger and falling rocks. The track was steep in places, but with care, it was perfectly safe.

Out to sea the lighthouse stood guard at the end of the Victorian harbour wall. A short walk around the paths at the foot of the cliff took me to the old promenade, where I paused to catch my breath again.

I looked around, hoping to find Harry Rook, the owner of the West Beach Cafe and Amusement Park. He wasn't in his usual spot, in the cabin by the entrance, wearing his distinctive red jacket, collecting car parking money and selling fishing and camping permits. Casual visitors, bumping into him as he wandered apparently aimlessly, would never guess he was the proprietor.

Tall, with a shock of white hair, he'd been a constant background presence in my life for as long as I could remember. Now, to my surprise, he had a more central role. I wasn't looking forward to telling him about the rabbit, to bringing back all those dark memories I'd prefer to leave undisturbed, but he needed to know. Perhaps the police needed to know, too. If so, I'd rather Harry dealt with them.

There was no sign of Harry; no glimpse of red anywhere.

Maybe he was on the beach? There was a simple old-fashioned iron railing protecting a sheer twenty-foot drop, and in the middle an opening on to old concrete steps down to a proper sandy beach. One of the few sandy beaches for miles around.

The steps were a bit crumbly and cracked in places, but still safe enough, with a secure iron railing to grab. In the middle of summer, it would be bustling with families with children, but out of season there were only a few fishermen, the odd walker, and me. Today, it was deserted.

I wondered if there'd been any particular trouble lately, while I was in hospital. No one would have told me then – that was for sure. But I knew Harry would be as concerned as I was. It felt good, I realised, that there was someone I trusted. Someone I could rely on.

The cafe was open so perhaps Tamsin would know where Harry was. Anyway, I'd been cheated of my picnic spot, so a coffee would be more than welcome.

Tammy was my best friend once. Still is, I hope. Tall and with glossy brown hair, she's always been sleek and fashionable – the kind of daughter my mother would have preferred, as she frequently mentioned. We had plenty in common, not just the beach and the Beacon. We'd played together as children, done homework together and passed our exams together. I'd not seen her much since I'd been back home, though she had visited me in hospital a couple of times.

There were few people around to keep Tammy busy in the late autumn and winter, although the café usually overflowed in summer. The remnants of the small fairground were already wrapped up in their winter clothes. The dodgems under tarpaulin, the hoopla and shooting booths shuttered and closed, the amusement arcade with its old-fashioned pinball machines and penny one-armed bandits was locked. At the far end the children's playground, the painted wooden roundabout, the swings, the see-saw, the climbing frame – all were deserted.

I took a deep breath and pushed the cafe door open, making the bells ring. Apart from Tamsin there was no one there.

"Good to see you open," I said, sitting at the counter on a stool, and smiling at her.

She didn't look up or say hello.

I persevered. "I was hoping I might find Harry here," I said. I paused, not wanting to worry her with the details. "There's been kids causing trouble on the Beacon, so I was wondering if he'd had any problems down here."

"Not that I've heard," she said. "Not seen Harry today, either."

She seemed offhand with me, but maybe I was being oversensitive. I asked for a coffee and a muffin. Mother wasn't due for at least an hour.

As the coffee machine hissed and gurgled, I picked the caramelised walnut off the top of my muffin.

"So why are you open?" I asked, as Tamsin put a mug of latte down in front of me. "Aren't you having one too?"

"Too busy," she said, still brusque. "Someone's coming to view the property later, and I have to spruce it up. Make it look like a thriving concern."

"Are you selling up?" I was surprised.

"We've had an offer," she said. "Aunt Julia wants Harry to sell. It's quite a generous offer."

"But you don't want to," I guessed.

She looked at me blankly and didn't answer, and turning her back on me again, carried on wiping down surfaces.

Something was wrong. The muffin was dry in my mouth, and I couldn't swallow. She didn't want to talk to me, and I didn't know why. Could it be to do with the nasty little ritual on the Beacon? I started my breathing exercises. Slowly breathing in, and counting, and slowly exhaling.

I had to be careful – the paranoia was building. She was busy, that was all. Worried about the viewing, her future. She would talk to me when she was ready. Not everything is about me.

"Well, I'd better be going," I said, finishing off my coffee. "If you see Harry, will you tell him I'm looking for him?"

She barely nodded.

"Anyway, I'd best get a move on, I'm expecting my mother."

I didn't mention Brookfields. Even with a friend like Tamsin, I couldn't take the look of concern, in case I'd gone off my head again. Perhaps that was why I was becoming more comfortable with Harry. He was one of the few people who'd seen me there, on the locked ward, who still acted normally with me.

I picked up my rucksack, swung it over my shoulder – being careful not to knock anything off the gingham clad tables – and waved as I left.

Some of my happiest memories were of summer holidays when my time was divided between wandering on the cliffs, or down here at the amusement park. Sometimes on my own, sometimes with Tamsin, or Grandma.

Grandma would often let me loose with a stack of old pennies, which you had to buy at the booth, to play on the ancient one-armed bandits. Every day I played until I lost everything, no matter how many times I won. I suppose there was a lesson in that. It was weird though, the way we spent so much time here, and never once did I see Grandma talk to Harry or Julia.

I walked along by the railings and smiled as the herring gulls peeled off one by one, moments in advance of my passing by. Some things stayed the same.

The place was deserted. A solitary fisherman still on the harbour wall, no parked camper vans, and no sign of Harry. The barrier was up and the stop sign was out by his hut, where he usually sat collecting car parking fees and selling fishing permits. His truck was parked there too, in its usual spot to one side, so it wouldn't block the way in or out.

Again I had that feeling there was something wrong.

Nerves strumming with tension, I walked towards the door of the hut, hoping desperately to see him sitting with his paper and Sudoku puzzle, or eating one of Julia's homemade sandwiches or pies.

He was there.

Harry.

My breath caught in the back of my throat, and I choked back rising panic.

Lying on the ground, with his hand on his heart. In the centre of a pentagram chalked on the tarmac. Everything was silent. All I could hear was my own heartbeat, drumming away in my chest.

He was gone. Harry was gone.

There was blood, too. Just a little. And another sharp stick, piercing his hand, through the palm. Exactly like the one that skewered the rabbit.

Without thinking, I grasped the stick. It lifted his arm off his chest, and I could see the point emerging through the back of his hand. I pulled, and it wouldn't budge, so I pushed the point with my finger and thumb.

Stupid, stupid, stupid. My finger dripped blood on the stick, on the ground. But it came out and I laid it down next to him, on top of a pile of coiled wire. Rabbit snares, perhaps.

What did it matter? Why was my mind registering this trivia?

I stumbled to my feet, and felt blindly in my pocket for my mobile, called 999 and asked for an ambulance, the police. I answered the questions impatiently. The responder asked me to check for a pulse, and I told her I already had. I was sure he was dead.

My finger was still dripping blood. As fast as I could, I backed away, walked twenty feet over to the grassy patch on the other side of the road way in. Then I threw up.

I grabbed another wipe from my pocket, thoroughly cleaned my hands and then put it in one of the burned-out oil drums that served as bins, and inadvertently, as feeding troughs for the gulls. The rancid, greasy reek of old chip papers made me retch again.

THREE

I COLLAPSED ON the nearest bench, pressing a tissue against the open wound, trying to staunch the bleeding, as I waited for the paramedics and police.

Thoughts whirled around in my head, on constant repeat. At least that kept my feelings at bay.

Helen wouldn't be in Brighton yet, then it would take her another thirty minutes out to Cuckmere. I thought about calling her mobile, but decided I couldn't face an inquisition. I'd be home soon enough – with any luck, before she arrived.

I wouldn't get to Brookfields to see Kelly now. I couldn't phone and explain, either. She'd read the stress in my voice and find some way to spin it into a paranoid fantasy. I could let one of the staff know, but they might easily make things worse. Anyway, it went against my deepest instincts to give them more power – the power of knowledge withheld over my already powerless friend. I hated that, when it happened to me. I'd have to deal with it later.

My panic was revived by the sound of sirens getting closer, coming down Beacon Road, past the new luxury apartments, the pub, past my home and Harry and Julia's place. The yellow paramedic van arrived first and blocked the exit by the far side of Harry's hut. A police car followed.

I stood and walked reluctantly back in their direction. The paramedics were already bending over Harry, but after the first flurry, there was no sense of urgency in their movements as they pulled back. The uniformed policemen from the patrol car started making busy with crime scene tape, after a hurried discussion about boundaries. They decided to block the way for traffic on the near side of the hut too, by the open door.

There was only one car in the parking area, apart from Harry's truck, and that probably belonged to the distant fisherman.

I felt useless. Invisible.

Another car pulled up, and a man got out – tall, with short cropped dark hair, but casually dressed. A detective, I thought, as he stopped to chat to the uniformed policemen, then took a close look at Harry. The victim.

The detective seemed familiar, but I couldn't quite place him. Perhaps it was just the situation, which seemed so unreal, like a TV detective show.

It was clear from the body language he was in charge.

He came over and introduced himself.

"DI Collingwood," he said. He offered his hand, but I couldn't bring myself to take it. I awkwardly stepped back, conscious of the blood-stained tissue stuck to my finger.

His face hardened, his grey eyes turned cold as he registered my inability to shake his hand, and took it as a snub.

"I take it you're the person who found the body. Where's your dog?" he asked.

"What dog?" I asked, bewildered.

"My little joke," he said.

"Not very funny," I said. "How do you know I found the body?"

I was making it difficult for myself, I knew. But I couldn't help it. My previous encounter with the police had not gone my way.

He looked around and shrugged. "No one else here, is there? Unless you reckon he called it in and went back to his fishing."

"Of course it was me," I said. "I'm shocked, angry, devastated. I liked Harry. He's been good to me. I've known him forever."

I was a second or two away from total meltdown. I started my breathing exercises again, closing my eyes.

"Are you alright?" he asked, at last showing a bit of sensitivity. "Let's walk, that will help. Gives the adrenalin something to do."

"Good idea," I said, and started to walk towards the railings. I could always grab them if I felt unsteady.

"Tell me about him." He carried on with the questions. That was his job, I supposed. Not looking after me. "Harry what? And what's your name?"

"Alice Hunter," I said, watching as he wrote it in his notebook. "Harry Rook. You must know him. He owns all of this." I gestured to the cafe, the amusement arcade, the play area. "I've known Harry forever. He worked here back when I was a little girl. He lives in the big old Victorian house you drove past, the one with the little turret. With Julia, his wife. Someone should tell Julia."

"Okay," he said. "We'll take care of all that, don't worry. Let's go over how you found him."

I let go of the railing, and started to walk along the prom. He was right, moving made me feel better.

"Why were you here?"

"I walked back from town over the Beacon. I live on this side of the road, opposite the Rook place. The detached house. It was my Grandma's home, until – well, she died last year. She'd lived here for ages, since my mother was a toddler."

He looked dubious, and who could blame him? Why was I telling him my family history? I was rambling on like an idiot. He wrote it down, all the same.

"I was looking for Harry," I said. "I checked out the cafe, had a coffee with Tammy—"

I changed direction, towards the cafe. "I didn't think. No one's told Tamsin. She'll be heartbroken."

DI Collingwood put his hand on my sleeve. I recoiled, and he let go.

"Not yet," he said. "The moment she comes out and sees us, we'll talk to her. It won't hurt, keeping her in the dark a little longer."

He was right.

I swallowed and nodded. But why hadn't she heard the sirens? Why wasn't she out here already? I kept my doubts unspoken. "I asked her if she'd seen him and she said not today. Which was odd. I should have realised."

I remembered the strange mood she'd been in; how distant she'd seemed. I didn't say that out loud, either.

"Why did you want him?'

"There was a rabbit on the Beacon. Dead. Nasty. Staked out with sharp wooden spikes, as if it had been tortured."

"Like the wooden stake by Harry?" he asked. Gentler now, coaxing.

"Exactly the same." I said. I took a breath. There was no one else to tell him – it would have to be me.

"In the clearing at the top," I said, falteringly. "There's a flat stone. There was a rabbit on there, like a sacrifice. Candle wax. The lot."

He looked bemused.

"There's a pagan tradition in the whole area," I said. "Goes way back. Some of my family too…" My voice trailed off, as I remembered all the things I didn't want to talk about.

He raised his eyebrows.

"Not me," I said too quickly, no doubt alerting him that there was something to find out. "My grandmother was involved – many, many years ago. Lots of locals were. Even the Stockmans. You know, our MP? His grandfather was… well. But lately, in the past couple of years – maybe longer, there's been trouble. The police were involved. It looked like someone was trying to revive the old ways, but it had a viciousness to it. The ritual sacrifice of small animals. Rabbits, mostly. Vandalism in the parish church, and the graveyard. I don't think they ever found out who it was. I don't suppose a few rabbits mattered enough for a proper investigation."

"It matters now," he said.

"What Grandma was involved with," I said. "And old Mr Stockman. It was more a religious thing, an appreciation of the natural world and the turning of the seasons. Ceremony and tradition. A spiritual path. This violence is not the same – although some people thought it was."

I was being defensive. That was another reason Tammy was not just my best friend, but almost my only friend when I was growing up. Being the granddaughter of Cuckmere's renowned witch, living in the Witch House, as it was known, had not been a route to popularity.

"I thought it was kids playing stupid games again. I was looking for Harry, so he could keep an eye out for them. It's my fault – if I'd been quicker, if I hadn't stopped to clean up after them, I could have stopped this."

"No," he said firmly. "Don't think like that. Let's not rush to any conclusions. The blood on the stake may not all be Harry's. Your rabbit killer could merely have found the body and run off."

After taking the time to chalk a pentagram? I thought not.

"The blood on the stake, some of it is mine," I said, holding my hand out, showing him the bloodied tissue. "It was stuck through his hand, through the palm. I know I shouldn't have, but I couldn't leave it there."

He frowned but said nothing. He called over one of the paramedics and stood back as my finger was disinfected and then bandaged up. I promised the paramedic my tetanus jab was up to date and he grunted. Then DI Collingwood produced an evidence bag for my blood-soaked tissue, which the paramedic bagged before going back to the ambulance.

"I know it was stupid," I said. "I shouldn't have." I choked back a sob, slipped off my rucksack, and sank onto the nearest bench.

He looked like he was going to pat me on the arm again, but he held back. Not as lacking in empathy as I'd thought then. A tad more kindness and I'd break down completely. I couldn't bear this. Losing control in front of people.

"I'm sorry," he said. "I'm going to have to ask you to take me to this rabbit."

"I moved it."

He couldn't hold back an exasperated sigh.

"Not fair," I said. "That was before I found Harry. I couldn't have known. I didn't want it to upset anyone."

He grinned at me, and I smiled back, almost forgetting, for a moment or two, the horror of the situation. Grandma would have said he was too young and handsome to be a detective. His charm works on most people, I expect. I shivered. I had a kind of premonition that DI Collingwood could be dangerous to me. I would have to be careful around him.

"Feel up to taking me over there now?"

"Sure," I said, standing up and putting my rucksack back on.

"Hang on a minute," he said. "I'll make sure that someone goes to talk to the woman in the cafe, and let them know where to send Scene of Crime."

"We're going up there," I said, pointing in the general direction of the path where I'd walked down the cliffs.

We walked towards the cliff path, past the information board with all the pictures of the local wildlife. He gave it a cursory glance and looked away. He caught my smile.

"What?" he said. "A gull's a gull. That's all I need to know."

"These are kittiwakes," I said, waving a hand towards their nesting area in the cliffs. "The ones back there are herring gulls."

"Doesn't make a difference, does it? I'm not going to charge them with anything."

A few more yards and we reached the bottom of the steep path. A notice said, "Beware of falling rocks. Do not use this path. Danger."

He looked down at his smart leather shoes, looked at the slightly muddy path, looked at me and shook his head.

"I don't suppose I have any choice."

"It's not that bad, going up," I said. "We can take the longer walk down the far side of the hill after you've seen, well, the spot where the rabbit was killed. I think that would be better anyway."

I really didn't want to end up responsible for the accidental death of a policeman.

I went first. Going uphill wasn't so slippery and he didn't have any trouble keeping up with me. He was barely affected by the brisk pace, especially considering he'd been worried about his footwear. Perhaps he was more worried about damage to the shoes than to him.

"Not far now," I said. "Over the next hilly bit, by the gun emplacement."

He followed me on to the grass by the side of the path and he slipped. I held out my hand to steady him, but he brushed it aside, clambered back up on to the path, pretending like a cat that he'd meant to do it that way all along.

Then I led him along the path through the bushes to the opening, and stood on one side watching as he took in the scene, looking at the large flat stone, and then walking to the cliff.

"This is where you found the rabbit?" he asked.

"There was candle wax too. I cleaned up the altar.'" I saw an eyebrow rise reflexively at my choice of word. I rummaged in my rucksack, and found the wipes I'd used. "Is this of any use as evidence?" I asked. He took it wordlessly and put it in a bag and then his pocket, and went back to examining the scene. I didn't tell him about the salt. How would they know that was me, even if they found it? I really didn't want to explain what it meant.

"What did you do with it?" he asked.

"I flipped it down the hill, that way," I said, pointing. "I used the wooden skewer."

I shuddered.

"Thanks," he said. "Pity you moved it but you weren't to know."

He took a deep breath and looked out over the sea, as I had done earlier. Even defiled, the peacefulness of the temple exerted its effect on him. I could see his tension dissipate. Maybe my banishing had worked its magic, a little.

"I've never been up here before," he said.

"How long have you lived round here?" I asked.

He shrugged. "Long enough."

He looked at his phone. "Wonder if I'll get a signal?" He did.

I looked away, pretending not to be listening, as he spoke to someone, presumably one of the uniformed cops he'd left with Harry. "I've marked the location with a bit of crime scene tape so the Scientific Support Team can find it. It's off the beaten track, in a kind of clearing. You have to walk under some trees towards the clifftop. The rabbit's gone, it was staked out on a big flat stone. Probably not important but if anyone fancies scrambling down the cliff, they could get lucky, I suppose. Otherwise, fingertip search around the clearing, see if anything turns up. And a thorough look at the flat stone, which appears to have been used for ritual purposes."

He turned to me. "I do hope you were right about the easy way down. Where does it come out? Then I can get Sergeant Parrish to pick me up."

"The far side of the Harbour View pub," I said.

"You get that, Bob?" he asked.

He hung up and put the phone back in his pocket.

"Lead on," he said.

Silently we climbed up as far as the Coastguard lookout at the top. From there it was a steep but easy walk down a winding tarmac path to the main road.

"What next?" I asked.

He looked at me blankly; not my business.

"I meant, do you need a formal statement from me?"

"Oh," he said, "Yes, I should have said. You can drop into the station tomorrow if you like."

"I'd rather get it done with," I said. "Tomorrow I have to do what I should have done today." And if I could miss my mother, that would be a bonus. I knew better than to say that out loud.

He looked at me blankly again. Clearly, he wasn't used to people talking to him like a human being. Perhaps there was a reason for that.

We carried on to the end of the path in silence. At the bottom, the police car was parked by the pub. One of the uniformed policemen was leaning against it, watching us approach. He stood up straight when DI Collingwood spoke to him.

They talked together for a while. Apparently, the forensics team were at the scene, and more officers were with Tamsin.

Finally, the DI turned to me. "I need to go back to the scene for a minute or two. You can wait in the car, and then we'll go back to the station and take your statement. Or we can drop you off there first, if you prefer?"

"No, it's fine," I said. "I can show you Harry's home. And I need to see if my mother's arrived…"

He looked hassled, so I gave up on that idea, and climbed into the back seat of the police car. The walk had calmed me some, but it was still a struggle to keep anxiety at bay, so I paid attention to my breathing while I waited for them to finish up at the crime scene. There was no sign of Helen anywhere, to my great relief.

As we came to an abrupt halt outside the police station, I had that eerie sense of déjà vu. I was in a police car looking at the back of DI Collingwood's head. I finally remembered where I knew him from.

The last time I'd been sitting in the back of a police car. The last time I'd seen the back of his head. The day I was admitted to Brookfields. The day I was sectioned.

I guessed he remembered me. Damn.

FOUR

DI COLLINGWOOD WAS taking his time. I'd brushed off his offer to call my solicitor – it was only a witness statement. I was stuck in a small interview room, with a mug of surprisingly good coffee. There was no one standing guard over me, and I was there voluntarily, but I felt trapped.

I was being foolish. That view of the back of his head must have triggered memories of being detained against my will last time.

All I could think about was finding Harry's body, and that wooden stake through his hand. Surely that hadn't been what killed him?

I'd seen worse than that in hospital. One patient had been an avid knitter, until the day she had calmly pushed a bamboo knitting needle through the palm of her hand. I was quite relieved when they took her knitting needles away. It might have been relaxing for her, but the constant click clacking of the needles drove me crazy. If there's one place where it's a bad idea to be crazy, it's on a mental health unit.

I drained the last sip of my coffee and took another look at my phone. I'd been stuck in that small grey room for what seemed like an age but was actually less than a quarter of an hour. I'd tried to call my mother a couple of times but there was no answer. I'd failed to do what she expected of me, and now she was punishing me.

I wondered how Tamsin was coping. In spite of the strange coldness between our families, she was still my oldest friend. Maybe even because of it – we're both rebellious. I couldn't help worrying about her, and I was still anxious about how she'd seemed so withdrawn from me lately.

Maybe it was because I'd been ill, or maybe it was because I'd grown closer to Harry since Grandma died. Everyone, including me, had been surprised when it turned out that he'd agreed to be a trustee, to oversee the Personal Management Company Grandma had set up. Tamsin might be jealous, but he was still her uncle (well great uncle, technically) while I was merely a legal obligation. Yet we had started to become friends – I trusted Harry, and I don't give my trust easily.

I decided not to mention it to DI Collingwood. It was an irrelevance. I'd just happened to find his body. Also, when people find out I'm loaded it changes how they treat me. It happened at school – another reason why Tammy and I became close. It may not be quite as bad as the stigma attached to being crazy, but still, it's uncomfortable. Yep, rich girl privilege. I have it covered.

Harry was dead. In my mind I saw him again, lying there on the grass. The stake. The blood. He was dead and I was sitting in a drab room in a police station with my brain spilling over with nonsense, and there was nothing, nothing that could make this better.

I couldn't just sit here. I needed time on my own. Time to let go, to feel, to cry. Without anyone watching me and passing judgement.

I stood up, scraping the chair legs across the floor. I opened the door, and the young female constable, who was sitting outside, stood up. Someone was watching me.

She spoke, "He won't be long, Miss. He called to say he's on his way back."

"Okay," I said. "Only I could always come in tomorrow if he's busy."

"I'd wait, if I were you," she said. "It will take up less of your time."

I went back into the interview room, sat down and started to do my relaxation exercise. Breathe in to a count of four… I hadn't even reached the first 'Breathe out' when the door opened and DI Collingwood walked in, with the policewoman from the corridor.

"Sorry to keep you waiting, but I thought it might be more efficient if I didn't leave it to DC King to take your statement. Saves me having to get back to you if I have any questions."

That seemed a bit diligent for a simple witness statement, but thorough was good. Harry was dead. A wave of grief washed over me.

"I spoke to Julia Rook," he said. "Tamsin is with her and other family members are on their way. Sergeant Parrish will stay with them, until the Family Liaison Officer is assigned."

"How are they?" I asked.

"Harry's brother is going to identify the body, as the widow isn't up to it. How well do you know her?"

"Hardly at all. Enough to nod to in the street." That was overstating it. Julia always completely blanked me, so any nodding would have been superfluous. "Tamsin and I were at school together. Best friends. But I hardly know Julia at all."

"That's a bit odd, isn't it?" he asked. "You grew up in the house directly opposite theirs. Neighbours."

"Not odd to me," I said. "My grandmother just didn't get on with Julia. They had nothing in common. Julia was all domestic goddess and charity lunches. Grandma was a businesswoman. Independent."

It didn't sound convincing said out loud. DI Collingwood looked at me, as if waiting for a better explanation. If there was one, I didn't know what it was.

"Okay," he said. "Let's get started. DC King, set up the recording equipment please, and will you take notes?"

DC King settled at the table with a pad of witness interview forms, and started to write, starting with my name and address.

DI Collingwood looked thoughtful, watching me. Then we went through it all in excruciating detail. From the phone call from my mother right the way to finding the body, and the moment he'd arrived at the scene.

"Will that be all?" I asked, after I'd read through DC King's notes and signed them. I tried to sound relaxed, but I was desperate to get away from his watchful gaze.

There was another silence, and the policewoman looked questioningly at him too.

"One more thing," he said. "It would be helpful if we could have a DNA sample, for elimination purposes, as you were at the scene."

"You have my blood," I pointed out, "Isn't that good enough?"

"Routine," he said. "You're not under caution, this is all voluntary. There's no compulsion. But you did say you'd do anything you could to help."

I opened my mouth and tried not to flinch as DC King wiped the cotton bud on the inside of my cheek.

FIVE

IT WAS TOO late to visit Kelly, and I certainly wasn't up to facing Brookfields.

On the steps of the police station, I checked my phone. There were still no missed calls from my mother. I left another message, saying I'd be home in half an hour and apologising for being late, but I couldn't help hoping she'd gone back to London.

The short walk home passed in a daze. I paid attention to my surroundings, a kind of mindfulness meditation, to keep my thoughts and emotions under control. I walked past the small parade of shops. The co-op, the off licence, the takeaway. Then the new marina development.

During those difficult months I was caring for my grandmother, as her bright colours and sharp edges had faded and dulled before my eyes, I'd seen the ramshackle old huts demolished, and the high board fencing erected, but it hadn't really occurred to me to wonder what was happening behind it. I was too preoccupied with watching Grandma dying to think of the future.

On the riverfront, the revamped marina was still home to several old fishing boats. They'd been joined by a few pleasure boats, though nothing like the ones you'd find in Brighton. It was aspiring to be something exclusive but hadn't quite reached it.

I looked up at the high-rise luxury apartments and wondered who my new neighbours were. They hadn't all sold yet, but the building was gradually filling up. It was an expensive looking development, all clean lines and reflective glass, but it was too aggressively modern for my taste. Even the penthouse flats didn't appeal, with their balconies and what must be a magnificent view down the river to the sea and towards the Beacon.

I'm all those things they said I was in Brookfields – shy, nerdy, old fashioned. I was happier in Grandma's villa than I would be in a shiny modern apartment.

I was almost home before I noticed it was happening again. All at once I was back in the world, all senses on high alert.

Someone was watching me.

I shivered and suppressed the urge to turn around and look. There was no need to give him the satisfaction, the knowledge that he'd unsettled me.

My pace quickened gradually, as if I was eager to be home. By the time I could see my house I was a little out of breath, not quite running, though the creeped-out feeling had disappeared. Either he'd gone, or my paranoia had dissipated.

All thoughts of being watched evaporated, as I saw the row of cars parked outside the Rook house. The drive was packed, so the family were there, but there were a couple of cars I didn't recognise, parked on the street – press perhaps? Across the road blocking my own drive was a van from the local TV news.

In the distance, by the hut where I'd found Harry, I could see the paramedics had left the scene, but there were still a couple of police cars, and crime scene tape draped across the entrance to the harbour and the beach.

I put my head down and headed for home, hoping no one had noticed me. They surely wouldn't have heard yet that I'd found Harry's body, so there was a good chance they'd not pay me too much attention.

Clearly that was too much to hope for. As I opened the gate, the horde of vultures descended. Well, there were only two of them, but it felt like a horde.

"Have you heard about Harry Rook?" a petite blonde woman asked, brandishing a microphone under my nose. She looked vaguely familiar, but I saw no reason to answer her, so I kept my head down and made for the front door.

I guessed it would get worse if they discovered I'd found the body. I wasn't about to tell them.

I was glad to close the heavy door behind me, and I waited to hear the satisfying click as it locked me safely inside.

Then my heart sank. It wasn't everyday paranoia. Or at least, I might be paranoid, but I was also being watched.

There were a couple of envelopes on the mat. One a standard business envelope that could be anything. The other was one of those that made my pulse race. Immediately recognisable. A parchment envelope. Expensive, heavy, cream parchment. Face up, with my name in beautiful hand penned calligraphic script.

I sighed, picked up the envelopes and carried them through to the kitchen table. So much for the fantasy of having time to relax and let my emotions catch up with me.

Then I walked upstairs, and through my bedroom to my bathroom. Straight away I had a hot shower, luxuriated in the heat and the steam until I started to unwind a little.

Only once I was dry and dressed in my silk kaftan and robe did I fetch a plastic pocket and my folder. Standing by the kitchen window, I held the suspect envelope up to the light. My name, as always, was perfectly executed. Alice, with a cursive loop on the initial; Hunter, with a calligraphic flourish beneath.

Moving to the table, I slit it open, slid out the contents. A rough textured post card, acid-free, substantial. My stalker is an artist.

Stalker. A word to trigger the meltdown I'd been holding at bay.

Heartbeat drumming. Blood pounding in my ears. Dammit, not again!

I grab the back of the chair, hold on tight. Sit down.

And breathe.

Calm.

Focus on the details, Alice. Cognitive behavioural exercises. Mindfulness conquers fear.

I study the card. It's a watercolour portrait of me, in profile, my mousy curly hair falling over my face. The Roman nose rather too prominent. It's me, alright.

All that energy and talent focused on me. The portrait had a warmth to it, though. Affection, even. It might have been flattering – except it was anonymous, one of a series, and revealed too much knowledge of my every movement. The absence of writing, of any meaningful communication, made it altogether more ominous. And the skill, the technique – it quite put my own pencil drawings to shame. What I wouldn't give to be so talented.

Had he – I presumed it was a he – been watching me today? Had he seen me on the Beacon? Had he seen me find the rabbit – or left it there, for me to find?

I shuddered. I was sure I'd have sensed it, that I'd have seen anyone else walking up there. He might have seen me start on the path – perhaps he'd been in town, behind me in the queue at the shop. He could have seen me lose it, dropping my shopping and fleeing in panic. Perhaps he was pleased, that he'd added to the stress that pushed me over the edge, time and time again.

I had to pause then and repeat the breathing exercises.

I couldn't turn to anyone for help.

If they knew how bad it was, they might want me back in Brookfields.

No, this was the return of the paranoia. The rabbit might be some kind of perverse gift for me, with some link to my background, my home. The Witch House. What if Harry was dead because of me? The identical stakes linked him with the butchered rabbit. But there was nothing to link rabbit and stalker.

My stalker has only ever sent me cards, pen and ink drawings, nothing at all threatening. There was never any hint of the pagan or ritual about it – no secret symbols. No reference to witchcraft. There was no need for me to pass this to the police, and risk them pushing me higher up the suspect list. There's a reason the word coincidence exists.

If my stalker had seen me, he might provide an alibi.

I imagined the possible consequences of feeding a delusion that he was helping me, that he was needed to watch over me, and shuddered.

Dr Lal, one of the more sympathetic doctors at the hospital had talked to me about paranoia, and how easy it was to let it get out of control. He'd told me a story about Robert Louis Stevenson, I think it was, who had experimented with imagining he was being watched and followed. Very quickly he had reached the stage where he had believed even the horses he passed in the street were taking a special interest in him. Everyone gets paranoid from time to time, Dr Lal said. It was an evolutionary adaptation. Interpreting every rustle in the grass as a prowling tiger makes us more likely to survive.

"Not once you've had a stay in a mental hospital, doctor," I'd said. He'd laughed, conceded the point. He even told me about the Martha Mitchell effect. Martha was the wife of a lawyer who was involved with the Watergate political scandal in America, who had been diagnosed as paranoid when her husband was, in fact, having her watched.

I'd seized on his words with some glimmer of hope. "So how can you tell the difference between a person who is afraid with some cause, and one who is paranoid, doctor?" I asked.

"Not so fast, Alice," he'd said. "Martha was being watched, but there's no doubt she was also genuinely troubled."

There's never a way out, once you're caught in that double bind. So I knew, if I reported a stalker, it was more likely to get me back on the ward, than him investigated.

Still, I slipped the card and envelope in the plastic wallet and filed it away with the others. One of Grandma's lessons had always been to document everything but keep your powder dry. You didn't have to use every weapon that came to hand, but it was a good idea to be prepared.

I turned to the other envelope. This one was business-like – franked and delivered by the postman. I opened it and read the letter. A flyer from the local estate agency telling me there was still significant interest in properties in my area, and if I was considering selling, I should contact them as soon as. I crumpled it up and threw it in the bin.

I went into the kitchen and contemplated the wine rack. I shouldn't really, given that it didn't mix well with my meds, but I needed a drink. I selected a bottle of Merlot, poured myself a glass, and took glass and bottle up to my bedroom.

Looking out of the window, the road was even busier than before. All the curtains were closed in the Rook house – perhaps as much to stop the snooping as a traditional mark of respect for the dead.

How was Tammy coping with the shock, the pain? In other circumstances, I would visit, but I knew Julia wouldn't want to see me.

Harry was dead.

I couldn't keep that image of him out of my head, lying there, staked like the rabbit. And that pentagram scrawled around the body – a final insult. Harry hated the whole pagan thing – I was sure it was one of the reasons he was at odds with Grandma for so long. It had taken me a lot of effort to convince him that Helen was wrong about what happened that night. That I had nothing to do with the poppet she found, and I certainly had no involvement in the outbreak of satanic inspired vandalism. I shouldn't have removed the stake from his hand. It was foolish. He was obviously dead, and I couldn't bear the sight of it.

He was a genuinely lovely man, though he'd been remote when I was growing up. I'd never understood the whys and wherefores of Grandma's feud with the Rooks, and I'd never plucked up the courage to ask him about it. Maybe it was partly her past history with paganism but it felt more personal than that. Anyway, no one could seriously suspect Grandma had ever performed blood sacrifices. Yet, somehow, they'd managed to set the feud aside, and he'd agreed to be the trustee and executor of her will.

That was something else that had pissed my mother off.

"Why didn't she trust me?" my mother had asked, during one of her rare visits to Brookfields.

Not a question that I could answer, especially as I was still hurt that Grandma hadn't trusted me either, that she'd tied up my inheritance until I was thirty. By the time I found out all the details of the will, I was on the locked ward, so I guess it looked like a perfectly reasonable decision to everyone else. I didn't see it that way.

Helen had handed me a pile of documents, and asked me to sign. It was routine paperwork, she said, to do with probate.

What did I care? Grandma was gone. I'd spent the last three years looking after her – as much as she would allow. She'd tried to pack me off to Uni, argued that she didn't need me, she could find carers and nurses. After a fight which wore her out so much I came close to giving up, she conceded. After she extracted a promise that I would get back to my education as soon as I could. That at least was easy, or so I thought. I hadn't expected to be recovering from a breakdown and facing panic attacks at the slightest provocation.

Perhaps I'd never know why she asked Harry to look after me. Now he was gone too, and I was on my own again. In the short time since Grandma's death, I'd come to rely on him for so much. Perhaps all grief is so selfish, I thought, before the tears finally came and I cried myself to sleep.

SIX

I WOKE TO the smell of smoke, catching the back of my throat. I couldn't move a single muscle. If I didn't move, I would burn in my bed. I couldn't scream and even if I could scream, there was no one to hear me. My heart was beating faster and faster and I had to move, I had to get out of bed, I had to escape from the burning house.

Somewhere in the back of my mind was a memory I couldn't quite bring into focus. A memory of a fire.

Night terrors.

I had them as a child. Not like this. Then I couldn't remember them, afterwards. Grandma had told me what they were like from the outside – that at first, she'd been terrified herself, swept away on the tide of my emotions. I would thrash around in bed, restless, a wild child. I would sit upright, inconsolable, and start to scream. There were people in the room, I said. People who were transformed into foxes and badgers, who had come to kidnap me, to take me away from my home, from Grandma. They planned to make me live in a cave under the Beacon and do housework, in some kind of mad mash up of Beatrix Potter and Stephen King.

She'd taken me to doctor after doctor and they'd all reassured her. It was nothing to worry about. I'd grow out of them. Just let me be and keep me safe at night – lock the doors and windows so I couldn't get out and wander the cliffs.

I did grow out of them. They only returned last year, when I was in hospital. A side effect of the medication, Doctor Lal had said. He'd experimented with my drug regime until he found a combination that didn't trigger them anymore.

Now I was home, and they were back.

As my panic receded and control of my muscles returned, I did my breathing exercises. Breathe in. Count to four slowly. Breathe out. Count and relax.

That wasn't enough. There was no way I'd get back to sleep – not without checking there was no fire. It was so vivid. The memory of the smell hung in the air, and even though the smoke alarms were silent, I didn't feel safe.

I checked the bedrooms and the bathroom, then ventured downstairs. The front door was locked, as was the library door. I checked the living room, and there were just a few ashes in the grate. As if someone had burned some papers. I reached out and there was no residual warmth. I touched, and it crumbled to dust. It could have been there for weeks. I didn't remember burning anything, but that meant nothing. My memory was addled by all the damn drugs the doctors insisted I still needed.

I went to the kitchen, put the light on, and filled the kettle. If I wasn't going to get any more sleep, I might as well have coffee.

While I was waiting for the kettle to boil, I unlocked the back door and stepped outside, to check the garden. The security light flooded the back of the house. Was there something rustling in the bushes, or was it my overactive imagination? Perhaps the were-foxes and were-badgers of my childhood. I smiled at my own foolishness, and stood breathing deeply of the sharp autumn air, reassured there was no lingering hint of smoke.

Still, in the middle of the lawn the patch of scorched earth rebuked me. I'd almost set fire to the Beacon that night, half a year ago now. I couldn't remember what happened, but it was impossible to deny with the evidence still scarring Grandma's beloved garden. It was no wonder my nightmares were now filled with flames and smoke, and not the scary monsters of my childhood.

I must have fallen asleep on the sofa, in the end, with the soothing murmur of the television in the background.

I woke with a stiff neck, and a ravenous appetite. I hadn't eaten the night before. There was bacon in the fridge, so I set it to cook on a low heat and I'd put the bread on the grill pan when the landline interrupted me. I dawdled out to the hall, hoping the ringing would stop and leave me to breakfast in peace. It was probably my mother, still angry with me for my absence the day before.

I picked up the phone and there was no answer. Probably a cold caller, I decided.

It was early. Too early. I was anxious about visiting Brookfields, and equally anxious about my mother. Where was she? When would she show up?

There were still no missed messages on my mobile, so I chickened out of phoning her again. I knew she'd be angry with me for not being here when I promised. The only thing I wanted to do less than apologise was explain my absence and start up another conversation about Harry and Grandma, stirring up all the resentment that entailed.

I went upstairs to my bedroom, for the best view of what was going on outside. Peering out of the window told me the crowd outside the Rook house had gone, but Tamsin's car was in the drive. In any other circumstances I'd have taken this chance to call and pay my respects, but I knew Julia wouldn't want to see me. Maybe not Tamsin either. I knew it was an excuse, as it had been the previous day, but I couldn't face them. Not yet.

Now I could smell burning.

I ran downstairs. The toast was charcoal, and some of the bacon had welded to the pan. I rescued enough to make a bacon sandwich – extra crispy. I sat at the kitchen table, eating and drinking tea, and dreading the day ahead.

As I cleared up the culinary disaster area, it suddenly occurred to me that the smoke alarm hadn't gone off.

That was weird.

I don't much like heights, but I dragged a kitchen chair to the correct spot, and carefully clambered up on to it. I unclipped the cover of the alarm. I could see loose wires, so somehow it had become disconnected from the alarm system. And the backup batteries weren't dead – they were gone. How could that have happened?

I sighed, and gingerly stepped down from the wobbling chair. Probably one of the cleaners had broken it and the repair had been overlooked. Or maybe it had been my mother, when she was staying here when I was in hospital. She was the single most domestically challenged person on the planet, after all.

I was pleased with myself that I'd so quickly found sensible explanations and not let myself be swallowed whole by paranoia.

This would need an electrician, not merely a replacement battery. Or maybe Mrs B's handyman would do.

A twinge of guilt reminded me I'd not been in touch since I was discharged from hospital.

My day was well and truly jinxed, it seemed.

I decided to make use of my early start by baking some brownies for Kelly. After my abject failure at gift shopping, it would be good to have something to take, along with the unopened bottle of body lotion I'd discovered in the bathroom cabinet.

As I measured out the flour and melted the chocolate, my mind wandered back to the day Grandma died. It was hard to make sense of it – my memories were fickle. I had glimpses, occasionally, where something came through. Like yesterday, seeing the back of DI Collingwood's head in the police car. There was still the patch of scorched earth in the garden behind the house where I'd built my bonfire – evidence to remind me that my orgy of destruction had actually happened. What other holes might there be in my memory?

I shrugged off the past; I had a promise to keep. I showered and dressed in my best clothes, even considered makeup, but then a burst of slightly hysterical laughter possessed me. I'd been free for days now, and still I was afraid that they'd not let me go.

Kelly had been released to outpatient care a couple of weeks before me, and she was already back on the locked ward. Older than me, in her early thirties, she'd taken me under her wing when I first arrived, lost and bewildered. She'd warned me it was a revolving door, and that everyone who she'd known had been marked for life by their time as a psychiatric patient. It was more than a label that followed you around and made life more difficult – it was a destiny.

I hoped she was wrong, and that it was her illness talking. Either way, I was determined that for me it would be different.

How would I explain my visit being a day late? Perhaps I could say I'd bottled it, that I'd been scared to come back. There was at least an element of truth in that. But I had to be careful: I didn't want to trigger an episode of paranoia. In her, or in me.

At the greengrocer's shop on Beacon Road I stopped, drawn by a bucket of beautiful white roses. They wouldn't be allowed on the ward. These were roses with thorns. So I picked out a bunch of tulips instead, and then on impulse, added the roses. Maybe I would take them home and brighten my living room. Or maybe I would pluck up my courage and take them across to Julia.

I dawdled so long I had to run for the bus. Fortunately the driver was not one of the sadistic ones, who wait until you are almost there and have relaxed to catch your breath before pulling away from the bus stop, leaving you standing there, lobster red. I paid my fare and sat downstairs, too winded to make for my preferred top deck seat.

The lower deck of the bus was surprisingly empty, and I had a double seat to myself. A rather large old lady paused, but then took the seat opposite as I studiously looked away.

I started to read, and was soon lost in a different world – the world of Roman Britain. In Brookfields I'd been laughed at and told it was pure escapism, almost as bad as a romance or science fiction habit. Why would anyone dream of studying classics and ancient history – did I want to end up being a teacher?

I'd rather be an archaeologist than a teacher, but I've never been able to work out what's so wrong about escapism. You only have to take the most cursory glance at reality to realise escape is the only rational choice.

Grandma was interested in history too. She'd declined her offer to read Classics at Cambridge when she became pregnant with my mother, and had been thrilled when I told her I planned to apply to the archaeology department at Oxford.

Mother wondered if she'd pressured me into living her dream and not my own, but that simply wasn't true. I'd been influenced, no doubt. I'd seen her enjoying Open University courses, and holidays were planned around her interest in the past. But I could understand why mother would think that I was doing it for Grandma. She couldn't see the point in anything earlier than Chanel.

Sometimes I wonder if unearthing the mysteries of the distant past simply seems more tractable than understanding my own life, my own family.

I was so lost in memory, that I didn't hear the kerfuffle at first but the sound of a boy's high voice, cracking and close to tears brought me back to the present. The driver was ordering him off the bus. It wasn't up to him. It was a matter of the regulations. The boy was fifty pence short of the correct fare.

"Won't hurt you to walk, a young lad like you," the driver said. I wanted to act, to do something, and started to steel myself to speak up, but before I could say anything, the old woman sitting opposite me went to the front of the bus and put fifty pence into the machine.

"You can't do that!" the driver spluttered.

"Looks like I did," she said. "Don't tell me there are rules and regulations saying everyone has to pay their own bus fare?"

The boy blushed, but said thank you politely, took the ticket and ran upstairs.

I smiled at her as she sat down again, and she grinned at me. "Random act of kindness," she said.

It was a happy reminder that there are, after all, still some kind people in the world. They're not all selfish jerks, like our Marlborough and Oxford educated Member of Parliament. However ridiculous it was after all that happened in between, I was still seething over his behaviour at the till.

I was envious of Mark Stockman, I suppose that was at the root of it. His easy confidence. Other lives seemed to go according to plan, while mine never had, right from the beginning. I hadn't been born into a storybook family. I hardly knew my father, I had no siblings, no normal family life. There was no material deprivation and no shortage of love, so I knew I was luckier than so many others. But I yearned for something I couldn't quite put into words. To feel I deserved my place in the world. To be free to be me, without always looking outside for validation and approval. To feel I was good enough.

My planned escape route had been college. If it wasn't for Grandma getting sick when she did, I would be a graduate of Oxford by now, perhaps moving on to postgraduate study. If it hadn't been for the months in Brookfields at least I'd be a student. Now all that was holding me back was my own failure of courage.

I knew I was really very fortunate by most standards. I had a home of my own, no need to worry about money, and I had a world full of opportunities. But I had lost the knack, if I ever had it, of feeling at home in that world, or any other. I couldn't even manage to buy bubble bath and body lotion without going into a full-blown panic attack.

Coming up to my stop on the outskirts of Brighton, I put my book away, stood up and rang the bell. I could see a few people waiting in the bus shelter anyway, so I needn't have rushed. Except I had an impulsive thought, and instead of getting off, I turned around and walked back to give the roses to the kind woman.

"Lovely," she said, "But are you sure you don't need them?"

"Not the roses," I said, "I had intended them for me, but…"

"Ah, your random act of kindness," she smiled.

"No," I said. "Not random at all."

Meanwhile, confused by my dithering, the people getting on the bus were blocking my way. The driver started to get testy again. "Are you getting off or what?" he yelled, in my general direction.

"Yes," I said, smiling through my panic. "Sorry to keep you waiting."

As he revved up the engine, I heard him mutter – loud enough for everyone to hear. "That'll be one of them loonies, then. Let out for the day. Makes me feel really safe, that does."

I stood at the bus stop listening to the sound of the bus's engine recede into the distance, my heart beating fast. I held my arm out in front of me, and watched my hand trembling.

I shrugged, swung my rucksack up onto my back, and set off in the direction of Brookfields.

SEVEN

WALKING PAST ROW after row of neat suburban houses. I wondered if the homeowners felt the same way as the bus driver. How much must their house values have dropped since their new neighbours moved in?

At least Brookfields wasn't one of those old Gothic asylums that look menacing, looming in the distance. Many of those are now luxury apartments, though the sales brochures don't tend to dwell on their history. It's not the kind of history that adds to the prestige – or the price.

This was a new building. When I first entered the lobby, a lifetime ago, it felt like, it still had the smell of wet concrete and paint. The architect had won awards. However, the physical assets might be superb, but the scrimping and saving was less immediately visible – as was the case in the nursing homes Grandma insisted on seeing, before I talked her into letting me look after her at home.

Another similarity – there simply weren't enough members of staff, which put everyone under constant pressure. That tends to sour the milk of human kindness at the best of times, and there are no best of times on a mental health unit. Staff turnover was high –anyone who could leave, did. As for the doctors, they were mostly competent and caring, although one in particular was positively medieval.

Taking a deep breath, I collected myself before approaching the front door. I rang the bell, my hand hardly trembling at all now, and the door opened to let me into the reception area. Tastefully furnished with pale wood and faux leather, it might have been the reception at any private clinic. There was someone talking to the woman at the desk, and it looked like she was there for the long haul, so I sat and flicked through a glossy magazine, trying to project an air of calmness.

At last the gossip fest was over, and I stood waiting for the receptionist to notice my existence.

"Visitor for Kelly Middleton, Hilton Ward," I said.

"Is it your first time here?"

"Sadly not." I wasn't going to volunteer the information that the last time I was an inpatient, not a visitor.

"You're familiar with the drill then. Sign in here, please," she said, pushing the book towards me and handing me an old-fashioned ballpoint pen, with the end badly chewed. I signed.

I did know the drill.

"I've brought a few things with me. Would you like to inspect them?"

She rummaged through the bag I retrieved from my rucksack. The tub of homemade brownies was inspected, brownie by brownie. Knowing my rucksack was full of all kinds of contraband, from my nail file to mobile phone, I decided to leave it at reception.

She escorted me down the corridor to the locked door to the ward and buzzed through. I could hear steps approaching the door, and the sounds of the locks clicking open. The receptionist handed me over to the ward sister, and I breathed a sigh of relief. Again, no one I knew.

"You're here to visit Kelly," she said, waving the receptionist back to her post. "Is she expecting you?"

"Yes," I said. "At least she was yesterday." I showed her the bag of treats.

She took me into her office and gave the bag a cursory glance. "That all looks fine. I'll put the tulips in a vase in the common room," she said. Then she paused and looked at me.

"She's really not very well, you know. Some people can't handle it, especially if they've only seen the patient when she was well."

"I've known her a long time," I said. "Last time she was ill…" My voice tapered off. Last time she was ill was when I met her. In here.

"How long has she been back here?" I asked, impulsively. I felt guilty. I'd been neglecting Kelly, because I didn't want to be reminded.

"A couple of weeks, this time," she said. "I'm sure you already know this, but she's going to ask you to help get her out of here. She's going to tell you she's well, that we've made a mistake. That she shouldn't really be here. That's not true."

"I understand," I said.

I did, too. From both sides. I understood how Kelly felt, because I'd been there too.

Before they'd been willing to discharge me, I'd had to conform to their way of thinking. I'd had to accept that my time in Brookfields had been necessary. That they knew my reality better than I did.

I'd jumped through every hoop. I'd put makeup on, to prove I wasn't depressed – even though I never wear makeup normally. I took my medication, even though it made me feel dull and lifeless, and made my hands tremble. I did everything they wanted.

It was a bit like prison, I suppose. They don't let convicted murderers out, unless they admit they're guilty. So where does that leave those who really are wrongfully convicted?

Same place it left me. I told lies so blatant you'd think they'd cotton on. I said what they wanted to hear. I sacrificed my integrity. It was that, or stay locked up.

"Okay then," she said. "Let's go down to her room."

One advantage of being on the locked ward at Brookfields – at least you got a room of your own.

At the end of the corridor, the nurse paused, and knocked on the last door. "Kelly, your visitor's here."

She turned to me, and said, "You can chat in her room, or in the common room, and there's a courtyard space if you want to smoke."

"Thanks," I forced a smile. Then the door opened and Kelly threw herself at me.

Shit, they've locked you up too, mate?" she said. "I thought you'd escaped."

"I'm just visiting, Kels," I said. "Remember, you phoned? We arranged it. Sorry, I'm a bit late."

She looked at her watch. "Nah. Visiting hours only started ten minutes ago."

I'd gotten away with being a day late then. At least for now. The nurse gave me a told-you-so look and turned and walked back to her office.

"I brought you some stuff," I said, and followed her into her room.

She grabbed the bag with delight and emptied it on the bed, as I sat on the lone armchair.

"No fags." She almost burst into tears.

"Kels, you gave up," I said. "You've not started again already?"

"Already? I've been banged up in here for days. What the fuck else is there to do?"

"I know," I said, "I'll bring you some next time. Why are you back here? What went wrong?"

"I'm fine," she said. "I thought you knew that." Her words were clipped, angry. She was about to flip. I touched her arm, tentatively, and smiled. It brought her back from the edge. I'd have to be more careful.

She looked around, nervously. "It's impossible to talk in here. Let's go outside," she said.

She nodded towards the TV, which was unplugged. The voices warned her off electronic stuff.

She caught my look. "Yeah," she said. "I'm paranoid as fuck, but tell me who they've locked up?" and she laughed. I laughed too. We shared that dark humour, and it had served us through some tough times.

Whatever else they'd claimed was wrong with me, at least I didn't have the voices. Kelly had once explained to me what it was like being her. All the jabbering voices in her head, offering a running commentary on her life. Some of them warning her of dangers, real or not. Most of them running her down, pointing out how hopeless she was, making her feel so bad that life didn't seem worth living. It was, I thought, a bit like living with my grandmother, or worse my mother, except that you could never ever escape the negative comments. You couldn't spend time on Cuckmere Beacon, gazing at the sea, or walking down to the beach, kicking off your shoes and having a paddle – not without the voices coming too.

In the courtyard there were a couple of guys smoking. She nodded to them and led me across to a bench, under the shade of a tree.

"Ha, you're wearing a skirt," she said, and had a fit of the giggles. "No makeup though. Are you worried they won't let you out?"

"Something like that," I said. She was in jeans. "Please tell me Dr Mansfield isn't on today."

"You missed his leaving do," she said. "It's still all points mean prizes, but at least now it's not so fucking old fashioned. Points are all for consideration and co-operative behaviour now, less for lippy and frocks."

"Ha," I said, "Could do with a bit more of that in the outside world." I told her about my experience in the queue in the department store. "Wouldn't it be wonderful if it were possible to apply a similar system of rewards and punishments outside the hospital?" I told her about giving the roses to the kind lady on the bus.

She laughed and laughed and coughed and laughed again, until she became aware that everyone was looking at us. "Shit," she said. "I'll have to calm down or else I won't be allowed visitors. It makes me too excitable."

"Sorry," I said.

"For fuck's sake, don't tell your psychiatrist about this plan," she sputtered. "Unless you want to end up in here with me again."

I laughed, but it made me realise our friendship had different rules now. She was inside and subject to arbitrary authority, while I was free. Not like the times we both got into mischief together, and both paid the price – if we were caught.

I longed to have someone I could talk to about finding Harry's body and how I felt. Someone I could confide in about my stalker. For Kelly's sake, I kept it all bottled up.

I took her into the kitchen and made coffee and we shared some of the brownies I'd brought with the other inmates in the common room, and a nurse's aide. That should gain her some points for social co-operation. I promised to visit her in a week, even though I knew and she knew I really didn't want to come back.

"Anything I can do for you?" I asked. "I'll bring cigarettes next time, but if there's anything else you need?"

"Somewhere to live," she said. "I can't, I won't go back to my family. If I have nowhere to go, I'll be stuck in this dump forever."

"What happened to your flat? I thought your sister was taking care of it for you?"

"So did I. That bitch, she told the landlord I was ill, and wouldn't be going back. She collected all my bills and did nothing about passing them on to me, or paying them."

I thought about it, and my heart sank. I could probably point her in the way of a bedsit, through Grandma's business partner, but then Kelly would become my responsibility. She'd find out about the trust fund, and think I was lying to her, that I wasn't who I said I was.

Brookfields had been a revelation to me. I'd quickly seen how sheltered, how privileged my childhood had been, and understood why Grandma wanted me to work, to appreciate the value of money. I'd thought I understood before, but I didn't really. Not until I saw it close up. My holiday job as a cleaner in the business had been no more real than Marie Antoinette playing shepherdess.

"I'll see what I can find," I said. "I should warn you, most landlords want tenants who are in work."

"What can I do?" she said. "There must be something. I wouldn't go to Maggie not even if the bitch asked me. Which she won't."

I grimaced in sympathy. I was lucky I'd had a home to go to – even though it was the scene of my precipitating breakdown. The terms of

Grandma's will left all the power in the hands of my trustee. Harry had briefly allowed my mother to stay there, so she could be close enough to visit me regularly. Not that those token visits were all that regular, once she found out she couldn't have what she wanted.

When I was finally allowed home, so much was missing. At first mother had claimed that I'd burned it all on my bonfire, but eventually she'd admitted to clearing out Grandma's things. She was helping me out, she said. Wardrobes full of vintage designer clothes had been emptied, and their contents given to the charity shops. Not that I believed that part – she knew what that stuff was worth. It would all have ended up on sale in her boutique in Islington.

It had been a struggle to get her to move back to her own home, in the flat over the shop, before I moved back in. Without Harry's help, I'd never have managed it. I had to learn to cope without him now, or become my mother's doormat.

Kelly had carried on talking while I'd zoned out.

"Any old dump would be better than this," she was saying. "A bedsit will do. Natural light would be fab, but anything, anything."

It made me so happy that she was taking her art seriously now. How could I let my self-consciousness stand in her way?

"I know someone who runs a property business," I said. "Don't get your hopes up, but I'll do what I can."

Close to the truth. I do know Mrs Banerjee, and she does run a property business. Half of which is mine, or will be.

"What's up with you?" she asked. "Jobhunting or college?"

"I'm not really ready for full time," I said. "One step at a time. There's a part time certificate course run by the local university. The Romans in Sussex. It involves some practical archaeological work as well. The open evening's coming up soon."

"I'd love to do a proper art course one day, in a real art college." She sighed.

"Keep working on your portfolio," I said. "There are all kinds of access courses. Something to work towards."

We both found it easier to dish out advice than to take it.

When she'd first said that the mental health unit was her art college I'd laughed, but gradually I'd come to understand that in some ways it was true. Being sectioned had actually gained her access to paint and canvas and teaching in a way that she'd never had in her home, or in her school.

"We could both be students together," she said, but I could tell from her tone she didn't really believe it. All that was in my way was anxiety – and that was quite hard enough. She had more difficult obstacles to negotiate.

I hugged Kelly and said my goodbye, all the time feeling like I was deserting her. The ward sister let me out and locked the heavy door behind me. I collected my bag and signed out of reception, all the time half-holding my breath, as if someone might spot I belonged on the other side of that door.

EIGHT

GLAD TO BE home, I pottered around in the kitchen, listening to the radio news. There was very little information; only a simple statement that the police were investigating Harry's death. They'd moved on to the weather when the doorbell rang.

I went to the front door and peered through the peephole. It was my mother. Either she'd forgiven me, or she'd heard about Harry's death. I braced myself, and opened the door.

She rushed over the threshold and grabbed me, subduing me with heavy perfume and an over-affectionate hug.

"I heard on the news, Alice," she said. "Why didn't you call me? I had to come and see if you're okay."

"Of course I'm fine," I said. "I left voicemail."

"There's no of course about it, not after last time," she said, obliquely referring again to what happened after Grandma died.

I could sense her looking at me for signs of disintegration. Just as well she wouldn't see the empty wine bottles in my bedroom.

I still hadn't forgiven her. She'd been so quick to call for help, to get me sectioned, to put together an entirely fictional narrative about witchcraft and poppets and ritual magic. All for my own good. What else would it be? What she hadn't done was agree to stay with me for a few days and keep an eye on me – oh no, she was too busy with her own life for that. She had a boutique to run. Mind, it had managed to run itself when she'd moved into the house a few months into my hospital stay.

Helen had been shocked when she found out that Grandma had left the bulk of her estate to me. She never seemed to realise that Grandma was still in control, anyway; it was all tied up in such a way that I didn't have any more freedom, no matter what my mother imagined.

I followed her into the living room, feeling my shoulders droop as my mood reached a new low. Tea would delay the inevitable inquisition.

I set out the tray, with teapot and milk jug, and thinly sliced lemon for mother. No mug – she would have been offended to be treated with any less ceremony than Grandma demanded. Plus it gave me an extra few moments of grace, to gather my courage to resist her questions. There is no right to remain silent where Helen is concerned.

I put the tray down on the coffee table, narrowly avoiding dropping it in my shock. Grandma's favourite cut-glass vase filled with white roses had been placed squarely in the middle of the table. Roses exactly like the ones I'd given away.

Without thinking, I blurted, "Did you bring the roses?"

I knew straight away it was impossible.

I'd blundered – given her a weapon. When she'd hugged me, she'd had nothing in her hands. She hadn't been in the kitchen, and I certainly would have noticed her reaching up to the high cupboard to lift the vase down, and filling it up with water.

She stood up, a look of concern on her face. It was about to begin. Again.

"I'll get some biscuits," I said, and retreated to the kitchen. Quickly, I tidied the wine bottles away into the recycling box, in case mother came in and started lecturing me about how alcohol wouldn't mix with my medication.

I took my time, selecting one of Grandma's china plates and opening a new pack of chocolate hobnobs. I took an extra moment to peek into the kitchen bin. Sure enough, there was the same wrapping paper that the florist had used on my roses, along with the snipped off stems and empty sachet of flower food.

I imagined the woman I'd given the flowers to on the bus tracking me down, and then breaking in and arranging them nicely for me.

Now that was crazy. But, however they'd got there, it must have been something equally crazy. Was it possible I'd had another blackout? Bought them on my way home, snipped off the ends of the stalks, opened the flower food sachet, put them in the vase – and erased every single step from my memory? I hadn't even been into the living room since getting home. Had I?

I took the biscuits in and put them on the table, a fake smile plastered on my face.

"Don't look at me like that. I forgot, that's all. I bought the flowers earlier, on my way home from visiting Kelly in Brookfields."

I don't like lying, but sometimes, with my mother, it's the only way.

"Oh. Was it a good idea for you to go back there, Alice?" she asked. All maternal concern. "You should forget all that, put it behind you. Make some normal friends, our sort of people, who won't drag you down."

Except I wasn't normal any more now, was I?

She didn't like Kelly – that was part of it. I shouldn't be mixing with someone who grew up on a sink estate, who did her clothes shopping at Primark.

I suppressed my rage, and poured the tea, my hands shaking a little. I handed her a cup and saucer.

"Should you be using the best china?" she said. "A mug would have been fine."

Whatever I did, it was always wrong. I was talented that way. "It's the meds," I said. "It's a common side effect, that's all."

"You must continue taking them, Alice. It's so important. We don't want to go back to Brookfields, do we?"

We? I snorted.

"I have side effects because I'm taking them, don't you see?"

She looked at me with such patently obvious disbelief I was tempted to fetch the pack insert. Then I realised the utter pointlessness of it all and sighed.

Then it began. She wanted all the details, and the story I told wasn't detailed enough.

"It said on the local news that you'd found the body," she said. "What were you doing there anyway?"

It was odd none of the journalists had tried to speak to me, in that case. I was sceptical – I must have missed that news report.

"I was walking back from town, over the Beacon. That's all."

I couldn't tell her everything. DI Collingwood had asked me not to tell anyone about the wooden stake, the ritual element and the rabbit, and I was doing as I was told. I knew my mother wouldn't be able to keep her mouth shut. Or more accurately, that she wouldn't choose to do so, if it suited her to blab.

She was more interested than I expected in the fact that the police had questioned me.

"I would have been petrified," she said. "Are you sure you're okay?"

"It was only a few questions. Where I'd been, who I'd seen. Stuff like that."

"So how come they took a DNA sample then? That makes it sound like you're a suspect."

"Purposes of elimination, the DI said. Because I found him. I touched him to see if he was still alive."

She shivered, perhaps repulsed at the thought of touching a dead body. It was hard to know with my mother what, or if, she was feeling.

"Please, please promise me you'll see your community support worker," she said. "For me, if you won't do it for yourself. It will make me feel happier. I don't want to have to worry about you all over again."

"I'm okay," I snapped. Almost losing my temper proved I wasn't, judging by the concerned expression. I clattered cups and saucers on to the tray, and took it out to the kitchen, counting to ten. It wasn't enough. It was never enough. I made a very rude sign with my fingers in her general direction. Just as well she couldn't see, or she'd know for sure Kelly had been a bad influence.

As soon as I went back in to the room, she continued her prodding and poking.

It was exactly like being a witch, I thought, not for the first time. Whether I floated or sank, I would always be guilty of something.

At least the ritual element of Harry's murder hadn't leaked into the news yet. If it had, Helen would not have been able to resist tormenting me further, questioning me again about the fire. She'd always refused to believe my denials about the wiccan fantasy she'd concocted. It didn't help that I'd finally given in to the pressures in hospital and outright lied about my interest. It's impossible to prove a negative – I found it much simpler to pretend a mild interest than to deny it altogether. And who wouldn't be interested, growing up in a house known as the Witch House, with the once notorious High Priestess of what the scandal sheets had called the Cuckmere Coven?

"Have you called on Julia Rook?" she asked.

"Have you?"

"Course not. I didn't find her husband's body, and I don't live across the road from her. She might have some questions for you, after all."

"Hasn't everyone," I muttered. Then audibly, "I've never understood it. I know my grandmother could hold a grudge, and I know there's some history there. What was it all about?"

She looked away. "I don't remember it ever being any different."

I knew the official version. Grandma worked for the Stockman family as a nanny. She'd stayed friends with old Mr Stockman after setting up her business and had seen him as a mentor. The agency she started supplied domestic staff, cleaners, nannies and gardeners to the local middle classes. It hadn't been easy, she'd told me, and at the start she'd been both boss and cleaning lady, whatever she had to do to make ends meet. The hard work and determination had paid off and she'd quickly become prosperous. Not quite rags to riches, perhaps, but she'd enjoyed telling the story that way.

The unofficial story included a shared deep and abiding interest in all things occult. Gabriel Stockman had been the centre of the local pagan community.

"Do you ever wonder," I said to my mother who had picked up the last hobnob, "if we might be related to the Stockman family?"

She choked on a crumb and started coughing. I hovered at her side, ready to try out the Heimlich manoeuvre, in the hope that I might be permitted to crack a rib to save her life. She waved me away impatiently and I ran into the kitchen for a glass of water and put it on the table in front of her.

She caught her breath and I relaxed. Two dead bodies in one week would certainly look suspicious.

Best not think like that, Alice, I told myself. She asked you to forgive her and you said you would. She's your mother and she only wants what's best for you.

Forgetting doesn't come easy. Nor does forgiveness, come to that.

"I've never heard anything so ridiculous," she finally managed to get the words out. "Grandma and old Gabe Stockman?"

Grandma was as far down the ladder from the Stockmans, as Kelly was from us. In mother's world view, that made it unthinkable.

"She never talked about him that way. I wondered, that's all. Why she quit her job to start a business. Wouldn't it have been easier, with a new baby, to be a nanny?"

"She would never tell me who my father was," my mother said.

"Is that what the problem between you was all about?" I asked. Daring, now.

"Partly. Of course it was. And she wouldn't let me take you back. I know I needed her help when you were small, but when I was settled, and could have made a home for you, she wouldn't allow it. She said it would disrupt your schooling. That you were happier living with her."

"I didn't know," I said, immediately awash with regrets. I'd known Helen had her own breakdown, all those years ago, although she'd avoided being sectioned. A suicide attempt that Grandma had believed was a cry for help. "Financial help at that," she'd said.

I thought she simply hadn't wanted me; that I was too much trouble. The way she insists I call her Helen – which I avoid by never calling her anything at all in her presence. But she had wanted me. I wondered what else I hadn't known.

"You always were her little blue-eyed girl. You never saw what it was like for me. I don't think Grandma ever forgave me for ruining her life simply by being born."

Impulsively, I hugged her. She stiffened, much as I had when she hugged me. It was hopeless. I resolved to try harder in future, if she would at least meet me half way.

"You never had any idea at all who he might be?" I asked.

She looked at the floor and fiddled with a button on her cuff, before lifting her face. She looked me straight in the eye.

"That's the first time you've ever asked. Think about that," she urged. "Grandma controlled everything, she always did. She even wanted to control what we could think about."

"There was always a walking on eggshells feeling," I admitted. I felt like I was betraying Grandma even my saying out loud that she wasn't perfect. Maybe Helen had a point.

"I asked her over and over. I hoped perhaps when she died, she would have left a letter, that perhaps she'd overcome her shame or embarrassment, for our sake. But nothing has turned up."

That sounded like a confession that she'd looked through everything – as she had denied before. I swallowed back my immediate response.

"You had the right to know. She should have told you."

"I might not have married your father, and God knows he was a poor enough choice, but his name is on your birth certificate. It's not a secret."

The least said about him, the better. I'd only seen him half a dozen times in my whole life, but it was enough.

"Anyway," she said, "I have to get back to London – I have a meeting with a collector this afternoon. But I don't like to leave you here all on your own. Not now."

Oh please, no, surely, she wasn't hankering to live here again?

"I like living on my own. But Kelly will need somewhere, when they discharge her."

I couldn't resist the teeniest poke back.

"Don't fall into that trap, darling," she said. "You don't want to be lumbered with that chav as a dependent, a hanger-on. You'd always be looking after her. You've done enough of that."

She simply couldn't help herself. My sympathy for her all but evaporated in an instant.

I thought back to the day I was admitted to Brookfields, and how Kelly had looked after me then. Now I could do something for her. I'd been wavering, but…

"I'll ask Mrs Banerjee. If one of the bedsits comes up, it would give Kelly some security and some independence."

"That old busybody. I don't know why you haven't persuaded her to retire. She leeched off Grandma for long enough."

"She's a partner in the business, you know that. She carried the entire load when I was in hospital, and she's still doing it now."

"She does well enough out of it."

It wasn't all about the money – it was about responsibility too. I'd been neglecting mine. Even if I was planning to check out the University course, I still had to do my part.

"Well," she said, gathering her coat and getting ready to leave. "You know what I think. I think you should sell up and start your own life somewhere new. Do what you planned originally. Don't bury yourself here like Grandma did. Cuckmere's a dead end. Go to Cambridge."

"Oxford," I said. "You came back, for a few weeks at least." I didn't point out I hadn't got much freedom when it came to selling up. That would have to wait until I was thirty. There was no point to starting up more arguments about the trust.

I knew she hated Cuckmere. She hadn't visited much when Grandma was dying, or when I needed her. I'd never understood why she'd spent those weeks living here when I was in hospital – it didn't make sense given that her life was in London. I supposed she'd been running away from something rather than to here. It was home to me, but it had never felt like home to her.

"It's such a pity that you can't make an effort with Julia Rook. She's your only near neighbour, and with a killer on the loose…"

With that seed planted, she swept out.

NINE

I SHUT THE door behind her and sighed my relief. She meant well but all she'd succeeded in doing was stirring up feelings I preferred to avoid, and now she'd reinforced my fears about being here alone. As if I wasn't constantly fighting paranoia without any help.

Back in the living room, I looked at the flowers again, still disbelieving my eyes. Was it possible I'd bought them and forgotten?

The flowers were real enough. Helen had seen them. I touched them, and could feel the soft velvet of the petals, the sharp jab of the thorns. Could I have imagined giving them away? My memory... I knew there were things I'd forgotten. Could there possibly be things I'd imagined that simply hadn't happened?

I carried the vase into the kitchen and grabbing a few sheets of kitchen paper from the dispenser, grasped the roses, and wrapped them. I unlocked the back door, walked down to the end of the lawn and flung them into the wooden slatted compost bins. I didn't want to see them again.

The hairs on the back of my neck stood up. I was being watched. Paranoia rising, I looked around but could see no one. The Rook house had no view of the back garden. To the north, the new marina flats overlooked the front of the house, but I could only just see the penthouse balconies. At the back, the garden was fenced in and the gate that would let me straight on to Beacon Hill was closed and padlocked shut.

The Beacon was public land and a nature reserve – anyone could be up there and could see the house. At this time of year the brambles were still fruiting, and I sometimes saw people scrambling down the hill with their Tupperware containers filled to the brim with blackberries.

On one memorable occasion I'd bumped into two bird watching nuns in full regalia, equipped with very high-tech binoculars. But today, I couldn't see anyone. That didn't mean there was no one there, however.

I shook my head, despairing at my over-reaction, and went back inside. On the counter next to the vase, which now held a little water and a couple of leaves, was a small card. It must have dropped out of the flowers, and I'd been so concerned with not scratching myself on the thorns that I hadn't noticed it as it fell.

Now I picked it up. Black ink, a drawing of a single rose. My stalker. Somehow my stalker had managed to break in to my house and he left me flowers. He went to the trouble to put them in a vase. Not only that, but they were identical flowers to the ones I'd bought earlier.

Had he also meddled with the smoke alarm? Heart pounding, I fought to control my fears. Breathing slowly, counting, trying desperately to hold on to my sanity.

I wasn't feeling particularly safe in my own home any more. I needed distraction from those recurring thoughts – the vivid images of Harry, lying there, the feel of the stake as I pulled it out of his hand, and these vague imaginings of being watched by some shadowy figure who wouldn't come into focus.

This wouldn't do. I opened another bottle of Merlot, and poured myself a glass. I carried it through to the living room. Perhaps it wouldn't hurt to skip the meds for today. I wanted to reduce my dependence on them anyway.

To take my mind off things, I turned on the TV, and channel hopped until I found something that would distract me. I paused long enough on the local TV news to be sure they hadn't mentioned anything about who found Harry's body.

I found a repeat of the Sussex Archaeology programme presented by Professor Matthew Buckley – who I would be seeing very soon in the flesh at the open evening for the course I wanted to take. His enthusiasm for his subject did a lot to reconcile me to the idea of not going straight for Oxford. And in the meantime, I could do my part to help Mrs B with the business. Grandma would have approved of that.

In some ways I was almost relieved my access to Grandma's estate was so constrained. I'm not rich. Of course, compared to many people I am, or I will be when I'm thirty. In the meantime, although I'm extremely fortunate, I am expected to work for a living – that I'd always understood. Part of that had involved spending school holidays working with Grandma and Mrs B – so that I knew the business from the bottom up.

"I want to be an archaeologist," I'd said. "I don't need to know how to run the business."

"I wanted to be an academic," she'd said. "You don't always get what you want. Always have a backup plan."

For all mother's resentment, Grandma had done plenty for her too. Not the education part – Helen had no interest in that, and had left school at sixteen, as soon as it was legally possible. She'd worked in Grandma's business for a while, too, but had eventually disappeared – and come back home holding the baby. Yes, that baby. Me.

Afterwards there'd been other failed businesses, then the current success. Troy – Helen's little shop in Islington. All of them funded by Grandma. I didn't know much about it, but I was there when Grandma had bought the premises for the boutique and the comfortable flat above, and I knew the Trust paid all the service charges and running expenses as well as a generous living allowance. Mother would be able to live perfectly comfortably, even if she pottered around in her usual amateurish way forever. I was determined to do better.

Realising I was still going over the same ground, round and round, and never getting anywhere, I went back to the TV for more distraction.

Later, from my bedroom, I looked out of the window across to the Rook house. All the visitors had gone now. There were no extra cars on the drive, and no journalists waiting to snatch a photo of the grieving widow. Only one light was on, in the window of the turret room directly opposite.

As I stood there, watching, a dark figure moved into the window, and looked back in my direction, before drawing the curtains closed. If anyone had a good view of my home, it was Julia. It was a pity I couldn't ask her if she'd seen a stranger hanging around with a bunch of white roses. In any case, it wouldn't help. The road between our houses was public and well-travelled, as it led to the beach. It would be so easy to blend in – carry a fishing rod, wear walking boots and rucksack, or walk with a dog. Seeing strangers was the norm.

I closed the curtains, making sure there was not the slightest gap, and went to bed. I tossed and turned, wondering how my stalker had managed to get into the house – with no broken windows and all the doors securely locked. Perhaps, somehow, he had a key. I would have to change the locks.

Had anything been stolen? I hadn't checked. How stupid I was. Especially as so many things had gone missing after Grandma died. As my mother had pointed out, when enumerating the reasons I needed to be detained under the provisions of the Mental Health Act, under stress I am somewhat less than reliable. I'd forgotten to lock the front door and had actually gone out to the shops leaving it wide open on more than one occasion. It was lucky that very little had disappeared.

Some of the missing things I had loved, like the local watercolours that had been in the hallway. Some valuable, like the jewellery and designer clothes. Some emotionally important, like the Roald Dahl book Grandma used to read to me at bedtime. Occasionally I would work my way through a cupboard or along a bookshelf, hoping I'd overlooked it, but it was nowhere to be found.

Grandma's small Tiffany revolver with the engraved silver grip had gone missing too. She'd kept it in the drawer by her bed, along with a box of ammunition. I'd pointed out that she wouldn't have time to load it if a burglar broke in, but she had resolutely ignored my suggestion it should go in the safe. If only I'd thought of that after she died. I hadn't dared report it to the police – I was sure Grandma hadn't got a licence, and in any case, I thought they might not believe me that it existed, after I'd been sectioned.

I wasn't going to sleep now; I was too restless. I dressed quickly, ran down to the kitchen, and put the kettle on for tea. I took it into the library. Still my favourite room, where I felt closest to Grandma, surrounded by her collection.

I turned the light on and made sure the shutters were closed. Then I lit the candle which always stood on the small table at the north wall.

I walked all around the room, touching books on the shelves as I passed, and remembering how Grandma had loved this room.

The bookcases held an impressive number of books on the ancient world and on archaeology. Grandma's special collection on folklore, behind lock and key. There were also cabinets full of what as a child I'd called Grandma's treasure. As an adult I knew better – I knew most of the artefacts were replicas. I'd even been there with her, when some of it was commissioned, after a visit to an exhibition at the British museum. She'd become good friends with a local silversmith and the reproductions he made were Grandma's one real extravagance.

Though not quite treasure, it was a valuable collection of museum quality replicas. My favourite items were a pair of silver platters, and a two handled Roman drinking vessel, that Grandma called a skyphos. The drinking vessel had an engraving of an unknown goddess, surrounded by dogs. Grandma had speculated that she might be a local version of the goddess Diana or Artemis.

From her intensity, I suspected that a similar goddess had played a part in the rituals of the local pagan group Grandma had presided over in her youth, but that was another of the subjects on which curiosity was forbidden. One of the platters depicted the god Bacchus, and the other Medusa. They took pride of place. She always talked of donating the collection to the local museum, but had made no mention in her will. It occurred to me now that it might be a sensible move, given that my stalker could apparently get into the house.

In the meantime, I'd best start being more careful with the alarm, and remembering to lock up. I snuffed out the candle before going back up to bed.

TEN

IT WAS AFTER ten the next morning when I was awoken by the sound of the phone ringing. Not again. My mother was virtually the only one who ever phoned me.

When the racket stopped, I picked up the receiver and dialled 1471. It was Mrs Banerjee's number. I felt ashamed of myself – I should have made the effort to go and see her before this.

I got out of bed and rang back, walking around the room. When she answered, I lied.

"Sorry, Mrs B," I said, hoping I sounded breathless, "I got in as the phone stopped ringing." I didn't want anyone to know I was spending so much of my time hiding from life under the covers.

"Thanks for calling back," she said. "I was wondering if you could lend a hand today. We've a few folk off work with a virus."

"Course I can," I said. I couldn't help feeling she was just keeping an eye on me, fulfilling her promise to Grandma to look after me. "Where do you want me?" I asked.

"Pop in to the office," she said. "And we can work out what hours will suit."

That wouldn't be a problem. I could fit it in between naps and panic attacks.

Did she know about Harry? I'd wait until I saw her in person, but I really didn't want another inquisition. Would Mrs B look at me searchingly, wondering if I might run amok at any moment?

I couldn't face the walk across the Beacon, so I cycled into town. On the High Street, as I was chaining my bike up, I saw Grandma's solicitor, John Harvey, coming towards me. I suppose he's my solicitor now. It just doesn't feel like it.

He saw me and raised his hand. My heart sank.

"Alice," he said, grasping my hand. "How lovely to see you looking so well."

I smiled and escaped his grip.

"I was so sorry to hear about Harry's death," he continued. "He's been a part of this town for so long. And a great loss to you, as well, my dear. Is there anything you need?"

"I'll miss him," I said. "I was beginning to get to know him properly. He was good to me."

I wondered if Mr Harvey knew I'd found the body. It seemed too ghoulish to bring up in conversation.

"It was fortunate I bumped into you," he continued. "We must have a word about the Trust, if you can spare some time. I know your mother is concerned – she's already been on the phone."

Ah. My mother. I'd been on the verge of putting him off.

"A few minutes," I said, "I'm on my way to see Mrs Banerjee."

He smiled. "Let's have tea and a toasted muffin then and skip the office. I think we'll be more comfortable."

I didn't tell him I'd have preferred the office – the tea rooms would be good practice in avoiding panic attacks. And I really didn't want my lawyer worrying that I couldn't cope out in the real world.

We found a table in the corner, and once I was safely barricaded behind a linen-draped table and a vase of carnations, I relaxed.

As we started on our tea, I had to ask.

"What did mother want? Surely she didn't think the Trust could now be broken?"

"It can't. You know as well as I do that Frances was stubborn, and she was determined you'd have until the age of thirty to grow up without the responsibility."

I noticed he didn't deny that was what Helen wanted.

"Until I'm safely past the age when I might hand it all over to the wrong man," I said.

"Is that what you think?" He sounded surprised, but didn't elaborate.

"Mr Rook as trustee too. I never understood that."

He sighed. "Mr Rook was reluctant enough to do the job, said he hardly knew you and it wasn't fair on you either, but after Frances talked to him... well. She was persuasive."

That was hardly news to me. I wished I understood her reasons though.

I was struck by a sudden thought. "Mr Harvey," I said.

He interrupted. "I think it's okay if you call me John now. I think we've known each other long enough."

"John, did my mother know that Harry Rook was the trustee?"

"Didn't he tell you? Oh dear. I told him he really should."

"Tell me what? Why do I feel like I know nothing at all about my own life?"

This was more than a one cup of tea conversation. I poured us both a second cup.

"Remember when you were in hospital, and your mother had you sign all that paperwork?"

"Yes," I said. "It was routine stuff, to make sure that all the bills were paid. The mortgage and council tax. To make sure the business could continue to operate in my absence. It was a temporary power of attorney, I think."

"And Harry came to the hospital to see you? With some more paperwork?"

I nodded.

"He had to move to protect your interests. Your mother wanted to challenge the trust, to close it down. She wanted to sell the house and the business."

"I knew that," I said. "Grandma said she would, and that she'd made sure it was impossible. I told her that, in the hospital, but she wouldn't believe me."

"But you signed the papers anyway? What if it had gone to court? What if Mr Rook hadn't stopped her?"

I looked down, ashamed. "I didn't much care, to be honest. Let it happen as it will, that was what I thought."

"It was not what your grandmother wanted." He sounded quite cross.

"But it was what my mother wanted," I pointed out. "I can see her point, can't you? I've been piggy-in-the-middle all my life."

"Perhaps Frances was right about the Trust then," he said.

"All that control, it didn't make her happy, did it? Not the best example of how life should be lived."

"Nor is your mother's," he said.

I knew what he meant. I'd heard her begging for Grandma's help often enough. To buy her out of one scrape or other. Usually money-making schemes gone wrong. She'd come dangerously close to a prison sentence once – I'm not sure how exactly, but Grandma made restitution and it was all hushed up.

But all the same, she was my mother.

"When I'm thirty, I will be splitting everything in half," I said. "With a chainsaw if need be. In my opinion, that should be happening now."

"Perhaps Frances was hoping that you would realise your mistake by that age," he said, with a wry smile. "She wasn't ungenerous, you know. Helen gets a monthly allowance, and she had a lump sum that has apparently all gone."

"I've told her already and I won't go back on my word. She's hurt, that's all. She and Grandma always had problems."

"They weren't all of Frances' making, but this problem is. I'm sorry, Alice. I have to tell you that she didn't sort this one out properly. I tried to tell her that she should make a decision about what would happen if Mr Rook should become unable to administer the trust. She simply wouldn't believe it possible. In the end she said he was the only one she knew would do right by you. So she left it in his hands. And now he's gone…"

"Who will be taking his place? It will be you, won't it? I'm hoping to resume my studies soon."

"Excellent. You're going to take up the Oxford place? That was specifically allowed for in the setting up of the trust. There can be no objection there."

He was avoiding my question. Not a good sign.

"I'm considering the local Romans in Sussex course first, with Professor Buckley. Only as a stepping stone, to let myself into it gently…"

I could see he was genuinely pleased – although he did feel the need to ask me if I was sure it was what I wanted to study.

"We all adored Frances, no doubt about it," he said. "But there's no denying she was a strong-willed woman. If you'd rather choose another subject, there's no need…"

A vision of Mr Harvey dressed in long robes and chanting appeared in my mind. He'd certainly known Grandma long enough for him to have been one of the Cuckmere Coven, as the tabloids dubbed it. Perhaps I should ask him about the rabbit, if he had any idea who was still involved with the old ways.

I shook my head. He wasn't the sort, was he? Then again, who would have thought Grandma was?

"No," I said. "I'm sure. I wanted to be an archaeologist when I was a child, and I never grew out of it."

"Any educational avenue will be fine. I'm not sure about any plans you might have regarding the business though."

"The new trustee?"

There was a pause. I could tell he didn't want to say it out loud.

"It may be a little awkward. The new trustee, well, it will be Julia Rook."

Oh great. I was going to have to deal with her now, whether I liked it or not. And she with me.

I shrugged. "Obviously you know there was some sort of feud between Grandma and the Rook family. Grandma patched things up with Harry, but not with Julia. If anything it got worse…"

He said nothing.

"Can you tell me what it was about?"

"No, I'm sorry, I can't."

"It would make it so much easier if I knew what I was up against. But she doesn't have to accept, right? She can't be legally forced to take on the responsibility."

"That's correct. However, I have spoken to her, very briefly, and she thinks it is her duty, because Harry wanted her to do it."

Could this week get any worse? I thought it was better not to tempt fate that way, and touched the wooden table, unobtrusively.

"I'll go to see her then," I said. "I wanted to pass on my condolences, but I was too chicken. Now it's going to look like it's self-serving."

He smiled. "You're not chicken," he said. "Look, you're here dealing with this. You've signed up for a course. You're making plans for the future. That all requires courage. It's not courage you'd need to break this damned tangle of a family feud. Heaven knows I tried hard enough, back in the early days."

I wondered what he meant, but didn't ask.

"Concentrate on getting on with your life," he said. "Forget about the past. Now it's time to live in the present, and look forward to the future."

I thought about that maxim about learning from history, but supposed it was still sensible advice. As ever, I made a joke to deflect my feelings.

"Forget about the past? Good advice for a future archaeologist," I said.

"Things have a way of working out," he replied, ever the optimist. "I expect Harry had hopes of reconciliation between the families."

That, I did know was true. "Julia was being stubborn, he said. He also said she'd come round in the end. He was sure he could charm her. He probably would have, in time. I'm not sure I can, though."

Mr Harvey insisted on paying the bill, and he walked with me until we reached his offices. I watched as he disappeared through the door to his building, then I continued on to Mrs B's, hoping she'd forgive me for being a little late.

ELEVEN

I HOVERED ON the doorstep of the photography studio and my doubts and fears were swept away by the warmth of Mr Banerjee's welcome.

"What a treat to see you again, my dear," he said, and not a word of my lateness or long absence. He showed me through into his cosy sitting room at the back of the studio.

"Make yourself comfortable and I'll call Mrs B down, and we'll have tea."

I didn't really need more tea, but I couldn't refuse.

"Still not retired, I see," I teased him. Sixty-five had passed him by some time ago, and every year he talked of retiring. He loved his work so much, he wouldn't ever give it up.

Mrs B appeared, summoned downstairs by the bell Mr B had installed in her office.

"So sorry I took so long to get here," I said, my guilt pre-empting any greeting. "I bumped into Mr Harvey, and he wanted a chat."

"Good," she said, enveloping me in a hug. "One less thing I have to nag you about."

I laughed. "That doesn't augur well. Shall I run away now?"

"I know your priority is getting back to your education," she said. "But in the meanwhile we could really use your help."

She left unsaid the part about it doing me good to have some responsibility. I could almost hear Grandma's voice filling in the silence.

I made my speech again about why I'd chosen the local course instead of going straight to Oxford. I felt a little like a child again, justifying my choices to the grownups.

Mrs B's eyes lit up at my mention of Professor Buckley.

"The one off the telly?" she asked. "He's a bit of a hunk, isn't he?"

I laughed. Mrs B had been trying to matchmake for me since I was sixteen. "He's much too old for me, but he's supposed to be an excellent teacher. And there's real archaeology in the course too. Actual digging!"

She looked perplexed. "If it's something you want to do, that's fine by me."

"It is," I said.

"Now what about the business? Have you thought any more about letting me buy you out?"

"I think we'll have to put that on hold for now. I don't really know what is happening with the Trust, so we may have to wait until my thirtieth birthday."

"I would like to get it settled, but I know it's not your fault. What was Frances thinking?"

"She was trying to protect me from myself, I guess. And predatory men."

"As if being thirty is any protection!" she said. "One day I'll tell you about my first marriage…"

Mr Banerjee harrumphed and she smiled at him. "I know, I know," she said. "I was lucky in my second choice."

"That was my good luck, not yours," he said.

"How old were you then?" I asked.

"Thirty-nine," she said. "But you don't have to wait that long. It's time you fell in love."

I grimaced. "Not yet," I said. "I have things to do first."

Mr Banerjee threw his hands up in mock despair. "Have some fun, girl! With someone wildly inappropriate. As long as you don't marry him." That last bit was in response to a glare from his wife.

"What?" he said. "Your family thought I was wildly inappropriate."

"And you still are," she said. "To business!"

I breathed a sigh of relief. I'd had enough of people cosseting me. I wanted the chance to mess up on my own for a while. Getting away to Oxford would have helped.

Still, I agreed to her plan to have me help out part time at first and work out something more regular once I knew what my course would entail. I had Grandma's sense of duty, after all.

"Your education comes first," she said. "It was what Frances wanted, and she shall have it."

"Everything else is running smoothly?"

"The cleaning and care business is growing faster than we can handle. I'm always looking for new staff – workers who can be relied on. But yes, apart from that. I do need to talk to you about the farm."

"Oh, I am sorry, I hadn't thought about that. I left you to deal with everything, didn't I?"

"It was no trouble at all, until the tenant farmer decided to end it all. Shotgun, in the barn."

"Steve Thornley? Oh no. Grandma adored him. And what about his son? What was his name now?"

"Daniel. He found the body."

"Poor boy. I must go and see him, and make sure he's okay. Is he still at the farm?"

"He disappeared, Alice. I'd have happily signed over the tenancy to him, debt or not, but he's only sixteen. He upped and left. I asked the police, and they said his clothes had gone, and his bike. He's on the Missing Persons register, but they don't seem to have made any progress."

"How long has he been on his own?"

"A couple of months now. There was some suggestion he might have gone to his mother, but no one seems to know anything about her. Steve had custody of the boy for as long as anyone can remember."

"So what are we doing with the farm? Any ideas?"

"I had it cleaned up, put all the Thornleys' belongings in storage, and left it empty. He'd let a lot of it run down. The few animals left, about a dozen sheep and some chickens and ducks, were taken on by a neighbouring farmer. I send someone out to look it over every week."

"The other properties?"

"Everything's ticking over nicely. The renovations on Number 18 are nearly finished. We might start to consider looking for the next wreck to add to our portfolio."

Kelly. I paused for a moment, but I had promised.

"While we're on the subject, there's one thing. I have a friend in the hospital who's homeless. I wondered if the new studio flats are all taken."

"There's a waiting list. But one of the tenants in the East Street house has given notice. He's got a job up North, moving back to be close to his children. But are you sure…?"

She faltered, trying to find a kind way of asking if I was sure we could risk our property in the hands of a nutter.

"I'll guarantee her rent personally," I said. "She's a good person, Mrs B. She looked out for me in there. I owe her."

"If you're certain. You know, this kind of favour can come back to bite you in the behind."

"I've been lucky," I said. "She hasn't. No support from her family at all, and the worst she's likely to do is paint the walls. She's an artist too, very talented. I'm trying to encourage her to apply to Art College."

"Lucky," she said, and muttered something about my mother and how supportive she hadn't been.

"Kelly needs something to look forward to. I'll be keeping an eye on her anyway, Mrs B. If she gets manic again, I will notice."

"Okay, then. If you're sure. The flat's due to be vacated at the beginning of November."

If Kelly was discharged earlier, she could always stay with me. Now that would upset mother.

No matter what had happened, I did feel very fortunate – when I thought of Daniel, the missing boy, and Kelly whose family undermined her and who'd left her homeless. Compared with them I had so much.

Grandma fretted before she died. Some days she'd talked about leaving a mess behind for me to sort out. At the end I think she was confused, because after all she had made sure I had Harry to help me, and John Harvey, and there was always Mrs B.

She could have had no premonition that Harry would die. I still didn't want to believe he was murdered – surely it must have been accidental. Perhaps he'd disturbed whoever was playing pagan games, drawing pentagrams, sacrificing rabbits. Maybe the shock of the stake going through his hand had provoked a heart attack. I couldn't imagine that anyone would deliberately want to kill him.

Grandma had been so worried she had made me promise that I would look after everything for her. Everything! How was I supposed to know what that meant? Then she tied my hands to make it impossible. But I will keep my promise, once I've worked it out.

TWELVE

A DAY'S CLEANING with Mrs B's crack team had actually done me some good. Not only had it worn me out, it had reminded me of how my life used to be before the anxiety and the panic attacks. To my surprise, my bleak mood had dissolved overnight, and I was actually looking forward to the open evening at the University, and especially to Professor Buckley's lecture.

First, I had a busy day ahead, with no spare time to hide away under the covers. More cleaning jobs, one office and two domestics, and my routine appointment with my mental health support worker, Claire. At least I could fit that in between times – it was on my route between one old lady and another.

My case worker's office was at the local hospital, so I didn't have to trek out to Brookfields.

I'd seen Claire twice since I was discharged, and I was hoping we could follow the most optimistic route through my outpatient care plan, and taper off the visits from fortnightly to monthly, and eventually stop them altogether.

As I'd said last time, "I want to get back to a normal life and put this behind me."

She'd smiled and said she understood, and that was what she wanted too. Somehow, I didn't feel reassured.

At least she was efficient, and I didn't have to spend much time in the waiting room, leafing through old copies of *Good Housekeeping* and *Hello*.

Our session started as it always did. How was I coping with life on the outside? With a heavy emphasis on whether I was taking my medication.

"Religiously," I said. "Every Sunday."

Perhaps the joke would cover up any signs that I was lying.

"Still the joker," she said, with a forced smile.

I didn't admit that when I came out of hospital it had taken me a few days to remember. I'd become institutionalised, accepting medication and food when it was put in front of me but forgetting how to look after myself. I'd missed a few meals too.

"Seriously, now." Claire continued. "You know medication is an important element in your care plan. If you're having any problems, any difficulties with side effects, that's what I'm here for. I can arrange an appointment with Dr Lal and we can try another treatment regime."

"No problems," I said. "I'd rather not be taking them at all, but I guess we won't be considering that quite yet."

"Perhaps we can taper them off when you've been stable a little longer," she said, which was pretty much what I'd expected she'd say, if not what I was intending to do.

I volunteered the information that I was working for Mrs B, that I would be attending the open evening at the University and was planning to apply for a place on Professor Buckley's course.

That earned me some brownie points, after I'd been cautioned on running before I could walk.

Then came the difficult part. I had to tell her about finding Harry. I knew if I ducked it and she found out there could be repercussions.

"There's one more thing I have to tell you," I said. "Did you read about the death of Harry Rook, the owner of the Cuckmere Amusement Park?"

"Yes," she said. "Shocking story. That's near where you live, isn't it? I hope you've not been too distressed."

"I found him," I said. "I was the one who found his body. He was a friend too, and more than that. Grandma made him my trustee."

I could see the doubts flitting across her face. Was I recounting some kind of grandiose fantasy, implying a relationship that didn't exist? Making myself the centre of a topical news story that had happened on my doorstep.

It was nothing, compared with some of the more florid fantasies I'd heard while I was on the unit. One young woman had been convinced the charming young Indian doctor was her brother (adopted – he was from Delhi and she was from Essex) and that he'd arranged for her stay on the unit to protect her from the CIA.

"I called the police," I said. "I did all the relaxation exercises I was taught as I waited for them to arrive. It didn't really help though."

Claire decided to believe me, but I had little doubt she'd be checking up on the facts later. "I'm so sorry," she said. "That must have been very difficult for you. If you need any extra support, please don't be afraid to ask."

She wasn't all bad. Her heart was in the right place.

I smiled at her. "I'm doing okay," I said. "I haven't felt the urge to set fire to anything. Yet."

She laughed then, a real laugh. "Oh Alice, what am I going to do with you?"

"I'll miss him. It's another link with Grandma gone. She asked him to look out for me. He was someone I could turn to with my problems."

"I hope you'll learn you can come to me, too," she said. "If you'd like an extra appointment, I can fit you in the same time next week?"

"The usual will be fine," I said.

"See you in two weeks, then." I could tell she was disappointed, but she didn't push it. I said goodbye, walking calmly out of the room when really, I wanted to run. Once off hospital grounds, I felt myself relax. It was as if I'd been holding my breath. I'd survived another encounter with the system and was still free.

Free to clean another old lady's kitchen floor.

After finishing work, I was late at the campus, still in my cleaning gear. I took the overalls off and carried them over one arm, struggling with my sense of direction as I tried to find the right building.

I could hear the lecture had already begun, but I didn't have the nerve to open the door and walk into the lecture hall late and have them all turn and look at me as I struggled to find the nearest seat.

Coward that I am, I hung around by the notice board. There were cards posted by various students looking for somewhere to live, which reminded me of Kelly and how happy I was to be able to help her. I knew how much it meant, when every day was spent locked in that drab, grey place. Kelly felt it more than most, when even in art therapy her every piece was scrutinised for evidence of her health. After one of her paintings had been dubbed too dark and depressing, she'd temporarily frozen and been unable to paint. As she put it, anything you write or draw or paint may be used in evidence against you.

Her love of art had come to her rescue, together with a realisation that not participating was equally liable to be seen as symptomatic. The classic double bind.

There was a postcard signed by the Professor himself, looking for a cleaning lady. I might have to give him a business card and recommend our services. Perhaps I'd talk to Mrs B about recruiting more students, if she was seriously under staffed. I still suspected she didn't really need me, and it was mostly a kind of occupational therapy.

The sounds from the lecture hall changed, and I heard people milling around. The door opened and a tall, blond, young man slipped out, nodded at me, and walked off briskly. I decided to risk going in.

The door groaned loudly, which alarmed me, but no one else noticed. They were all gathered round Professor Buckley at a couple of big tables at the side of the room. The Professor wasn't quite what I was expecting. He wasn't as old as I'd thought, or as tall as he seemed on TV. Perhaps in his late thirties, he was clean-shaven, with cropped dark hair, and was casually dressed. He was also gorgeous. Mrs B was right about that.

There weren't so many potential students as I expected either. I'd imagined a much larger group. There were a dozen or so people, all ages. Some not much older than me, if at all. A couple of tall young men, and a bearded grey-haired pensioner. A few middle-aged ladies, who looked as if they'd escaped from the Women's Institute and should be more interested in jam making and knitting than grubbing around in the dirt. Now who was guilty of stereotyping? I slapped myself mentally on the wrist.

I hovered at the back of the group and listened to their questions and the Professor's answers. He seemed like quite a relaxed guy, and not as intimidating as the people who had interviewed me at Oxford. Still I was too nervous to join in. The group all picked up application forms from the table, and as if following some unseen signal, moved as one and flowed out of the room.

I picked up a form myself, and found a pile of handouts too, that I'd obviously missed out on by being late. I picked one up, thrilled to see that it included a reading list. Perhaps some of the books would be in Grandma's library, and I'd be able to get started straight away.

The course promised lots of practical work, as well as visits to local sites of interest – Fishbourne and Bignor Roman Villas. There was a lecture series and a fair bit of essay writing. I was quite excited by the prospect, and it sounded challenging enough to give me the confidence to take up my place at Oxford. If I passed. If I survived.

When I left the lecture room the hallway was all deserted. They'd all moved on, perhaps to the bar. What had my mother said about having a normal social life with normal friends? On the whole, I suspected a group of wannabe archaeologists wouldn't count by her standards.

I wandered down the hall, feeling moderately pleased with myself. I'd made progress, I had the application form, and a reading list. Okay, so I hadn't actually spoken to anyone…

As that realisation brought me back down again, a door at the end of the corridor opened, and Professor Buckley came through it. He was on his own and looking rather distracted.

My heart in my mouth, I took the chance that fate offered me.

"Professor Buckley." I said, too quietly to be heard.

My mouth was dry, my heart was beating fast.

"Professor Buckley." Now that was better, almost a shout. He turned round, looked at me, and waited for me to catch up.

"I was only wondering..." I said, nervously.

He smiled at me, a very calm and patient smile. "About the cleaning job?" he asked. "It's still open." He reached into his pocket and gave me a card.

"Call on me tomorrow, at eleven. I'm late already, sorry, must fly."

With that he rushed out of the building, leaving me equally embarrassed and amused. It was my own fault – I'd come dressed in work clothes, holding my nylon overalls in front of me like a shield. I looked more like a cleaner than a prospective archaeology student.

Perhaps mother was right and associating with Kelly had me sliding down the social ladder. And to think I worried about coming across as posh and privileged. I laughed.

THIRTEEN

THE NEXT DAY at the appointed time, I walked down the seafront looking at the house numbers, hoping I was in roughly the right place. As I'd expected, the house was beautiful – a tall Regency terrace, with a basement and several stories, all white-painted stucco facade and black wrought-iron balconies.

There were a couple of similar properties in Grandma's portfolio, both divided into bedsits and in need of some renovation.

I'd dressed in my best clothes – smart tailored black trousers, leather ankle boots and silk shirt. I wanted to shake up his perceptions, and that was a bit worrying in itself. Since the Dr Mansfield regime, I'd more or less rebelled against the desire to create a good impression, and preferred to slouch around in my old clothes. Or maybe their theory was right and it was a symptom of depression. However, it was unlikely now that Professor Buckley would hand me the scouring powder and a loo brush and leave me to get stuck in.

That was what I told myself, as I rang the bell. I was shaking so much I thought my legs might literally give way.

He opened the door and looked at me without any sign of recognition.

"I was at the open evening, last night," I said. "You gave me your card and told me to call at eleven."

"The cleaner?" he said, doing a double take. "You don't look like a cleaner. Err, come in, please."

He moved aside, and I brushed past him as I stepped into the hall. I managed not to reach out and use the wall to steady myself, but I still felt alarmingly wobbly.

What was the advice they gave at the hospital? Admit how you're feeling and it gets easier. It was worth a try.

"I'm sorry," I said. "I feel a bit nervous, and I was stupid last night not to set you right, but you were in a rush."

"I was," he said. "I made the mistake so I should apologise."

I noticed he didn't though. Most people don't apologise all the time like I do. Something to work on.

"I did look like a cleaner," I said. "I was late after a hard day and didn't have time to change. I might be of some help with the cleaning issue, but really I was hoping for a quick word about the course."

He ushered me through to a large living room. It was as I imagined a Professor's house – every flat surface overflowing with papers, and every wall lined with full book shelves. The sofa and easy chairs looked comfortable, but there was no space to sit. He hastily gathered together the papers on the nearest chair and gestured for me to sit down, while he pulled up the office chair from his desk and sat on it backwards, with his legs akimbo, and an easy smile on his face and asked me to begin.

Even though I was developing a bit of a crush on him, I started to feel more relaxed. I tried my best to sound all business like.

"First off, about the cleaning. Unless you're keen to employ a student, I can recommend Cuckmere Domestics, my Grandmas business. Well, technically it's mine, now, so I suppose I'm touting for business, but it really doesn't matter, so if you'd rather—"

"You're not in sales, are you?" he asked, laughing.

"I'm not," I agreed, ruefully. "Grandma was the businesswoman of the family. But it is a good service, if you feel inclined."

"I was hoping to find a student, so there'd be some mutual benefit," he said. "But no applicants as yet, so you could give me a card. But you didn't get all dressed up for that, so tell me, what is this about?"

I blushed but didn't reach for an excuse.

"I was late for your lecture, but I do want to sign up for the course. I was planning to study classical history and archaeology, and I was offered a place at Oxford four years ago, but life had other plans."

I paused, but he didn't ask. I was relieved – I hadn't had much practice talking about it yet. I'd have to deal with it eventually, I supposed.

"I'm planning to take up that place next year, but I need to let myself in gently. I know this isn't a full-time course and that suits me, but I wondered how much of a commitment it is. How much time will it take to really get the most out of it?"

He grinned.

"I think the course will suit you very well. I was worried for a moment there, that you wanted an easy ride, to get away with as little as possible. There'll be plenty of opportunities for practical work – we liaise with sites across the South East that are looking for volunteers, and sometimes we do our own excavations."

"Great," I said. "In that case, I've filled in the application form. Shall I leave it with you or mail it in?"

"I'll take it," he said. "If you need any help with applications for financial support?"

"No, I'm fine," I said.

I noticed he was looking at my necklace, so I took it off and passed it over to him.

"I found it when I was eight," I said. "On the cliffs, out at Cuckmere Beacon. I was so excited. That's how I got hooked on history and archaeology."

He was weighing it carefully in his hand and turning it over.

"Interesting setting," he said, looking at the filigree pentagram on the back of the casing.

"My grandmother had it made for me," I said. "She was friends with a silversmith – a craftsman who made copies of ancient artefacts for museums and collectors."

"It's a lovely thing," he said, looking up. "The coin is unusual. Would you mind if I kept it for a few days? I'd like to take it to my pal at the British Museum and see what he thinks. I think you have a very special artefact here."

I didn't know what to say, how to deny him, but my silence was enough.

"I can see you don't want to part with it," he said, gently. I braced myself for the manipulation to follow, but he handed it back to me, and I hung it around my neck. "And you say it was found in Cuckmere? Are you absolutely certain?"

"I remember finding it…" my voice trailed off.

"But?" he prompted.

"I did wonder if Grandma might have planted it, to get me interested."

"I thought your grandmother was a businesswoman?" he said.

"She certainly was, but she always regretted dropping out of her own studies. I never quite understood why she didn't go back to it once she had the chance."

"I'd be interested to see where you found it, nevertheless. One of the first things you will learn on the course is that context is often the most valuable part of any find. Archaeology is about understanding the past – we're not mere treasure hunters."

"Of course," I said, smiling. I knew enough not to mention he reminded me of Indiana Jones, or how many times I'd watched those films in my childhood.

"You could come up to London with me, if you'd prefer to hang on to it?" he offered.

Ah, here it was. An offer I couldn't refuse – even though I was nervous. If I couldn't handle shopping in Cuckmere, how would I handle London?

"I might take you up on that," I said. "I haven't been up to the Museum since, well, for a long time. Is it that interesting a coin?"

"I do think it might be," he said. "Only one way to find out. I'll give you a ring to arrange a time, then, when I've spoken to my friend. Is your mobile number on the card?"

"No, that's the business. But it's on my application form," I reminded him.

"That's right, I'd forgotten. You know, we do a pretty good degree course here, so if you change your mind about Oxford... But there's no need to think about it now."

More flattery, already. He didn't even know if I was good student or not. All about the coin, then.

"I must go," I said, looking at my watch. "I have an appointment at noon, and I don't want to be late."

I said my goodbyes, improbably pleased that I'd be seeing him again. I knew how silly it was, but I knew it was a good sign. Grandma would have been glad I was getting on with my education, as I'd promised her, but not quite so happy I was attracted to my new Professor.

So much so that I'd agreed to the day in London so easily, in spite of my fears. It would be interesting to find out something about my coin. Maybe it would confirm that Grandma had planted it for me to find. That would be so like her – mother would call it controlling, but to my mind what mattered was the intention. An object lesson for an archaeologist though.

It was a trinket to interest a child – no different than the play doubloons hidden in the sand at the Pirate Island adventure park from some childhood holiday. I hadn't liked having to give them up, I recalled, even if they had been replaced with chocolate ones. I laughed, as I connected the dots for the first time. It wasn't long after that holiday that I'd found the Roman coin. I guess I had my answer already.

FOURTEEN

I LIED – there was no appointment. I needed to get out of there before my inner coward chickened out of the projected trip to London. I didn't have any work scheduled, so I decided to go home and have a meltdown in private.

On impulse, I got off the bus outside the police station. I wanted to know how the investigation was going. Perhaps they'd found the person with snares and stakes and portable ritual paraphernalia, and discovered it was all some horrible accident. It was bad enough knowing I had a stalker, without thinking there was a murderer out there too. Worst case scenario, they could be one and the same person. I had to tell the police, I decided, even if they did take it as further proof I was unreliable. A nutter. What if it was connected and I'd held back?

I visualised DI Collingwood's expression as he told me I'd obstructed a murder investigation, because I was embarrassed to make a fuss.

Steeling myself, I crossed the road, walked straight into the police station and spoke to the Sergeant on the reception desk.

"May I speak to DI Collingwood, please? Alice Hunter, it's about the murder. Well, it might be, I suppose."

Way to go, Alice. Start off by undermining yourself.

"Is it or isn't it?" he asked, putting me on the spot.

"I don't know. That's the point. It might be related." I was talking too much. The way he was looking at me didn't help.

He called through and after a quiet conversation, told me that DI Collingwood was too busy to see me, and that I could come back the following day, or make a statement now, if it was important.

"I'll do it now. It doesn't really matter who I talk to," I said. "Only I spoke to DI Collingwood last time."

He sent me into a small side room and a couple of minutes later, the young policewoman – I recognised her as DC King – came and took my statement.

"I thought I ought to tell you, in case there is a connection." I explained to her about the stalker I'd had since coming out of hospital, how he had secretly sketched me on the Beacon and clearly knew the local area very well.

"I don't know if he was around that day. But maybe he had something to do with the rabbit, he might be the local pagan oddball, or he might be a witness."

She scribbled some notes and then paused and looked at me. "Is there anything else you think might help us?" she asked.

"No, I don't think so. I wouldn't even have thought of my stalker if it weren't for the flowers."

I decided again not to mention Grandma's pagan connection. It would only draw attention to too many things I didn't want to think about, let alone talk about.

"That does seem very frightening, Miss Hunter. Not the sort of thing you'd be likely to forget."

She left a long silence, and I said nothing. I couldn't bring myself to explain why I hadn't wanted to talk about it. In case I was imagining it, in case it wasn't real, in case it was real but no one believed me.

"You're living there on your own? Why not stay with your mother?" she continued.

I laughed at that. "I'd prefer to stay in Cuckmere."

DC King raised an eyebrow, as if that were unreasonable. I got defensive and babbled on. "I'm getting used to being on my own but living with my mother would drive me crazy."

I winced at that particular cliché, and she saw me wince. I wasn't surprised that they knew. I suppose they had to check everyone out.

"It's real you know, not imagined. I have a folder with all the postcards. I can bring them in if you want."

She smiled, a bit too quickly. "I'm sure DI Collingwood will want to see them, but he's busy right now. He doesn't have time to talk to all the witnesses himself, you know. We'll be in touch. Thank you for coming in."

I felt a bit taken aback. She sounded like a receptionist trying to protect the doctor from a hypochondriacal patient. Or was it something else? Did she think I was the stalker here, chasing after her boss? Perhaps she had a thing for him. He was certainly attractive enough.

She walked with me to the police station main door, seeing me off the premises, as if making sure I wasn't going to hang around.

Walking down Beacon Road, I shivered, as if I was being watched. I turned around, and looked, but could see nothing out of the ordinary. Except – wasn't that DI Collingwood, slipping out of sight, going into the police station? With DC King, right behind him.

Perhaps he was only now getting back to the station, and that was why he hadn't had time for me. Or perhaps…

Paranoia was creeping up on me – if not my stalker, or the police.

Shaking the uneasy feeling off, I called in at the off licence and bought a couple of bottles of wine. It wouldn't do to leave too many spaces in the wine rack in case my mother decided to do an audit, but she'd never notice I'd replaced good reds with cheap plonk. I'd better stock up on the good stuff too sometime. I also bought some more roses from the greengrocer, this time for Julia. I would do the right thing, even though it would now look like doing the wrong thing.

In the shop white roses again seemed the most appropriate choice.

On impulse I spoke to the shop assistant. "I bought some of these roses from you the other day. Tuesday, I think it was. You don't happen to remember someone coming in and buying some right after me, do you? I know it's a long shot…"

"No, sorry," she said. "Intriguing question!"

I stumbled a bit on my explanation. I hadn't thought it through properly. "Someone left a bunch on my doorstep," I said.

"A secret admirer, how romantic."

I summoned a smile, deciding not to disillusion her.

FIFTEEN

I INTENDED TO strengthen my resolve for the coming visit to Julia, perhaps with strong liquor, or at least a cup of tea, but when I approached home, Tamsin's car was parked on the Rooks' drive. It was too good an opportunity to miss.

Tamsin answered the door. She looked startled to see me there, as well she might, but she saw the flowers.

"I'm so sorry, Tammy." I said. "He was a wonderful man, and I know how it feels to lose someone so close. I thought perhaps I could give these to Julia?"

"Thanks," she said, standing squarely in the doorway. "It must be hard for you, remind you of – But now might not be the best time."

Even now, she still sounded cold, as if she was pushing me away. I was hurt and struggled to hide it.

A voice came from behind her.

"Who is it, Tammy?" Julia said.

Tammy stood aside.

Julia's face dropped. She'd aged ten years in a few days. I was struck with pity for her. I hope I managed to hide that too, and my guilt. Here I was, making her life more difficult.

I held out the flowers.

"I wanted to give you these and say how sorry I am for your loss."

I got the sentence out and although trite it made sense, but her reaction didn't. She didn't take the flowers, and she didn't refuse them either.

"You'd better come in, girl," she said, and walked back down the hall, spine erect. Tammy half pulled me in, and closed the door behind me, whispering in my ear.

"She hasn't slept. Don't upset her."

I glared at her then. That was sure to be my intention, visiting a grieving widow to upset her.

Tammy backed off. "Sorry," she said very quietly, "I know. I'm worried about her. That's all."

I whispered back, still angry. "I'm trying to do the right thing."

"What are you two whispering about? Come in here please, instead of acting like naughty children."

Tammy grimaced at me then, on automatic, and for a moment I felt like my friend was back. Then her expression went blank, and she virtually pushed me into the room ahead of her. Julia was sitting by the fire, in an armchair.

I stood in the middle of the room, my weight shifting uneasily from one foot to the other, as if I were in the headmistress' office.

Julia sat in silence. She knew how uncomfortable I felt, and she liked it.

"Mrs Rook," I said. "I should have come sooner. I am truly very sorry for your loss. I was only beginning to know your husband. He was a good man, and he took time to make my life easier. I will miss him."

"Good speech," she said. "Did you commit it to memory?"

"I am sorry," I tried again. "I knew you and Grandma weren't friends, and because of that I made a mistake. I should have come straight away. I'll go now. What shall I do with the flowers?"

"Don't be ridiculous. You're here now, and we have things to discuss. Give them to Tamsin. She'll take them into the kitchen, and while she's at it, she'll spend a good fifteen minutes making coffee."

Tamsin took the flowers and disappeared.

"Please sit," Julia said.

I sat on the other easy chair, facing her. I saw her reaction too late and realised it was her husband's chair I was sitting in. Harry's chair. I was still living with furniture that was unthinkable for anyone but Grandma, so I knew how Julia must feel. I started to rise, and she waved at me, impatient.

"Sit," she said. "Yes, it's Harry's chair, and you're the first who's had the temerity to sit there since he died, but he's not coming back. I'll have to get used to it."

"Sorry," I said. "I didn't think."

"Say what you have to say."

I paused and thought. There was no easy way into this, but I realised that my selfish instincts had been leading me astray. Now was not the time to ask about the trusteeship, and whether she would give it up to someone else.

"I should have come that day," I said. "The policeman, he wouldn't let me go and talk to Tamsin, and then later after I gave my statement, the police were here, and journalists milling around outside."

"Tell me how he looked," she said. "Tell me the details. Harry's brother identified the body – the family ganged up and wouldn't let me see him."

She saw the look on my face and smiled, "Impossible to imagine, I expect. I do usually get my way. I suppose I was afraid. I suppose I wanted to remember him as he was alive. That morning we argued, and he slammed the door on his way out. Just the way we fought all those years ago when we first met. I want to remember him that way."

"I'm sorry you argued," I said. "That must be difficult. I did with Grandma too…"

There was my gift for saying the wrong thing again. I should never have mentioned Grandma.

But Julia smiled. "Oh no, we fought all the time. It was nothing serious, only the way we always were. He was simply full of life. He stormed off to attack the day as he always did."

"Have they said anything yet about how he died?" I asked. 'I got the impression from DI Collingwood they were treating it as murder, but…"

"They haven't said, exactly. I've pushed on cause of death but it's still with the coroner. Tell me what you saw."

"I thought at first he'd had a heart attack," I said. "His hand was on his chest, but when I got closer—"

Too late, I remembered I'd promised DI Collingwood that I wouldn't mention the stake through his hand, or the rabbits, to anyone.

I faltered. "I'm sorry," I said. "I can't say any more. The detective asked me not to."

At that point, Tamsin appeared with a tray, which she placed on the coffee table.

I decided it was time to make my escape.

"I must go now," I said. "I am sorry, Mrs Rook."

"Yes, yes, you've said that often enough," she said. "I daresay I'll be seeing you again. As we haven't even started on the real reason why you're here."

This was never going to be easy.

Tamsin walked me to the door. "The fact that she isn't in floods of tears doesn't mean she isn't hurting."

"I know that," I said.

Tamsin carried on, as if I hadn't spoken. "Already there's been another offer for the business and the house. In person, this time."

"Lovely timing," I said.

"Oh yes," Tamsin said. "Sympathetic, and thoughtful. It will help her to get over it, he said. Move away from the scene of the distressing incident."

"He?" I asked.

"Mark Stockman."

"Ah," I said. "I bumped into him in Tweedies the other day but he didn't recognise me. Our new MP, I gather."

"Yes," she said. "Cashed in on the popularity of the Marina development. Julia was all in favour, you know. She was ready to sell, although Harry wanted to stay put but Stockman pissed her off. She's keeping him hanging for now. She's probably holding out for a better offer. A great negotiator, my Auntie Julia."

"Do shut that door, dear, it's getting draughty." The imperious voice echoed in the hall.

"Aunt Julia calls," Tamsin said, and turned to go.

I reached out and touched her on the arm, and she shrugged me off.

"I don't know what I've done, Tamsin," I started.

"I have to go," she said. I thought she'd started to relax with me again, but she was still pushing me away.

She closed the door on me.

I walked slowly across the road towards home. I wondered how much Mark Stockman wanted this land. How much rested on this development.

Then I laughed at myself. He was a business man, and ruthless like all the Stockman family, I guessed. He wasn't some kind of Sussex mafioso.

To my relief there was no letter waiting on the doormat, and no flowers in the living room. I made a quick circuit of the house, checking every door and window.

Then I settled down in the library. I lit the candle and joss stick, sat cross legged on the rug and did my meditation practice. It took me so long to achieve even a basic level of calmness, I realised that I'd been neglecting the one routine I really needed.

As I put a simple meal together in the kitchen, I replayed my meeting with Julia. It hadn't gone too badly, considering. Unsurprising that she was sure that I'd only mustered the courage to go and see her because of the trust, and that was partly true. She was, however, perfectly capable of holding on to a pointless grudge for decades. Exactly like Grandma.

I put the chicken stir fry in a big white bowl and settled myself on the sofa in front of the TV and watched Mary Beard talking about Pompeii. I skipped the wine, having taken my pills that morning in a fit of remorse.

As the final credits rolled, my phone chirped.

A text message from Professor Buckley wondering if I would be able to join him the next day on a trip to the British Museum.

I replied at once, before I lost my nerve. *Yes. That would be brilliant.*

His response was simple. *Train at 9.40. Meet at station. Don't be late.*

Okay, I typed, holding back on a smiley, although I was grinning from ear to ear.

In spite of everything, I was really looking forward to the next day. I couldn't remember when I'd last felt like that.

SIXTEEN

THE TRAIN WASN'T busy. We settled down opposite each other, juggling take-away coffees.

"Who are we going to see, exactly? I know you said he was a coin expert."

"Sam Jones," he said. "Romano British artefacts. We were at Cambridge together. We had the same ambitions, we went on the same digs, we applied for the same jobs, but our paths diverged. He had a skiing accident, and was paralysed from the waist down, and could no longer do the fieldwork that had been his passion. Now, he's the first person they turn to when some amateur with a metal detector turns up a hoard. He often gets involved in cleaning up coin collections and valuing them for the coroner. I'm sure he'll be interested in this one. If it is what I think it is."

"Grandma told me that it was a pretty average Roman coin. Thousands of them all over the place, she said. You can buy them on eBay."

"If I'm right, your grandmother was telling fibs. It's true that a lot of Roman coins have been found in Britain, but relatively few of them gold. Nero in near mint condition is even more rare."

The rest of the journey passed very quickly as I encouraged him to talk about the digs he had been on, like the fan girl I was, and asked how much the students on the course I'd signed up for could expect to get involved in fieldwork. He was quietly amused by my enthusiasm, and it took my mind off the butterflies in my tummy at the prospect of dealing with the crowds at Victoria Station.

Then there was the tube.

I endured.

At the museum we left our bags in the Members' Cloakroom, and Professor Buckley asked the attendant to let Sam Jones know his visitors had arrived. We were obviously expected as we were nodded through with barely a glance.

The Professor set off down the corridor at quite a pace, and I had to rush a little to keep up with him. When we reached the small room where his friend worked, I was out of breath.

He knocked at the door and a voice said, "Come in, come in." The Professor moved aside to let me pass, then followed me into the room.

A huge man, with red frizzy hair and beard, was sitting in a wheelchair at a desk that was piled high with papers.

"I'm Sam, and you must be this old reprobate's student," he said, smiling and holding his hand out.

I took his hand and shook it. His grip was firm.

"Hello, yes, Alice Hunter," I said, smiling. He was such a big bear of a man, and so welcoming that my nervousness receded.

"Not quite a student yet," Professor Buckley said. "But by the end of next week she will be. New class, fifteen in total."

"Excellent," Sam said. "That should be enough to provide all the slave labour you need."

"There'll be a few volunteers from the town," the Professor replied. "The local archaeology group is quite active."

"As it should be," he said. "Okay then, future archaeologist, let's see your coin."

I took my necklace off over my head, and handed it over.

Sam took it and looked intently at the pendant. He rolled over to the desk and turned on a lamp – a bright one, with a daylight bulb.

Both men had their heads bent, looking down at the pendant – ginger shaggy mop and dark brown cropped hair almost meeting in the middle of the table. Sam pulled a magnifying glass over and looked closely. Then he pushed it across to the Professor who looked too.

Professor Buckley beckoned me forwards. "Don't hang back, Alice. This is your party. Come and have a look."

I marvelled at the clarity of the portrait of Nero, and the worn letters of his name.

"May I take it out of its protective cage?" Sam asked.

Professor Buckley spoke up. "It's really personal, Sam. A gift from her grandmother. Recently deceased."

"I have lots of stuff from Grandma, but this one is different." I explained again, told the story of how I'd found it.

"Interesting," Sam said. Then, echoing the Professor's first reaction, "I'd like to see the place it was found."

"I said that!" Professor Buckley said. "Shall we have a closer look?"

"Certainly," I said. "Grandma used to say that scholarship is more valuable than any treasure."

"A wise woman," Sam said. "We academics believe that is the case, but it's a rare person who isn't seduced even a little by gold and glamour."

He rummaged in his desk for a moment, then said, "Why don't you two go and have a wander, perhaps Matt's favourite Room 49."

I smiled, "Grandma's favourite too. Roman Britain."

We started to walk down the corridor, when the Professor paused, and said, "Oh, I forgot. You keep on, and I'll catch up."

A few minutes later he found me, standing and gazing with awe at the great silver dish from the Mildenhall Treasure.

"A spectacular find," Professor Buckley said.

"Grandma loved it. She used to fantasise about how wonderful it must feel to find something as stunning as this. To be the first human being in many hundreds of years to lay eyes on something so special."

"I suppose every archaeologist dreams of finding something so magnificent. The reality, of painstakingly excavating post holes and occasionally finding a Neolithic flint axe head, or a medieval leather shoe is rewarding in its own way, but we all dream."

We wandered around the room, pausing to look at the wooden writing tablets from Vindolanda, and the occasional fragment of mosaic. I stopped by a particularly beautiful example of a Roman drinking vessel. "Grandma has one of these," I said. "Very similar in style, but hers is a replica. There's a silver statuette of a goddess, perhaps Demeter, or the Romano British version. Two platters, a fluted dish, and some silver spoons. The originals are in an American museum, I think – years ago she was commissioned to help them acquire some Roman silver for their collection. The replicas were a thank you."

"Where are they now?" Professor Buckley asked, with real interest.

"She bequeathed them to me personally," I said. "I've kept her collection intact. I thought perhaps I might donate them to the local museum, if they would be interested in displaying replicas. They aren't authentic, but they are beautiful pieces."

"I would like to see them, if I may."

Perhaps he would have some idea of what best to do with them, I thought. I'd been thinking of seeking professional advice, and here it had fallen into my lap.

"Any time."

At that point his phone buzzed.

"Ah," he said, "Sam's ready for us. Unless you'd like to wander some more?"

"I wonder what the verdict is?" I said.

Back in Sam's room, my coin was on the table, still under the magnifying glass, but now without the pendant around it.

At least, I thought it was my coin.

I had a sudden burst of panic. I'd so easily left it alone with someone I didn't know at all, persuaded by someone else I could hardly say I knew well.

I reasoned with myself, as my counsellor had taught me.

This was the British Museum. Professor Buckley was well known. I was being paranoid again. I started my breathing exercises.

"Anyone in there?" Sam's voice penetrated.

"Sorry, miles away." I managed a smile.

"If it's alright, I'd like to keep it here for a few days, and ask some of my colleagues for their opinion. It could be very exciting indeed, if it is what I think it is."

"May I?" I asked, nodding towards the disposable gloves on the bench. I put them on and picked up the coin and had a close look at it. It was still the same one, I was sure of that. I didn't have to say yes, I thought. Then I relaxed and put it back on the bench and put the gloves back next to it.

"Sure," I said, as if I'd never had any doubts.

He handed me a folder, with a receipt and a detailed description and photograph of the coin and had me sign a copy for his records.

"Modern technology makes this all so much easier," he said. Then he beckoned the Professor to him and handed him my gold pendant. "Your idea," he said. "You give it to her."

Professor Buckley looked at it. "Looks great," he said. "Even though we know it's not quite the same."

He put the pendant round my neck, explaining as he did so. "I asked Sam to replace the coin with one of the replicas the Museum sells. It's only gold plated so I know it isn't the same, but really, you can't carry on wearing something so valuable. Certainly not once people know…"

Oh.

That kind of exciting.

I looked at the pendant and it did look very similar, although the replica was a bit shinier to my eyes, even though it had gone through some fake patination process.

"What a lovely idea," I said. "Thank you both. How much do I owe you?"

"No charge," Sam said, and the Professor looked awkward. I contented myself with saying thank you rather than keep on through that whole embarrassing ritual, but as we left the museum, I made sure he saw me put a generous donation to the museum's upkeep in the collection box. I didn't want to feel beholden. I had enough of that in my life already.

It was mid-afternoon when the train pulled into Cuckmere station, and Professor Buckley didn't seem to be eager to get away, so I risked asking him if he would like to see Grandma's collection.

He looked at his watch. "I have a faculty meeting at five, but I'd love to have coffee and run, if that's okay?"

Of course, it was, so we took a taxi back to the house.

If he noticed my paranoid scrutiny of the front door and the post I picked up from the hall floor, he said nothing.

"Perfect location," he said. "So close to the sea and the hill. No wonder you grew up interested in history – the landscape here is steeped in it."

"Yes," I said. "Grandma loved this place, and walked on the hills around here until a few months before she died. In her last week I pushed her wheelchair up the tarmac path of the nature reserve. The look of pure joy on her face when we reached the top of the cliffs is one of my best memories."

I'd pushed her wheelchair right up to the stone altar, and she'd asked me for a few minutes alone. I'd left her in the clearing and waited within earshot until I heard her call my name. I understood that in some way this was an important moment for her.

She'd always been careful to protect me from her other life. I knew there was some kind of scandal stirred up by the tabloid press about the Cuckmere Coven. There'd been a kind of feud between the vicar and the group, and he'd denounced Grandma from the pulpit, going into full flood about the Whore of Babylon. She didn't let it bother her – just started going to another church. But it had caused problems for Helen in her childhood, and she always resented that.

In mine, there were vague rumours at school about how I was the witch's granddaughter and it was best not to cross me. I put up with the nastiness for a week or two, then decided enough was enough. I'd borrowed Grandma's special ritual pentagram and worn it under my school uniform, hidden under the blue checked blouse. The moment I heard the chief bully start up again, I fished it out and made sure the whole gang had a good look. Then I fixed her with my stare and started chanting, nonsense words, under my breath. That very night her home was broken into and all the Christmas presents from under the tree stolen, along with TV and laptop. It had nothing to do with me other than the power of suggestion. Life is full of co-incidences, and there was pretty much bound to be something bad happen for her to link it to. I was lucky, or unlucky, that it was so memorable.

I didn't know how that would return to haunt me after the incident with the fire.

"Sorry," I said, as the Professor coughed to catch my attention. "I was remembering Grandma and thinking how thrilled she would have been to show you her collection."

"It's a pity she didn't contact the University," he said, out of politeness, as I turned off the alarm. I wondered why she hadn't — perhaps it was merely an issue of trust. Not finding trust easy — that was certainly a family trait — learned if not inherited.

I showed him into the library and encouraged him to potter around, giving me time to put the kettle on and check all the locks and windows without him thinking I was crazy. He made straight for the display cabinet. I fished the brass cabinet key out of its hidey hole behind one of the rows of books and handed it to him.

"Take them out if you like," I said. "There's cotton gloves in a box on the shelf there. Grandma was old fashioned. I'll make the coffee. Milk, sugar?"

"Black," he said. "Unless it's instant."

"I think I can stretch to the real stuff this once," I said, but his attention was already focused on the silver.

In the kitchen, I ground the coffee and started the drip filter before wandering around checking the locks. Looking out of the window in the back door, I could see there was something on the lawn, something I couldn't quite make out.

I unlocked the back door and ventured outside.

Staked to the ground, right in the middle of the burnt-out patch of the lawn, was a ginger cat. A dead ginger cat. And laid out around it was a pentagram made out of ribbon, like a ritual version of a crime scene.

I stood stock still, and automatically did my breathing exercises. Four breaths in, hold, and then out. And again. I could feel my heart beating faster, and I fought the urge to scream, to turn and run back inside. I was intensely aware that someone might be watching. What kind of reaction did this person want from me?

One thing was for sure, they didn't want me to stay calm and practical. Stubbornness gave me strength. So I carried on breathing slowly, and I looked around, on the off chance that I might catch a glimpse of someone or a clue as to where they were. I decided that I'd take a walk around the hill at the back as soon as I could and check out all the spots that overlook my home. Maybe there'd be some evidence that someone was watching me.

I took my phone from my pocket and took some quick photos – a close up of the cat, and some of the whole scene, and the stake.

Then I ostentatiously started to make a call for anyone watching to see. I aborted it at the last moment – I decided it would be better to talk to DI Collingwood in person, as soon as I could. It was all too similar, to the way the rabbit had been staked out, to the pentagram scrawled around Harry's body. The wooden stake was exactly like the one I'd foolishly pulled out of Harry's hand. The pentagram was more evidence as the police had not, so far as I knew, released the information. There could have been gossip, I suppose. It's the sort of thing that leaks. But surely, the cat was most likely killed by the person who'd killed Harry.

Could it be my stalker?

I wished I knew.

I wondered who had lost their pet. There didn't seem to be a collar, but maybe the animal was micro chipped. Later I would make sure someone checked, but for now, I was going to go back in and heap chocolate biscuits on a plate and take a tray of coffee into the library. I didn't want the Professor to know what was going on around me. I wanted a normal life, a normal future, without being connected with all this occult nonsense and a murder.

"You were a long time," he said, as I put the tray down on the low table by the fireplace. My hands were shaking a little. "Sorry," I said.

He'd barely looked up from the silver he had spread out on the table. The skyphos was in the middle, but the fluted dish and the spoons were there too, and a pile of coins. I must remember to show him the replica jewellery, which Grandma had stored in the safe in her bedroom. It was all still up there, I supposed, but I hadn't looked. I really ought to do a full inventory and see if the museum wanted them.

"Are you sure, absolutely sure, that these are replicas?" the Professor asked, finally looking up and then walking across to the fire. He sat in the armchair facing me, coffee in one hand and chocolate hobnob in the other.

I laughed. "Yes, I'm sure! Do you have any idea how much they'd be worth if they were the real thing? The skyphos alone would be hundreds of thousands of pounds.

"More, in that condition," he said.

"Well then. No, I'm sure. Grandma was friends with a silversmith. She took me to his workshop. I saw him making these things."

He picked up a second biscuit and started to eat like he was a starving man. I realised we'd neither of us eaten a proper lunch, only a snatched sandwich in the station.

"Some of the coins, they're possibly real, but not especially valuable."

The doorbell rang, before I could make a fool of myself by offering to cook him a meal.

"Excuse me," I said, stood up, and went to answer the door.

Standing there on the doorstep were DI Collingwood and DC King.

"Oh, good," I said. "I needed to talk to you. Do come in."

Neither of them smiled, or spoke, but they followed me in, and I led them through to the kitchen.

"I was going to call you," I said, "when my visitor leaves. But as you're here…"

I opened the back door.

"I don't think you realise, Miss Hunter, this is not a social occasion. We didn't come here for a tour of your garden," DI Collingwood said.

At that moment, Professor Buckley came out of the library, and stood in the kitchen doorway, a quizzical expression on his face. I wanted to explain, but it would have to wait.

"Don't be ridiculous," I said. "There's a dead cat, and you'll want to see how it was killed."

I remembered in time my promise not to mention the stakes and the ritual elements.

"Stay here," DI Collingwood said to DC King, and then followed me into the garden.

"Oh," I said helplessly. "It was here, fifteen, twenty minutes ago. Staked through its body. Exactly like the rabbits. The pentagram was ribbon – well, obviously chalk wouldn't work here. So he was prepared."

It was gone. There was nothing to show it had ever been there.

"Enough of this," he said. He hustled me back inside, before I had a chance to say any more. It was on my phone, I remembered. I got it out and scrolled to the pictures and showed him.

DI Collingwood pursed his mouth and passed the phone to DC King, who also looked.

"Enough of the distractions," DI Collingwood said. "Let's get down to brass tacks, shall we? You made a statement on Monday, and you came in to the station again yesterday to tell us some detail you overlooked. Is there not a lot more that you damned well know you should have told us, Miss Hunter?"

Some detail? I knew my instincts were right when I felt them watching me as I left the police station after reporting my stalker. I knew they didn't believe me.

Professor Buckley was still looking on, bemused.

I was sure my expression was much the same as his. What on earth was DI Collingwood on about?

"I'm sorry for the interruption," I said to the Professor. "Hadn't you better be getting to your meeting?"

It was a bit brusque, but I wanted rid of him. I'd been humiliated enough.

"I had," he said. "But I think you should call a lawyer, don't you?"

"But that's not really necessary, is it?" I looked to DI Collingwood and DC King for confirmation.

DI Collingwood squared his shoulders. "Alice Hunter," he started. "I am arresting you on suspicion of the murder of Harry Rook. Anything you say—"

The rest of the caution passed me by, although I knew the gist of it from too many police dramas on TV.

I sat down on the nearest kitchen chair, my legs suddenly unsteady. I started again on the breathing exercises.

DC King passed me a document. "We also have a warrant to search your property, Miss Hunter. Looking for any evidence that might relate to the death of Mr Rook."

"What does that mean?" I asked. "What evidence could there be?"

"We'll be the judge of that," DI Collingwood said. "But right now we're taking you to the station. The rest of the team will be here any time now."

The Professor got his phone out and started to make a call. "I'm calling my lawyer right now," he said, "and cancelling the faculty meeting."

"You don't have to do that," I said, weakly.

"I do," he said. "Who else is going to keep an eye on everything here, while you are being questioned?"

"Thank you," I said. I hadn't even thought of that.

It wasn't me he was looking after, sadly. It was Grandma's collection. I was glad there'd be someone there to watch the police. But who would keep an eye on the Professor?

SEVENTEEN

SILENT AND IN shock, I followed DI Collingwood out to the car. He opened the back door and I got in. At least he hadn't handcuffed me, but I could imagine all too well how it looked. Not quite as bad as the last time he had driven me away from here – that had required restraints and I'd been making a lot of noise. So I've been told.

I looked up at the Rook house and could see Julia standing at the window, watching. Would anyone have warned her I was going to be arrested for murdering Harry? I was pretty sure she hadn't known the day before, at any rate. I couldn't quite get up the nerve to ask. What did it matter anyway? Everyone would know soon enough.

It wasn't a long journey, which was perhaps as well. I was soon standing in front of the custody sergeant and handing my possessions over.

"My phone," I said to DI Collingwood. "You might want that separately, in evidence."

"Thought you'd forgotten how to speak," he said. "Why the phone, especially?"

"The dead cat. I took a photo."

"That won't be our primary interest. A man has been murdered, Ms Hunter."

I was ready to scream with frustration. "That's why the cat and the way it was staked out matters, for fuck's sake. The pentagram?"

He looked at me, one sardonic eyebrow raised. "Not so sweet and innocent after all," he said.

I pulled myself back from full meltdown. "I'm sorry I swore," I lied through gritted teeth. "It's frustration."

He shook his head, as if incredulous, but asked the custody sergeant to put my phone in an evidence bag, separately.

DI Collingwood asked if I wanted my case worker present, as I was a vulnerable person.

I felt like he'd slapped me in the face. Did he think I was crazy, that I'd had some kind of psychotic break and murdered Harry?

Breathe in, count to four… I couldn't complete the exercise. So much for the idea that regular practice would mean it would become automatic in a crisis.

"My solicitor, please. John Harvey, I don't know the number but they're on Cuckmere High Street." I clipped the words out.

A police constable escorted me to a cell, the door slammed behind me, and I was locked up. Again.

So far, I reasoned with myself, it wasn't as bad as being taken to Brookfields. I was as confused about what was happening, and on top of that I was desperately upset over Harry's death, but I wasn't out of my head. I was raging, but at least I hadn't been forcibly restrained and injected with an unwanted sedative.

Under a layer of pine disinfectant, the cell had a faint whiff of stale vomit. The blanket on the cot smelled reasonably clean, though, as I held it up to my nose gingerly, holding it in two fingers. I lay down and closed my eyes, and resumed the breathing exercises. At least some of the time it stopped my mind going round and round over the same ground, asking unanswerable questions. Breathe, and count.

Every so often I heard a click as the custody officer peered through the grille into the cell.

I was still hyped up and stressed when the door opened, and I was led out of the custody suite and into a small interview room. I was expecting to see DI Collingwood, but instead, there was Mr Harvey.

I was so relieved and pleased to see him, I almost burst into tears. I didn't want to seem crazy. I had to stay calm. I held my tears back.

"Sit," he said. "And listen very carefully to my words, my dear. I can't represent you, because at some point I may have to become a witness for your defence. I can't explain now, and I know I'm being obscure. Please remember, and it will all fall into place. I promise."

Now a tear did escape. What the fuck? The person who was supposed to help me now couldn't help me and was talking in riddles.

"I've brought a young colleague with me who has no such conflict of interest. You will be properly looked after, my dear girl, I promised Frances I would."

He offered me his handkerchief and I blubbed into it. I felt my face become all blotchy. Another skill I hadn't inherited from my mother – the ability to cry while retaining a perfect complexion.

"That's better," he said. "Don't worry. Crying's not a problem, let it out. I wish you'd told me you'd found Harry's body – that's all."

"I thought you knew," I said. "I heard it was on the news. I assumed you knew."

"Never mind that now," he said. "I shouldn't have said anything. Suhad Khalifeh will represent you. She's a good lawyer, with wide experience in criminal cases, from her last job in London. We were lucky to get her. But please, use your head."

He patted me on the shoulder and walked out, and in walked a tiny and elegant woman in bright scarlet, with high heels and a black leather briefcase.

I admit it, I was surprised.

"Not what you expected?" she asked, smiling. "Funny, I never used to get that when I worked in London. Follow my boyfriend out to the wilds of Sussex when he got work in the Brighton hospital, and all I get is these looks like I'm an exotic species."

I blushed and apologised. "I thought all lawyers wore navy pinstripes. Certainly all the ones I've seen at Harvey and Smithsons."

"Not anymore," she said. "Now to work."

She asked me what had led up to my arrest and if I had any idea what might have prompted it. I explained about finding the body, how I'd long been a neighbour of the Rooks, and about Grandma's feud, but that no – I really couldn't imagine.

"Besides, the feud was over, it must have been. Grandma had asked Harry to be executor of her will and a trustee, when she knew she was dying," I explained.

"Yes, Mr Harvey told me a little about that, but not in any great detail," she said. "So what happened when they took your statement. On the day you found him, right? Did they give you a warning, anything about incriminating yourself?"

"No, they were clear it was a witness statement. DI Collingwood said it could wait until the following day, but I preferred to get it over with. I answered all their questions about Harry and the Rooks and how long I'd known him. I might not have mentioned the trustee part because it didn't seem important."

"That may have been an error," she said. "Had there been any dispute between you and Mr Rook about your inheritance? Had you any issues with how he performed his duty?"

"No, not at all," I said. "I told Mr Harvey that he was very kind. He came to see me in hospital – you do know about my time in hospital?"

She nodded but seemed unfazed. Relieved, I carried on.

"He was on board with my educational plans. We were having discussions about the business side, but nothing had been decided."

"Is there anyone who can confirm that all was running smoothly?"

"Mr Harvey. And my mother, I suppose. Although perhaps it's wiser not to talk to her. She's still angry about Grandma's arrangements. Perhaps Julia. Harry's widow."

"No one else? None of your friends, no one without any reason for bias?"

"I don't talk about it," I said. "In the hospital – people would have thought it was a delusion. It was bad enough that I had a posh accent, that I speak in complete sentences. Out of the hospital, people treat you differently if they think you're spoiled. Poor little rich girl stuff."

She made another note, scrawling with a fountain pen in a leather-bound notebook.

"I suppose the worst part is the stake. I couldn't bear to see it sticking through his palm so I removed it."

"Foolish, but understandable. We can put that down to emotion."

"They took samples of DNA and fingerprints and so on, for exclusion, and they let me go home."

"You agreed to it? They didn't caution you, or anything?"

"They might have done. I was a bit out of it." She scribbled something down. "It was routine, they said. There was no pressure. I volunteered the DNA sample, I think."

"That may work to our advantage. We may as well see if they're ready to interview. Remember, you don't have to answer, but they'll give you all the warnings. It will all be recorded. Oh, and Mr Harvey said to remind you to use your head."

I wasn't sure it was working – that was the problem.

DI Collingwood was too busy to talk to us right away, and so I was taken back to my cell for half an hour and provided with regulation refreshments. Strong builder's tea, and an egg and bacon sandwich. It sufficed.

Then DC King returned and escorted me upstairs. At my request, we made a detour to the ladies, where I managed to pee in spite of feeling hemmed in, supervised, watched. Again, like hospital, but then it was suicide watch, rather than a fear that I'd abscond. Cooped up in Brookfields, one especially hot day, Kelly and I had made a run for it, after scrambling through the loo window. We'd stayed out late, picnicked in the park and had a drink in the nearest pub, until the nursing assistant who'd been supposed to be supervising us tracked us down. We all three sneaked back in through the laundry – so that none of us would get into trouble. Luckily, we hadn't been missed.

In the interview room DI Collingwood and Ms Khalifeh were already at the table. She was smiling at him rather too enthusiastically. Flirting. He was very attractive, I supposed. I swallowed my irritation. I couldn't afford to look crazy right now. Or guilty.

I called on my breathing exercises, and forced myself to stay calm.

I'd been arrested for murder. It really hadn't sunk in yet.

I sat down next to my lawyer, and DC King took her position by the recording equipment. This time, I wondered if there were people watching us unseen, from another room. Did there need to be a two-sided mirror as in the TV dramas? Or just a camera?

Shut up, butterfly mind.

"Start the recording please, DC King."

"For the record, I remind Miss Hunter of her rights." He rattled them off again. "Do you understand?"

"Yes," I said.

"Unlike last time, when you were here solely as a witness, you are now under arrest. It has been explained to you that we can keep you here for twenty-four hours, at which point we may ask the court to extend the arrest time to thirty-six, or ninety-six hours. At any point during this process we may release you on police bail, release you altogether, or charge you with a crime. We may also decide that it might be necessary to remand you into custody, for your safety, or because you pose a risk of flight, or because there is a risk you may commit another crime or attempt to cover up your role in this one."

"Do get on with it," Ms Khalifeh said. "You've been through all this already and she's said she understands."

"I needed to be absolutely certain," he said. "We need to be sure Ms Hunter understands the seriousness of her position."

"She's spent the last hour or two locked up in a cell. I think she has the picture."

I knew what he meant though. He was suggesting that because I'd been in a mental hospital that I wasn't bright enough to understand what was going on. Or alternatively, that I would be canny enough to wriggle out of the charge by reason of my mental health.

Or was that my paranoia kicking in?

"You are under suspicion of the murder of Harry Rook," DI Collingwood continued. "That is why you are here. Before we go any further, do you have anything else you'd like to tell us?"

Like a confession, perhaps?

I remembered what I'd been thinking. "I told you everything I could on Monday," I said. "Then I came in again a couple of days ago, to tell you about my stalker. In case there was a connection. And I was going to call you about the dead cat," I said. "As you know."

"Ah yes," DI Collingwood said. "The dead cat. It may surprise you to know that no such cat, dead or alive, has turned up in our search. Nor has anyone in the immediate area admitted to owning a ginger cat. Dead or alive."

"You saw the photograph," I said. "I didn't imagine it."

"I don't think you imagined it, Miss Hunter. Far from it. I think you created it, you killed it and displayed it, as you did the rabbit. As a distraction."

"How could I have created it?" I asked, my voice rising. "Look, you have my phone. You have the photo. It must be time stamped, or something. Or am I some kind of master phone hacker now? I was with Professor Buckley most of the day. When I found the cat, he was in the library, and I was making coffee – I can only have been out of his sight for ten minutes. Please check up on it."

"He's already confirmed most of what you say. But you didn't mention the cat to him, which in the circumstances seems a bit odd, wouldn't you say?"

"Would anyone want to share that with their new Professor?" I asked. There wasn't much else I could say. My voice started to break with emotion. I was pleading with him now, beyond reason. "Please keep on looking. I didn't touch it. I took the photograph and went inside. Please, it will help to clear me."

"And the ritual element? In Harry's murder, and in the rabbit and the cat killings.'

I fell silent. Clearly, he'd found out about my family history.

"You're quiet, now," he said, clearly satisfied with my lack of response. "Do you have nothing to say?"

"You've clearly made your mind up so what's the point?"

Ms Khalifeh touched my hand, gently. I looked at her, and she smiled, reassuringly.

"I think I need to have a private word with my client," she said. Collingwood looked disappointed, as he obviously thought he had me on the ropes. She smiled sweetly at him and he gave in with good grace.

"My grandmother used to say that you catch more flies with honey than vinegar," I said. "I'm not very good at remembering."

My lawyer grinned wickedly at me. "Admit it, you thought I was flirting with him, earlier."

"He is very attractive." I laughed, responding to her attempt to cheer me up.

"Tell me what this is about, Alice. How can I help you if I don't know what's going on?"

"DI Collingwood told me not to tell anyone about the crime scene. You know, when I found Harry."

"You can tell me, Miss Hunter. I'm your lawyer. It won't get any easier if you put it off."

She was right.

"There was a ritual element to the killing. A chalked pentacle was drawn around Harry's body. And on the same day, on the Beacon, I found a rabbit, sacrificed. A chalk pentacle on the old altar, and fresh black candle wax."

"I don't understand."

"Today, in my garden, there was a cat killed the same way. And a pentacle made out of ribbon draped around it."

"That sounds horrible."

"The police think it was me. They think I killed the rabbits and the cat. They think I killed Harry... because. Well, because my grandmother was a witch."

Ms Khalifeh was silent.

"This isn't my illness talking. This is truth – ask Mr Harvey. Well, she wasn't a witch precisely, although that's what the locals call it. She was High Priestess of the local pagan group. Years and years ago. There was some kind of scandal and it was all over the tabloids. A new vicar in the village took against the old ways and tried to ban followers of the old ways from the church. So the meetings, the sabbats, stopped – some say it went underground. Nothing was heard about it until a couple of years ago when it all started up again."

"What started up? You have to spell it out, Alice."

"There were chalk markings on the church, pentagrams like now, only upside down. I don't suppose you can say which way is up on the ground, but you can on a gravestone. Candle wax. Sacrificed animals, rabbits mostly, in the cemetery behind the church. Satanists, people said. It was in the papers."

"I don't understand why suspicion would fall on you?"

"I never understood really. Well, it was supposed to be about Grandma, and her feud with the vicar. It was ridiculous because it was just a personal thing. She never stopped going to church and even returned to the local congregation when the old vicar retired."

"I know about the bonfire, and you being sectioned, Alice. Mr Harvey told me."

Her voice was very gentle, and understanding, and somehow that made me want to rage. I didn't need treating with kid gloves, I wasn't fragile. Or maybe I was. Maybe that was what made me so angry.

"There were some ritual elements about the bonfire. Candle wax was found. There was a half-burned poppet. My mother – she said she thought I'd been doing ritual magic. Necromancy. An attempt to communicate with Grandma. Then, while I was in hospital, the sacrifices stopped. No more candles on the church doorstep. No more rabbits on the gravestones. And it's started up again now. Obviously, I am the culprit."

"I take it that's not a confession."

"What? No. I mean, according to the local rumour mill. Maybe the doctors believed it. Mother can be very convincing. She likely convinced herself. Of course I'm not a Satanist, and Grandma certainly wasn't either. In her view, the Old Ways were about honouring the Divine Feminine, not about turning away from God."

But maybe, just maybe, that was why Tamsin had been so weird with me. Maybe she believed it too.

"Are you up to restarting the interview?" she asked me. "Remember you don't have to answer any questions if you don't want to."

"I'd rather get it over with," I said. "I don't remember the fire, but it might have been some of Grandma's stuff I was burning. I was grief stricken, that's all. And I have never sacrificed a rabbit or any other animal, or chalked pentacles anywhere. It wasn't me. That I know. But I can't prove a negative."

"They need more than rumour and local gossip to prove you're a witch," Ms Khalifeh said. "Chin up."

DI Collingwood and DC King settled themselves back into the room and the interview started up again.

"About the dead cat, and the ribbon pentacle," he said. "You said you didn't touch the cat. Can you explain again why you took the stake out of Harry Rook's hand?"

"I don't know. It wasn't rational," I said. "It seemed so wrong, and after the rabbit. I don't know, I wish I hadn't."

DI Collingwood sighed. "We know about your connection to the Cuckmere Coven, Ms Hunter. Your grandmother was the Head Witch, and local rumour has it that you've followed in the family tradition."

"I'm not a witch, and come to that, neither was Grandma. She was High Priestess of a local group who practised the old rites and followed a high magic traditional path. It's not witchcraft. It's not Satanism. It was, as I understand it fairly boring religious stuff with lots of meditation and a bit of dressing up."

"No ritual sacrifices?"

"I really can't imagine Grandma slaughtering rabbits for kicks."

"And you? There's been some very unpleasant goings on in this area for the last couple of years. Only there was a long gap, which happened to coincide with your stay in hospital."

"It wasn't me."

"Really? Is that all you've got?"

"It wasn't me. And you can't prove it was."

"We certainly will be looking for evidence. That's our job, Ms Hunter."

"I thought you were looking for Harry's killer. This psychopathic blood sacrifice nonsense should have been investigated when it started, not brushed aside as a local curiosity. If these vile people graduated from desecrating churches and sacrificing small animals to killing Harry, it won't be Grandma's responsibility, and it won't be mine."

Ms Khalifeh put a hand on my arm, and I realised I was starting to lose it. So I deliberately slowed my breathing and tried to relax.

It wasn't easy with DI Collingwood looking at me, and with the video camera in the background, recording all of this. No doubt my body language would condemn me too.

"Seriously think again, Ms Hunter. What else have you omitted to tell us?"

Was he dangling for a confession? Did he think that because I'd had a breakdown I would fold, give in under pressure – and make his life easier?

Then I remembered.

"Mr Harvey reminded me. Harry Rook was my trustee. My grandmother asked him to look after my financial affairs until I'm of age to take control myself."

DI Collingwood leaned forward, a satisfied smile on his face.

"Now we're getting somewhere," he said. "Mr Rook was an obstacle, wasn't he? You had plans and he was in your way. Plans about what to do with your inheritance."

"No, it wasn't like that at all," I said. "We were in agreement. It was an easy relationship – Grandma knew what I wanted and she chose someone to guide me who would share her views and mine."

"Do you deny that there have been offers on your property – quite generous offers I understand, and that Mr Rook has blocked the sale?"

"I didn't want to sell," I said. "It was Grandma's house and it's always been my home. I'm happy living there."

DI Collingwood looked at his notes in the manila file in front of him.

"There have been two attempts to sell the property. Both blocked by Mr Rook."

He took two plastic envelopes from the file and pushed them over the desk at me.

"Is that your signature? Here, and here?"

"Yes," I said. "Look at the date. That was when I was in hospital."

"So you admit that six months ago you wanted to sell the house? Your childhood home that you are so attached to?"

It was my mother, I wanted to say. It would seem like shifting blame. It didn't matter anyway. This was a nonsense. I closed down and said nothing as he went on about the house.

Then he changed tack.

"You told me your grandmother and the Rooks had a long-standing feud. If that was the case, why did Mr Rook agree to be your trustee?"

"I don't know," I said. "Grandma didn't tell me. I simply don't know."

Was this when I was supposed to use my head? Pity I couldn't find the on switch. All I had was bewilderment.

Ms Khalifeh spoke up, again.

"Are you going to get to the point, DI Collingwood? Have you actually got any evidence, or are you thinking you can push my client until she makes a false confession? You've said yourself that she's vulnerable. Stop badgering her."

He looked at her, clearly narked. Then he looked at me.

"Miss Hunter," he said. "When were you going to tell me that Harry Rook was your grandfather?'

What the fuck?

Mind games, now?

He pushed some paperwork across the desk at me. DNA test results. I couldn't understand the science bits, but I certainly understood the wording at the bottom. 'There is 99 percent certainty that this DNA test is from someone who is directly descended from the victim, Harry Rook.'

I pushed it to my lawyer.

I'd heard that DNA could give misleading results. Perhaps this was one of those times. Perhaps there had been some mix up at the lab?

DI Collingwood could read my mind.

"There was no snarl up at the lab," he said. "I had a phone call asking me to double check, as the forensics expert noticed the relationship when there wasn't supposed to be one. To be on the safe side, we're going to have the test repeated. DC King?"

She came forward and under the watchful eye of my solicitor another swab was taken, put into a prepared evidence bag, sealed and signed by all present.

"Have you got anything to say, Miss Hunter?" DI Collingwood asked.

I hadn't. I was in shock, I guess. Thoughts spinning round and round in my mind. If Harry Rook was my grandfather, then he was my mother's father. Frances, my grandmother – had an affair with him. Five years before she moved into the house opposite his home. Opposite Julia's home.

Had Julia known? She must have done, I realised. And Mr Harvey – that was what he'd promised Grandma not to tell me.

"I don't understand," I said. "I need a break."

"Don't try that on, Miss Hunter," DI Collingwood's tone was scathing. "You knew, or you'd recently found out. You felt betrayed. You had motive."

"I need a break," I said. I didn't trust myself. I didn't trust anyone. Mr Harvey knew, and hadn't told me. How dare he tell me to use my head? I wanted to scream with frustration.

"How did you find out?" Collingwood asked. "Did he tell you?"

My solicitor spoke up. "My client has been clear; she needs a break."

The interview was wound up, and I was led back to my cell, which still smelled of stale vomit overlaid with disinfectant, where I lay down on the cot and thought. This time there was no way to stop the thoughts spinning around in my head.

EIGHTEEN

THE RATTLE OF the grille in the cell door roused me from fitful sleep as the custody sergeant checked up on me. I was confused for a moment or two about where I was, and then surprised I had eventually managed to fall asleep.

Harry was my grandfather.

I understood now why Grandma said she'd left a mess for me to untangle. Mr Harvey had known all along, and not told me. She must have made him promise. Harry too.

My whole life built on lies – and everyone but me knowing the truth. Except my mother. I don't think she knew. For the first time I had a glimpse of how she must feel. Rejected. An outsider. The one who didn't belong.

I felt a flash of anger. I'd liked Harry, and barely got to know him, yet he was my grandfather. My father was not worth knowing – mother had made sure I knew that much. He hadn't been seen for years, but he was a layabout. Sometimes I thought she'd picked him deliberately for the qualities that were most likely to enrage Grandma.

When my mother found out she was pregnant, he'd pressured her to have an abortion. She hadn't been able to bring herself to do it, she told me later, even as she expressed regrets that she hadn't listened to him. "He was right, it would have been the wisest move. I thought Grandma would understand and support me," she said. "Because it had happened to her, hadn't it? But she told me that she'd found her way through it on her own, and I must do the same."

"I'm sure she didn't mean it like that," I said. "It was thoughtless. She didn't mean to hurt you." Just as you didn't mean to hurt me, I thought, by saying it would have been better if I'd been aborted.

"You were her blue-eyed girl – you have no idea," she said. "She told me I was a whore, that at least she'd been engaged to be married. My father, her so wonderful choice, called it off at the last minute. That was all she said, she wouldn't tell me more, however much I asked."

So my mother hadn't known Harry was her father. Could she have found out since? I didn't think so. She'd have told me. She'd have delighted in twisting the knife, in showing me how imperfect Grandma was.

Once upon a time Harry and Grandma had been engaged. Julia must have known. That was what the feud was about. It was probably why she was so angry with Harry for agreeing to be my trustee. But she must have realised I was in the dark – Harry talked to her about everything.

Was that the theory the police were working on? That Harry had told me he was my grandfather, and that I'd snapped and murdered him?

I had to say as little as possible – I had no choice. There were so many pieces missing from this jigsaw and I had no way of understanding what was going on.

The cell door opened and I was brought a tray of food. Cold, chewy toast and a mug of tea. I asked to use the bathroom and was allowed to splash my face with water and freshen up, but I still felt grubby and dishevelled.

By nine o'clock, I was back in the interview room with DI Collingwood and DC King, waiting for Ms Khalifeh.

She was immaculate in a black pinstriped skirt suit today, perhaps to conform to my expectations. At least DI Collingwood and DC King looked like they'd had as little sleep as I had.

"Okay," DI Collingwood said, once the recording equipment was set up again and I'd been reminded of my rights and the caution. "You're expecting us to believe that you didn't know until yesterday that you are the biological grandchild of Harry Rook. The man who lived in the house across the road from you. All your life."

"It doesn't matter if you believe it or not," I said. "Rather it does matter, but it doesn't change reality. I didn't know. I still don't know, really know. But it does make sense of some things that confused me."

"Your grandmother was Frances Hunter, is that correct? And you are the biological daughter of Helen Hunter, her daughter?"

I paused. Took a deep breath and then another as the world was pulled from under my feet.

"I think I am," I said in a voice that sounded hollow and small, as if it came from a long way away. "But I don't actually know."

As if through glass I saw Collingwood's expression soften, as if he could see how devastated I was by these revelations. Then his professional mask slid back into place, and I wondered if I'd imagined that fleeting moment of humanity.

"You are badgering my client again," Ms Khalifeh spoke. "It's fairly obvious to me that unless she is an exceptional actress, this information has knocked her for six. If the only evidence you have against her is that she didn't tell you Mr Rook was her grandfather, then I suggest that your case is very thin indeed."

DI Collingwood bridled. "Ms Hunter found the body. She interfered with the body at the scene of the crime. She held back vital information from our enquiry."

"Information that she didn't have," Ms Khalifeh pointed out.

I spoke up. "Look, ask my mother. She knows that I didn't know about Harry Rook. Ask my lawyer, Mr Harvey."

Ms Khalifeh closed her notebook and straightened it on the desk. "It's impossible to prove a negative, Ms Hunter. If you think about it, you must see that."

"Of course I can. It's just frustrating. I didn't kill Harry," I said. "I had no reason to kill him. I was getting to know him, and if I had found out he was my grandfather, I think I would have been pleased."

Now there I surprised myself. I observed that idea from all angles. Yes, it was true. I was angry. So much had been kept from me by all of them. You'd think I'd be used to that by now.

DI Collingwood said, "Okay. Tell us more about this Trust. Your grandmother left pretty much everything to you, but you aren't to get control of it until you're thirty. Why was that?"

"Good question. Grandma had some disappointments in her life. She didn't trust people much. In particular, she didn't trust men. She wanted me to be old enough to know my own mind."

"Why didn't she leave it to your mother? Apart from a miserly stipend?"

Ms Khalifeh said, quite calmly, "A more than generous amount in most people's terms. Miserly it most certainly is not."

Miserly was my mother's word – so they had talked to her already.

"It's not property though." DI Collingwood said. "The house and the farm were left specifically to Ms Hunter here, as well as some knick-knacks. And the business interests. All that was left to Helen Hunter was a lifetime's interest in the flat and her boutique."

I wondered why mother hadn't mentioned that the police had talked to her. Perhaps they'd asked her not to.

"A flat in Islington, London," Ms Khalifeh pointed out drily. "Spacious, with two bedrooms, two baths. It would probably be valued at more than the house and the farm together. The flat is above a boutique, and that was left to Helen Hunter's use as well."

This I could answer. "Grandma asked her, and she didn't want the use of any of the Cuckmere properties. She chose London. Grandma had bankrolled three businesses over the years – the previous one a restaurant also in London. She lost it in a poker game, I think. Or that might have been a joke, I don't know. Mother hates Cuckmere. She didn't want to be trapped here. Even in my childhood, she was hardly ever around. She would disappear for months at a time. Once she was gone for almost three years."

Under his breath, DI Collingwood muttered something that sounded like a heartfelt agreement.

"One more time, why did you remove the stake from Mr Rook's hand?"

"I can't explain it logically," I said. "It was instinctive. It felt wrong to leave it. I don't know. I wish I hadn't. But I am sure he was already dead when I found him."

He sighed and stood up.

"We'll take a short break now," he said.

"I don't need a break," I said. "I'd rather get on with this."

"I do," he said. "Would you like to stay here or go back to your cell?"

"Here, please. But I do need the loo."

"DC King will look after you. Then she will come back here and stay with you until I return."

He stalked out. I felt quite sorry for DC King, but she escorted me to the toilets then back to the interview room and arranged for a tray with tea and biscuits.

"How long can they keep me here?" I asked Ms Khalifeh. I knew she'd said, but I was losing track of time. I was beginning to feel an urgent need of a shower, and a sleep in my own bed.

"You've not been here a day yet, and they could ask for an extension of thirty-six hours. But I don't think they will. Unless they've got any evidence they haven't mentioned, it's all circumstantial."

There was barely time for a cup of tea and a digestive biscuit before he came back with a list.

"Okay," he said. "These are the items we have taken from the cottage under the terms of the search warrant."

I looked at the list.

My laptop.

Some papers from Grandma's study – financial stuff mostly, I thought.

My folder with the stalker postcards.

One of my sketchbooks.

That was all.

"Professor Buckley was there when you took all this?" I asked.

"Yes, he signed this off. He was still studying your grandmother's collection of replica antiquities," DI Collingwood said. "He locked everything up, and the property was secured when we left."

I hated having no choice but to trust them.

"Okay," he said. "I am releasing you without charge, on police bail. The terms of your bail will require you to wear an electronic tag at all times."

"What does that mean?" I asked.

Ms Khalifeh replied, "They don't have enough evidence to charge you, so they are going to let you go while they try to find some more. It means the clock stops ticking and at any moment they can pick you up again, and the clock starts again while they question you."

"That's right," he said. "And there are a few conditions to your bail. First, you will sign in here every day, at ten a.m."

"Can we make that half past eight?" I said. "I'm starting a course next week, and I have work too."

He crossed out ten o'clock, and wrote down eight thirty, with a sigh. I could tell from his expression he thought I was being difficult for the sake of it. "In addition, you must find somewhere to stay other than your Grandmother's house. In the circumstances we would prefer not to leave you living on the doorstep of the victim's widow. We'll also be asking for a curfew."

"Julia," I said. "Did you tell her you'd arrested me?"

DC King spoke for the first time. "We had no choice," she said. "I'm sure you understand that she doesn't want to see you right now."

Or ever again, I expected. I needed to see her though. Perhaps Tammy would help me. I kept my silence.

"Do you have somewhere you can stay?"

"I'll manage," I said.

"The moment you do, you let us know the address and we'll be over to make sure it's acceptable," he said.

Ms Khalifeh spoke. "Are you going to insist that Ms Hunter's bail is contingent on her wearing an electronic tag?"

DI Collingwood nodded. "We think it's for the best. Given her personal history, and the proximity of her home to the widow's home, we will be requesting a place for Ms Hunter on the trial for the new GPS tags, so that we can track whether she strays into the exclusion zone, as well as imposing a curfew."

Ms Khalifeh looked at me. "Are you willing to accept the electronic tagging as a condition of your bail? It's so unusual, I'm sure we'd have grounds for appeal. There's no reason to suggest that you might abscond. You're of previous good character, and there's no compelling evidence against you, or they'd have charged you."

DI Collingwood spoke up. "Ms Hunter has a history which leaves us with some concerns. If she doesn't voluntarily accept the electronic tagging, then we may seek custody. It's for her own good."

Isn't it always?

I nodded. "I'll take the electronic tag, thanks. I don't want to be locked up again. Even if it is for my own good."

DI Collingwood grimaced.

"Remember that we need to approve your place of residence. We'll escort you to the house first, so you can collect what you need. Is that clear?"

"Yes, thank you."

I looked at Ms Khalifeh.

"You don't drive, I gather," she said. "We'll go in my car then."

The police car with DI Collingwood and DC King pulled up ahead of us. As Ms Khalifeh parked, I watched as they got out of the car, and parted ways – DC King crossing the road to the Rook house.

The door opened, and Julia Rook stood on the step looking across at me. I was used to it, but I felt an extra chill in her gaze, and I shivered.

DC King had my sympathy, having to tell Julia Rook that they were releasing their prime suspect on bail.

Ms Khalifeh spoke, and I realise I'd missed what she said.

"Come on," she said. "Let's go get your things together."

The police search hadn't made a terrible mess of the house – things were subtly out of place, but it wasn't wrecked. I imagined the presence of Professor Buckley had helped.

I went into the kitchen and threw away the milk and the perishables and put the bin bag outside. I looked longingly at the wine rack, but didn't want anyone to know I was drinking while taking my meds. Or not taking them.

Then I went up to my room and packed a couple of cases, which I dragged downstairs to the hall. I went into the library to collect some books. Grandma's display cabinet was beautifully arranged. No gaps, it all looked perfect and balanced, apart from one thing. The silver skyphos was gone.

NINETEEN

MS KHALIFEH AND DI Collingwood were transfixed by Grandma's display cabinet, as was DC King, who had returned from the Rook residence.

"It's like a museum in here," she said. It was, I supposed, but where they saw it as a museum because of all the Roman stuff, to me it was a museum devoted to my grandmother.

On the top of Grandma's escritoire there was a note with my name on it. "Alice, I have it safe. Please don't worry, it's all in hand. Phone me when you can, Matt."

I crumpled it into my pocket. "I'm ready," I said. "Shall we go?"

"Not so fast," DI Collingwood said. "We'll have to check your suitcases, I'm afraid."

"Why not a full body search while you're at it? Before or after you have a good rummage through the underwear I've packed," I said.

He coloured slightly but said. "Probably for the best. DC King will do all the rummaging."

I followed DC King into the sitting room and she closed the door.

"We're doing our jobs, that's all," DC King said, after searching me.

"You don't have to look like you're enjoying it so much," I grumbled. "Anyway, you've searched the house. What could I possibly have in my case, or on my body, that you haven't already seen?"

"It's procedure," she said.

"DI Collingwood seems to enjoy making me squirm," I complained. "I want to know how Harry was killed, and who killed him. But your DI seems convinced I'm guilty already."

"We have to be objective. We can't afford to be sympathetic, especially—" DC King broke off, suddenly.

"Especially what?" I asked, intrigued.

She ignored me and bustled me back into the hall with her lips zipped shut.

Back in the hall I asked DI Collingwood how long I was going to be on police bail.

"As long as it takes," he said.

"So long as you spend some time looking for the real killer," I said. "Had you thought perhaps that the stake through his hand might be some kind of accident and the shock triggered a heart attack? That wouldn't be murder, would it?"

"Is that a confession, Ms Hunter?" he asked. "Did you put the stake through his hand? Is that why you had to pull it out?"

"Don't be ridiculous," Ms Khalifeh said. Perhaps it was for the best her words drowned out my muttered, "Fuck you."

DI Collingwood heard me anyway. I could tell from his sour expression. "We are still waiting for the results of the post mortem, Ms Hunter," he said, opening the front door.

I tried one last time, starting with an apology for losing my temper.

"I was beginning to care for Harry Rook. It looks like he was my grandfather. If he was murdered, I really want his murderer caught. It wasn't me. I don't care if you don't believe me, so long as you investigate all the other possibilities. Thoroughly. Look for other suspects. Please."

"Don't tell me how to do my job," DI Collingwood said. Then he shrugged. "You simply can't help yourself, can you?" He walked out without waiting for an answer, followed by DC King. She looked back, with half a smile, as if to say she'd warned me.

"That went down well, Ms Khalifeh," I said.

"Call me Suhad," she said. "I know we have a professional relationship, but it looks like it won't be a short one." She sighed dramatically, and after a moment, I laughed. Mr Harvey was right – she was good to have on the team.

Between us we dragged the cases over to her Audi and put them in the boot, all the time under observation from the police car.

In the car, Suhad said, "Mr Harvey will want to have a chat so I suggest we make for the office first. Where next is up to you. Although you will want to be relatively close to the Beacon Road police station, if you're signing in at eight thirty every morning."

"Sounds sensible to me," I said. "Mr Harvey first and then perhaps you could drop me off at Mrs B's. The photographer's on the High Street."

"I'm seeing you safely settled in some place suitable," Suhad said. "I need to be sure as soon as possible that it will acceptable within the conditions of your bail."

"I don't need babysitting," I grumbled, but I was relieved not to feel quite so alone, at least for now.

Soon we were all sitting around Mr Harvey's desk. The receptionist offered coffee and biscuits, but Suhad suggested something more substantial might be welcome.

"They do good bacon sandwiches in the coffee shop on the corner," the receptionist suggested.

"We'll all have one then, please," Suhad said. "If you don't mind? I am a good Muslim woman, but even so I do enjoy a good bacon sandwich."

Mr Harvey added, "And the occasional glass of champagne."

"Not before noon," she quipped. "I am English after all."

I did feel much more human after laughing and eating, but we were soon back on emotionally shaky ground.

"I am so sorry that I couldn't tell you," Mr Harvey said. "I was bound by my promise to my client. I warned her that something like this would happen."

Involuntarily, my eyebrows rose.

He saw and smiled ruefully. "Not that I was expecting Harry to die in suspicious circumstances. No, I meant that there would be many situations when you would need to know. I thought she should have told you years ago."

"Does my mother know?" I asked.

"No. At least, Frances certainly didn't tell her. No way she'd have given Helen any more ammunition." He looked at me with a concerned expression. "It's not for me to say, child, but someone has to. Your mother is not the nicest of people."

"But she is my mother," I said, defending her again. "Frances was a wonderful grandmother, but I get why my mother is so difficult. It wasn't ever easy for her. There was the stigma of being a bastard. Helen always cared about what people thought. She and Grandma – they were chalk and cheese. Grandma would never understand how much mother simply wanted to be accepted."

"Your loyalty is to be admired."

"I wish we knew how Harry died," I said. "I wish I'd known he was my grandfather. I wish…"

"I was wondering about hiring a private investigator," Mr Harvey said.

"Maybe," I said. "But won't that risk getting in the way of the police investigation? DI Collingwood might think I'm guilty, but he'll do his job."

Suhad chimed in. "I agree, at least for now. Let's hold and see what happens. If the post mortem comes back with natural causes – well, then, we're probably in the clear."

"I'd like to know who my stalker is," I said. "It's been preying on my mind."

"Why didn't you raise it earlier?" Mr Harvey asked.

"I was… afraid… that no one would believe me."

"Now, that was silly," Mr Harvey said. "Certainly we would."

Suhad spoke up for me. "That's not been Ms Hunter's experience, however."

I smiled at her. She'd forgotten. Or was being professional in front of her boss. "Call me Alice, please. I guess it's time to face it. All those rumours about me being responsible for Cuckmere's outbreak of satanic vandalism have come back to haunt me."

"No one really believed that, surely," Mr Harvey said.

"Apart from my mother, my doctors, half the village…" I shrugged. He looked outraged.

"Oh yes," I said. "When you're crazy, people will believe anything of you. I had a breakdown after Grandma's death. I imagined all sorts of foolish things. I heard footsteps and voices in the house when I was alone. I had a bonfire in the garden, during a drought, and I could have set fire to the whole of the Beacon Nature Reserve. I burned valuable antique furniture for no good reason. And now they'll all believe I'm a murderer."

Suhad said, very gently. "In the light of your stalker, we might consider perhaps that not everything was in your mind. It's possible that someone broke into the house when you were alone those nights after your Grandmother's death."

She paused.

"Or I could have been bonkers," I said.

They both looked thoughtful. All at once I realised how very tired I was.

"Enough," I said. "I'm exhausted and I have to find somewhere to stay."

"You are more than welcome to our spare room," Mr Harvey said. "Rose would be delighted to fuss over you."

I smiled. "Very kind, but I'm sure Mrs B will have somewhere. Then all I'll need is a laptop and a phone. The police are holding on to mine."

"I'm sure there must be a spare laptop in the office you can borrow," Mr Harvey said. As I shook my head, and started to refuse, he stood up. "No, I'll go and search one out. The least I can do."

Suhad stood up too. "Let's go, then. I can get you a phone if you like, while I leave you at Mrs B's. Unless you want to shop for the latest smart phone and agonise over the features."

"Nope, I am betting on the police returning mine before long. A simple pay as you go will be fine."

As we left his office Mr Harvey came through from the back of the building, carrying a laptop bag and beaming. "State of the art," he said. "Frances wouldn't have wanted anything to get in the way of your continuing education. When does that course start?"

"Next week," I said. "And thank you. Thank you for everything."

He hugged me, which was a first. I hugged back, then followed Suhad back to her car.

"You know," she said, "I suspect Mr Harvey had a bit of a thing for your Grandma."

I snorted with laughter, but on reflection she was probably right. Grandma had that effect on a lot of people.

Mrs B came up with the perfect solution for where I could stay.

Her first suggestion was the flat she'd suggested for Kelly. It had been vacated and hadn't been cleaned and refurbished yet, but that wouldn't be much of a problem.

"Oh no, I completely forgot to tell her," I said. I'd neglected my friend, and I knew how important it was for her to have hope. I would try to remember to phone her later.

"Why don't you live at the farm?" Mrs B asked. "You'd need a bit of furniture but we can quickly sort the basics out. It's not too far out of town, there's a bus route almost on the doorstep, and you could cycle to the police station, or walk across the fields. There's an old path across the fields, a ley line I think Frances called it. One of those tracks that has been used forever. She used to rhapsodise about how people had probably walked along there in Neolithic times. There's a stone, about half way up the path, with a bottom-shaped depression, that the locals call Rest and be Thankful. It's very peaceful, and you won't get journalists on the doorstep, or at least if you do, they'll be easy to spot.

"What kind of state is it in? I could really do with a hot bath and some home comforts. I'm not so sure about camping out at a derelict farm."

"It's not derelict, only a bit old fashioned," Mrs B said. "It's barely lunchtime now. We can have it all cosy in no time at all."

Suhad arrived back with my temporary phone, and Mrs B recruited her to the task at hand. We went shopping and bought some towels and bedding, and Mrs B sent a cleaning team off to spruce up the farm and turn the water and heating on, and she set her handyman on collecting various bits of furniture from storage and transporting them in his white van. Suhad also persuaded DI Collingwood to let the driver collect my bicycle from home, supervised by DC King.

When Suhad and I pulled up in the farm yard the van was there, as well as Mrs B in her BMW. The cleaning team had already been and gone.

It looked quite homely. In the kitchen there was a simple old oak table and four old wooden chairs. The fridge was ancient but working – and when I opened the door, I found it was full – milk and butter, cheese, eggs and bacon. There was a vegetable rack full of produce, and there was a cupboard packed full of tins and jars, and packets of rice and pasta.

There was no wine. No alcohol at all. I wished I'd risked bringing some from home, but I'd known it was impossible, being watched by the police and by Suhad. Not that they would have stopped me, I didn't think that. But it would have shown them that I'm a rule breaker and that would not work in my favour. I'd kill for a glass of wine, though. An unfortunate way of phrasing it, for a suspected murderer.

In the living room a fire blazed away – next to it a stack of logs and a gas poker.

The carpet must have been there forever, an old faded red square surrounded by bare polished boards at the edge of the room. An amazingly ugly three-piece suite, a solid 1950s design, dominated the room. It was dark red fake leather, carved or embossed with an intricate floral pattern, with thick cushions, covered in dark green velvet. The far wall had obviously been knocked through, creating an archway into the dining area dominated by an ancient solid oak table with leaves that could be pulled out, and four old oak chairs. Green velvet curtains hung at the windows.

Upstairs, the bathroom was clean and bright, and a towel already hung on the towel rail. The front bedroom had an extra wide futon base bed and a couple of cheap canvas storage units in place of a wardrobe.

"I know you'd rather have the old stuff, but this was all we had available," she said.

"It really doesn't matter. You've done so much for me."

We went back downstairs and warmed ourselves in front of the fire.

"It's a cold house, with there being no central heating," Mrs B said. "We might arrange to have some storage heaters installed if you're here for long. But in the meantime, there's plenty of logs in the barn, and you can camp out on the sofa if it's too chilly upstairs."

I shivered. How long would it be before I could go home?

"I can't see any smoke alarms," I said, after a quick look around.

"Easily fixed," Mrs B said, and straight away was on the phone to the handyman to come over and sort it out.

I was touched by how willing she was to help me, and without calling attention to my paranoia. I'm not normally a demonstrative person, but I was overwhelmed. I flung my arms around her and hugged, and felt a tear or two start to crawl down my cheek.

"I think that's the first time I've seen you cry, Alice, and I've known you since you were a toddler. Now please take care of yourself. Are you sure you'd rather be on your own? If you change your mind, call and you can be in our guest room in no time at all."

"That's very kind," I said. "But I do want to be alone. Not in a Greta Garbo kind of way, but it's important to me, to prove I can cope."

"I understand," she said. "You are so like Frances."

Maybe like Harry too, I thought. I wondered how long it would be before everyone got to know. For now, I was keeping it to myself. I decided I'd best mention that to Suhad, and Mr Harvey.

Suhad had brought the new bedding in and was making up the bed with flat sheet and hospital corners.

"You're really not the average lawyer," I said.

"We sleep in beds, you know. We don't hang upside down from a rail."

I laughed.

"That reminds me," Mrs B said. She disappeared out to her car and came back with a beautiful coverlet. It was bright colours, orange and red and turquoise, and completely covered with parallel lines of stitching. A kind of quilt.

"It's a kantha," she explained. "Made of recycled saris. I thought it would add a touch of colour."

She gave me another quick hug, and was gone, repeating her earlier words, that any time I wanted company I should call them first.

I had plenty of offers, considering I was now suspected of murder. When I was simply crazy, not so many.

TWENTY

IT WAS DARK by the time the handyman had finished, and I was alone. I had a hot bath, washing off the grime of the police station. Then I curled up on the sofa, with the kantha wrapped around me. I'd called the police and told them where I was. DI Collingwood had been surprised I was sorted so quickly and told me he'd arrange for the tagging to be done in the next couple of days. In the meantime, he warned me to abide by the curfew and to keep out of the exclusion zone.

I was looking forward to exploring the farm and the surroundings the following day. Mrs B had told me not to rush back to work – she had my jobs covered. That confirmed my suspicions that she'd been worried about me spending too much time alone, rather than desperate for my help. All the same, I insisted that once my tag was in place, I would get back to it. I didn't say it out loud, but I didn't want to sink back into hiding under the bed covers all day.

I was still trying to make sense of everything. I was exhausted, but in that state of being too tired to sleep. My mind kept going over and over the same ground and getting no further. I wished I had something to distract me, but I hadn't thought to bring any books.

In the library I'd been distracted by the missing skyphos. I had no radio or television. When I booted up the laptop, I realised I had no Internet either. That was first on the to-do-list the following day – go and get a mobile dongle. First after the police station, I reminded myself.

The skyphos. My paranoia about the Professor had been triggered again, but I was getting better at reasoning myself out of it. Perhaps so good that I'd be perfectly capable of reasoning away justifiable fears. How does one ever know the difference? Without my own phone and laptop, I had no one's contact details, so I couldn't get in touch with the Professor for information – and reassurance. I desperately wanted to ring Kelly too. I looked in my wallet and discovered Suhad's card, so she was the only one I could call.

She gave me Mrs B's number and willingly agreed to Google the number of Brookfields for me, and promised she'd put some pressure on the police to get me my own mobile back as soon as possible. I could tell from her tone that she didn't hold out much hope, but it was touching that she was willing to try.

I phoned Brookfields and asked to speak to the sister on Hilton Ward. Fortunately the one I'd met when I visited was on duty, and she remembered me. I hoped she hadn't seen on the news that I was a suspected murderer. Perhaps it was as well I didn't have a television.

Kelly was not easy to talk to. I asked how her case conference had been and she was evasive. I guessed that meant that they had decided she wasn't ready to leave yet. I told her twice that I had arranged somewhere for her to live. I described the studio flat in the old Victorian building on the sea front in Cuckmere and stressed that it would be ready for her to move in by November. It would all work out. There was no rush. When I repeated it the second time, the message got through and I was glad I rang. I persuaded her to find a pen and paper and write down Mrs B's phone number as well as mine, in case I wasn't easily available when she did need a flat. She was very much more cheerful when we said goodbye, and that cheered me up in turn.

I felt guilty for not phoning my mother, but I wasn't quite ready to deal with her yet. I did want to ask her if she knew about Harry, but not on the phone. It was a conversation I could only imagine face to face – and anyway, I needed to see her reaction, not just hear it. Not that it would necessarily help. My mother is the kind of liar who doesn't have a tell – because she lies to herself most of all. At least, that's my working theory.

I wandered round the house, turning all the lights on and considering every room. Although the place was old and shabby, it did have the feeling of somewhere that had been a home. Only one room, upstairs, gave me the shivers – a sense of familiarity.

On impulse, I rolled back the rag rug which covered the bare floorboards. There was a pentagram on the floor, in faded paint. Daniel? I wondered. But surely at sixteen he was too young – Grandma's coven certainly wouldn't have accepted an initiate so young. He could be a solo worker, perhaps.

More likely it was his father, or even his aunt. They were of the right generation, and the connection would explain why Grandma had been so generous with the rent.

I sprinkled a little salt, in the room and around the outside of the farmhouse too, and performed a small banishing ritual. It helped me feel at home, and safe – no different, in all truth, to the psychological exercises they taught me in hospital.

I didn't think I'd ever been to the farm before. Perhaps once, long ago – at Christmas. I remembered sitting at a big scrubbed wooden table in the kitchen, with the boy, Daniel. I was about fifteen, and he would have been eight, or nine. There were three hot mince pies on a plate in the middle of the table, and a jug of hot blackcurrant squash, mimicking the adults' mulled wine.

We had one mince pie each and then each of us eyed the other, neither reaching for the last one. Then we had both reached out simultaneously and smashed the pie on the plate. He wailed, and his mother came over, and shouted at us both.

The dog was watching, all big eyes and drooling tongue, as she cleared the mess away into the bin.

His mother gave the dog a bone shaped biscuit. "Good girl, Tess," she said. "Not like this pair."

But she was laughing. Tess, yes, I remembered the collie. That was what the farm needed now, a dog. I could use the company.

"Your mum's a good cook," I'd said to him.

"My mum's gone," he'd said. "That's my auntie."

I shivered.

Poor Daniel. Now his Dad was dead and he was alone. I would have to talk to Mr Harvey and get something sorted about that private investigator. I thought about how my Grandma's death had sent me into a tailspin, and I had every advantage. Poor kid, only sixteen. Someone needed to be in his corner.

There really didn't seem to be anything very special about the farmhouse. It was far older than my home. It was decorated in old faded floral wallpaper and painted woodchip. The woodwork was all white gloss and had been done recently – obviously part of Mrs B's plan to make it into a rental property. It wasn't old in the interesting sense of having history. It was old in the sense of needing a lot of attention.

I put another log on the fire and lay on the sofa again, pulling the kantha quilt around me. There was so much to think about, so much to organise.

Why had Grandma chosen to live so near the Rook house? I knew from the family stories, and from leafing through old photo albums I'd unearthed after her death, that they'd moved in when my mother was about five. Before that, they'd lived in a flat in the town centre. Was Grandma still seeing Harry? Were they carrying on an affair so blatantly in front of Julia? No wonder she was so bitter and cold if she knew her husband's daughter was living across the road. Especially as she had no children herself, and it was common knowledge how much she had wanted them.

More than anything I wished I could talk to Julia. I felt sure she had some of the answers I needed. It was against the conditions of my bail for me to approach her, and in any case, she wasn't going to talk willingly with me, now that I was suspected of her husband's murder. If only Tammy would talk to her for me. I set that problem aside for another day.

I must have fallen asleep on the sofa, still ruminating. I woke up with a start, unsure where I was until I saw the fire was still flickering in the hearth. My heart was beating very quickly, and my ears strained. I was sure I could hear something.

I wished I had Tess with me now.

I pushed the quilt off me and carefully, quietly, stood up in my stockinged feet. There was enough light from the fire to see where I was going, so I carefully padded over to the kitchen door. Again, that sound, something moving. I wasn't alone in the house.

Something clattered to the floor – a knife, perhaps, from where I'd had a sandwich at the table and not cleared up.

I put the kitchen light on, fully expecting to see someone in the room with me. My stalker, perhaps.

Only if my stalker was a kitten, who had indeed pushed a knife to the floor, and was now helping itself from the tuna tin I'd left on the table.

How ridiculous, to be terrified by a kitten.

I found a saucer in the cupboard and opened a tin of sardines, mushing half of them up for the kitten. The rest I put in a bowl in the fridge. Then I put both empty cans in the bin with the lid firmly down and did the dishes.

It was a little past two when I was finished. Even though it was comfortable, sleeping on the sofa seemed like a minor defeat, so I turned the kitchen light off and shut the door on the kitten. The fire was all but done, so I ran upstairs and was very soon settled in my bed, and fast asleep.

The following morning was a blur. I barely had time to dress and had to run to catch the bus at the end of the lane. I was signed in on time by a grumpy desk sergeant, who told me to make sure I was at home that afternoon. Well, not home exactly.

When I asked for permission to collect some more of my things, he told me I'd have to wait until DI Collingwood was available. I waited half an hour and gave up – another day would do as well. I had things to do, and I couldn't put them off. I tried not to think about how I hated shopping, and especially not to dwell on the panic attack I'd had last time I'd shopped in Tweedies. It would be far quicker than traipsing around town, so I told myself to get a grip and get on with it.

First, a mobile dongle, together with some reassurance that I'd be able to set it up. It was easy, the salesman said. I wrote his name down and a contact number, saying I'd be in touch if I got stuck, and he blanched. Sometimes it is fun to scare people a little. I bought some speakers for the laptop too – at least I'd be able to bear listening to music now.

That was entertainment sorted, but I also treated myself to a pile of books and magazines. Once they were packed into my old rucksack, I was ready to go home. I'd had to pause to do my relaxation exercises a couple of times, but I'd coped.

At least, everything was fine until I was half way down the High Street. The strap on my rucksack snapped.

Grandma, I thought, you may have deprived me of knowing my grandfather, but you left me well provided for financially. I was lucky that shortage of funds wouldn't make this difficult time any harder, and I turned around and trekked back towards the outdoors shop. I would buy a new rucksack.

That was when it all went wrong. I started to feel a bit conscious of people staring at me, hoping it was only because I was so heavily laden, carrying my broken rucksack gingerly from the unbroken strap.

I bumped into Tamsin by the counter in the shop.

Literally bumped.

"Oh, I'm sorry," I said, reaching out to steady her.

"Sorry doesn't really cut it," she said. "Murdering bitch."

I let the rucksack carefully down to the floor. I didn't know what to say. I thought Tamsin knew me. We were friends. Second cousins, actually.

"Tamsin, I didn't kill Harry. Why would you think that?" I was impressed that I got complete sentences out. That I sounded calm and reasonable when I wanted to burst into tears.

"I thought I knew you," she said. "Turns out I was wrong. I didn't know you at all."

This time I was sure it wasn't paranoia. Everyone really was watching us.

Breathe and count.

Eventually, I thought, I would get to the stage where I wouldn't be able to take a breath without that steady count of four in, four hold, and four out.

I could find no words. How could I prove myself innocent? She didn't know me. I didn't know myself any more. I'd never known myself.

She walked out of the shop, leaving her purse on the counter. I went to pick it up, to chase after her, but the look on the cashier pierced me, as he snatched it away. As if I was a thief, as well as a murderer.

"We don't serve your kind in here," he said.

I swung the rucksack over my shoulder by its surviving strap, and walked out, slowly. I was moving like an old lady. I crossed the road and sat down on a bench in the middle of the park, to collect myself.

A ghost of a laugh escaped. So much for all the self-talk telling me that there was no reason to have a panic attack in a shop – that nothing bad could happen to me while shopping. I felt convinced that people were watching me again. I started up the breathing exercises, then reluctantly dragged myself to my feet.

I stopped off at the off licence and picked out a couple of bottles of wine. Pretty much the only thing the farm wasn't well stocked with – for my own good. Isn't everything?

It was a long walk back to the farm with a full, but broken, rucksack.

TWENTY-ONE

BACK AT THE farmhouse – I couldn't find it in me to call it home – I was exhausted. I knew it wasn't merely the walk and the stress of shopping. It was the effects of the last few days catching up with me.

I couldn't settle. Even after my hurried banishing rite last night, I didn't feel secure. I didn't really know the farm well enough. From the outside, the farmhouse still had the unlived-in look of the previous day and I decided that was a good thing.

I locked myself in and the world out, cleared the fireplace and set myself a new fire. The gas poker was efficient and for now there were enough logs. Mrs B had said there were plenty in the barn. I'd have to bring more in later. It was cold, so I pulled the heavy curtains closed, to make the place feel cosy.

I was expecting visitors, so I made myself a quick sandwich lunch and then settled myself down at the dining table. Laptop plugged in and ready to go, I got the mobile dongle out of its box, and started to set it all up.

I'd hardly begun when there was the sound of a car engine outside, followed by a knock at the door. I peered out of the kitchen window, and as I expected it was DI Collingwood.

I let him in.

"The tagging crew not here yet then?" he asked.

I looked around the room. "Nope," I said, "Can't see anyone else here." Then I thought better of being a smartarse – I didn't need to alienate him any more than I already had. The way things were going, before long I'd have spent more time with DI Collingwood than with anyone else since I'd been discharged from Brookfields.

"Would you like a coffee?" I asked.

"Yes, please," he said.

He stood by the window, looking out at the yard and across the fields to the river as I put the kettle on.

"It's isolated here," he said.

"It was passed as acceptable," I said, immediately on the defensive.

"That wasn't what I meant. I was thinking of your safety."

For the first time, I looked him in the eye, startled. He flushed, and he looked away. So did I, thoughtful now. Biting back an impulsive comment about how I was supposed to be the dangerous one, I busied myself with kettle and mugs.

As soon as we sat down with our coffees, both of us unusually quiet, we were interrupted by the sound of another vehicle pulling up outside. I opened the kitchen door and watched as two men got out, the shorter one carrying what looked like a heavy tool bag. Like a plumber, I thought.

I offered them coffee but they were in a rush, they said. They had other customers waiting.

"This one is for the GPS trial, right?" the man with the bag said, looking at DI Collingwood.

"Yes, that's right," Collingwood answered. "Curfew between six p.m. and six a.m., and a permanent exclusion zone in the area around the victim's home." He sounded relaxed, now he wasn't on his own with me.

"If you could show us where the landline is, we can install the control box," the taller man said.

"It's in the hall," I said. The guy with the heavy bag followed me and settled on the floor.

I went back into the kitchen.

"Please sit down," the taller one said. "And if you can put your right foot up in this chair, I can fit the bracelet."

I did as I was told, and first he handed it to me to inspect. It looked like a bulky watch, really. Nothing special.

"Does it come in any other colours?" I asked.

"Like I've not heard that before," he said. He smiled, anyway, and set to fixing it around my ankle.

"Done," he said. "Stand up and walk around in it for a minute and see how it feels."

"It feels weird."

"You'll get used to it quickly enough and forget it's there. At least that's what they tell us, when they break curfew."

"Will I be able to go out to the barn, to fetch logs in?" I asked.

"Not during curfew, then you have to stay strictly inside the house. But during the day, you can go anywhere as long as you stay out of the exclusion zone. Here's a map, to make it clear."

I looked at the red circle on the printout. It covered the Rook house and Grandma's place, the Harbour View pub, and all around that end of the road. I could still walk on the Beacon, almost as far as Grandma's back garden. I could still go down to the beach, but only if I walked over the Beacon to get there.

It wasn't a large area. It was my home.

"You can shower with it on," he said. "But no long soaks in the bath. If you take it off, or tamper with it, we will know. If you enter the exclusion zone, we will know. There'll be a call to your landline and if you don't answer in fifteen minutes, you'll get a visit. If you're found to have tampered with it deliberately or to have broken the rules, then your bail will be revoked, and you may end up in custody."

"I understand," I said, in a small voice.

This was worse than the hospital. They'd been so relaxed and jokey at first that I'd been able to pretend it wasn't serious. But it was. I was a murder suspect.

The shorter man came back from the hall, his bag packed.

DI Collingwood had been watching in silence. Now he spoke. "All done?" he asked.

"Apart from the test to make sure it's working," the short guy said.

"Okay," DI Collingwood turned to me.

"Pop outside for a few minutes, would you?"

"It's not six o'clock," I said.

"We'll set the timer after we know the equipment's working."

I went outside and wandered around the outbuildings for five minutes until they called me in.

The phone was ringing. The short guy answered, and then hung up.

"Okay," he said. "Timer's now set. We're all done."

DI Collingwood showed them out, then picked up his mug and mine and put them in the sink.

On the doorstep he paused and turned back.

"My phone number," he said, holding out a card.

I took it, feeling bemused.

"If you're worried, ring 999 first, but then call me. Understood?" He didn't give me time to answer. "I'm off then," he said. "Unless there's anything?"

"You could set my mobile dongle up," I suggested, pointing to the laptop.

"Such a comedian," he said, as he left.

Would he prefer it if I cried, I wondered. Another similarity between being a mental health patient and being a murder suspect. Your emotions were someone else's business, and you knew they were always marking them against some unknowable ideal scale. Did I pass or fail?

Two hours, and much frustration later, fuelled by a much-needed glass of red, I had the mobile dongle working, and no tears.

What I wanted to do was check out the course details and the reading lists. Instead, I did the dutiful thing and set up my email. I hoped I could remember my password. Fortunately user support at my ISP was helpful and before long I had downloaded hundreds of emails.

Dozens, anyway. Most of them from my mother. Why wasn't I answering my mobile phone or my emails? She knew I'd been released on bail but the police wouldn't tell her where I was, only that I was banned from going home, and that for now Grandma's house was off limits for everyone unless accompanied by a police chaperone.

Not a word of concern for how I was, or a single question about what I needed. There was no avoiding it, so I emailed her a reply. I told her the police had my phone and my computer and I'd only now been able to get access to my email. I didn't tell her where I was but asked for her phone number. 'And any others you think I might need – helplessly out of touch without my own phone,' I typed.

And yes, I did get a little bit of a thrill from knowing that my reticence would have irritated her beyond measure.

Another email from Suhad – this one asking if there was anything she could help with. I emailed to thank her for the offer, and that she could be sure I would indeed take her up on it – but for now I was taking it easy.

Finally, the one I saved for last, one from Professor Buckley.

"Heard that you were released. Hope everything is fine, and that you got my note – your skyphos is in the safe at the University. Anything you need, do ask, and I hope we'll see you at the first lecture next week." His sig file thoughtfully included a link to the course details, and some preparatory reading. I smiled when I recognised that I'd already bought the first book on the list, and that it was sitting next to my laptop on the dining table. And then his PS, 'Seriously if there's anything you need, let me know.'

I didn't email him back. I was feeling a bit fragile and didn't much want to see anyone, but I did key his phone number into my phone. A ping informed me I had another email, and it was from my mother. It was brief, and to the point. Her phone number, with a note that it was the only one I needed and would I call her straight away. Where was I? It was so rude and uncooperative of me not to answer any of her questions. I could hear her voice in my mind as I read.

I tapped her number into my phone, my finger hanging over the call button, then thought better of it.

Instead I picked up the Romans in Sussex book, and carried it into the living room. I snuggled down under the kantha and started to read.

I was deep into Julius Caesar's view of the Britons, when I heard a knocking at the door. The doorbell didn't work, so the heavy door knocker was a necessity. I stayed put. I wasn't sure who it was, but I didn't care. I didn't want to see anyone.

I grabbed my mobile and turned the ring-tone off not a moment too soon. Incoming call. My mother. I would lay good money on it being her – she'd probably tracked down Mrs B and demanded to know where she'd hidden me. Mrs B could have warned me, I thought, as she had the landline number.

I was glad I had the curtains drawn and the lights off. She wandered around the house and rattled at the windows. I wondered if she would go so far as to break in – but she wasn't likely to do that if it involved any physical strain. Her main objection to me studying archaeology was the prospect of me getting my hands dirty. "Grubbing around on hands and knees in the mud" as she put it.

Just in case though, I set the book down on the back of the sofa and pulled the kantha up over my head. I would pretend to be asleep. It didn't muffle the noise very much and she hammered on the kitchen door one more time before giving up.

After an hour of dozing on the sofa, I began to trust she'd gone, and I risked getting up and putting the light on.

I checked the laptop and there was another angry email from my mother.

I rang Mrs B, and she apologised. "Your mother was dead set on visiting you, and I really had to tell her where you were. I am sorry."

"That's okay, Mrs B. I know she's impossible to refuse. Did she say what had her so worked up?"

"Something about the house, I think. She wanted to go and make sure everything was okay. She didn't like the idea of it being left empty."

"Funny," I said. "She had no problems with it being empty while I was in hospital."

"She did go round and make sure everything was okay every week, and we had the cleaning crew in regularly too."

She visited the house more often than she visited me then. I bit that comment back. Mrs B was being scrupulously fair – I knew what she thought of mother and what that cost her.

Now for answering mother's email. That was tricky.

"Finally persuaded Mrs B to tell me where you were living. The old bitch loves having power over me, you really should have let me know where you were. How do you think it feels knowing that everyone else knows, and not me? You always find new ways to break my heart. I came out to see you and for all the talk of how tired you were, there was no one in, so I suppose you had a better offer. I'll be out there again tomorrow morning. I really need to talk to you."

I emailed back. There was only one possible approach.

"Sorry, I was in, but fast asleep. I should get the doorbell fixed. Why didn't you knock? I have to sign in at the police station early tomorrow but should be home later. See you then."

Oh well. A lot could happen to divert me from my plans for the day, but I would have to see her eventually – I might as well buckle down to it.

I heard the email ping again but shut my laptop down to avoid any more instructions.

Instead I wandered into the kitchen, cooked myself a bowl of pasta with a jar of tomato sauce and tinned tuna, and ate at the dining table while reading my book. I checked my pillbox and realised I hadn't taken them again. I flushed them down the toilet and helped myself to another glass of red.

I hadn't told mother I'd registered for the course yet. Perhaps that would keep her off some more irritating topic the next day.

TWENTY-TWO

AS FAR AS I could tell, my high-tech ankle bracelet survived my morning shower. Still half asleep, I waited a few minutes in case, but there was no phone call so I ran to catch the bus.

Signing in at the police station was brisk and no nonsense, and I was done in minutes. I knew I wasn't allowed back home, but I had to test the limits of the exclusion zone. I walked down Beacon Road until I could see the pub, the Rook house, and my home. There was no one around, but I felt vaguely guilty about being in the vicinity. According to the map which I'd studied carefully, if I walked up the tarmac path as far as the Coastguard look out, I could then walk down to the beach, keeping well out of the exclusion zone the whole way.

I walked almost as far as Harry's kiosk, my heart beating faster and faster the closer I got. Where there used to be a blackboard with the times of high and low tide and the prices of fishing permits and overnight camping, now there was a police poster, asking for any witnesses or people who had been in the area on the day of Harry's death to call the information line. There were some remnants of crime scene tape still straggling and various bits of litter – crisp packets and cola cans, mostly. Knowing how he would have hated that, I paused and pulled my gloves on, and collected and binned it all. It was a small gesture, but I knew I was doing it for him.

It wasn't enough. He deserved better. One of the things he deserved was to have his murder properly investigated. If the police wouldn't do it, I would. I would see Mr Harvey and get the go ahead on hiring a good private detective agency. At the very least they could find out who the rabbit and cat killer was, and maybe track down my stalker too. I was also seriously concerned for Daniel. In some obscure way, living in his home made me feel responsible for him. I knew Grandma would have worried too.

Sometimes I felt certain DI Collingwood would do his job and investigate it all properly, and sometimes I was equally sure he thought I'd made up a stalker to divert their attention from me. Hiring an investigator might help me stop driving myself crazy with my doubts and paranoia.

A plan had been developing in the back of my mind since Tamsin had confronted me in the outdoor gear shop. I walked back along the seafront to the cafe, intending to go in and have a coffee and a muffin, and talk to her. Maybe I could make her understand it was a mistake, and that I would never have done anything to hurt Harry, no matter what anyone thought. I needed Tamsin's help. Without her as mediator, I would never get to talk to Julia.

There were no lights on in the cafe, but the door was open. It was early, but Tamsin usually opened for the fishermen, and there were plenty of them in the distance on the breakwater.

There was a sign tacked to the door. I thought at first it said, For Sale. Closer up, I realised my mistake.

Large red letters.

SOLD.

I knocked on the door and walked in. "Tamsin," I said. "Are you there?"

I could hear voices, male voices. Then I saw him, Mark Stockman, walking towards me, coming out of the kitchen. Following him an older man, in shabby suit, talking nineteen to the dozen.

"Well, it doesn't matter, the whole place will be demolished by then—" Stockman said, then he saw me and stopped abruptly.

"What do you want?" he asked.

"Coffee, a walnut muffin, and a word with Tamsin."

"Tamsin?" he said blankly. Then, "Can't you read? The sign's big enough. The cafe is closed. There'll be no more coffee here."

"It says, *sold*," I said. "That doesn't mean quite the same thing as no more coffee. I suggest you try for a little more clarity in your signage, Mr Stockman."

"Do I know you?" he asked.

I ignored his question. "You may have bought the cafe, but I don't think you'll have so much luck buying the Hunter house."

"That's what you think. I'm in negotiations as we speak. It will be mine before the month's out."

I laughed out loud. I'd rattled him, and he'd told me what I needed to know.

"You're not in negotiations with the owner," I said, and turned to walk away.

"Oh," he said, as I walked away.

His tone told me he'd worked out who I was. I was glad I had managed to puncture his self-importance, however briefly.

Now I actually wanted to talk to my mother. What was the betting she wouldn't turn up? It was as if she had some instinct to frustrate me.

I walked back by the fastest route. Up the Beacon, down to the bus stop, then straight to the farm. I walked quickly and tried not to think about Harry and the animals. It was about as effective as not thinking about a monkey climbing a stick.

Mother was leaning against a car, smoking. My heart sank, and I realised I should have wondered how she'd managed to get out to the farm the previous day. Helen having wheels was a premonition of hell on earth. As I approached the yard, she tossed the stub of her cigarette and crushed it with the toe of her red stiletto. Ideal footwear for visiting a farm.

"I thought you'd given up," I said.

"It's the stress, darling. Having my daughter arrested for murder has left its mark."

"I didn't do it, you know."

"I said you'd been arrested, not that you were a murderer."

She followed me into the house and squealed and jumped when the kitten ran past her and straight outside.

"Not a cat. You know I'm allergic."

I'd forgotten, if I ever knew. Perhaps the kitten would get a reprieve after all.

I made coffee, while mother wandered around the farmhouse. We settled in the living room, sitting in front of the fire. I poked around with it, and put the last log on.

"Bit of a comedown, darling," she said. "It's tons better than the squat I was living in at your age, though. Your beloved Grandma wasn't quite so generous with me as she has been with you."

"When you were my age, I was two," I said. "I was living with Grandma by then."

"I did what was best for you," she said. "I couldn't possibly have a child living with me in those conditions. Fungi grew in colonies on the wall in the kitchen – it really wouldn't have been healthy."

I held my tongue and didn't mention all the times she had just disappeared off the radar in my childhood.

"She had me over a barrel, darling – that's the truth of it. She wanted you, that was what it was all about. A second try to shape a child in her own image. She did a better job with you than me. You're so much more malleable. But at least I was never arrested for murder, no matter how disappointed Grandma was in me."

She really wasn't holding back. It was my own fault, no doubt. I should have dropped everything as soon as she wanted to see me. I should have phoned her last night. I was paying for all the ways I'd let her down and ruined her life for the last twenty something years.

Only one thing for it. Change the subject.

"Did you know Mark Stockman has bought the Cafe? Tamsin said Harry didn't want to sell any more than she did – they both loved that place, but Julia didn't wait long."

She took the bait.

"Already? That is fast work even for Julia Rook. Harry'd be spinning in his grave – if he wasn't in a mortuary somewhere being scrutinised for evidence that you killed him."

Nice image, mother.

I pushed her, again. "Stockman also said he was in negotiations to buy Grandma's house. Do you know anything about that?"

She stood up and took another cigarette out of the packet.

I put up my hand. "Not indoors please, I can't bear the smell." She put it back in the pack and sat down and started tapping her fingers on the table. An angry beat.

"Stop harping on. I was only doing what I thought was best. Your trustee, the great and glorious Harry Rook, made sure I knew exactly where I stood – how little influence I could expect to have over my own daughter's life. He was downright rude."

I wish I'd known him well enough to have asked him what he said. All he'd told me was that he'd sorted it out, and made it clear to Helen that she couldn't sell the house. With or without my permission.

"Anyway, Mark Stockman is obviously planning another major development project. He was talking about demolishing the cafe and the arcade. Another bit of my childhood gone."

"Don't be so sentimental. It's not healthy. Mark has great plans for the area. It will create jobs, encourage tourism, raise Cuckmere from the dead."

Mark, was it?

I'd already known who he was in negotiations with – but it's always comforting to have one's suspicions confirmed.

Over my dead body was he getting Grandma's house.

There was one thing I really needed to know, and that was not going to be easy. How old was I, when I worked out that mother's truth was a strangely amorphous thing that shape-shifted from one moment to the next? Too young. It was one reason why I loved my Grandma, in spite of everything she had kept from me. Yes, there were gaps in the story she told, but they were out in the open. "I don't want to talk about it," she said. "It's too painful." But nothing she said was pure fabrication. It might be ordinarily fragmented and biased, but it was never completely invented.

Looking back, perhaps the gaps were the most treacherous lies of all. Grandma's refusal to acknowledge those things that had hurt, to keep silence, was a kind of self-containment that I'd seen as strength. Now, I was less sure.

As for me, what was my relationship with the truth? Where did I stand? I didn't often lie, I told myself. I didn't go out of my way to lie, at any rate. But I had turned away from truths I didn't want to face. I was complicit. I colluded with every fantasy rather than risk a tantrum. I'd grown braver as I grew up – although never brave to the point of confrontation. My strategy was to keep silent and bottle everything up. Perhaps mother was right then. Perhaps I was like Grandma.

Time to grow up.

I sat down opposite her at the table.

"Did the police question you?" I asked.

"Why would they question me? I wasn't the one who found his body and disturbed the crime scene. I didn't pull a stake out of his hand."

"So they did question you. I know that wasn't mentioned in the news. In fact, DI Collingwood made a big deal of asking me not to mention it to anyone. Anyone at all."

She glared at me. "He might have said that to me too. But talking to you doesn't count. How could it? I mean, you're my daughter. And you were there, so obviously you know."

"Have you mentioned it to anyone else, by any chance?"

She remained silent, lips thinning. I wondered who she'd told. I wondered if I could get that particular information across to DI Collingwood without looking like the kind of person who would stitch up her own mother, which was probably the kind of person who might murder their own grandfather. Probably not. I grimaced.

"Why would I kill Harry? I mean, I understand why the police might think I would, but why do you believe it possible?"

"I don't, Alice. I don't think you're a murderer. Not when you're in your right mind, of course not."

I stood up and turned away. My hands were shaking. My heart was beating so fast I thought it might leap out of my chest. What was this feeling? I don't think I'd ever felt it before. Not mere anger. This was pure rage.

If she said anything else, I might just kill her with my bare hands. For the first time, I really felt capable of it.

Maybe I was. Maybe I'd killed Harry in some kind of fugue state and forgotten, like with the bonfire.

It was always mother who made me feel this way, who made me doubt myself. It was the first time she'd undermined me to the point where I thought I might be a killer.

My rage surged again.

I had to do something with the adrenalin that was coursing through me.

"It's cold," I said. "Stay there, I'm going to fetch some wood in." I picked up the empty log basket.

I didn't look at her but walked out of the living room. I heard her get up to follow me, and I turned round and said, in a very cold and controlled voice, "No. Stay."

For once, she did as I said and retreated very quickly. I felt a strange piercing of something akin to joy, that I'd scared her for once, instead of the other way around. Perhaps I was my mother's daughter.

I carried the log basket into the barn, where the logs were stacked against one wall waiting to be chopped. I took the axe off the wall. It was in perfect condition, sharp and had been recently cleaned. There was an oily rag and an oil-soaked bucket of sand too. Someone knew how to look after tools properly.

I placed the logs one at a time on the big old circular slice of tree stump that was clearly used for the purpose. I swung and I split them, log after log, until the basket was full with suitable sized pieces for the fire. Then for good measure I split some more kindling and topped up the basket with that.

As I cleaned the axe with the rag, I heard the barn door open. I looked up, expecting to see my mother, and feeling rather glad that the strenuous exercise had worked off my murderous rage. Instead, I saw a boy's face, under a fleece hat. He was a skinny kid, dressed in navy from head to toe, and he was as surprised to see me as I was to see him.

"Daniel?" I said, but he turned and ran. I dropped the axe and ran after him, but by the time I reached the yard, there was no sign. He could be anywhere, I thought. He knew this place inside out. There were lots of outbuildings, a chicken shed, even a tumbledown small labourer's cottage as well as the barn, and he was probably camping out in one or another of them.

I couldn't deal with it now – I had to get back and face my mother and ask her one final question. I would deal with Daniel later.

I finished cleaning the axe and put it away. I wondered if I ought to hide it, but I thought it better not to act scared and treat Daniel as a criminal. Whatever else, I was living in his home. He wasn't much more than a child, and a child who'd lost his father. I knew what it was like to feel alone.

Perhaps the kitten was his, too.

The basket was too full for me to carry, so I emptied half of it out and staggered across to the farm with a much lighter load.

I found my mother in the dining area, looking at my books and playing with my laptop. I could see she'd moved my meditation candle too. I guess she was looking for more evidence to prove I'm still crazy. I still couldn't quite believe that when I was admitted to Brookfields, she'd told everyone that I was involved in witchcraft. She'd used Grandma's collection as evidence. She'd claimed I'd made a poppet of her and bound it in twine, and then burned it on the bonfire. And she'd implied I was the person behind the rash of satanic vandalism in Cuckmere.

No wonder DI Collingwood thought I was the murderer.

If I had the courage of Grandma's convictions, I would explain the vast gulf of difference between High Magic and Wicca, and between either of those and Satanism. Although it is hard not to admire the sterling political work of the American Satanist movement right now, with their fight for religious freedom.

"You were a long time," she said, after checking my expression and deciding to risk speaking to me.

"Chatting to a neighbour," I said.

At that she did look at me as if I was crazy. "That kitten," I elaborated. "Feral, I guess. Living in the barn."

It turned out I could lie.

I fed the fire – it was still glowing, so I threw some of the thin shards of kindling on top, then arranged the logs precisely.

"Stop playing with that fire. You're as bad as your father."

She hardly ever mentioned him. I suppose we're all living in the past. It was my father who'd taught me to light a fire, and to chop wood. It hadn't exactly been an idyll, the couple of weeks I spent with them both when he came back into her life. He took us camping. Nothing could have been better designed to torture Helen. He wasn't the ogre she painted him. I'd never seen him since, but that was hardly his fault as he'd died in a car accident a couple of weeks after he left her, the second time around.

It was my fault that he'd left her, she'd said. Both times. Every moment they spent together they'd fought, although I was pretty sure they'd made up as passionately'

But when I was on my own with him, we'd had fun. I was almost as good as a boy, he had teased, when she said something rude about me being all grubby, and how he must be ashamed to have a daughter like me.

It wasn't him who was ashamed.

Perhaps after all he'd been a good man, and I'd judged him by my family's standards. What a little snob, to judge him on his lack of money. If he was good, that gave me some hope. I had his genes too, his blood running through my veins as much as Helen's.

Still, she'd given me the opening I needed to ask her that question again. This time I knew the answer.

"Do you ever think about your father?" I asked, watching her very carefully. Did she know?

"What a peculiar question," she said, avoiding the direct answer.

"Not really," I said, preparing to twist the knife. "You mentioned my father, and I was thinking, we have that in common. Growing up without a father. We've both had mental breakdowns. Do you think, perhaps, it was why you attempted suicide that time?"

It was her turn to rage. She stood up and towered over me as I sat in front of the fire.

"I never did anything of the kind," she said. "It was an accident, I knocked the bottle of painkillers over. Your grandmother overreacted."

Like you did, I thought, when I was sectioned.

"Growing up without a father?" I said. "That didn't bother you at all?"

"That wasn't my choice. Your father walked out of my life before you were born. As soon as he turned up again, I told him about you, and I fought for him to get to know you. I stood up to Grandma, who said you didn't need that loser in your life. In fact, I wouldn't be surprised if she paid him to go away again. Like the first time."

I snapped. "You can always twist everything around, can't you? Nothing is ever your fault. It's always Grandma's or mine."

"I'm sure I don't know what you mean," she said. Her lips had almost disappeared in a narrow strip, and she was containing something, holding back. "I know you're under a lot of strain with the arrest and everything so I'm cutting you some slack, but you are dangerously close to crossing a line, madam."

She really did sound like Grandma when she was crossed. Right down to the 'madam' at the end.

I didn't ask her again, and I didn't reveal what I knew. I wouldn't get a straight answer, either way.

Sometimes what mother didn't say was more illuminating than what she did say.

TWENTY-THREE

EVENTUALLY HELEN LEFT me in peace with my books, but not before grumbling at length about the course. Why had I signed up for it without talking to her first? Why wasn't I taking up my place at Oxford? She ridiculed my fears of being overwhelmed, and said I was running away from life again, exactly the way I had when Grandma became ill.

Looking after Grandma was my way of showing I loved her – it had nothing to do with being scared of going away to University. Mother had disappeared on a month-long Buddhist retreat on some remote and craggy Scottish island, learning non-attachment. I never dared ask if she'd been leading the retreat; non-attachment being her one natural talent.

On the day Grandma had her first stroke, I was off gallivanting (mother's word) around Oxford. The Ashmolean, the Pitt Rivers Museum. I was in my element.

Getting home and finding the house empty and fearing the worst from the note on the kitchen table had been devastating. That was when I decided no matter what the results of my A-Levels, I was staying at home to look after Grandma. At some unconscious level I felt that so long as I was with her, she would be safe. It was always when I wasn't there, that bad things happened.

I shook the memories off and had settled down to work again when someone else knocked at the door. I was startled – not too many people knew I was there. I contemplated hiding, but the knocker clattered again, so I dragged myself away from the table before whoever it was started prowling around the house looking in through the windows.

I answered the door, hoping that it wouldn't be Daniel. It had been a long and emotionally fraught morning, and I couldn't take any more of it.

To my relief, it was Professor Buckley. I'd answered his email about the skyphos and told him then I'd moved in to the farm.

"I was passing, and I wondered how you were doing. I thought perhaps you might like a little company."

I grinned at him and looked pointedly down the lane and then to left and right.

"Okay, I wasn't passing. I wanted to see the farm. When you said your grandmother thought it might be a Roman site, I thought it was wild speculation, but now I've seen her collection…"

"Let me put my shoes on," I said. "I could do with stretching my legs. So long as we're back by six…" I showed him the tag on my ankle, quite enjoying the awkwardness of the moment. The great Professor Matthew Buckley, TV personality and man of the world, had probably never been alone with an accused murderer before. "Unless you want a coffee or something first?"

I let him into the kitchen and he sat at the table while I pulled on my thick socks and walking boots.

"Not quite all the comforts of home. But it will do. I didn't kill him, you know." I said. "I liked him, he was my… friend."

As far as I knew the news of my relationship with Harry wasn't public knowledge yet. For some reason, I felt the longer it stayed that way, the better off I'd be.

But even though I was brave enough to say it out loud, I wasn't brave enough to look the Professor in the eye and see his reaction.

I followed him out of the house and locked the door behind me. We walked along the lane, and up by the side of the barn. I kept my eye out for him, but there was no sign of Daniel.

"Your grandmother must have been a very good businesswoman," he said, looking around the farm. Even neglected, it was still a substantial property.

"She was," I said. "She started off as nanny to the Stockman family. Her charges were the father and aunt of our current MP. She doted on them. Somewhere at the house there's a whole album of photographs – there are more of them than of my mother."

"How did a nanny end up going into business for herself?"

"Mr Stockman helped her out at the beginning, I think. She was single and pregnant and had to drop out of University before she even began. She found him a replacement nanny before she quit, and the idea started there. At first, she was the only worker, but by the time my mother came along she had several workers on the books. It's still a thriving agency. She renovated properties too, long before those TV programmes made it popular."

"She must have been very driven," he said. An understatement if ever there was one. Then he was off, attracted by the landscape.

"That's not a natural slope, is it? Absolutely fascinating."

Before I could say anything, he'd scrambled up on top of the fence to get a better view.

"Yes," he said. "If only I could get a bit higher."

"There's a pretty good view from up the hill, there," I pointed. "With binoculars. Grandma thought this whole area was full of Roman stuff. Perhaps a farm, and there's definitely evidence of a road. Straight across it goes, parallel with the South Downs Way."

He clambered down, grinning. "She was probably right too. This whole area was over-run with Romans. It wasn't only the famous sites we know about like Fishbourne. There were lots of Romano-British settlements – from individual farms and villas to towns and fortifications."

We tramped companionably a little more along the side of the earthworks and then turned to look down the slope towards the farm.

"It wouldn't be at all surprising if there's been a farm on this land back through the centuries, all the way back to the Romans and before," he said.

At the top of the hill we took a path to the east, walking towards the river. A couple of times the Professor stopped and looked at the landscape.

"This certainly has the feel of a Roman road'" he said. "Is all this on the farm?"

"Yes," I said. "When I was a child, this whole area used to be full of sheep. I wonder what happened to them all."

"What happened to the farmer?"

"I don't know exactly. It seems that while I was… away… after Grandma died, something went wrong. He committed suicide."

"It's really not healthy to be close to you and your family, is it?" he said.

I flushed with anger, bit back a retort.

"That was a stupid thing to say," he said. "I'm sorry, it came out all wrong. Let me tell you about the coin. I heard from Sam today."

"Do tell."

"Sam is certain it's authentic. Not many have been found in Britain, but one was recently discovered at Vindolanda, the fort on Hadrian's Wall."

"I read about that," I said. "I thought at the time it sounded similar to mine."

"Yours, Sam tells me, is in very much better condition. It's such a pity we don't know the context, because that condition means it was probably lost much earlier than the Vindolanda coin, which had been in circulation for maybe three hundred years when it was lost. Your grandmother didn't have any provenance for her collection, did she? I mean, she must have some paperwork somewhere, documents of where she bought the various replicas, and valuations for the insurance company. That kind of thing."

"I don't know. I'm not sure there is any insurance. Anything like that – maybe the solicitor has it? I can ask him. I can't check out the house though. I'm not allowed."

"It would be an interesting line of enquiry. They really should be insured."

"I would much rather sort them out so that they can be donated to a museum."

"Not a bad idea," he said, looking at me thoughtfully. "But not yet. I know you have a lot of other stuff on your mind."

"I am looking forward to starting the course."

"I feel an idea coming on," he said. "I'm thinking this might be a great location for our first field trip. A literal field trip. I'd need to do some preparatory work, to see if it's suitable – just me and a couple of grad students. We could come over here and do a proper survey. Walk the field, maybe even use a metal detector, or some other high-tech archaeological toys."

"Heresy!" I said, laughing.

"Technology isn't the problem, it's technology coupled with ignorance and greed that's the problem."

"We've all used a computer to make bigger mistakes faster and more efficiently."

He grinned. "Perhaps we've walked over the Cuckmere Hoard on our way up here today."

"Wouldn't that be something?"

"Who can resist buried treasure? Even if we do really know the real treasure is to be found in what we can find out about the past."

"Grandma used to read to me at night. My favourite Roald Dahl book was always the one about the Mildenhall Treasure. I used to dream that one day I might find something equally stunning – something that would change what we knew about our history."

"We've all been there," he said. "Me, when I was on my very first dig as a volunteer digging up a Roman farm in Peterborough, alongside Ermine Street, the Roman road from London to York. I became an expert on the construction of Roman post holes. One of the most boring, painstaking kind of archaeological grunt work. Meanwhile, a couple of fields away, a farmer ploughed up a buried cache of early Christian silver. I was so envious."

"I hope this doesn't prove too much of a disappointment," I said.

"Oh, I'm not disappointed. Far from it. Looking at your earthworks, there might be the potential for something very interesting. And maybe, for once, I might have found a sympathetic land owner."

I laughed. I didn't think of myself as a land owner; that sounded so strange.

"How Grandma would have loved this," I said.

TWENTY-FOUR

I WAVED GOODBYE to the Professor. Watching his battered old Volvo estate disappear into the distance, I started to feel strangely optimistic, given what was going on in my life. He had behaved as if I was a perfectly normal person, not a flake who was suspected of murder. He was charming and fun to be with, and I didn't want that to end. He made me feel like I was too. A useful contrast to my own mother, who obviously thought it was entirely possible that I'd murdered Harry in cold blood, and then wiped it from my memory, in the same way I'd forgotten setting the bonfire.

I hadn't asked him about the skyphos. I was beginning to genuinely trust him – and not because I now had an email record making it clear he'd taken it from the house.

It had been a long day. After an early start, signing in at the police station and a succession of visitors. I'd missed lunch, so I ate a protein bar and pottered around the kitchen planning dinner.

I still couldn't relax. I had to take some kind of action. I lit a candle and meditated for a few minutes, opening up to my intuition, then I rang up the police station and asked to speak to DI Collingwood.

He answered the phone, sounding wary.

"Sorry," I said. "Is it a breach of protocol to phone up the police officer who arrested you for murder, to ask how the investigation is going?"

"You didn't check with your lawyer, did you? I advise you to talk to her. Remember that warning I gave you?" He rattled it off again.

I felt guilty – it hadn't even occurred to me to talk to Suhad first. Perhaps because I knew she'd try to stop me. In spite of everything that had happened, I had more faith in Collingwood than was sensible. I was beginning to make a habit of trusting people.

"Stop," I begged. "Just one thing. I know you questioned my mother. I want to know, did she know that Harry Rook was her father?"

He snorted into the phone. If I ever wanted to be a comedian, apparently I had the skills.

"Don't your family ever talk to each other?" he asked, when he was capable of speech. "In what world does it make sense that you haven't discussed this?"

"In my world," I said. "Or rather in the world of my family. I wish you'd met my Grandma. Perhaps then you'd understand a little."

"You were close to her, I know," he said, sounding oddly sympathetic. Must be a quirk of the telephone line, when I couldn't see the slight sneer or quizzical expression which coloured nearly every conversation. "I remember that night..."

Oh. That night. He did remember driving me to Brookfields then. The night, a week after Grandma died, when I was sectioned.

I was spending too much time dwelling on that missing night again. I thought once I was out of hospital I could forget about it forever – put the memory, and the lack of memory, away. It had obviously influenced what DI Collingwood was thinking when he arrested me.

"Yes," I said. "That night. I was hysterical, and angry, and I kicked you. I remember that. I am sorry. I was sorry pretty much straight away. But remember, you didn't see me in the three years I was at home, nursing Grandma through her illness. You weren't there the night she died – when my mother was sitting with her, and I was away at a friend's wedding, the first time I'd left her in months. You weren't there when the will was read and my mother went batshit crazy when she found out she was getting an allowance, and that I was the major beneficiary. You didn't hear what she said when she discovered Grandma had left Harry Rook and Mr Harvey in charge of the trust."

"I'm sorry," he said. "I didn't mean to upset you. You must talk to your lawyer."

And he hung up on me.

My only chance of finding out whether my mother had known about Harry blown in one slightly hysterical phone call. Perhaps I should have talked to Suhad. I called her at the office, but she was in a meeting with another client.

I was back to looking out for myself, I reckoned. I was the only person for whom that should be, or could be, a full-time job.

It was only five o'clock, so I went back out to the barn.

Everything was where I'd left it. The axe hanging up, the greasy rag on the floor next to the bucket. The logs I'd chopped but couldn't carry in a loose pile in front of the rest. I made a show of piling them up, in case someone, Daniel, was watching. But even though every nerve in my body was on high alert, I had absolutely none of that sense you get when there's someone else around.

I explored the barn. The stacked logs, with a locked cupboard alongside – I guessed it was some kind of tool store, but I couldn't immediately see where the key might be. A couple of big old brooms. A sack of chicken feed, but as far as I knew no chickens. Bales of hay, stacked high. Everything looked neat and tidy and as it should be, but I had a nagging feeling I'd missed something.

I started to move the hay bales. They were heavy and awkward, but manageable. There it was. Behind a row of bales, a comfortable nest. A den. A way through round the back that only needed one bale to be moved – not the half dozen I'd dragged aside.

There was a bright orange rucksack, stuffed full. A couple of overflowing boxes. One of the boxes held a Calor Gas stove and camping gear, and cans of spam and beans. The other was stuffed with clothes, a couple of sketchbooks, some artists' postcards, a tin of art pens and a box of chalks. The moment I saw them, my heart stood still, and I knew what I would find if I looked inside.

I was right. Pen and ink drawings. The latest of the kitten. Earlier ones of the Beacon, the beach and the lighthouse. Some pages had been torn out. I carefully put it back in place, and stepped over the rolled up sleeping bag, several blankets and a couple of pillows. There was even a saucer with some cat food in.

Trying to control my rising panic, I started to replace the bales of hay so that Daniel wouldn't know I'd found his hidey hole.

Daniel. My stalker.

I didn't know whether to laugh or cry. He was only a kid, for heaven's sake. I'd been terrified of a grieving kid.

If things got worse, I could add more space alongside and move into the barn myself. For a moment I almost considered it as a serious option. I grabbed the nearest broom and swept the floor area around the hay, sweeping all the dust and broken bits of straw into a dark corner and under the bales of straw.

Everything looked undisturbed, as if I hadn't even been there. I didn't want to frighten him off – he obviously needed help. If anyone could imagine how the death of his father had affected him, it was me. If I couldn't show some compassion, then who would show me any?

But what if he'd killed the rabbit and the cat, staked Harry's hand to the ground, and killed him? Maybe I should be scared. What kind of person does that? Perhaps I could talk to Collingwood?

No, I couldn't believe the kid was a killer.

I chopped a bit more wood, so that it would look like I had a reason to be there. I found a small basket and filled it with kindling, and carried it across from the barn to the house.

The microwave clock said five to six, I was only just in time.

There was no sign of Daniel, but still I locked myself in and settled down for the night. I also inspected the cat-flap, and discovered it was lockable. I was pretty sure the kitten was outside, and I meant to keep it that way.

I made a coffee and switched the laptop on and searched for the website of the local paper.

That was probably a mistake.

There was a photograph of me from my schooldays. I suppose it was lucky they hadn't found anything more recent but given the reaction to me in the Cuckmere outdoors shop, I was all too recognisable. The story opened with how I'd found Harry on the beach, and after dwelling on my subsequent arrest had mentioned the fact that I'd been sectioned and had spent some time in a locked psychiatric ward.

There was a paragraph which implied I was more than a nutter, I was the local Satanist. There were references to the fact that I'd grown up in The Witch House, and to my Grandma's interest in magic and her reputation as the head of the local coven.

"A source close to the suspect" had kindly provided a timeline of the incidents of vandalism and pointed out that it had all stopped while I'd been in hospital and started up again soon after my discharge.

None of it was untrue. It was the inference which was wrong – and impossible to prove wrong without finding out who the vandal actually was.

I didn't look at the comments.

I was the ideal hate figure. I had grown up in a beautiful home, with a rich grandmother. I had inherited her business. On top of that, it turned out I was a dangerous psychotic nut case and probably a Satanist too.

There was an up-to-date photograph of my mother too – she had clearly talked to them. "My daughter is very fragile, please leave her alone," she was quoted as saying. "Let the police do their job." Thanks, Mom. Way to make me sound guilty. Already rehearsing her role as mother of the killer.

Imagine what they'd make of my chopping firewood with an axe. The mad axe woman of Cuckmere. Once they discovered Harry was my grandfather, I'd be Cuckmere's answer to Lizzie Borden.

My email pinged, distracting me from my catastrophising, with a lovely message from Professor Buckley saying how much he'd enjoyed the exploration, and confirming the details for the site survey. There would be forms I had to sign, but other than that, I only had to show up. And finally, what did I think about doing an aerial survey as well?

I emailed back.

"Not a chance. I have extreme acrophobia. I'll watch though, and you can take photographs and video, right?"

He replied pretty much straight away, laughing at me and promising that he and his pal would take plenty of pictures, but he thought I might prove braver than I expected.

I was very touched by his playfulness, sure he was mostly being kind because he felt sorry for me. He'd been there when I was arrested. By now he'd probably read about me in the paper, or seen the local news reports. Still, he was treating me like a normal person. Or maybe like a person who could grant him access to an interesting Roman site, a cynical voice in my head whispered. It was all a little too good to be true.

TWENTY-FIVE

I MISSED THE freedom of being at home. I had no TV and limited music, although I could use the laptop. I'd settled on the sofa with my feet up, reading the course textbook, and when I looked up at the clock, it was past eight. It was too far to pop down to the Indian, even if it hadn't been past my curfew. I could have phoned and asked them to deliver, but I was trying to keep my location reasonably private. After being recognised in town I felt very vulnerable.

Grumbling quietly to myself, I made beans on toast. There was no wine left – I'd have to order some to be delivered – it was a long way to carry bottles to the farm. Still, it meant I might as well take my meds. I was planning on tapering them off, after all, not going cold turkey.

I couldn't stop wondering what to do about Daniel. I'd made his life more difficult by moving in here. On the other hand, he had been trying to get my attention with the poems and sketches and the flowers – and now he had it.

The police had collected my stalker folder when they searched Grandma's house and had also taken one of my sketchbooks. To compare the drawings, I supposed. I wondered what kind of iron control a person would have to have, to make lousy drawings in her own sketchbooks, and to forge consistently better stalker sketches.

I half-wished I was that kind of person.

If only I still had the folder maybe there'd be a clue to understanding Daniel. Dr Lal, my psychiatrist at the hospital – the good one, not the crazy drunk who treated us like experimental subjects in a large Skinner box – he'd told me that delusions often have a certain internal consistency, rather like a poem or an abstract piece of art. He believed if he could uncover the hidden meaning, then he would be able to help the person understand the delusion and cross the bridge back to reality. It was a fascinating conversation even if he was convinced I was on the wrong side of that bridge, and was trying to understand me through a cobbled together tale of witchcraft and Satanism which was actually more to do with my mother's venal imagination than with reality. In the end I had co-operated with his treatment plan, or else I'd still be in there. I'd even admitted to an interest in Grandma's High Magic, although I'd had the sense not to confess to the vandalism.

I wondered now, though. Perhaps something in me was seriously broken. Perhaps my brain's wiring had shorted, and I'd killed Harry and then somehow erased all memory of it. Perhaps I was my own stalker, and I'd conjured Daniel into existence with my imagination.

I was dozing on the sofa in front of my fire, again, when I was startled awake by a noise. Metal scratching on metal. Definitely not a kitten – not since I blocked up the cat-flap. The thought of having a kitten startling me into a state of high alert constantly had overcome my scruples as soon as I was sure Daniel was feeding her.

Slowly and silently, I padded in my stockinged feet into the kitchen. Someone was fiddling with the lock. I panicked. Daniel had probably still got a key. I picked up the heavy skillet from the cooker top.

I heard the lock click and saw the door handle move down. Quick as I could I pushed it down and pulled the door wide open, holding the skillet above my head, expecting to see Daniel.

"Kelly! What are you doing here?"

"Put that fucking pan down and let me in," she pleaded.

"Why didn't you knock?"

"I did, several times! But Mrs B told me you were lying low and probably didn't want visitors."

I must have actually fallen asleep then.

I let her in and then locked the door behind her.

She dropped two plastic carrier bags stuffed to bursting point on the floor in the corner. Then she flitted round the kitchen, the living room and dining room, touching everything with apparent delight. Even the 'vintage' red plastic sofa.

"Brilliant! I love it."

"What are you doing here?" I asked.

She looked around the room again. "TV?" she said. "Laptop?"

I showed her my set up on the table, strewn with textbooks. "Look," I said. "I'm powering it down now. Hardly anyone knows that I'm here, so no one will know you're here, other than me and Mrs B."

"Okay. It's probably safe. I did a runner, Alice. When the cops turned up asking questions, I knew you needed me."

After her last bid for escape, Kelly had never forgiven her sister who had, as she put it, grassed her up. I didn't want to lose our friendship. I would have to contrive some way to persuade her to go back voluntarily.

"Do you want something to eat? I can do you beans on toast." Food would buy me time to think.

"I could eat a scabby horse. Why didn't you tell me?"

"Why didn't I tell you what?" I asked, as I opened a can of beans and put them in the saucepan on a low heat.

"That you'd found a body. That you'd been arrested for murder. You could have told me, you know. I know you're not a murderer."

I put the bread under the grill, holding back the tears. Kelly believed in me.

"I wasn't arrested until a couple of days ago, Kels. Until then, it didn't seem that important."

"Someone was murdered and you didn't think it was important? You're supposed to be the fucking sane one. Don't worry, I didn't say a word to the cops."

Oh dear. If she'd clammed up, they'd be sure there was something to hide.

I put her beans on toast on the kitchen table and gently encouraged her to sit and eat. I sat opposite, my elbows on the table and my head in my hands.

"I didn't want to upset you," I said. "I'm sorry, I know it was stupid. I really wasn't expecting to be arrested."

"We're mates," she said. "I spilled my guts about my own fucked up life and you didn't trust me with yours. That wasn't right."

"No, it wasn't," I said. "It was stupid, and thoughtless. And I really do need someone to talk to."

"I'm waiting," she said.

I piled the empty dishes up and we took our coffees through to the living room. She was delighted by the open fire and asked, like an eager child, to be allowed to add some logs.

It was a relief to be able to tell someone the whole story. Unvarnished.

"So he was your grandad, and you never knew? Wow," she said.

For something to amaze Kelly in paranoid mode, it had to be really quite a long way out of the ordinary.

She understood what had been going through my mind. Her thinking was clear, so long as nothing crossed over into her paranoid fantasy world.

"Did your mum know that Harry was her dad?"

"I don't think so," I said. "But no one will tell me, and I'm uneasy about asking her directly. I gave her a chance, but she didn't take it."

"Ah," Kelly nodded, with a knowing look. "She didn't pass The Test. Like my sister."

Sometimes it was hard for me to know where the line was in Kelly's world too. It was all too easy for me to assume that the stuff about her sister was paranoia. But the fact that she was paranoid about the CIA tracking her through the Wi-Fi didn't mean her fears about her sister were unfounded.

"I started to doubt myself too," I told her. "You know, maybe I had some kind of blackout, maybe I don't remember."

Kelly said, "I know you're not a killer. When Janey went full psycho and lashed out at you, you stood there and took it."

"She didn't know what she was doing," I said.

"Sticking up for a pal, though, you'd be full on. No messing."

She grinned at me, and we both remembered. One of the new members of our art therapy group, Johnny, had filed the end of his paintbrush into a sharp point. He had started by ripping apart Kelly's canvas and flinging it to the floor. Then he had started slashing at her face. Her cheek was cut open, and the blood dripped onto her spoiled canvas.

Everyone else was standing back. Johnny moved forward, towards Kelly, and I launched myself at him. I put my arms around his neck, and wrapped my legs around his waist, like a demented piggy-backer. I stayed there. I hung on, ignoring his attempts to shake me off, and his cursing and threats of more violence. I had no choice really – if I had let go, I knew he would turn that improvised weapon on me.

It probably wasn't as long as it felt like, before the tutor returned with three orderlies. They separated us, two of them marched him off, one took me back to my room, and I was sedated. For my own good.

The following day I had an unpleasant interview with Dr Mansfield. The Skinner box man – everything for him was a matter of classical conditioning. He patiently explained to me that my actions had been faulty and as a result I would lose perks like Art Therapy for a week.

"What did I do wrong?" I asked. "He was attacking Kelly. She was bleeding, he stabbed her!"

"You should have waited for the orderlies to arrive," he said. "It's not a free for all. We can't have patients disciplining each other."

"I wasn't disciplining him. I was stopping him from doing more damage."

I lost another two weeks Art Therapy then, for refusing to abide by the behavioural code.

Kelly brought me back to the present. "Unless your grandad was going for someone with a shiv, there's no way you'd have done him in. So who the fuck did?"

"I can't think why anyone would want to hurt him," I said. "It doesn't make any sense."

"Family are the most likely," she said. "I've watched Law and Order you know."

"That's me then. His granddaughter – though I didn't know it."

"We ruled you out already," she said, mock-glaring at me. "Your mam then. His daughter."

"She wasn't even in Cuckmere at the time. She phoned me from Victoria Station."

"I'd better write this down." She grabbed my notebook from the table. "Romans in Sussex?" she asked.

"I've registered for the course. With Professor Matt Buckley."

"Yum," she said. "He's gorgeous. Can I register too?"

"Possibly not," I said. "As you're on the lam. Anyway, Art College is the plan. Remember?"

"Back to it. Any other kids?"

"Impossible to know for sure, in the circumstances. It's supposed to have been the tragedy of their married life, Harry and Julia. They both wanted children, but..."

"The widow. If she'd just found out?"

"Julia must have always known. It explains her feud with Grandma. I don't see an easy way to ask. It's a condition of my bail that I stay away from her."

"Other family members?"

"Too many to mention. His niece Tamsin used to work at the seafront cafe with him all the year round. Her brothers worked the amusement arcade and the rides in the summer and at weekends. They're both away at Uni now."

"This Tamsin, was she there on the day?"

"Yes, I had a coffee and a muffin in the cafe with her. She can't have done it – she was far too calm. And she was my friend. I thought."

"Was?"

"Until I was arrested for murdering her uncle."

"Your cousin, too, then."

I hadn't had time to properly think that one through. There was so much uncharted territory here. No wonder I felt completely cast adrift.

"The only other thing is the marina development. Mark Stockman has been trying to buy Grandma's house and Harry and Julia's. The company bought the cafe, the whole amusement park – within days of Harry's murder. He didn't want to sell, and Tamsin didn't, but Julia did."

"The same guy who wanted to buy your house when you were in hospital?"

"Do you remember that?" I said. "I'd forgotten, really."

"You were a bit out of it. Your mum nagged and nagged until you signed anything she put in front of you."

"She was doing it to make my life easier, that's all. She thought the responsibility of it all was too much for me."

"Yeah, right," Kelly said. "That wasn't what that guy said who came to see you, once he realised you had no idea."

"That was Harry," I said. "My grandfather."

"Oh. You didn't say," Kelly started. Then, "Course you didn't. You didn't fucking know. Wowee. Your Grandma must have been some lady, to keep all this quiet for so long. And living across the road too."

"It must have been deliberate. My mother was about five when they moved in."

Kelly laughed. "She must have been very deeply hurt, and she made sure he was too. Good on her."

"I hadn't thought of it as revenge," I said. "More a kind of advanced stalking. Or perhaps they were still involved, having an affair. I wish she was still alive, then I could ask."

Kelly put the pen and notebook down. "No wiser, are we? I understand now why the cops picked on you."

"Thanks!"

"Not that way," she said. "Only you were at the scene, you found the body, and then there's the weird history."

"I know," I said. "But I didn't do it, and I haven't even told you about my stalker yet." I told her it all, from the first postcard, to finding the den in the barn.

"A suspect, then," she said. "Why aren't you out of your head terrified? Why haven't you dobbed him in to the cops?"

"I know him, or I did. He's a kid." I said. "I know he's grieving. I don't happen to think locking someone up is the right thing, even if they have gone off their head with grief. I'd like to talk to him first, really, and see if I can help him."

"I'll tackle him then," Kelly said.

"Maybe tomorrow," I said. "But we must be careful not to scare him away. I don't want him to suspect I know where he's hiding."

After a heated discussion we agreed that Kelly would sleep upstairs in the bedroom, and I would stay on the sofa downstairs.

"You sleep in your bed, I'll take the sofa," she said.

"It's been my bed for exactly two nights," I pointed out. "And one of those nights I spent mostly on the sofa anyway. I have to sign in at the police station at eight thirty, so—"

"Too early for me," she said looking at her watch. "Considering it's nearly three now. And I don't lose points if I sleep in tomorrow."

"Don't count on it," I said.

TWENTY-SIX

ALTHOUGH I TIPTOED around the following morning, when I put the kettle on Kelly rushed downstairs wide awake and full of plans. Perhaps she *was* still a bit manic.

"I'll tag along, if you're sweet with that. I wanna get to know this place if I'm moving here. After you've done your thing at the cop shop, you can show me your gran's house and where you found the rabbit and everything."

"I suppose I can point it out from a distance," I said, reminding her about my electronic tag.

"Damn. I forgot. Sorry."

We caught the bus, and she chattered the brief journey away, happy to be free. I still hadn't thought of a way of suggesting she should go back.

I left her looking in the shop windows and promised I'd be back in a few minutes. Signing in with the desk sergeant took no longer than usual, but then he asked me to wait. Apparently, DI Collingwood wanted to see me.

I was shown into the same interview room as before, and waited patiently, wondering what would happen to Kelly if I was about to be rearrested. I supposed I could explain to Suhad, but that would risk her rushing Kelly straight back into hospital. It was selfish of me, wanting her around – it was so good to have someone on my side.

After fifteen minutes or so DI Collingwood walked in, looking rather the worse for wear. He had dark shadows under his eyes.

"You look tired," I said. "I hope you're not losing sleep over me."

He didn't rise to the bait, so I carried on.

"Shouldn't I call my lawyer before we talk?" I asked sweetly.

"Very funny," he said.

He passed me a phone, and I looked at it. Mine.

"I thought you might find it useful to have this back," he said.

"Thanks. Anything on the cat?"

"Not a thing. Nor has a ginger cat been reported missing. But an analysis of the photograph shows that the stake matched the earlier one."

"Does that help to clear me?" I said, feeling a rush of hope.

"I'm afraid not." For a moment the human being trumped the policeman. "Professor Buckley was certain you hadn't had time to kill a cat and dispose of it, but in any case, you might still have killed the rabbit on the Beacon, or indeed, impaled Mr Rook."

"You didn't think it was me on the day," I said. "You saw how upset I was. Trust your instincts."

At that he snorted and looked me in the eye. "Be careful what you ask for, Alice," he said. This time I looked away first, blushing.

"That's not how police investigations work," he said, kindly. "If you had killed him, you would be upset. You touched all the stakes. Every single one."

"You found the third one then?"

"Yes. They all had your fingerprints. The Professor was very passionate in your defence. You've made a conquest there."

I blushed again, and he laughed.

"He's old enough to be your father. He isn't your father, is he?"

"No, he is not. Weren't there any other fingerprints on them?"

"Not even a partial," he said. "People are not always what they seem — that's the first lesson we learn on this job. One may smile and smile and be a villain."

"You want to believe me though. I can tell," I said, ignoring his flight of Shakespearean fancy.

He half smiled at me, then shrugged off his inner human, and became all brisk policeman again.

"Right. Now you're all tagged, I thought it might be easier if we changed the conditions of your bail. Unless circumstances change, you can sign in once a week from now on. On Friday mornings."

"It's Friday today," I said. "So not until next Friday, then?"

"Correct. Don't go getting your hopes up that it means anything. It's standard procedure."

I turned to go.

"Aren't you going to say thank you?" he asked.

"What for?" I asked.

"Your phone," he reminded me.

"Oh, that. Thank you for returning my property, which you kept because you suspect me of brutally torturing small animals and of murdering my own grandfather. Because I'm a nutter. Thank you for that."

For a fleeting moment, he looked hurt.

I let the door swing shut behind me. I walked out of the police station with my head held high, and a feeling of quite childish satisfaction, as if I'd come off best for once. That quickly faded. Why did I so easily get thrown off balance emotionally? Why did I lash out at the person who could help me? I normally have more self-control.

I was expecting to have a real search on my hands looking for Kelly after my promised ten minutes had turned into an hour, but she was pacing up and down and looking frantic. I waved, and she saw me and ran towards me.

"What took so long? You didn't tell them about me, did you?'"

She was talking nineteen to the dozen. I put my hand on her arm and steadied her.

"Breathe," I said. "Breathe and relax."

She shook me off, "Don't you start on that crap." But with a visible effort she dragged herself back from the brink. "Sorry. I went off the deep end there."

"Don't be sorry," I said. "I know what it's like. I keep trying to reason myself out of paranoia, but when you've actually been arrested for murder it turns out paranoia feels perfectly rational."

"So what gives?"

"Nothing major. DI Collingwood wanted to see me so I had to wait. He gave me back my phone, and said from now on I only have to sign in once a week, instead of every day."

"Brill," she said. "You're not a suspect anymore."

I said nothing.

"Tell me why you look like a wet weekend?"

"I'm still the chief suspect. It means the tag is working, I guess. Maybe they're not so worried I'm cracking up any more. I think signing in every day was the equivalent of me being on suicide watch."

She paused, thinking. I could see the cogs move. "You know what you were saying about being paranoid? This is the far side of that line."

I started to laugh, and then found I couldn't stop. Everyone was looking at us, which brought me back to my senses. Anyone who saw me laughing could interpret it as glee that I'd gotten away with murder.

"What the fuck was all that about?" Kelly demanded.

"I was thinking, if there was a list of all the people in the world who are equipped to have a rational discussion about paranoia, we wouldn't be on it. Not even at the bottom."

"Who'd make a list like that?" she asked. "Other than Dr Mansfield."

At that, I started laughing again.

"Come on," she said. "Show me your house, and the scene of the crime. I always wanted to be a private eye."

We walked past the shops and along the path next to the river, which always had that peaceful feeling associated with going home. Now I felt a sense of dread. I didn't feel watched though. Perhaps only because I knew Daniel was likely at the farm.

"I can't go any further," I said. "But there it is," I pointed it out to her, as I stopped at the bend in the road, and the house came into view.

"Oh, it is pretty," she said. "You didn't tell me you were loaded."

I could tell she was hurt that I'd kept things from her, but I didn't know what to say.

"Dumb luck," I said. "My grandmother started a business. She had a talent for it."

"No wonder your mum was pissed about the will," Kelly said.

"On the other side of the road, that big old house with the gables and the little turret, that's where the Rooks live. And you see at the end there, the little wooden hut—," my voice faltered a bit. "That was Harry's hut. Where he worked, day in and day out. Taking money for parking and fishing licences. Chatting to the customers."

Kelly paused, to take in the view.

"You can walk past the house, if you like, and I'll go the long way round."

"Sorry," she said. "I'm a nosy bitch. I'd rather walk with you."

"It's okay Kels," I said. "The choice is yours, I don't mind."

I meant it too, but still she chose to walk with me.

As we walked up the Beacon and past the coastguard station, an old Land Rover pulled up and a man in coastguard uniform got out. He looked at us and nodded when Kelly gave him a cheerful hello but continued on his way.

"He could be a witness," she said. "Maybe he's seen someone watching your house."

She was about to chase after him, but I put my hand on her arm and stopped her. "Remember, I promised the cops not to say anything about the rabbit and the stakes."

"Do you really need to keep that promise? What are they doing for you?"

"I have to keep the promise for my own sake. I told you, because I know you're not involved. You don't know anyone else in Cuckmere, and you were safely locked up in Brookfields when it all happened. Anyone who knows about the stakes and the rabbit – they had to be involved, right? Except for me, and the police. And the police aren't even sure about me."

"Maybe we could ask generally? If they've seen anything unusual up here?" she suggested, but when I shook my head, she reluctantly agreed to leave it for the time being.

We kept walking up the winding tarmac path through the nature reserve. It was steep, and hard on the knees, and Kelly squawked a little at that. We stopped and rested on one of the next benches.

"You can see the back of the house from here," I said. "See that patch there – right in the middle of the lawn. That's where I found the cat."

"Basically someone, anyone could sit up here and enjoy the show," she said.

She was right.

Grandma's house had a great view over the Rook House, and in its turn was overlooked from pretty much all this side of the hill.

"There'll be a pretty good view from those flats the far side," she said. "Especially those high balconies."

"That's part of Stockman's marina development," I said. "You can see why he'd be interested in buying the Rook House, and Grandma's."

A few people passed us walking dogs, but not many. Although the herring gulls were still producing copious amounts of pink guano, the blackberry season was almost over, and there were few sloes to be had, so the Beacon was pretty much deserted now. It was entirely possible that someone could have spent a lot of time here watching me, or watching the house, and I would never know.

I led the way down the winding rabbit path to the seafront, and Kelly followed me. We walked as far as the cafe, now all shuttered up and obviously closed.

"I'm not going any further," I said. "I don't want to risk getting too close to the exclusion zone." I shivered, looking past Harry's hut, to the spot where I'd found him.

Kelly said, "Harry wasn't like any boss I've ever known. Actually working. Who would know he was the owner?"

"I think all us locals knew," I said. "But visitors often had no idea. He enjoyed talking to people. He was that kind of man."

In the distance, beyond the kiosk, I could see someone coming out of the Rook house. To my relief, whoever it was started walking in the other direction. It was enough to make me hurry Kelly along, though. I would feel more comfortable once we were out of sight.

We peered into the cafe through the shutters and cursed that we couldn't have cake and a coffee. I realised I still hadn't done anything about trying to contact Tamsin, and now I had no excuse – I had my phone back. It needed charging though. Shit! The charger was in Grandma's house. Perhaps I'd be able to buy another in town.

I looked at Kelly's shoes – she was wearing trainers. They would do, for the walk over the hill and the cliff back to town, and I really would prefer not to have to walk back the way we came.

We walked back up the steep hill, and I pointed out the place where I found the rabbit but didn't venture off the main path. When we reached the top, we turned and looked back down on the way we had come, catching our breath and enjoying the view out across the bay to the distant white cliffs.

We walked the rest of the way into town over the grassy cliff top paths until we reached the promenade. On impulse, Kelly persuaded me to have lunch in a cafe, her treat. I was reluctant, but as she said, I couldn't hide away forever. Swings and roundabouts. With her company, I couldn't run away if it all got too much for me. With her company, it was much less likely to be too much for me.

As we sat in a window seat, sipping lattes and waiting for our jacket potatoes with cream cheese and ham, we watched the world go by, which was relaxing until I was reminded that the world included my mother. She walked past the window with Mark Stockman at her side. They looked like the best of friends, chatting away merrily. Like a character in a bad spy film, I picked up the menu and hid behind it, hoping that if she looked in the window, she wouldn't see me.

"You hungry or something?" Kelly asked.

"Thinking about pudding," I said. "Chocolate brownie, maybe."

Our food arrived then, so she didn't tackle me on my lie for a minute or two. When I confessed who I'd seen walk past, she was cross. "We should have followed them," she said.

"No point. I know what's going on. She's stringing him along into thinking she's his best chance to buy the property. She thinks that if I end up in prison, now Harry's dead, that she can gain control of the trust, and look after my affairs."

"Why would she think that?" Kelly asked.

"I suppose that's my fault really," I said. "I didn't tell her it was impossible, and that Grandma had specifically ruled her out in the articles of the Personal Management Company."

Kelly thought for a moment or two. "Are you daft? You should have told her there was no chance."

"I thought it was kinder. I didn't want to hurt her feelings."

"Does she worry about hurting yours?"

Good question.

"If you're suggesting my mother would do anything to get her hands on the money, then that is paranoid. She would certainly take advantage, if it came to it and I was sent to prison. But she wouldn't do anything to cause that. That's crazy talk."

Kelly grinned at the resurrection of one of our feeble jokes but pressed on. "Is it really crazy, mate? I mean, when you were in hospital, she tried then."

"That's just mother," I said. "She was probably short of money and didn't think it through, that's all."

"I still think you should find out what she's up to." Kelly was stubborn.

"I agree. But talking to my mother never helps. More useful to make an appointment with Mark Stockman and quiz him."

"Will he see you?"

"I reckon he'll leap at the chance. If I tell him I'm considering selling the house."

"Sneaky," she said. "But you aren't really going to sell, are you?"

"I don't know. I wasn't, but I really don't know any more. I don't even know if I can, without Julia's consent."

As we drank another coffee, I said, "I'd like to call in and see Mr Harvey, my lawyer. You could come with me, or stay here, or do some more window shopping."

"Better not. They might know I'm on the run... I'm probably giving off vibes, or something."

I understood. I was a bit worried too.

"I'll go walkabout. Explore a bit. Back here in an hour?"

I tried to hand her my phone, and some cash, asking if she could find a replacement charger.

"Ew, do I have to?" she asked, automatically pulling away from me. I'd forgotten how paranoid she was about mobiles.

"Sorry. Look, I'll take the sim card out, how about that?"

With some difficulty I juggled the phone in one hand and clicked the back off, and carefully put the sim card into my purse. This time she took the phone, although still a bit reluctantly.

I pointed her in the direction of Tweedies, at the other end of the High Street to Mr Harvey's offices, feeling relieved I'd found a way to avoid braving the store. When I looked back, Kelly was already out of sight.

TWENTY-SEVEN

"I KNOW WE said hold off on the private detective," I said. "But I've changed my mind."

Mr Harvey and Suhad looked at each other, and he said, "I'll tell her."

My heart sank.

"We thought the same. With that in mind I approached Mrs Rook, and made the suggestion that the Trust should indeed hire a detective agency. Mrs Rook was not at all in favour, and in fact, she declined to approve the expenditure."

That didn't sound so terrible.

"How expensive can it be?" I asked. "Surely I could pay a retainer from my allowance?"

"I'm afraid it's not as simple as that. Mrs Rook has effectively suspended your allowance. For now, you only have access to whatever is in your current account."

I didn't know how much that was, but I knew it wasn't much.

"Can she do that?" I asked.

"Not indefinitely. But she can use the law to cause us a considerable amount of trouble in the meantime."

"And you weren't going to tell me?"

"We thought it best not to worry you," he said. "I was hoping we would be able to sort it out before you even realised there was a problem."

I lost my temper. I didn't trust myself to speak, so I slammed out of the office without a word and walked down to the seafront. I crossed the main road and the Promenade, and stood on the beach, watching the waves beating hopelessly against the pebbles until I calmed down. Then I turned and walked back up to the lawyer's office.

Mr Harvey and Suhad were drinking coffee, and the receptionist brought me one too.

"I do wish you would all stop protecting me. It really isn't helping, keeping me in the dark."

Suhad spoke up. "For what it's worth, Mr Harvey, I agree with Alice. She isn't a child, and she is your client now. Her grandmother is gone."

There was a tense silence, for a moment or two.

"You're both right," he said.

"There go any plans of absconding to South America. I can keep myself in baked beans for a while, but that's about it. And no investigator."

"Haven't the police taken your passport?" Mr Harvey asked, as if he thought the South America quip was a serious option.

"Not yet. I'm sure it's on DI Collingwood's to-do-list."

We talked a while and eventually I was reassured that the blip in my finances was truly a minor problem, and that they weren't humouring me.

"I'm sorry, Alice," Mr Harvey said. "I am hopeful that once Julia is over the shock of her loss, she will be more reasonable."

"So long as I'm not found guilty," I said. "I can imagine my thirtieth birthday. I'll be in Holloway, and finally allowed access to my funds."

I was joking, but they were fussing around me so much I almost started to believe it was likely.

As I left the office, I smiled to myself a little. I should have a meltdown more often – it was more effective than behaving well. It was way past time that I stood up for myself. Then my fears bubbled up to the surface again. Perhaps now they would start to believe it possible that I snapped and killed Harry in anger. Unless I did. What if there was more than one hole in my memory?

"You raised your voice, Alice. That's not a first step on the path to murder, whatever the timid child inside you thinks. Get a grip."

Now I was talking to myself. Out loud.

Kelly was nowhere in sight, so I wandered back to the seafront, this time paying attention to my surroundings.

On the north side of the coast road a string of old houses, mostly Georgian and Regency at this end of town, but further out Victorian and even a few Edwardian. I crossed again to the long wide promenade and the sea, and this time sat on the nearest bench and looked out at the waves, crashing up onto the pebbled beach. It was cold, but a couple of hardy souls were paddling.

I huddled closer into my fleece hoodie and looked at the sky. Grey clouds hung low over a dark slate sea. It would probably rain later. I worried briefly about Daniel – so far, his nest in the barn was shelter enough but as the year grew cold as well as wet, it wouldn't be so much fun.

I was so lost in contemplation I didn't hear anyone approach, until I heard my name. It was Tamsin.

"I thought it was you," she said, when I looked up and smiled. My face on automatic.

"Hello, Tammy," I said.

"Don't smile," she said. "I haven't changed my mind. I wanted to tell you face to face. I don't want to hear from you again. You were arrested for the murder of my uncle. My father's uncle. We can't be friends and I won't be your cousin. I feel betrayed. I don't suppose you can understand, but that's how I feel. We were never friends if it was all based on lies."

She stalked off, head held high, and I longed to chase after her, to ask her how she thought I'd felt, when I found out that my whole life had been a lie.

So much for me standing up for myself. I continued to sit and stare at the sea.

How was it possible that the people who knew me best could suspect me of murder? I didn't have anything to gain. Tamsin might though. Maybe she was in Harry's will. She'd always wanted to be able to set up her own café.

I couldn't believe that of her, no matter what. She loved Harry, and she was grieving. I knew how that felt. I couldn't stay angry with her for long. I was just hurt.

By the time I'd dragged myself out of the depths, I was late to meet Kelly. I raced back to the cafe, where she had already ordered another latte and was sitting reading a magazine at the window seat.

I joined her and told her the news – there would be no investigator, as Julia had cut off my funds.

"I wish I could do my bit," she said. "I can spring for a fish and chips supper if you want."

"It'll be fine," I said, trying to retrieve the situation. I didn't want to be loading Kelly down with guilt. "She can't stop my basic allowance for long, only until a set of audited accounts have been prepared. Anything else – she can be obstructive on a whim. It's so frustrating. I can't understand why she doesn't want to discover the truth."

"Perhaps there's a good reason," Kelly said.

It was possible, I suppose. It would have been perfectly feasible for Julia to simply walk back to her home. No one would even have noticed her. She was almost as constant a presence at the West Beach as Harry. Tamsin was weird with me that day, too. She could have confronted Harry at his cabin and gone straight back into the cafe.

I still couldn't believe it though. I knew how much they both loved him.

As we finished our coffees, it started to pelt down with rain, so we caught the bus back to the farm. Walking up the lane, I finally asked Kelly the question I'd been avoiding.

"Will they be missing you at the hospital yet?"

She looked guilty.

"Probably. They said I wasn't well enough for a week's leave. There was one way to prove them wrong."

"So you did a runner?"

"I'll go back Sunday. It's been worth it, hasn't it? I've not been acting really crazy, have I?"

"Unless you count playing at Sherlock Holmes, I suppose not. But still, they won't see it that way. Merely doing what you want without their permission is proof you're not well, as far as they're concerned."

"Dr Lal isn't like Mansfield. He'll get it."

"I hope you're right," I said. "Because I have sorted out that flat for you. It's a lovely attic flat – there's a skylight in the bedroom, and room for a studio."

"That's wonderful," she jumped up and down and hugged me. "Why didn't you say earlier? Can we have a look?"

"I told you on the phone, remember? Perhaps another time, as you're not officially out of hospital yet."

"I haven't got a damage deposit or anything," she said. "I'll start job hunting right away. I'll get the cash, just you see."

"We can worry about that once you are properly discharged," I said.

Our mood was considerably brighter by the time we got back to the farm. There was no real reason. Kelly was still on the run, and I was still on police bail, and we were both soaked to the skin.

"Did you find a charger?" I asked.

"I forgot," she said. "Errr, I splurged."

She gave me a small box with a charger, and a weird looking pouch, which contained my phone.

"The man in the techie shop said it was easier than taking the sim out," she explained. "It's made out of a special fabric that has metal woven into it, and it blocks the GPS thingy, so they can't see where you are."

I carefully put the sim back in and put the phone on to charge. "I wonder," I said, 'if it would work on my tag? Best not try it, I don't want to give them an excuse to lock me up."

"You can get them for laptops too," she said, pointedly, as I turned the laptop on. She didn't run away or go upstairs, but she did look highly uncomfortable fidgeting on the sofa.

I had an email from mother, talking about Mark Stockman and what a great offer he was willing to make on the house. I opened a browser window and Googled Stockman's property company and wrote down the phone number.

Back to my emails, and there was one from the Prof, saying he'd managed to borrow the fun toy, as he'd hoped, for Friday, and if that was okay perhaps we could do the site survey then. I emailed back my enthusiastic agreement. A ping a moment later and there was the group email inviting all the course members to an extra-curricular fieldwork assignment and giving directions out here to the farm.

I looked up the home page of the manufacturer of my new phone case, and on impulse ordered the laptop version as well, putting it on my credit card with fingers crossed I'd be able to pay the bill when the time came. If it made Kelly happy, then so be it. Out of curiosity I did a search to see if it would work to block my electronic tag and as I suspected there was one major drawback. It would draw attention to me because it would block the signal. There were articles about spoofing a signal to cover up where I was, but that was so far beyond my capability as to be pointless. While I was online, I decided to buy myself a new rucksack too. That was essential – I'd quickly become tired of lugging my old one by one strap. And I couldn't resist adding a sketchbook and some soft pastels as a surprise for Kelly.

Sensitive to her anxiety about the electronics, I unplugged the laptop and checked my old phone. It was sufficiently charged now to get my messages. Dozens from my mother. A few from the Professor, asking what was going on and telling me about the skyphos. Several from journalists. I deleted them all.

TWENTY-EIGHT

IT WAS STILL within office hours, so I dialled the number of Stockman Properties.

"May I speak to Mark Stockman, please?"

"He's not available right now, so perhaps I could help?" a young-sounding female voice replied.

"Perhaps you could take a message," I said sweetly. "Alice Hunter would like to talk to him about his interest in buying her house, on Beacon Road opposite the Marina development."

"The Hunter house? I'm sure that's not necessary. He's already in negotiation with the owner."

Bingo! I dug a hole, and she fell right in.

"I'm the legal owner of the property," I said. "Whatever my mother may have told Mr Stockman, she does not have the authority to act on my behalf."

Her response was indistinct, but she sounded flustered.

"I suggest you check your records for what happened last time." I hung up.

Kelly said, "Bitchy! Not like you."

"She sounded so sure of herself, but I suppose it's not really her fault. My mother is pretty convincing."

We were both chopping vegetables for a stir-fry, when the phone rang.

"Mark Stockman speaking." He sounded smooth and charming, but I thought I could detect a note of irritation in his voice. "I understand you wanted to talk to me about the Hunter house."

"Yes, indeed," I said. "But if you're serious, we should do this face to face, don't you agree?"

"Certainly I'm serious. I've been trying to buy the damn place for the best part of a year. All I've had is the brush off. Frankly, I'm fed up of being played. My offer is more than fair, and it's been on the table for long enough. Take it or leave it."

He was irritated. I smiled.

"And yet you've never spoken to the person who has the authority to sell."

Not that I did, really, without Julia's say so, until the Trust expired.

"I understood your mother was acting on behalf of the Trust, as with the other properties she had on the market. Okay, then. Let's meet. How about tomorrow morning, nine o'clock sharp, at the house? I have to be over that way anyway. The demolition of the amusement arcade starts tomorrow."

I could have wept. Perhaps I really would want to sell the house, after all. And what did he mean, the other properties mother had on the market?

Damn. The house was still off limits. I shouldn't be arranging to meet Mr Stockman there. I agreed anyway. I could ask Collingwood along too. It would be the perfect opportunity to see if he had been following up any other leads.

This time, I didn't phone DI Collingwood directly. Instead, I called Suhad.

"I should have called you first," I began.

"What have you done now?" she asked.

"Nothing yet. Except I have made an appointment for tomorrow morning, to see Mark Stockman over at Grandma's house. I also need to pick up a few things, if that's possible."

Suhad agreed that she'd try to arrange it. "I can't see any reason why not," she said. "Although perhaps you could have given more notice."

"I'll re-arrange, if it's not possible," I promised. "I don't mind messing Mark Stockman about, but he suggested tomorrow morning – and for me, the sooner the better."

In spite of her worries, Suhad rang back to say that DI Collingwood would be there by eight thirty, to give us a little time to chat before Stockman arrived.

Talking over an early breakfast the next morning, Kelly pointed out that much as she'd like to see the house, she'd really prefer not to attend a meeting with a lawyer and a cop present. "Just thinking about it makes me itch," she said, wrinkling her nose.

"Suhad's lovely, but I get your point."

I reminded Kelly she had a spare key, so could wander and explore in my absence, then I grabbed my broken rucksack, ran down the lane and caught the bus.

I arrived a bit early. I hung around on the bend in the road, outside the exclusion zone, willing Suhad's car to appear. Even so, I was startled when a dark blue car pulled up, and a voice called my name. DI Collingwood.

"Get in," he said, as I stood there dithering. So I did.

"Alarmingly sensible of you," he said. "I was surprised not to find you waiting right outside, upsetting Mrs Rook."

"I don't see why," I retorted. "I've been following all your rules; however pointless I think they are."

He glanced at me with a sardonic smile. "Apart from the one about not talking to me without your lawyer present."

I shut up and sat with my head facing firmly ahead, but not before I caught a glimpse of his smug expression out of the corner of my eye.

As he parked by the front gate, Suhad pulled up directly behind us.

"I came to collect you at the farm," she said. "I didn't realise you had someone staying there with you?"

Ah. Poor Kelly. I hope she wasn't too worried.

"An old friend," I said, deliberately vague. "Sorry you missed me. What did she say?"

"Only that you'd left already. Seemed a bit shy."

"Probably not awake," I said. "We were up late chatting last night."

DI Collingwood was holding the front door open, waiting for us, not quite tapping his foot. We followed him inside.

The house had only been empty for a week, but it already had that sad air of a place neglected. I didn't feel at all like I was coming home. It wasn't only that I had to be accompanied by the police, it was something more intangible, more emotional.

We sat at the kitchen table.

"What was it you wanted to collect?" DI Collingwood asked. "Let's get it over with before this estate agent chap arrives."

I laughed to hear Mark Stockman described thus and was only sorry he wasn't there to hear it himself.

DI Collingwood's phone rang, and he excused himself to answer it. He sounded annoyed.

"The tag's working," he said, after he hung up. "But the system is not. I put in a request last night for them to switch off the exclusion zone for a couple of hours this morning, and it wasn't done."

"I hope that doesn't mean you have to lock me up and throw away the key," I said, only half-joking.

"Just this once, we'll let it go," he said. "Good to know it works, right?"

"I didn't even know it was in doubt."

"Back to my question, what is it you want to collect?"

"A couple of Grandma's books for my course. Some paperwork for Professor Buckley," I said. "I'm trying to arrange a home for Grandma's collection of replica Roman silver, perhaps at a local museum. He's taken a couple of pieces to a Roman Artefacts specialist, a conservator at the British Museum, and he wanted to know if there was some paperwork concerning their provenance, and stuff like insurance details."

"I see," said DI Collingwood. Not really seeing, and not much interested.

Suhad perked up though. "Can you do that, give the stuff to a museum, without Julia's permission?" she asked, anxiously.

"Yes," I said. "Check with Mr Harvey if you like, but the collection wasn't ever part of the Trust. It was left to me personally. As were all the contents of the house. The house itself, and the farm, the share in Grandma's business – that's all in the trust."

DI Collingwood looked interested and spoke to Suhad. "Have I understood that correctly?" he asked. "I understood that Harry Rook was Alice's trustee, but hadn't gathered that it passed to Julia."

I answered before Suhad could get a word out. "Yes," I said. "Doesn't exactly give me the strongest motive for murdering Harry, does it? To replace a trustee who was co-operative, with one who is actively trying to block my every wish."

DI Collingwood asked, "Did you know that Julia would be Harry's successor?"

"No." I had no choice but to admit it.

"I don't think anyone did," Suhad said. "I've seen the paperwork and apart from ruling out Alice's mother, every single thing was left to Harry's discretion, and he obviously had his own lawyers. There'll always be a representative from our legal practice on the board, and Mrs B from the business."

"Mrs B?" he asked, getting his notebook out.

"Mrs Banerjee. Can usually be found in her office at the photographer's studio on the High Street."

He wrote it down. At least if he went to see Mrs B, he would get a rosier view of my family, including me, than he would have had from Julia. Until he asked about Helen, anyway.

"Your grandmother doesn't appear to have trusted your mother," he observed. "Do you know why?"

I refrained from the obvious answer – that it doesn't generally take long for anyone to find out that my mother isn't trustworthy. "They were never close."

"You don't know of a specific reason?"

"I tried to keep out of it," I said. "It wasn't easy, being in the middle."

I changed the subject. "Can I go and hunt for the papers then? They'll be in the library, I expect."

I didn't wait for an answer, but opened the library door and went in. I took a deep breath and relaxed. Now that did still feel like coming home.

They followed me into the room. Suhad went straight to the bookshelves, and DI Collingwood to the silver cabinet. I said nothing but waited quietly for a little payback.

I'd forgotten how loud the alarm was. Suhad stepped back from the books she was touching, as if afraid that she'd set it off. DI Collingwood put the silver spoons back down in the cabinet. He was red in the face – anger, rather than embarrassment.

"Turn the alarm off, now," he said.

I walked over to the library door and typed the number into the keypad. The dreadful shrieking noise stopped. I suppose a bit of me hoped it had disturbed Julia as well as pissed off DI Collingwood. Childish, but rewarding.

"Phone the security company?" he said, through gritted teeth.

I picked up the library phone and selected the right autodial. "False alarm, sorry," I said to the person who answered. She asked me my security question, and I gave the correct answer, and all was calm again.

DI Collingwood was glaring at me, and I felt my cheeks flush, but I didn't apologise. I did give him a pair of cotton gloves from the box beside the display cabinet. "Grandma always insisted," I said.

We were interrupted by the loud clatter of the door knocker. Mark Stockman was exactly on time.

Suhad said, "I'll let him in, while you find those papers."

DI Collingwood went back to the silver cabinet. I heard Mark Stockman's voice, but not what they were saying. I decided I would have to rummage through the papers afterwards.

I stood up as Suhad preceded Stockman back into the room. DI Collingwood nodded at him and went back to handling the silver as if he was fascinated. Perhaps he was.

"Mr Stockman," I said. "I'm Alice Hunter."

He smiled, and it was a real smile, and I realised how much of a politician he was. He knew how to turn on the charm.

He shook my hand with warmth, held on a moment or two too long.

"So pleased to meet at last Ms Hunter," he said. I thought I saw a flicker of recognition showing he must remember me from the café, but he pretended otherwise.

"Call me Alice," I said. "No need to be formal. After all, I've seen your father's baby pictures."

"Ah yes," he said. "The family connection. Do, please, call me Mark."

DI Collingwood looked interested, so I explained, for his benefit.

"Grandma was nanny to the Stockman family, before she started her business."

"I was very sorry to hear about her death," Mark said. "I came to the memorial service. If you recall?"

I didn't remember any of it. They had let me out of Brookfields for that, although I was so doped up that I was hardly conscious. Mrs B had looked after me; my mother had kept her distance.

"No," I said. "I was a bit out of it that day."

"Yes. I understand from Helen that you nursed Ms Hunter in her final illness, and that the strain proved a little too much. I'm sure she appreciated it though."

He was admitting to first-name terms with mother too, then. How cosy.

"So," I said. "I understand you've been talking to my mother about the house?"

"We got talking at the memorial service. The Beacon Road development was reaching completion, and I was looking for the next project. I was already in talks with Harry Rook, so…"

DI Collingwood dropped one of the silver spoons, and everyone was silent for a moment.

"Mr Rook didn't want to sell, did he?"

"No, he didn't. But he was coming round to it – he was well past retirement age and knew he couldn't carry on forever."

"His niece, Tamsin – she wanted to carry on though. And other family members were keen too, I think."

"I don't think anyone was really as emotionally invested as Harry. Julia consulted everyone concerned, I assure you. I didn't exert undue pressure, take advantage of Harry's death. She came to me."

I wished I could ask her, to see if that was true. Perhaps DI Collingwood would be able to do so. If he thought it was important. Having so little control was frustrating.

"If you were to buy this house, what would you do with it?" I asked.

"I don't think that would really be any of your business, but if you want to know, it would probably be demolished. I intend to create a luxury new development, and the style of the house isn't in keeping with the architect's plans."

"I see. Grandma loved this house. Will you be demolishing the Rook place too?"

"It's not been decided yet, but it's likely. Victorian gothic isn't quite what we're aiming for, either. That won't pose a problem, will it?"

I looked at Suhad, and she nodded.

I said, "Let's talk."

I sat in Grandma's chair and he sat on the sofa, with Suhad next to him. DI Collingwood was still trying to play invisible, but Mark Stockman hadn't really shown any interest in who he was. I wish I knew whether that was because Stockman knew and didn't care, or whether he'd written him off as unimportant.

"I don't know what my mother has told you, but she really doesn't have the authority to sell the house. I'm not sure anyone can, before the trust Grandma set up ends on my thirtieth birthday. It's possible, perhaps, with the go ahead from my trustees, but it would involve going against Grandma's expressed wishes."

"I understood Helen has authority to act on behalf of the Trust. That she's a director of the Personal Management Company."

Suhad and I spoke at the same time. I gestured her to continue.

"No, Helen Hunter has never been in a position to act for the Trust. I'm afraid there's been some misunderstanding."

His face fell. For all his polish, he wanted this house so much that for once he couldn't control his expression. That was interesting. I thought about what Kelly had said about my safety, and decided it might be best to leave the possibility open.

"I'll be straight with you, Mr Stockman. I don't have strong sentimental ties to this house. I am quite keen to sell it, no matter what your plans are. I don't intend to stay in Cuckmere. I'm aiming to take my place at Oxford next year, and after that, who knows? I will be seeking to break the trust. My memories of Grandma don't reside in things, well, not this particular thing, anyway." I caught myself fiddling with my pendant, even if it wasn't the real coin.

"May I look?" he held his hand out. I slipped the chain over my head and handed it over.

"It's a Roman coin," I said, having decided not to elaborate on the whole story about how the real one was at the British Museum. "I found it myself, when I was eight. This part of Sussex was heaving with Romans, you know."

"On the Beacon?" he asked.

He was looking at the coin very closely. I didn't offer to show him how to open the pendant and take a closer look at the coin, in case he had any real knowledge and would spot it wasn't authentic.

"It was a long time ago," I hedged. "I was only eight. We used to explore the whole area. We found some fossils too, ammonites, in the chalk cliffs over at Seven Sisters."

"I see," he said. "I thought there were Roman fortifications up here on Beacon Hill?"

He handed the pendant back to me, and I put it back around my neck.

"Probably," I said. "You should ask Professor Buckley – he's the expert. There was a road along the coast, in Roman times as now. There was possibly a villa on the farmland over by the river, to the north of town. He's considering applying for a grant to do an excavation, if the preliminary studies look exciting enough."

A slight exaggeration, but I could hope.

"Is this farm another of your Grandma's properties then? Because if it would sweeten the deal, I would be prepared to make a fair offer to include the purchase of that and any other local property."

"That's very kind. It's too far away to be of any interest for your new development, though. On the wrong side of town."

"It's a serious offer," he said. "We always have a variety of projects on the go."

"It's all down to Julia Rook," I said. "And Mr Harvey and Mrs Banerjee, but I can talk to them myself."

Suhad spoke up at last. "I don't think you should bother Mrs Rook, Alice. It's an awkward situation all round, but you should leave it to Mr Harvey for now."

"Sorry," I said. "I wanted Mr Stockman to know that there was no more reason for him to negotiate with my mother behind my back."

He looked taken aback, but I quickly reassured him. "It's alright," I said. "I know how persuasive she is, but it's my decision, not hers."

"I understand" he said. "Families…"

I longed to ask him about his grandfather, but it wasn't the right time. Anyway, he was unlikely to know what I wanted to know. Was he sweet on my Grandma? Had he invested in her business? Where had her start-up capital come from?

"If you're planning to demolish the house, I don't suppose there's much point in asking if you'd like to take a look around?"

"No," he said. "But if you can spare a few minutes I would love to have a look at your Grandma's collection. I'm hooked on local history."

DI Collingwood stepped aside, and went to the far side of the room, as Mark and I went through the cabinet. He loved the spoons, and asked about the missing skyphos.

"Fancy you knowing about that," I said. "It's with Professor Buckley at the moment."

"I have a photo," he said. "Of my grandfather, your grandmother and the Roman silver jug."

"I'd love to see it," I said. "I haven't seen many photographs of Grandma when she was younger."

"He was very fond of her, I think," Mark volunteered. "I know that silver jug meant something to them both."

"She told me he put her in touch with the silversmith who made the reproductions," I said. "That was what I was looking for when you came in, the paperwork and the insurance details. For Professor Buckley."

"Are these all replicas?" he asked. "There's an unknown goddess on the skyphos, at least not one that's mentioned in any history books."

"Most of them, and made by the same man," I said. "The coins are real though, I think she bought them from a London dealer. The silver spoons are real too."

"Is it okay if I touch them?" he asked.

"Yes," I said. "Best with these gloves though." He pulled them on, and picked up a spoon with enough reverence to have satisfied Grandma.

"Amazing," he said. "To think someone treasured these spoons so long ago."

I warmed to him then. He was genuinely interested and not merely trying to charm me into selling. He put the spoons back and pulled off the gloves, then stood up.

"Thank you," he said. "I'll be off now but be sure I'll be in touch again."

"Thank you for coming," I said. On impulse I added, "If and when I do sell, I promise that you shall have first refusal. Any fair offer considered."

He smiled then, a proper smile that reached his eyes, and shook my hand. Suhad walked with him to the door.

DI Collingwood said, "Did you mean that?"

"Yes, I did. I liked him. Didn't you?"

"Typical politician," DI Collingwood said. "All charm and no substance. He really fooled you with that fake interest in the Roman stuff then."

"You looked interested enough," I pointed out.

"I was trying to keep out of your way," he said. "Now find those papers and I can get back to work."

"I thought babysitting a suspected murderer is your work," I sniped.

"I didn't think you were here for the pleasure of my company."

That hit the mark, and I grinned at him as he fought the impulse to snap back at me. But I did as I was told and went back to the roll-top desk and worked through each cubby hole.

Fortunately Grandma had been quite well organised, and all the paperwork concerning the silver was bundled up together. I found it as Suhad came back into the room.

"I don't think that was wise, offering him first refusal," she said.

"If I sell," I pointed out. "If I do, who will give me a better offer? It seemed reasonable to me. And it will stop him talking to my mother."

"Fair point," she conceded.

"Take a look at these papers, and see what you think," I said. She and DI Collingwood sat on the sofa and started going them through them.

"Wow," she said. "Have you seen these prices? And that was for a reproduction, made years and years ago. It was thousands then, and now it's insured for a hundred grand."

"Yes," I said. "If it were the real thing, it would be more than a million."

"Where's the real one?" DI Collingwood asked.

"An American museum, I think. Grandma went on holiday when mother was a baby. It was originally found in someone's attic and bought by an American collector who donated it to the museum. It had some kind of tax advantage, I think."

"If that's all, we can lock up and go," DI Collingwood said. "I see no reason why you shouldn't take these. We'll add them to the list of items you've removed from the house, but I really can't see how they'd be connected with Harry Rook's death."

"Thanks," I said. "You'll be ready to admit I'm innocent soon."

"Never that," he said, with half a smile. "Not guilty, at best." He put his policeman face back on, sharpish. "But I grant you, it was interesting to hear all the stuff about the family not wanting to sell up. Don't think I couldn't tell what you were doing there."

I was rather pleased he had cottoned on.

I put all the silver away and made sure the cabinet was properly locked and the alarm reset. I quickly collected a pile of books on Roman Britain, and on a sentimental impulse, looked once more for Grandma's copy of The Mildenhall Treasure. It was in a short story collection, I knew, but could never remember what it was called. It was still nowhere to be found.

I packed the books and papers into the rucksack and followed Suhad out of the house and watched DI Collingwood double lock the front door. He stood by the gate as I climbed into the passenger seat of Suhad's car, and he was still watching as she drove off. I resisted the impulse to wave. He wasn't the only one watching though. When I looked back, he had crossed the road, and was standing at the door of the Rook house, talking to Julia.

TWENTY-NINE

"DI COLLINGWOOD WAS unusually forthcoming," Suhad said, as she drove me back to the farm. "I think he's a bit soft on you, actually."

I remembered him flirting with her in the interview room when I was under arrest. It wasn't his way to pull the bad cop routine, I suspected. He preferred to charm.

"He shouldn't have criticised Mark Stockman. Very unprofessional."

She laughed. "I think he was pushing your buttons, to see how you'd react. He's definitely smarter than you think. He knew you'd set it up to demonstrate that Stockman had a motive."

"I should hope so too. I didn't go to all that trouble for nothing."

"Strange how so many people are suddenly interested in the Roman stuff," she said. "And strange how it didn't go missing when you were in hospital."

"Some things did. Mostly the vintage clothes, and some trinkets that weren't in the safe. Including an Egyptian necklace, a real one, which Grandma said should really be in a museum."

I didn't mention the silver Tiffany revolver It wasn't licensed, for one thing, and I felt guilty about that. But also, I didn't want to worry her. I'd had enough of people looking after me. I can look after myself.

"That's not just a trinket, Alice. It sounds like a serious theft. Did you report it to the police?"

"I did, on the day they had me sectioned. It was dismissed as a delusion, that I thought Grandma had been an Egyptian princess. They wrote it down but didn't take much notice."

"Insurance?"

"It turned out it wasn't insured. That didn't help. I suspect it was too valuable – any insurer would have insisted she keep it in the bank, but she wanted to have her treasures around her. I used to tease her that she was an upscale version of a hoarder. But isn't that what all collectors are?"

Suhad was silent for a moment or two, before speaking in a more serious tone. "I think you should do something about your mother. I know it's difficult, but she shouldn't be allowed to get away with this habit of helping herself to anything she fancies from the house."

Do something? What exactly? Some problems are intractable. One reason it's so much easier not to talk about them.

"It's not all her fault," I said, wondering when I'd switched from defending her to myself, to only defending her to other people. "She was so deeply hurt by Grandma's will, and who can blame her? They always brought out the worst in each other. I can hardly take her to court, if the police didn't believe me."

"It's not just the necklace though, is it? She sold all the couture clothing. Mr Harvey acquired a copy of the catalogue from Sotheby's. It wasn't merely a few frocks through the boutique."

Suhad had been doing her homework.

"She needed the money," I pointed out. "What was I supposed to do?"

"And she's still trying to sell the house. Mark Stockman confirmed that today."

"She didn't succeed."

"It doesn't have to be official," Suhad persisted. "We could set up a meeting with her and Mr Harvey. A sort of intervention, with a legal edge."

Everybody wants me to do things their way. Why is that? "I think there are other things to worry about right now," I said.

"I'm your lawyer. It's my job to protect your interests."

"I'll think about it," I promised.

Luckily at that point we had reached the end of the lane, and she dropped me off, apparently content for now with my vague concession.

It wasn't quite so easy to shut down my inner voice. I'd been brushing off Mrs B and Mr Harvey's concerns for ages, but Suhad was more persistent. She was also an outsider, not influenced by Grandma. That gave me pause for thought.

Back at the farm there was no sign of Kelly. I put the kettle on, carried my coffee through to the dining table, and started going through the various papers I'd collected. By the time I'd added up the numbers on my fingers, I was more determined than ever to sort out some kind of home for them in a museum. I didn't want to live under the same roof as something quite so valuable any more. It was increasingly hard to believe how I'd taken them for granted for so long.

I fired up the laptop and emailed the Professor. It was useful to have someone knowledgeable and interested to discuss things with.

"I have the paperwork for Grandma's collection – the receipts and the insurance documents. I thought I might try to trace the silversmith. He could still be alive – he wasn't much older than Grandma."

He emailed back pretty much straight away. "Is there an address on the receipts?"

Silly me. There it was, in black and white. I Googled and there was still a jeweller's operating there, but no guarantee that he was still involved with the business.

I emailed. "The jeweller's is still there, in the Laines in Brighton. I might catch a train and go over there this afternoon."

"I'm busy today," he replied. "But if you can bear to wait until tomorrow, I'll give you a lift. If you can stand an insatiably nosey companion?"

"That would be great. You'll have better questions than me. And perhaps you could bring the skyphos?"

That last part slipped out and surprised me. I really did want the reassurance of seeing it again.

We arranged a time for him to pick me up, then I pottered around the house, restless, wondering where Kelly was. Perhaps Suhad showing up had spooked her. As I wandered around the yard and looked up the lane, a delivery van arrived with my parcels. Once I had them inside, I opened the box with the rucksack straight away, and put the others aside.

My original plans for the day scuppered, there was more research on my to-do list. It would have been so much easier to have a private detective to do all this properly, but needs must.

Having tackled the train to London with the Prof gave me much needed confidence. Ironically, being accused of murder had actually helped me learn to face the social anxieties I'd been avoiding dealing with since leaving hospital.

At my next appointment with Claire, I'd have to tell her how effective it was, if only to see the look of horror on her face. I suppose it was exactly what should happen in theory. Enduring and even enjoying an experience that would have provoked a full-blown panic attack was positive feedback, and was helping me get off the downward spiral and on to an upward one.

So long as it didn't lead me straight to prison.

I picked up my textbook on the Romans in Sussex and put it in my new rucksack, along with a bottle of water, a banana and a couple of energy bars – as if I was preparing for a Himalayan expedition rather than a simple trip to London. Then I spiralled into a panic, wondering about the electronic tag.

I checked the paperwork again, and as far as I could tell I was okay to go to London. Anywhere, in fact, except the area around Grandma's house. So long as I was back in time for my curfew and when I had to sign in at the police station. The only drawback was that the police would know where I'd been. Would that be a problem? Would DI Collingwood check up to see what my movements were?

If he did, perhaps it would prompt him to do some investigating of his own. That wouldn't be a bad thing.

I left my bicycle chained up at the station car park and was soon on the train to London. Everything went swimmingly until I arrived at Victoria station. The rush of the people, the noise – it was all too much. I couldn't face going down the escalators and dealing with the tube – I'd been slightly claustrophobic even before Brookfields. I found a relatively quiet spot out of the flow of pedestrians, and did my breathing exercises, and then joined the queue for a taxi at the front of the station. Damn the expense – my sanity took precedence.

"Upper Street, Islington," I said to the driver. "There's a boutique, called Troy." I gave him the postcode.

It took me ten minutes of being stubbornly monosyllabic to communicate that I didn't want to talk. He tried the weather, my shopping plans, and politics before he gave up.

I'd only been to the boutique and flat once, with Grandma. It was so long ago now, I wasn't entirely sure I would recognise it.

I didn't.

It wasn't called Troy any more, for one. Nippers?

A cowardly voice in my head suggested I ask the cab driver to take me back to Victoria, but I ignored it, climbed out of the cab and paid him. I grabbed my water bottle out of my rucksack and wandered over to the window. Baby stuff. High end baby paraphernalia of all kinds. A most expensive old-fashioned perambulator, and a range of modern buggies. Hand crafted cots and high chairs. Wooden toys and expensive teddies. Designer baby clothes too.

This was not my mother's shop. No way had she transformed Troy into a baby boutique.

I presumed she had sublet, and I wondered if that was true of the flat as well. Was it even allowed by the terms of the Management Company? How I wished this problem was in the hands of a reassuringly expensive and competent private investigator.

A couple of doors down, I paused by the entrance to the flats above the shops. I read all the names by the buzzers. Twice. Number 16, the little card that used to say H. Hunter now said M. Papasavas. I suppose she could have married a Greek without telling me, but somehow I didn't think so.

I decided the most sensible approach was to try the shop first and ask. For a start it was less likely that someone would be home in the flat during working hours, and in a shop people had to talk to you, especially if you were buying something.

Today was going to be far more expensive than I'd planned. Credit card to the rescue again.

The bell jangled when I opened the door and went in, and a middle-aged olive-skinned woman looked up from behind the counter and smiled at me. That was hopeful, I thought. She could easily be called Papasavas – so two birds with one stone and all that.

I looked at the teddy bears and stuffed toys, but the cheapest was ninety pounds. That was ridiculous as the price for a simple question, however personal. I browsed the rack of baby clothes and found a very pretty polka spotted red dress for a baby. A bargain at only thirty-one pounds and ninety-five pence.

"Didn't this place used to be a vintage fashion boutique?" I asked. "Troy, wasn't it?"

"We've been here a few months now," she said. To my relief, she seemed happy enough to chat.

"You've saved me an extra shopping trip to buy a present for my god-daughter, but I was hoping to see the old owner. Helen. Does she still live in the flat upstairs? Sixteen B, wasn't it?"

"Oh no," she said. "I'm sorry you've had a wasted journey. We bought the flat as well as the boutique."

I looked down, hoping I'd disguised the shock I was feeling. I'd been worrying about having to explain how I knew Helen so well but didn't know she was no longer here, but there was no need. Perhaps if I decided against archaeology after all, I could train to become a private detective.

"Credit card?" she asked, offering me the machine.

Some private detective, I thought, as I caught myself in the nick of time, and paid in cash instead. She might have noticed that the name on the card was Alice Hunter.

"If you could wait a moment," she offered. "I have her contact details here. I'm sure she won't mind me passing them on."

She tapped on her phone keyboard and grabbed a pen and a small notepad. She wrote down my mother's mobile number, and then as I watched, wrote down the address of Grandma's house.

"She was sad to give up this place," the woman added. "She had to go back home to look after her daughter. Doolally, I gather. Very sad."

"That's how I know her," I said. "Through Alice. Thank you for your help."

"I hope the dress fits your god-daughter," she said. "Don't forget to say where we are."

"Don't worry, I'll tell everyone," I said. "It's a lovely shop. I'm sure they'll want to see it for themselves."

The journey home was not long enough for me to work out the ramifications of what I'd discovered, even though there was a delay at Gatwick. I was sure it was completely against the terms of the Trust for my mother to sell up without the express permission of Harry Rook and Mr Harvey. Neither of them had said anything to me.

I wondered where my mother was living now. No wonder it had taken so much time to get her to move out of Grandma's when I came out of hospital.

How had she done it? Working that out was beyond me. Definitely a task for Suhad, or Mr Harvey.

I cycled back to the farm with only half an hour to spare before my curfew. I hung my rucksack on the back of the chair and got out the baby dress and put it on the table, together with the handwritten note of my mother's mobile number and the address of Grandma's house.

As I put the kettle on, I heard Kelly coming down the stairs.

"You were ages," she said. "I was worried about the damn curfew."

She saw the baby dress on the kitchen table and did a dramatic double take. "Is there something you ought to tell me?" she asked.
"Oh yes," I said. "We'll need coffee."

THIRTY

WHILE I WAS waiting for the Professor, I phoned Mr Harvey. I'd have preferred to talk to him face to face, but this mattered too much to wait for the right opportunity.

"I went up to London yesterday," I said to him after we exchanged the usual greetings. "I went to Islington, to the boutique. Did you know it specialises in top end baby gear now?"

"No," he said. "That doesn't sound like Helen. I thought she enjoyed the vintage fashion business. She's stuck with it longer than anything else."

"I thought so too," I said. "It's being run by a Mrs Papasavas, I think. Has the Trust had any dealings with her?"

"No," he said, sounding comfortingly mystified. "Mind, I don't deal with the day-to-day admin."

"Mrs Papasavas is living in the flat too," I said. "In fact, she says she bought both the business and the flat."

"That's impossible," he said. "You must be mistaken."

"That was what I thought, especially as the Trust pays the service charges and the business rates for the shop and so on."

"Ah," he said. "That's all paid as part of Helen's allowance. She made a huge fuss not long before Frances died about not being trusted to do it herself, and we changed the arrangement. Your grandmother agreed. She signed all the paperwork. Nothing was ever done without her agreement."

"Did you talk to her?"

There was a pause.

"I'm not sure," he said. "I think we'd better check this out with the Land Registry, hadn't we? I'll set Suhad on to it straight away."

"Best not mention it to mother," I said. "Not yet, anyway."

"Yes, yes. Certainly."

He sounded very worried, and I felt guilty. "It's probably nothing," I said. "I'm probably being paranoid again."

"I hope so," he said.

In some ways, I did too.

The Professor arrived while I was on the phone with Mrs B, apologising for another afternoon when I was too busy to work. I let him in and made him a coffee, while he looked through the documents I'd retrieved from the house. He was as fascinated with Grandma's papers as I was. He looked up and caught me looking at my watch.

"Okay, let's be off then," he said. "You're impatient to find this silversmith – and I can see why."

Professor Buckley chatted as he drove. "There was nothing about your coin in those documents. It's such a pity, because without a context its historical value is next to nothing. If we could prove it was found in Cuckmere, that would be really exciting."

"I'm not sure about the provenance of any of it anymore," I said.

He parked in the multi storey, a short walk from the jeweller's.

I hovered uncertainly, looking in the window at the relatively ordinary range of commercial rings and necklaces. There was some antique silver – a Regency teapot or two – as well as a couple of pieces that were described as top quality reproductions. There were no antiquities though. Nothing Roman.

"Let's get on with it, then," he said.

I opened the door and went in. The shop was empty of customers, but a young woman was sitting behind a counter, polishing silver. When she heard the tinkling of the bell, she grabbed a wipe and cleaned her hands off, standing up as she did so.

"Can I help you?" she asked.

"I hope so," I said. "I found these receipts in my grandmother's personal papers for some silver reproductions of Roman antiquities. I was hoping to talk to the person who made them."

"That's a first," she said, taking the papers. She started flipping through them. "Yes, these are ours. I didn't know that we went back quite so far."

She read a bit more, concentrating. I felt my excitement building. There was something here.

"That's the boss's signature, right enough. Hang on—"

A couple of minutes later she came back, with an old man who seemed vaguely familiar.

"This is our Mr Rushton," she said.

He held out his hand and clasped mine when I offered it.

"Young Alice," he said. "I wondered when you'd come. Don't you remember me?" He seemed genuinely pleased to see me. "You do have a look of Frances, you know. And this is your young man?"

I blushed. "No, he's my Professor, I suppose."

"You suppose? Shouldn't you know?" the old man teased.

"The course hasn't started yet, that's all. He's an archaeologist, interested in Grandma's collection."

"Is he now? And wouldn't Frances have enjoyed that? Come through."

We followed him into a small room furnished with a couple of wooden chairs and a workbench.

"Don't you remember me, Alice?" he asked again. "You came to my workshop a few times with Frances."

"I don't remember coming here," I said. "Somewhere out in the country, I think."

"This isn't my workshop – I do a bit of tinkering here, that's all. Changing watch batteries. Fixing safety chains. Sizing rings. The real work I do in my workshop, out beyond Lewes, on the road to Eastbourne."

"That would explain it," I said.

"Frances was a regular visitor, you know. A fascinating lady. So interested in the work, and a stickler for authenticity."

"We'd love to visit," Professor Buckley said. "Is there anything you can tell us now? It's the silver skyphos we're really interested in."

"Ah, that. Yes, I consider that to be one of the best things I've ever made. The real one is in a museum somewhere, I understand. Frances had a collection of photographs of it from every conceivable angle. All the details, weight and everything – so precise it didn't matter so much that I was only allowed access to the item itself for a couple of hours. Mind, she was a charmer, that one, she could talk anyone into anything."

Except for the one thing she'd really wanted, I thought. She'd not been able to charm Harry into marrying her.

"Is there any way of telling your copy from the real thing?" Professor Buckley asked.

"I should think not! Frances was insistent," he said. "Except for my maker's mark. I always include that – not to do so would be unprofessional."

"But you remember Frances was clear that it shouldn't be visible?"

"She didn't want me to include my mark at all," he said. "She wanted the replica to be identical to the original. I understood, but I'm a silversmith specialising in reproduction work. It would be professional suicide to risk gaining a reputation as a forger."

He went out into the sales area and came back carrying two Georgian teapots.

"One's mine, and one's the original. Take a look and see what you think."

The Professor picked one of them up and turned it over, and I did the same with the other. "A crowned leopard," the Professor said. "That's early London, I think?"

"Correct," the silversmith said. "And the other symbols show the silver content, the letter is for the date, and there's the profile of George IV."

"So this is the real one. And on yours?" he asked.

"A set of scales with the numbers 925, an uncrowned cat, and a fancy letter M. So the M is your mark?"

"Yes," he said. "That M can be found on all my pieces, together with the assay mark."

"The Romans didn't use marks," I said. "So where did you put it?"

"It's there alright," he said. "I wanted to place it under the handle but Frances persuaded me not to do so. We devised a very clever way to hide it in plain sight. The medallion of Medusa on the front, surrounded by ivy leaves, the M is disguised in the folds of the clothing. I doubt anyone has ever noticed – but you would if you compared with the original."

"Could you recognise it now?" Professor Buckley asked.

"Undoubtedly I would."

The Prof reached into his bag and brought out a package wrapped in soft fabric. Mr Rushton unwrapped it carefully, smiling with pleasure. I was relieved to see it again, and with a witness present.

"Here," he said, picking up the skyphos. "Right in the middle of this—"

Abruptly he cut off the sentence.

"But that's impossible," he said. "There's no mark there."

He took out his magnifying glass and looked again.

"Is there any possibility the mark has been removed in some way? Polished out of existence?" Professor Buckley asked.

"What do you think I'm looking for, man?" Mr Rushton responded tetchily. "No there's nothing there."

"What does that mean?" I asked. "Is this the real one? Impossible, surely?"

"It's either the real one or a damn fine reproduction," Mr Rushton said. "Better even than mine."

The Professor started to wrap it up. "There's only one way to find out. Someone has to track down the exact location of the one in

America, then go and take a look at it. As I doubt the police will agree to you leaving the country, Alice, it will have to be me."

I spoke to Mr Rushton. "Any idea which museum? A name, a city, anything to narrow it down?"

He was shaking his head. "Sorry," he said. "If I ever knew, the memory is gone."

"It wouldn't be in your records, would it?" Professor Buckley asked.

"I can look, but my dealings were with Frances. If it's not in her records—"

"I haven't seen anything," I said. "I have no idea where to start."

"We have to report this to the police," Mr Rushton said. "I can't be complicit in a fraud. I have my reputation to consider."

"Absolutely," I said. "I'll talk to my lawyer and start the ball rolling, but you can be sure we'll make it clear it was not your doing."

The Professor spoke. "We wouldn't even know if you hadn't said it was the real thing. So not to worry on that score."

Mr Rushton looked relieved. I felt more worried than ever.

"In the meantime, what the hell are we going to do with it?" I asked.

"Apart from us three, no one knows," Professor Buckley said. "Where do you think it will be safe?"

"Your friend at the British Museum seems the obvious choice," I suggested.

So that was agreed. We decided it would be fine at the Professor's place overnight, and straight up to London in the morning.

THIRTY-ONE

I WAS QUIET on the way back to the farm, thinking over what we'd found out.

"How does all this make you feel?" Professor Buckley asked, as we approached the turn to the farm. "What will you do if it turns out that your grandmother was somehow involved in a massive fraud?"

"I'm still coming to terms with being accused of murder," I said. "Somehow this must be connected, surely?"

"You're getting ahead of yourself," he said. "One step at a time. And remember, your grandmother was a good businesswoman. Maybe it will all become clear as we take a closer look."

"I'm afraid it will become only too clear, Professor," I said. "I've always felt the inheritance carries a responsibility, but I never imagined—"

He smiled. "I think it's time you started calling me Matt, outside class at any rate," he said.

"Thanks, Matt," I said, touched by his kindness. I kept it to myself that I'd become comfortable with thinking of him as the Prof.

He refused my suggestion of dropping me at the end of the lane. I was trying to protect Kelly and maybe even Daniel. Instead, he insisted on driving all the way up to the farmyard.

"I'll take the skyphos up to London tomorrow," he said. "I'd have done it days ago if I'd thought there was the slightest chance. For now, sleep on it and we'll talk again. Don't let yourself get overwhelmed. One thing at a time."

I smiled gratefully at him and got out of his car.

"Are you going to trust me with it?" he asked.

"You've had it a few days and not disappeared with it yet."

"Yet." He shook his head. "You're a foolish young woman. No wonder your grandmother put everything into a trust. You've no more sense than a kitten."

"That's where you're wrong," I said, and smiled. My confidence in myself was returning. "It's not that I didn't think it through. I made a decision. So far, it looks like a good decision."

He shook his head, mock stern, but was smiling as he drove off.

I unlocked the door and went inside. I couldn't see Kelly, but I felt the house wasn't empty.

"Kelly, I'm back. I'm on my own."

The larder door flew open, and she came out, laughing.

"Thank fuck it's you. I was shitting bricks after that lawyer yesterday."

"No need, is there? You agreed you're going back Monday. A week's leave, you said."

"Yup" she said, looking at the ground. Then she brightened. "Let's make the most of my freedom while I still have it."

I looked worried. "You're worrying me, Kels," I said.

"Nothing that exciting. Just a bit of fun. I'm still allowed some fun, aren't I?"

"Site survey on Friday – does that sound like fun?"

"Yes!" she clapped her hands. "Do you think we'll be paragliding?"

"You might be," I said. "I won't."

"Wimp!"

There was no way of denying it. I've always been scared of heights. Even standing on a chair to change a light bulb is challenging. I can clamber around on the hills and cliffs all day though – so long as my feet stay on solid ground, I'm fine.

"I was worried I'd be stuck here on my own if you'd been arrested again. By that dishy cop. Well, not exactly on my own. I met Daniel today."

"What?" I said. "Tell me."

"You tell me yours first," she said. I knew how stubborn she was, so I gave in, once she'd reassured me Daniel was okay, and he hadn't taken off in a panic at being discovered.

"He's fine. Cross my heart. Now talk."

When I'd finished, Kelly said "Your gran was a real dark horse, then. All that bling in an ordinary house. As if it was a china tea service or something."

"I'm beginning to wonder if there is anything ordinary about the house at all," I said.

"What do you mean?"

"It seems obvious now that she moved there because it was so close to Harry Rook. What on earth were they up to, the pair of them? And right under the nose of his wife. No wonder Julia's so angry."

"Maybe."

"Do you think I was daft, then, for trusting the Professor with the skyphos?"

"It's not your problem any more. But—" she cut off, mid-sentence.

"But what?" I demanded.

"Are you the only one who knows? I mean, it's worth a lot of dosh and there's already been one murder. Yeah, yeah, I know, paranoia strikes again."

"No, that wasn't what I was thinking," I said. "' was wondering earlier if Harry knew about the Roman stuff and its value. And who else might know? Perhaps that could be another motive."

"Or perhaps you want another motive to talk to the gorgeous DI," she teased.

"Will you stop that? Matching me up with every male in the general vicinity. No, I'm not the only one who knows. Professor Buckley would have to do away with the silversmith too, and his mate at the British Museum expects him to have a fake skyphos, which is not something he could conjure out of thin air."

"He has a silversmith," she pointed out.

I laughed at the ridiculous scenarios she was spinning out of random thoughts. "I'll email Suhad and Mr Harvey and keep them up to date with what's happening. I've been thinking about what the Prof asked, and I think that now I know, I have a duty to put things right. The real skyphos needs to be in a museum – maybe the museum that currently has the fake, maybe not. It's not simple."

"We could sell it and run off," she said, wistful.

"But who would we sell it to? Probably we would end up like one of those people who tries to hire a cop to murder their husband."

"One of us would have to get wed first. Toss a coin? The Prof, or the DI?"

"Neither." I mock punched her. "Seriously now, I can't imagine how Grandma could have become involved in all of this. Where did she get the silver? How did she work out how to sell the thing to an American museum? She had a whole army of skeletons in her cupboard – not merely the identity of my grandfather."

"Harry Rook. He must have been in on it, I reckon."

"It seems likely. I don't know. It's impossible. Now, tell me about Daniel."

"After you left with the Prof, I heard a car in the lane," she said. "I ran for the barn. He was there, and I realised that he must have seen me, so I asked him to help me hide."

"Sneaky."

"I was terrified, so I didn't even have to pretend. So I was obviously no threat."

"What did you tell him?"

"The truth. That I should be in hospital, and that you know. That you're a good friend, and that you haven't turned me in yet, although you are worried."

I grimaced. "I wouldn't you know. Unless you were really in a bad way and I could think of no other way to help you."

"I know. But you'll wait until I'm really off my nut. No one else would."

I suppose that was exactly right. Maybe if I hadn't been there myself…

"What did he say?"

"He told me about his dad and what he did. That he had nowhere to go. He's fucking angry about his dad, the farm, everything. Who can blame the poor sod? It's his home, and you moved into it."

"You talked in the barn?"

"No, I made him a coffee. Once your mother had given up. In the house. That's not a problem is it?"

"No, no, of course not. I just think – poor kid. It was his home."

"I didn't mention the stalking or anything, I thought it best not to let him know that you knew it was him, or that he was living in the barn. But he volunteered that to me, oddly enough."

"That's weird."

"Not that weird. He was telling me there was room for me, if I didn't want to go back to hospital. He's lonely, I reckon. Not talked to anyone properly for weeks, if not months. When did his dad die?"

I felt ashamed – I didn't know. "When I was in hospital, that's all I know. I was out of it." I was making excuses, but it was also true. "I wish I could do something to help him."

"We'll manage something. He's tired of it. He's young though, not sixteen yet. He doesn't want to go into care."

"Oh no, I didn't realise he was that young."

Poor kid.

"Did you ask him about the dead rabbit, and the cat?"

"I was impressive. I did that Columbo bit, right at the end." We watched a lot of telly on the ward. Columbo had been my favourite, Cagney and Lacey hers.

"And another thing? But without the mac…"

"I asked if he was any good at hunting – assumed that as a farm boy he would be. Thought he might have an air rifle. He volunteered that he's set snares in the past, but swears he hasn't hunted over on the

Beacon Hill – I didn't mention the rabbit, honest," she was looking at my expression.

"He wouldn't admit it though, if he'd been trying to frighten me. Or someone else."

"True but he wasn't lying. I don't think he knew Harry Rook was dead either – he looked shocked He had no idea you'd been arrested."

"That is interesting. Thanks for that, Cagney."

"He trusts me. He made me promise not to tell you where he's holed up. I didn't tell him you already knew. I promised we wouldn't call the cops on him either."

"I wish you hadn't done that. Maybe he could help clear my name?"

"You need to get him to trust you. Talk to him. Perhaps we can find a way to help. Track down his long-lost auntie or something."

"Has he got a long-lost auntie?"

"Dunno. I didn't mean a real auntie."

"Do you think you could get him to talk to me?"

"Give him time. When the cops don't show, then there's a chance."

"Okay," I decided. "Not until after our archaeological adventure then."

She smiled.

While Kelly started chopping vegetables and measuring out spices, I remembered the parcels I still hadn't opened. I grabbed the kitchen scissors and set to them, putting the sketchbook and pastels on the kitchen table and then stacked the packaging materials in the recycling.

"What's that?" she asked, as I sat down at the table.

"I bought a few things I needed," I said, "New rucksack, and some bits and pieces. While I was at it, I added in a sketchbook and pastels for you."

She stopped what she was doing at the cooker and came over to the table. She sat down opposite me and looked at the art supplies.

"You stupid cow," she said, quietly.

"I thought you didn't have anything with you, and while I'm studying..." My voice trailed off as I saw she was really angry.

"I'm sorry," I said. "I can see you're angry, but I don't understand."

"Your sort never do," she said. "You've never had to take charity."

I was hurt. "It's not charity," I said. "It's a gift for a friend."

"Just a spoilt little rich girl," she said. "Already I can never pay you back. How do you think that makes me feel?"

I picked them up and put them on the kitchen dresser, out of the way.

"You know where they are if you change your mind. But no matter, I can always use them. I'm sorry I upset you, Kels. I really didn't—"

The smoke alarm interrupted my apology. I sprang into action and threw a damp tea towel over the flaming pan, and then I asked Kelly to remove the battery from the alarm, fetching her a chair. The smell of burned curry was overpowering, so we opened doors and windows and retreated to the living room.

"I'm sorry," she said, laughing from sheer relief. "I didn't mean to try to burn your house down."

"Oh God," I said. "Imagine if we'd needed the fire brigade. We'd both be back in Brookfields in no time."

After we stopped laughing hysterically, we gave in to the inevitable and ordered an Indian from the takeaway.

"I really didn't mean what I said, you know. It's a sore nerve, that's all, that I can't pay my way."

"Kels, you don't have to worry. I do get it, or at least I'm trying to. But you have no idea how much better I've felt since you arrived. I felt so alone. And you know you pretty much saved my life in Brookfields."

She shrugged it off, but it was the truth.

I went back to my studies, and Kelly picked up the sketch book and opened the pastels and started to play with them.

I warned her I was going to use the mobile dongle – but only for a few emails. She didn't even seem to mind. Getting all involved in this was good for us both, I thought. I should get myself accused of murder more often.

My email pinged as soon as I logged on. From the Prof, Matt, with a few attachments. Photographs of the skyphos, and an email describing our visit to the silversmith and what had transpired. Adding that he was taking the skyphos up to London for safe keeping, but that so far he'd had no luck tracking down the location of the replica. Perhaps there'd be something in Grandma's records?

Well, that was interesting. Even before I'd done anything he'd acted sensibly, making me feel safe. All the same I did what I planned and emailed Suhad and Mr Harvey, and forwarded them the photos of the skyphos, together with the news that it was the genuine article.

I thought back to the wording of Grandma's will and the trust. I'd ask to read it again, but I was pretty sure that Grandma had intended me to put this right. That was why she hadn't left it to mother. She knew I cared about the historical record. Just like she did. That was why she made me promise when she was dying.

THIRTY-TWO

NEXT MORNING I was woken up by my phone. Again. I hid my head under the duvet until it stopped ringing, but it immediately started again so I gave in to the inevitable. Suhad had read my email and wanted me to come in to the office for an urgent consultation about Grandma's collection. Apparently, Mr Harvey had turned up some new information about the boutique too.

I was slightly amused that I was on police bail accused of murder, and yet still the rest of my family's stuff took precedence. Grandma's collection called for an urgent meeting. My mother's boutique. Even in the middle of my own personal disaster – and really, this one was beginning to outperform being sectioned – they still cast a long shadow over my life.

Kelly decided to stay at the farm, but she walked with me down to the bus stop. I suggested she try to talk to Daniel again, but she said it was best not to pressure him too much, and reluctantly, I agreed.

Mr Harvey and Suhad were all business.

First on the agenda, my mother's boutique.

"We've done some preliminary investigations," Mr Harvey said. He had dark shadows under his eyes and looked very sombre. "It appears that the properties concerned are indeed now officially owned by a Mrs Papasavas. Our first look at the documentation shows that they were sold by your Grandma's Personal Management Company back in May."

"That was when I was in hospital," I said.

"However, Mrs Papasavas didn't purchase the properties until July." He paused.

"Strange," I said.

"We uncovered the middle step at the Land Registry. Ownership of the property was first transferred to a company with a very similar name, Hunter Family Investments. The new company had all the same officers, Company Secretary, Directors, the whole shebang. Including me. I didn't provide the signature, although it does look right."

"That would be around the time my mother was living at the house," I said, struggling to keep my voice even. "She would have had access to everything."

"Shortly after the new ownership was filed at the Land Registry, ironically accompanied by filings of new paperwork intended to minimise the chances of fraud, another director was added to the new company."

"My mother," I said.

"I'm afraid we've let you down, my dear. This fraud was perpetrated on our watch, and we didn't spot it."

I tried to reassure him. "The timing was perfect," I said. "The accounts were filed at the end of the tax year as usual, and in normal circumstances this wouldn't have been uncovered until next April. It's not your fault."

"Thank you for your confidence, Alice. It's still our responsibility. You can be assured we will take all the necessary legal steps to put things right."

"Absolutely," I said. "I would like the chance to speak to my mother first, if that's okay. In case there's some explanation."

He nodded, and I relaxed. The last thing I needed was for her to be spooked.

Next. What to do about the collection that was still in the cupboards at Grandma's house. After some discussion we agreed that Suhad would contact the Metropolitan Police's Art and Antiques unit for advice, and meanwhile we would go together and bring everything to the office and put it in the safe.

"I'm sure DI Collingwood will enjoy this extra call on his time," I said. But Suhad phoned and arranged for DC King to meet us there instead. At my prompting, Suhad reminded her to sort out the exclusion zone. I didn't want to be arrested for noncompliance with the terms of my bail.

"Even if the rest of it is real," I said, "Only the silver platters would be of exceptional value. And the skyphos."

"I don't understand how Frances had the genuine article," Mr Harvey said. "I can't even begin to imagine what it means."

"Were you wise to entrust it to Professor Buckley?" Suhad added. "Surely if anyone knows how to sell something of that sort privately, it would be him."

"He asked me the very same thing, why I trusted him."

"Clever," Suhad said. "Too clever, maybe."

"Look what he did," I said. "He took the photos, he emailed them to me from his usual university email account. The silversmith knows too. This is not the behaviour of a thief."

Drily, Mr Harvey added. "I'm glad that at least you thought about it."

"Mostly I'm worried about what it means about Grandma. May we have a look at the terms of the will again, please?"

Mr Harvey looked quizzical, but asked Suhad to fetch the file from the office.

She switched on the computer, and found the electronic file, smiling and tutting at Mr Harvey's old-fashioned ways.

He grumbled. "I prefer the paper version." He read the relevant sections aloud to us, in that serious legal tone that last time had been somewhat drowned by mother's hysterical reaction. *It should have been me* was the sentence I most clearly remembered from that day.

"Finally, my Roman antiquities. I leave this very special collection to my granddaughter, Alice Hunter, secure in the knowledge that she will care for them better than I have. Restoration is a difficult task, but it is not one beyond her ability. I am satisfied by whatever decision she makes as to their disposal."

"Very interesting," Suhad said. "I notice there's no mention of reproduction antiquities there."

"Restoration is an interesting choice of word," I said.

Mr Harvey sounded a bit grumpy. "There was no reason to analyse the precision of the language so clearly. I saw the insurance documents. The skyphos was clearly valued as a fine reproduction at a few thousand pounds. What would the real thing be worth?"

"According to Professor Buckley, it's hard to judge, but we are talking about more than a million. His friend at the British Museum is the expert."

They both looked at me.

"Are you sure?" Mr Harvey said.

"That was a while ago. Do the values of antiquities go down as well as up, like the stock market?"

None of us knew.

Suhad, tentative now. "Is it possible that the murder of Harry Rook had something to do with this? Did he know, do you think?"

"I don't know. He never came to the house – at least, not while I was there. Before or after Grandma died. When we met to talk about the trust we usually did it in the cafe, Tamsin's place. He explained to me then, he wouldn't do anything that hurt Julia and she didn't want him going into Grandma's house."

"He must have done so once," Mr Harvey said. "She was pretty much bed bound when she talked him into taking on the trust."

"That must have been on one of the days Grandma persuaded me to take a break," I said. "She made such a fuss about me needing some time for myself that I gave in. Who knows what else she got up to?"

Suhad laughed. "She must have been some lady. I do wish I'd been able to meet her."

"Anyway," I said. "It can't have had anything to do with that, can it? I don't think killing Harry would accomplish anything that couldn't be more easily accomplished by a bit of breaking and entering."

"I still think we should let the local police know," Mr Harvey said. "In case it is connected to the murder."

"We've no real evidence of any criminal activity yet," Suhad pointed out. "All circumstantial, and only relating to Frances Hunter. I think we hold fire while we gather more information. But I will arrange an informal chat with the Arts and Antiques guys."

"Storing the items here and entrusting the most valuable to Professor Buckley and the British Museum is probably wise," Mr Harvey said. "It demonstrates that you have every intention of dealing with this legally and in the open."

"The most important thing, I think, is that Grandma intended me to sort this out. I know what she valued. Many times when we were in museums she said the same thing. The objects have a value that goes beyond their beauty and the craftsmanship. She valued knowledge for its own sake. I think she wanted me to make some kind of restitution, perhaps because she couldn't face the music herself."

"I never knew Frances to back off from a fight," Mr Harvey said. "But perhaps you're right. She certainly was making some kind of statement in that will – though it wasn't something I noticed when drawing it up, or at the reading."

"One more thing," I said. "The replica of the skyphos is probably in America. Professor Buckley is trying to track it down. And when he does, he's planning to go to America to try to find out what happened and to negotiate a solution. I'd really like to go too."

Suhad spoke. "Alice, I really think that's going to be impossible, unless the police make more progress on the murder inquiry. I'm sure that you won't be allowed to leave the country while you're on bail and accused of murder. I don't think you'd get an American visa, either."

I hadn't thought of that – had simply hoped I could charm DI Collingwood into giving permission.

"Is there anything we can do to find out what's happening? Do they know yet how he was murdered?"

"Sorry, Alice. That's not how it works. They won't tell us anything until they're good and ready."

I thought about stamping my feet and saying it wasn't fair, but restrained myself.

"The other thing, is, well, do you think we ought to tell Julia about the Roman stuff?"

"Absolutely not," Mr Harvey said. "It was made completely clear in your grandmother's will that her antiquities collection was a personal bequest and separate to the Trust."

"Okay," I said. "I wondered if she might know anything about it. Although I don't think Harry did…"

"She's also continuing to be difficult about your allowance and your other plans," Mr Harvey said. "It's a lot of nonsense but she was trying to make out that the Trust in your name should be forfeited because your murder of Mr Rook makes it ill-gotten gains. All nonsense, even if you did murder Mr Rook."

"Which I didn't."

"Certainly not," Suhad said hurriedly. "Mr Harvey was speculating about the law, not about your innocence. Of which we have no doubt."

"Thank you," I smiled. "I did know that was what he was doing. I don't mind."

Suhad threw up her hands in frustration.

"You should mind!" she actually raised her voice. "You're accepting all this too easily. Scream and shout. Let rip for once. You have to fight to clear yourself, not give in to it all."

Mr Harvey looked at her and smiled. "That's not very lawyerly, my dear. In fact, that's the first time I've seen it get to you. Perhaps Alice is handling it. I don't see what else she could be doing."

"I know what you mean, though, Suhad," I said. "I feel it too. Like I am swayed by every breeze. I don't feel in charge of my life at all."

"None of us is," Mr Harvey said. "Control is an illusion, and we are all subject to the whim of the forces of nature. Right now, you're being buffeted by a dramatic storm, and not the usual occasional showers."

THIRTY-THREE

BACK AT THE farm, Kelly went off to explore, and I settled down with my books. She was looking forward to the planned site survey and had decided she wanted her own sense of the place first.

I settled down to studying, reading about what it was possible to deduce about a society from the objects that survived. In one experiment, a group of anthropologists analysed the debris left behind by a Cree Indian temporary camp. Simply asking the Cree themselves about the conclusions showed a startling degree of misunderstanding. How much more must we get wrong about civilisations long gone? We can't ask the Romans and Britons who lived in Cuckmere all those years ago what the artefacts we uncover mean, how they were used, why they were discarded – and the stories we're able to piece together will probably have some truth, but we will never know how much.

It was exactly the same problem as the one posed by the way my life was unravelling, I realised. I was trying to piece together Grandma's life from the evidence that was left – and I could no more ask her in person about the skyphos than I could interrogate the original Romano-British owner. The family stuff was even less tangible. Whatever I worked out would be frustrating – always incomplete.

As I couldn't go back to the house, I didn't even have proper access to all the things she left behind. I was sure of one thing though. Unlike the Romans, Grandma had left clues for me. She knew how I thought, how my mind worked. That should give me an advantage. But she hadn't known Harry would be murdered – she'd assumed I'd be able to consult him. There could be many, many missing pieces. Nor could I talk to the one person who knew Harry well – his widow.

I sent an email to Mr Harvey, explaining my thoughts, and wondering if he might, at some point, talk to Julia and ask what Harry had known about the silver. But then, even if he knew everything, he may not have been able to share it with his wife.

As I clicked send, the door opened and Kelly came in, hot and breathing fast. She'd been running.

"Get your skates on," she said, when she finally caught her breath. "Guy. Metal detector. Lane."

I pulled my shoes on and followed her, walking briskly. At first there was no one in sight, but in the distance a movement caught my eye. A dark green Barbour and boots, a tall man. Mark Stockman, maybe? Or someone associated with the Professor. I knew it wasn't him, as he was in London.

"Daniel says he's seen him before," Kelly said, puffing and trying to catch her breath. "With the metal detector. Up on the Beacon."

"Did he recognise him?"

"No, only that he was posh," Kelly answered. "Might be Stockman. I wasn't close enough to see."

"I'll check with the Professor that he hasn't sent anyone over," I said, getting my phone out. I sent a text, and a few moments later the phone rang.

"Is there a problem, Alice?" The Prof spoke, without introducing himself.

"Not really," I said. "My house guest saw someone wandering the field and the lane with a metal detector. I wondered if you might have sent someone?"

"No, I'd have told you," he said. "It doesn't look as if anything's been disturbed, does it?"

"I hadn't thought of that. Give me a few minutes to have a look around and I'll call you back."

I explained to Kelly, and we scrambled over the earthworks, and had a quick look around the field, then back down the lane. There was no sign of anything unusual.

I phoned him back.

"I wonder," he said. "Perhaps it would be possible to arrange some kind of security?"

"There's no funds for that right now," I said.

"I was thinking more of student volunteers, camping out in turns."

"Wait and see, perhaps." I wasn't keen to have Daniel spooked, but couldn't exactly say that out loud. "Whoever he was, he left quickly enough when he saw Kelly, metal detector and all. Perhaps he won't come back, now."

"Promise me you'll be careful," he said. "Let's not forget there's been a murder, and if it was anything to do with your Grandma's collection, you could be in danger."

"I don't think anyone could possibly know," I said. "Only you, me, Kelly, the silversmith and the lawyers."

"Plus whoever Frances told," he added. "Maybe Harry, and whoever he told too."

"I don't think Frances told anyone," I said. "If she was going to confide in anyone, it would have been me."

"Keep an eye open," he said. "Promise?"

I agreed.

"If there's any more visits or any disturbance, we'll sort out that camping rota, alright?"

"Yes, sir," I said to the unresponsive phone. He'd already hung up.

"That's it," I said. "I've had enough of this. I'm going to Mark Stockman's office now. You coming?"

Kelly grinned. "Try and stop me," she said. "I'm your sidekick. And I can call the cops if you don't come out again."

I laughed but made sure she had my spare phone before hustling her down to the bus stop. In its protective case, for her sake, and only to be extracted in a real emergency.

The receptionist was frosty. Perhaps she recognised my voice from the phone call.

"You really should have made an appointment," she said. "Mr Stockman is often out on-site visits. You might have had a wasted journey."

"Is he available?" I asked, smiling sweetly.

"I'll check," she said, and knocked on the office door. A couple of minutes later she was back.

"He'll see you now," she said. As she sat back down, I could hear her disgruntled muttering.

Mark Stockman was all smiles.

"Hello," he said, grasping my hand in both of his. "What can I do for you today? Or do you have good news for me, on the matter of the sale of your properties."

"No, not yet," I said. "I wondered if you'd had any luck finding those photographs of Grandma."

"Sit down, sit down," he said. "As it happens, I do have them here. I found them last night and brought them in to the office. I was going to call you. I just hadn't gotten around to it."

I sat, and as he opened the desk drawer, took a surreptitious glance around the office. Dark green Barbour hanging on a hook by the door, and muddy boots next to them. But no sign of a metal detector.

He opened the photograph album at the page marked by the wide black ribbon. He looked down and smiled, and turning the album around, pushed it across the desk towards me.

"There's a few here, from the nineteen sixties. Including a visit to the US."

As I opened the album, a loose photograph slipped out of the first folio.

I'd seen very few of Grandma as a young woman, and here she must have been in her early twenties. She was dressed in a long white robe and wearing some kind of crown, fashioned out of what looked like silver leaves and twigs. Her hands were crossed on her breast and she was holding a ritual athame. I took a closer look, and smiled. It was the same silver bladed knife I'd seen her use so many times in simple banishing rituals. What a pity it wasn't the skyphos! And behind her, Stockman's grandfather, similarly clad but with a simple gold band around his forehead.

I looked up to check Stockman's reaction.

"I've never seen any photographs of the Cuckmere Coven before," I said. "Thank heavens they aren't sky clad."

"I was hoping you might fill in some of the gaps in my knowledge," Mark Stockman said. "A colourful part of my family history, and yours."

My attempt to embarrass him had clearly fallen short – he was still determined to be charming. Well, he still wanted the house.

"Grandma wasn't keen on talking about that time in her life," I said.

"Oh? I understood you were personally involved in the local pagan community."

So the charming mask had slipped. All this could be in reference to was the outbreak of satanic vandalism, and the implications in the local paper.

"If there is still a local coven, I have no knowledge of it. I thought you might."

I looked at him, hoping to see some discomfort, but there was none.

I turned a page in the album, to see another photograph of Grandma. She was beautifully dressed. I recognised the Balenciaga coat as one my mother had sold when I was in hospital. For the first time, I realised how angry I still was about that. That she had given me no choice in the matter, no option to pick out a couple of pieces to keep. That coat was one of Grandma's favourites. I wished I still had it.

Smoothing over the tension, Stockman spoke again. "It must have been some kind of business trip, and your grandmother was needed to look after the children."

I didn't say anything, but I knew Grandma had quit her job much earlier. Not to mention the general unlikelihood of the average nanny wearing couture.

"You have a look of your grandfather," I said, looking at him. I hadn't seen it before, but the resemblance was clear. The same dark hair and eyebrows. The same slightly wide nose and sharp chin.

Stockman laughed. "I've spent my whole life being told I'm a chip off the old block." He looked at me, slightly critically.

"You do remind me of someone," he said. "But I can't put my finger on it. It's not your grandmother though."

I was silent for a moment. I knew who it was now. I'd always been slightly disappointed that I was nothing like Grandma, had long harboured hopes that like the ugly duckling I would grow up transformed, to be like her and Helen, sophisticated, in the Lauren Bacall mould. False hopes, as it turned out.

"Like my father's family, I suppose," I prevaricated.

"I am sorry. Is that rather difficult for you?"

I laughed. "Not in that way, no. I'm not embarrassed. It's more that I've never known them."

"Good. There's never any reason to be ashamed of where we come from," he said.

A well-judged response. I could see why he'd been elected. He moved on swiftly. "On the next page, they're at a museum," he said.

I turned the page, and there it was. The skyphos, with Grandma on one side and Stockman's grandfather on the other. Underneath the photograph, the name of the museum. I smiled.

He was looking at me rather intently, I thought.

"Are you sure there wasn't something going on between them?" I asked. "Seems a bit odd, off to the US together. And your grandmother nowhere to be seen."

"She didn't like having her photograph taken," he said, stiffly. "I'm sure there was nothing like that. It was just business. My grandfather lacked knowledge about the antiquities, and he asked your grandmother to go along as his adviser, I think."

Either she was a nanny or his antiquities adviser. Interesting how the story shifted.

On the next page, was another photograph of them, with a much younger silversmith, but clearly it was the man I'd met. Mr Rushton. It was all starting to hang together.

"Would it be possible to have some copies of these?" I asked. "I have so few photos of Grandma from those days."

"Certainly," he said. "It would be my pleasure. I will get some copies made at the photographer's on the High street."

Always good to send business Mrs B's way.

"In the meantime, if you have a photocopier, I would appreciate one now," I said. I knew I was pushing my luck, but he was keen enough on buying the house to keep me sweet. He buzzed for the receptionist and asked her to deal with it. In a few minutes, she was back, with a handful of colour prints, and the photo album. She passed everything to Stockman, and he dismissed her with a nod of the head.

"These are actually pretty good," he said, passing them over.

"So they are," I said, looking at them. With the scan, the notes underneath the photograph were also reproduced.

"Thank you," I said, standing up. "It was very kind of you to dig those out for me, and to make the copies."

"Our families have obviously always worked well together," he said. "Long may it continue."

He walked with me to the front door of the offices. "Please do call by, any time," he said.

He had that practised charm of the politician, but to be fair to him, he did sound as if he meant it.

Kelly bounded up to me as soon as I came out of the marina offices.

"You were a long time," she said. "I was getting worried."

We went back to our favourite cafe and sat at a quiet table with coffee and cake. I showed her the pictures and told her I thought Stockman genuinely seemed like a decent sort.

"Don't be daft," she said. "He's a politician."

"Maybe that's a touch cynical?" I said. "Anyway, he is right, our families have worked well together. Grandma always had a fondness for the family."

"That was the grandfather and father though, not this guy," she warned. "Maybe, looking at this—" she waved the picture with the skyphos at me. "Maybe the Stockmans have something to do with the big picture."

I scoffed. "If it was the Stockmans who were dodgy, how come it was Grandma who had the real silver?"

Kelly frowned. "None of it really adds up."

She looked again at the photograph of Grandma in her ritual getup. "She was a stunner," she said. "And she looks so regal. I love the headdress, too. Do you still have it?"

"It might be in the house somewhere," I said. "Perhaps it's something which goes with the position. She was High Priestess."

"Witchy woman," said Kelly.

"Let's forget about it for a while," I said. "How about we walk across the Beacon to the beach?"

Walking along the cliffs, I felt a change. Something in me had shifted. Perhaps I would be able to sell Stockman the house. There was a kind of freedom in living at the farm. I had a fresh start – a chance to make my own kind of life. All that was in my way, apart from being under suspicion of murder, were a few ties to the past. Maybe they could be severed.

Kelly was still fascinated though, looking down from the coastguard lookout at the back view of the house.

"I wish I could go in there," she said. "It's impossible to imagine what it must have been like, living so close to the man she loved."

"I don't think she loved him during my lifetime," I said, drily. "I don't see it as some great doomed romance."

"There must have been some deep emotion there."

I didn't know. I couldn't get my head round it. I've never really had those kinds of deep feelings for anyone – only a succession of crushes.

I suppose I'm afraid of intimate relationships – and considering the examples I've had, for good reason.

We walked down the hill to the beach, and sat on a bench, looking out to sea. More of the amusement arcade had disappeared – demolished. Everything really was changing.

Gazing at the horizon relaxed my eyes, and briefly, I closed them, oblivious to the world around.

I felt that prickling sensation at the back of my neck, of being watched.

A familiar voice spoke. I opened my eyes.

"It's the Hunter girl," Julia said, from behind us. "Enjoying your walk? I don't know how you can live with yourself."

I stood up, turned round, and faced her.

"I didn't kill him, Julia. That helps."

"I'm calling the police," she said, tapping away on her mobile keypad. "I'm sure you are breaching the conditions of your bail, walking here, talking to me."

I shrugged.

"I haven't been near Grandma's house," I said. "I'm outside the exclusion zone. I didn't knock on your door. I didn't approach you. You came here to talk to me."

She put her phone away.

"No, go ahead. Call them," I said. She stood looking at me like I was nothing. Less than nothing.

"Grandma's house," she said. "Is that what you call it? The local kids call it the Witch House. We called it the Bitch House. That was Harry's name for it, and it was spot on, wasn't it? Three generations of women, none of them capable of love. All bent out of shape and twisted by hatred."

I flinched.

"The truth hurts," she said. "Good."

"Try this truth then," I said. "Harry agreed to be a trustee. He looked after my interests. He asked you to give me a chance, didn't he?"

She looked at me and stayed silent.

I raised my voice, insistent. "Didn't he?"

"Yes," she said. "But then you murdered him."

"Julia, please. Think about it for a moment. I asked for funds to pay a private detective, and Mr Harvey tells me you refused, on the grounds that you couldn't in all conscience pay to have someone work to clear my name. I'm asking you in person this time. I'm pleading with you. You choose the detective agency. You and Mr Harvey. You give them clear instructions that they are to search for the truth, nothing less. Because I cared about Harry too. Even though I didn't know he was my grandfather while he was alive. I liked him. I trusted him. I thought of him as a friend. And I want to know who killed him. I want justice for him. I'm sure you do too."

I could hear Kelly muttering behind me. "Perhaps you can't handle the truth."

Julia had ignored her until now.

"And who are you, exactly? Are you trying to say I murdered my husband?"

"No one. Alice's mate."

"Exactly. No one. Why would I listen to you?"

"Because if Alice hadn't found the body, family are always the first suspects. Maybe you're on the suspect list already. A private detective might clear you too."

I decided to add my halfpenny-worth. "People are already talking about how quickly you sold the business." Well, it was true. Kelly and I were people.

She was silent, looking at me, looking at Kelly, weighing things up.

"Can I ask you something? One question?" I said.

"You can ask," she said. Which was progress of a sort.

"Does my mother know?"

"Does she know what? That Harry was her father?"

I said nothing.

"Answer me first," she said. "Then I'll think about it. Why aren't you asking her?"

This was difficult. I'd not said it out loud to anyone, not even myself, but my suspicions were growing, taking on a life of their own. I was still hoping I was wrong, and that I wouldn't have to confront Helen.

Talking to Julia felt like a betrayal, but I had to do it, for my own sake. I had to try to find out. Somehow, I knew the only chance I had was if I stuck to the truth.

I smiled, because that reminded me of something Harry once said, that I hadn't understood at the time. "You're so like Julia. Even though it would annoy her beyond measure, you really are like two peas in a pod. I've never known anyone else with such regard for the truth. Who would tell the truth and shame the Devil."

"I could ask her, but I couldn't trust her answer. I know you will tell the truth, if you know it."

"How do you know that?" she demanded.

Funny. The one thing that had seemed to make me so vulnerable, admitting I didn't trust my own mother – that had almost no impact on her.

"Harry," I said. "He talked about you a lot. He wanted me to get to know you. I already said that."

"I know he did," she snapped. "I told him what I'm telling you. I have no interest in getting to know any of Frances' brats, daughter or granddaughter. As for your mother… Harry didn't tell her, because I asked him not to do so. He didn't tell you for the same reason. Even though he begged me, I wouldn't allow it. You claim that you didn't know, so I guess that means Frances didn't tell you. Would she have told your mother something she wouldn't tell you? I would guess from the terms of the trust that she thought more highly of you than of your mother. Does that help?"

"Not really," I said. "I'm pretty sure there are other people who know, but not many."

"Who else?" Julia demanded.

"DI Collingwood and the police, for starters. Did you tell them?"

"I didn't volunteer the information," she said. "But when the DNA evidence came back, I couldn't lie."

Ah, so she could lie by omission then. I guess none of us avoid that one, even if we do have a fetish for the truth. All those things I'd never said. Maybe one day I would say some of them, if only to see if the whole world really would implode. Sometimes I think the world is held together by a network of lies, and that a single spoken true word could make the whole edifice collapse, like a game of ethical Jenga.

"I think Mr Harvey may know. Although he wouldn't tell me, because I expect Grandma asked him not to."

"Don't you think it's been hard enough, all these years, without all and sundry knowing? With your grandmother and her architecture of revenge under my nose. Seeing your mother, and then you, grow up – and all that time I failed him as a wife. I failed to provide him with the child he wanted."

"I hadn't thought about it," I pointed out. "I haven't had time for it all to sink in properly. I've been accused of murder. I've had limited capacity to consider how everyone else's life has been affected. How much time have you spent wondering what it's like to suddenly discover your life has been built on a huge lie?"

She nodded, slightly.

I hit back. "I do know my grandmother was difficult. I loved her, yes, but she was hard work. But she wasn't the only one in this. If Harry was my grandfather, then he had sex with her. I'm guessing he betrayed both of you."

"She must have known he was spoken for," Julia said. "It wasn't a secret that we were engaged. It was in the local paper."

"He certainly knew," I pointed out.

We both eyed each other in silence.

I tried one last time. "I didn't kill him, Julia."

She was silent for a moment or two.

"Neither did I," she said.

Kelly spoke, "Me neither." Simultaneously, Julia and I turned and glared at her.

"Seriously, I don't think either of you did. I believe you both.'"

Something about Julia's stance relaxed, and I felt some of the tension drain from me too. I wasn't expecting a miracle, but I felt reassured. There was a change. A softening. And if Julia could start to believe in my innocence, then there was still hope.

"I'll talk to Mr Harvey," she said. "We'll sort out that detective. I want to know who killed him too." Then she turned and walked away.

"Thank you," I called after her.

She didn't turn round, but I heard her voice. "Take care, Alice," she said. I think that was the first time I ever heard her address me by my name.

We watched as she disappeared in the distance. Her shoulders slumped as she walked past the hut, and I felt a stab of guilt that I had even wondered. Harry had loved her, I knew that. I guess she'd loved him too.

Kelly said, "Shall we walk back to the farm?"

"I thought you wanted to see the house?"

"Now you're getting a proper detective, you don't need me."

"Don't be silly, I'll always need you. Without you here, Julia would never have opened up so much."

"I did nothing," she said. "But let's go home."

She strode off in roughly the right direction, and exactly as DI Collingwood had, she paused to read the Nature Reserve information board.

"Kittiwakes," she said. "I thought they were seagulls."

"No such thing as a seagull," I said, parroting Grandma's words. "The everyday ones are herring gulls. The kittiwakes are smaller."

THIRTY-FOUR

THE PROFESSOR AND a couple of my fellow students were coming over to the farm for our first site survey the next day. Introduction to Fieldwork. Anticipation made it difficult to fall asleep.

Kelly was up before me, sitting at the kitchen table drinking coffee and reading the paper.

Rubbing my eyes and yawning, I said. "Is there any coffee left?"

She started, and hurriedly folded the paper over. "I'll get you one," she said, jumping to her feet. "You sit down."

She carried the newspaper over to the recycling bin, hesitated a moment, then put it down on top. All the time she carried on talking, abnormally cheery for the time of day.

"Scrambled eggs?" she asked. "Or toast and jam?"

"Kelly," I said. "What's in the paper?"

She picked it up, reluctantly, and put it in front of me.

"Sorry," she said.

I laughed. "You weren't subtle. But it's not your fault. It's better I know the worst."

"I suppose," she said. "It's horrible."

"I saw what people were saying online. It can't beat that."

But it did.

The first thing I recognised was a school photograph. It was the one the paper had used when my school had shared the news that I was one of the pupils at Cuckmere High School offered a place at Oxford University.

"Secret history of woman arrested in connection with the murder of Harry Rook."

"Alice Hunter is currently on police bail, after being arrested in connection with the death of Harry Rook. The Cuckmere Herald can exclusively reveal hitherto unknown details of her family life, and her breakdown that led to her being sectioned under the Mental Health Act."

Ugh. It was all innuendo. The damning words from my mother that had been in the online version of the story were repeated. It all made me look as if I was a danger to society, implying the fire had been some kind of unhinged attempt at arson, deliberately attempting to send the Beacon up in flames.

There was a reference to the Cuckmere Coven. There would be. Without accusing me outright, the story highlighted that the outbreak of satanic vandalism had strangely stopped when I was in hospital.

The meat of the story was simply that I came from a broken family, the product of two generations of unmarried mothers. That when I discovered I lived across the road from my secret paternal grandfather, Harry Rook, it had a catastrophic effect on my already fragile psyche.

There were all kinds of seedy speculation about the relationship between Harry and my Grandma. Imaginative speculation that Harry might also have been a member of the Cuckmere Coven and that there had been skyclad hanky panky on the Beacon. How living in a house of adultery had warped my mother's life, and then mine.

There were more photographs of my childhood. All from school. And all of this information had been provided, it said, by a source close to the Rook family.

Julia, I thought at once. Then realised that was impossible – she wanted the news of Harry's paternity kept private even more than I did. I didn't think my mother had anything so sentimental as childhood photos of me, although I suppose it was possible. On balance, I thought it was more likely to be Tamsin. No wonder she had resisted all my attempts to talk to her, ignored all my texts.

I'd almost forgotten Kelly even existed, and I was startled as she coughed when I started tapping on the keypad of my phone.

"Who are you texting?" she asked. "I'm not being nosy, only if it's the paper, silence might be the best strategy."

"Tamsin," I said.

"You think it was Tamsin?"

I put the phone down and looked up.

"Who else could it be?" I asked. "It couldn't be Julia. She doesn't want anyone to know. Tamsin is the only other person who knew about Harry, who would want to hurt me, and who would have my school photographs."

"Will texting her help?"

"It will make me feel better," I said.

I pressed send.

"I'm really glad that no one seems to have worked out where I'm living," I said.

"Me too," said Kelly. "I don't want to be outed either."

"You're a friend who's staying with me," I said. "It's not as if you have a brand on your forehead."

"Escaped lunatic?" she suggested. "I could have a tattoo."

"People would think it was a joke," I said. "Unless they knew you."

"Isn't it against the law," she said, "For newspapers to publish stories when there's going to be a trial?"

"Maybe," I said. "I'll call Suhad and ask her."

After a short conversation I was a bit reassured. Suhad would send the local newspaper a strongly worded letter, telling them that if they were to continue that I would have no choice but to sue them.

"There's every possibility that today's story crosses the line, maybe even breaching the Contempt of Court Act. I don't think they will do it again, and once this is all over, you might well have a case against them for defamation."

"The main thing is to stop them from doing it again," I said. "I can't bear how people will look at me now."

Kelly heard the crack in my voice, and stood up, put her arm around my shoulder and squeezed.

I felt comforted, both by Kelly's hug, and Suhad's promise that she'd deal with it. Even if she was humouring me.

"Anyway, we have some fun today, to take our minds off this bollocks," I said. "You're coming along, right?"

"So we're paragliding then?" Kelly asked.

"Do I look crazy?"

We both dissolved into giggles, as usual, patching up the open wounds the only way we knew how.

As we tidied up after breakfast, we heard a car draw up outside. They were early – it was only half-past eight. We both grabbed our coats and almost ran outside into the cool October sun. It was a fine day for it.

The Prof got out of his car and crossed the yard to meet us. There were a couple of vaguely familiar faces – probably students from the open day. "Good, that'll be Sam," he said, as the noise of a second car approaching interrupted us.

I introduced Kelly and the Professor. "Another amateur archaeologist?" he asked. "Most of our volunteers are at their day jobs today, so the more the merrier."

Soon I was in the front passenger seat of Sam's car, watching Professor Buckley, Kelly, and the two students walking up the lane. Well, the rest were walking – Kelly was almost bouncing. Her initial shyness with the Professor had quickly dissipated.

"We'll let them get ahead," Sam said. "I don't want them to think I might run them over, however many points I'd earn." He grinned. "Anyway, I wanted to talk to you."

That sounded ominous.

"Your coin. A rough estimate, it's worth around fifty grand. You can put it back in your pendant if you like."

He handed me the coin in a small velvet purse.

"I don't think I can. I had no idea." I put it in my jeans pocket. I would have to think about what to do with it later.

"It's a pity that we can't be sure about where it was found," Sam said.

"Sorry," I said.

"What for? It's not your fault." Sam continued, "I was pretty excited by it, nevertheless. It's not often that such a rare Roman coin shows up."

"Maybe it didn't – this time," I pointed out.

"What do you think your Grandma's game was, exactly," he asked. "That skyphos. Well, I am speechless."

I put my head in my hands.

"I really don't know," I said. "I can't get my head around it. I became interested in archaeology and history because of Grandma. Specifically, because of that coin. I thought she was an amateur history buff. She talked about how she wished she'd had the chance to study…."

"And you were to do that for her," he said, gently. "Are you sure it's your own dream you're pursuing, and not hers?"

"How can I be sure?" I asked. "It's been my dream for so long…."

He smiled. "Doesn't matter really," he said. "I thought it was important someone asked you to think about it. Matt certainly wouldn't – it's only a lack of interest in his subject he would have doubts about."

I laughed. "And you?" I said.

"I love it too, but I am aware there are other worlds. Don't forget you have choices. Right now it seems clearing up the mystery around your grandmother seems to be a driving necessity."

I nodded. "I don't know if Matt told you, but I've tracked down the museum in the US, where they have a skyphos that must be the fake one. Perhaps there's a loose end there that will unravel some more of it."

"That's a start," he said.

"There's a connection with the Stockman family too. Our local MP. His grandfather was in the photographs of the skyphos, along with my Grandma." I didn't mention the other photograph.

"Ooh, a juicy scandal might prove a threat to his political career. Rising star of the right, isn't he? Perhaps there's some leverage there?"

"Maybe. But he does seem awfully interested in the Roman stuff. We saw him up the lane here with a metal detector, at least we think it was him, and he's been spotted on the Beacon too."

"Ah," said Sam. "Hoping to discover where your grandmother unearthed her treasures, perhaps? Even if he doesn't know she had the real skyphos. You might try to find out what his family stories were about the museum visit and the photos."

"I tried talking to him, but he didn't say much," I said. "I thought they might have had an affair, his grandfather and my grandma. He wouldn't tell me, that's for sure. He wants to buy Grandma's house."

"If the Professor's right, perhaps it's the farm he should be after."

"He is, too." I'd forgotten that – and another piece clicked into the jigsaw. "At our last meeting he added it in to his offer, to sweeten the deal."

My phone pinged. A text from Tamsin. *No idea what you're on about.*

"Excuse me a moment," I said, then I tapped out an answer.

School photos in the Herald? Had to be you.

That, she ignored. An admission of guilt, or remembering she'd said she wanted nothing to do with me.

Someone who used to care about me was doing her best to do me harm. No wonder I was hurting.

"Sorry," I said to Sam. "I'm a bit preoccupied. I don't know if you know…" I paused, not really wanting to talk about it.

"Matt told me about your arrest," he said. "But you've not been charged, have you? I'm sure it's all going to be okay."

"There doesn't seem to be any other suspect, that's all," I said. "There don't seem to have been any witnesses. And now there's a story in the local paper…" I couldn't quite bring myself to talk about the mental health issues.

"Let's go and see what they're up to," he said. "And there's a toy in the car for us to play with."

I directed him up the lane, and we parked by the gate into the North field.

The Prof, Kelly and the two students had clambered up onto the steep embankment and were looking over at the field, but as soon as Sam parked, they clambered back down and mobbed the car.

"Steady on," Sam said, "Give me a bit of space."

As I got out of the passenger side, the rear doors opened at the push of a button and Sam's wheelchair reversed and he made his way down the automatically lowered ramp.

He saw me admiring the huge tyres and rugged construction of his wheelchair and grinned. "Much more fun than my office wheelchair, isn't it?"

The Prof smiled at me. "This is Alice," he said, introducing me to the two students. "And these are my grad students, Adam and Babs."

I recognised Adam – he was the tall blond student who had rushed out of the lecture theatre on the open day, when I'd been hovering in the corridor, too scared to go in. Babs might have been there too, but I didn't remember her – she was short, with red hair and quite bubbly.

We all said hello, but were interrupted by Sam.

"Okay," he said, "You can unload the toys now."

"What is it, exactly?" I asked.

"A drone," he said, grinning.

"A hexacopter, to be precise," the Prof said. "It's a rather special beast that has been adapted for archaeological use. It can fly over the site, and take aerial video, which we can then examine at our leisure, to determine if this is an appropriate site for an exploratory excavation, and if so, where would be best to start."

"Not only at our leisure," Sam said, grabbing his iPad. "We can watch it all on here as we go."

The Prof took charge and directed us all, and we soon had the hexacopter unpacked and in the air. We all gathered round Sam's chair and looked at the landscape around us from a very different angle.

"See these lines," the Prof said, "and these right angles? That's definitely a sign of some kind of human intervention in the landscape. We can hazard a guess at Roman because of the suspicion that there have been some interesting Roman finds in this area."

"And on the Beacon," Adam said. "There are some coins in the local museum, found up on the Beacon in the Second World War," he added.

I smiled at him. "I spent my childhood scrabbling around up there because of those coins," I said.

"Did you find anything?" Adam asked.

I was evasive. "I did find a coin," I confessed. "But now I think it's possible my grandmother planted it there."

Adam laughed. "That was kind of her," he said.

"It's an interesting idea though," I said. "Perhaps we should consider having the drone survey the Hill too?"

"Not a bad idea, Alice," the Prof said.

"Hey, what's that?" Professor Buckley asked. "I'll take the 'copter in closer, for a better look."

We all watched intently as the hexacopter circled around the area.

"The ground's been disturbed, and recently. You've not been doing any freelance digging, Alice?"

Before I could answer, Kelly said, "That guy with the metal detector was up this way. The developer. We didn't check the far side of the field."

"Mark Stockman," I said. "I can't really see him actually getting his hands dirty, though."

Babs said, "That was why we were going to camp out here. I was going to ask you where – our gear is in Professor Buckley's car."

"Looks like up by this field might be a good spot," I said. "If it's really necessary."

"It looks like it might be," the Prof said. "But let's find out more. We have enough footage to study later, now, so let's put the 'copter away, and have a very informal exploratory dig in that disturbed patch of ground."

I was worried about how Sam's wheelchair would cope over the rough ground into the field, especially as it was muddy, but he and the Prof got on with it, after directing the rest of us in the proper packing away of a hexacopter.

Babs went to back to the Professor's car, and brought a couple of buckets with various tools, and Adam collected a rucksack. He unpacked some finds bags and pens, and pegs and tape. I was reminded of the crime scene technicians, after I'd found Harry's body.

Breathe.

Count.

This was upsetting. My anxiety returned with a vengeance, making me realise it hadn't been as bad the last couple of days.

The worst that could have happened was the destruction of a potentially valuable archaeological site. The damage was small and contained. He was an archaeological vandal. But so was Grandma.

Without the hexacopter's aerial view, we might never have spotted the disturbed ground. It was well off the beaten track, on the far side of the fallow field. Sam and the Professor both started to take extensive photographs of the area, and then under direction, Adam, Babs and Kelly staked out a large square, with metal pegs and string.

The Prof cut a square section outside the staked-out area, where the ground had not been disturbed.

"This is for comparison purposes," he said. "Let's see if it shows up anything of particular interest."

The cross section was photographed, and the layers discussed. The earth was filtered through a huge sieve – as if we were gardening or panning for gold. There were a few loose flints – all unworked stone. Nothing of any interest.

Kelly said, "This is exciting. I'm hooked."

I mock punched her, knowing she was drooling over the Prof rather than the digging.

Now the Professor moved to the disturbed earth. "Think of it as a learning opportunity,' he said, kneeling and calling us all to watch. As he worked, he described the process of using a trowel, and the things he was looking for. "It's not only a matter of artefacts," he said. "Especially in a case like this when it's possible that something was there and has been removed. We compare the colour of the earth to our cross section and see how much the layers have been redistributed. We can see here, for instance, that it's a relatively shallow disturbance, and – Oh!"

We all peered closer, but I couldn't see anything.

"I've never seen anything like this before," he said. He carefully used the trowel to move more of the soil to one side, and I saw a glimpse of bloody fur. My stomach turned, and I heaved. I ran to the edge of the field and threw up in the hedge. It was the marmalade cat that had been staked to my lawn. I knew it, even though I couldn't prove it.

I grabbed a tissue and wiped my face and shoved it in my pocket, then walked back to the group, who all looked at me, concerned. Kelly came across and put her arm around me.

The Professor continued to work, until he had uncovered the whole thing. The dead cat. He stood up and looked at me. "I'm thinking what you were thinking, aren't I?" he said.

"If you were, you'd be throwing up by the hedge," I joked, grimly.

"It's more of a crime scene, than an archaeological find. I think I should call the police. What's his name? DI Collingwood?"

Adam spoke up. "A dead cat, that's not a crime, is it? Okay, it was wrong to bury it on your land, but…"

The Prof looked at me, and I nodded permission.

"Alice has a stalker," he said. "She found a tortured cat in her garden the day she was arrested. Only in between her finding it and the police turning up, the cat's body disappeared."

"Crikey," Adam said, baffled.

Questions were running through my head at speed. Who could have buried it here? Why? Did they expect us to find it? Was it, I thought, feeling absolutely chilled with fear, part of a plan, to prove me mad and get me sectioned again, or to somehow frame me for Harry's murder?

THIRTY-FIVE

"I STILL THINK I should call the police," the Professor said. "Are you sure it's the same cat, Alice?"

I really didn't want to look any more closely, but I stepped forward and looked down.

"It's the same colour," I said. "And isn't that dried blood in the poor thing's belly, where it was staked to the ground?"

"There's no wooden stake. I don't want to disturb anything though, if the police may want to take a look."

"Best ask them," I said.

"It will confirm the existence of the cat," the Prof said. It was kindly meant, I thought.

I said nothing. It might to him, and to me. To the police it might confirm something worse. Perhaps they would think it some bizarre ritual. Or that I tracked a ginger cat down after I was released and buried it here, then arranged for it to be found to exonerate me. Or maybe they would think I'd done it to prove to them I wasn't crazy.

I knew I hadn't put it there, but someone had. Was I intended to find it? Not many people knew I was at the farm, which made the list of suspects very short.

Kelly was convinced Daniel hadn't killed a cat – she'd been sure of that. Yet he had drawn the stalkerish pictures. He knew how to snare rabbits, and he had snares. There was a link to him somehow. I had to speak to him.

As the Professor tried to raise a signal on his mobile, and the others huddled around trying not to look at the cat, I took Kelly quietly aside.

"I really do need to talk to Daniel," I said. "I know you said it wasn't a good idea to push it, but I have to know about the cat. I have to ask him if he was there when Harry was killed. If…" My voice trailed off. I didn't want to say it out loud. I knew what it was like to be falsely accused – I didn't want to rush in and do the same thing to someone else. Especially not to a grief-stricken child.

"I don't think it's him," she said. "But he can't camp out in the barn forever. I'll try."

I bit back my instinctive response. Her situation wasn't exactly the same – Kelly was an adult, and I knew only too well what she'd face when she went back. Daniel was different. No matter what he'd done, he was a minor. He needed a home and emotional support. I wondered where his mother was.

I knew where mine was.

She was walking across the field towards us. There was someone with her. I couldn't recognise who from this distance, but I could tell my mother from the way she moved. Who else would walk through a muddy field in stilettos?

I didn't want her to see the cat. I didn't want her questions, I didn't want the worried look on her face. I didn't want the suspicion and all the fuss that would ensue. Somehow it would all turn out to be my fault in some way I couldn't defend.

"I think we should move back to the farmhouse, and talk there," I said to the Professor. "My mother's here, and I'd like to deflect her. The fewer people know about this the better."

"Right," he said. "Anyway, I can't get a signal. Coffee break in the kitchen, then?"

"Perfect," I said.

I left them to pack up the tools, and I set out across the field to intercept my mother, trusting that they would follow.

Oh my God, I recognised her companion. It was my case worker, Claire. Gee, thanks mother.

My mother and Claire stood still, waiting. Kelly had caught up with me.

I whispered to her, "Does she know you? It's my case worker, with my mother."

"I don't think so," she said.

"Best not take a chance. If you go via the lane, you can be back to the farmhouse before us all."

The Prof must have heard me, and decided I wanted time alone with my visitors, because he shepherded everyone down the lane. I heard Sam's car start up, and saw Kelly get into his passenger seat. That would give her a bit more time to get out of the way."

I slowed down, not even deliberately. It was automatic, the way one slows down the closer one gets to the dentist's, but even so, I reached them in a matter of a minute or two.

"What brings you out here? I'm not due to see you for at least a week," I said, looking at my mental health worker, but including my mother. I'd been seeing far too much of her recently too.

"No need to be rude, Alice," my mother said. "Claire's only doing her job."

"Who says I was speaking to Claire?" The words slipped out before I could stop them. My mother said nothing, but I was pleased to see it cost her some effort. Her lips became thin and pale.

"Shall we walk back to the farmhouse, and we can have a coffee?" I tried to put some warmth in my voice, but it was too late.

"Your mother was only worried about you," Claire said. "That's why she contacted me."

Oh dear, I was going to pay for that slip of the tongue. Already a black mark against me. Before I knew where I was, I'd be 'lacking insight' into my own condition again.

"Why don't you show us what you were doing?" My mother, showing an interest in archaeology now? Wonders would never cease. "Wasn't that Professor Whatsisname off the telly?"

"I told you I'd signed up for the course," I said. "Remember?"

"I thought it was only an evening class to get you back into the swing before trying for Oxford again," mother said. "I didn't realise it was serious."

I shrugged. What was the point?

"I hope it's not putting you under too much stress," Claire said. "You do need to pace yourself. No need to run before you can walk."

I picked up speed, walking faster across the field. Metaphorical defiance. Perhaps that would be a new symptom.

They kept up with me but didn't have enough breath for talking. Good.

When we reached the lane, I could see the rest of them piling through the farmhouse door. I kept up the pace, worrying a bit now about Kelly.

At the door, I waited politely and followed them in.

The Prof, Sam, Adam and Babs were sitting round the kitchen table with coffee. There was no sign of Kelly – she was upstairs, I hoped.

"I hope you don't mind," the Prof said.

"Not at all," I said, then introduced everyone. "This is my mother, and Claire. Her... friend," I added. The long pause signalled I was lying.

Claire's eyebrows shot straight up, in exaggerated surprise.

"If you'll give us a few minutes, we need to have a brief chat. Then I'll be back to join you," I said, with my biggest fake smile.

I ushered them into the living room, then followed and shut the door carefully. In a quiet voice, I said, "This has got to stop. I am not doing anything wrong. I am busy getting on with my life. I spent enough time in hospital. I am getting my life back together."

"You seem angry," Claire said. "More angry than this visit warrants. Your mother is worried about you and I can see why. For instance, why did you lie to everyone about who I am?"

I looked her in the eye. "You know why."

"Living a lie puts you under more stress, don't you see?"

"I'm not living a lie. How can I be – they've read the paper!" I said, exasperated. "But I don't see the need to remind them constantly. I'm

Alice, the nutter. People come to check up on me all the time in case I go crazy again."

"Another thing. Yes, your next appointment with me is in a week's time, but you are supposed to let me know of changes in your circumstances."

"Last time I saw you was directly after I found Harry. I was going to tell you next week about the new address, which wasn't my choice, anyway. The police requested I move from Grandma's, because of it being so close to Julia's home."

"You were arrested for murder, Alice. That's stressful for anyone. For someone in your position, it's a serious threat to your stability."

"I was arrested but not charged. I didn't kill him."

"You sound paranoid, Alice. Are you taking your medication?"

I opened the door to the kitchen and noticed everyone was quiet. I had perhaps raised my voice. I smiled faintly and went to the kitchen drawer, collected my pill box, and my repeat prescription form and the boxes of tablets.

I took them back into the living room, closing the door behind me, and carefully placed them on the table.

"Let's do a full audit. It's all here. You will be able to work it out, from the pills that are left in the boxes, and the next due date on the repeat prescription form from the doctor."

I knew there'd be the right number there, more or less. Any doses I'd skipped had been flushed down the loo.

"I don't think that will be necessary," Claire said, but my mother was already counting.

Claire put her hand on my arm. I stood there rigid, not daring to respond as I wanted to, and shrug it off. Not wanting to be humoured into submission.

"I think it's time to consider a voluntary admittance," she said. "To get you through this difficult patch."

I ignored Claire and looked at my mother, who was still counting. I knocked the pills out of her hand.

"I'm not the one who can't be trusted with pills, am I, mother? Remember?"

For a moment her face revealed her true feelings, but she got it under control. I don't think Claire saw, which was a pity. It would have been educational for her to see what real anger looks like.

"So now you care about my stability," I continued. "A word from you last time, a promise that you would stay with me for a few days would have been enough to keep me out of hospital."

"You still resent me for that, don't you?" she goaded. "I had other commitments. I couldn't drop everything to come and look after my adult daughter."

"You always had other commitments. Why not now? How is the boutique managing in your absence?" I paused, but there was not a glimmer of nervousness on her face. She was such a good liar. "Why did you bring Claire here today?"

"You mean, what made me think you're losing your grip again?"

"If you like."

"How about this? I hear from Mark Stockman that you're talking to him about selling the house, when you know perfectly well that you can't sell until you're thirty."

I wondered how hard to push her, now that her true worries were coming out, however much she disguised them as concern for me. She was selfish as ever. I made a superhuman effort and bit back the accusation. She wanted to sell the house herself.

"That's not entirely true," I pointed out. "The trust can be broken, with the permission of the trustees."

She stood up and got right into my face.

"You think Julia Rook is going to co-operate with anything you want? You are deluded, my dear daughter."

I wasn't as controlled as I believed. The floodgates opened.

"You thought you could sell the house without my permission last time I was in hospital. Harry Rook stopped you. This time, I've spoken to my lawyer and made it clear that you are not to over-ride my wishes.

Mark Stockman got the message too. So getting me sectioned is not going to work out, mommy dearest. If you need money, all you have to do is ask, and the trustees will consider your request. As Grandma wanted."

She looked at Claire, and said, "See, it's exactly as I said. She's slipping into paranoia again."

Then I looked at Claire. "My mother has no right to come to you with concerns about my health. She forfeited those rights when she handed me over to my grandmother when I was a toddler. There were times I didn't see her for months, years on end. A teenage girl needs to see her mother – I couldn't even phone mine. No one knew where she was. I won't admit myself voluntarily. I am not unwell, I am taking my medication. I am co-operating with my outpatient care plan."

Claire started to look uncomfortable and fidget nervously. Surely they weren't considering sectioning me? A spell in hospital was not what I needed – either for my health or for the sake of proving my innocence. If I admitted myself voluntarily, people would believe either that I'd snapped and killed Harry, or that I was trying to weasel out of the judicial process.

I thought about trying to explain this to Claire but faltered. It would be interpreted as more evidence of paranoia.

My mother said, grudgingly, "It looks as if she's taken her medication. Although she could be flushing them away every day."

I hoped my guilt didn't show on my face.

"Talk about me as if I'm not here, why don't you?" I said. Fortunately, the doorbell rang before she had time to reply, and I opened the door to the kitchen.

Professor Buckley was standing at the open door, and I could hear him talking. I recognised DI Collingwood's voice. So he'd come to look at the cat. I really needed to get rid of my mother and my case worker.

I turned to Claire and said, "I think you should leave now. It looks like we're going to be busy for a while. Perhaps we can continue this at a more convenient time? Your office, at our next scheduled meeting, works for me."

They followed me into the kitchen in time to hear DI Collingwood say to Professor Buckley, "We're not here to see a dead cat. We're here to take Ms Hunter in for further questioning."

THIRTY-SIX

CLAIRE STEPPED FORWARD. She thought she was doing the right thing, to her credit. I thought she wasn't.

"You'll have to make arrangements with the hospital if you need to question Ms Hunter. We were about to collect her things and take her to be re-admitted to Brookfields."

"If you would wait a moment, DI Collingwood," I said, and turned to Claire and my mother.

"I'm going with the police now. I was released on bail, and I am under arrest. It is in my best interests to do this. I have a lawyer, and she will be with me in the interview. I will have someone who is fighting my corner, and who will advise me throughout. That's more than I get in your world, however well-meaning you may be."

My mother looked about ready to explode, but Claire looked a little shamefaced. Perhaps I had got through to her a little.

I then turned to DI Collingwood. "Before we go, I would appreciate it if you would take a few minutes to look at the dead cat. I think it may be the one that was in Grandma's garden the last time you arrested me."

After a short discussion, Collingwood agreed. It was decided that he would walk over to the excavation with the Professor, then decide what action to take. If any.

I was left at the farmhouse with the other policeman to keep an eye on me. Everyone else sat and stood around looking uncomfortable in complete silence. I gave Sam a house key, and returned the coin in its purse, saying that I hoped they would all keep an eye on things while I was gone.

"If Adam and Babs camp over," I said, quietly so my mother wouldn't hear, "They'll want access to the house for water and the loo and so on."

Sam took key and coin and nodded. "That's very trusting of you," he said.

I had trust issues, alright. I would trust anyone and everyone before my mother. "I'm the one who's been arrested for murder. I don't think I'm the one who's trusting."

He patted me on the arm and smiled. That was kind. All the same, they must have doubts. No smoke without fire.

After that, I sat quietly with my thoughts until DI Collingwood returned.

"Let's get you down to the station," he said. "Have you called your lawyer?" he sounded irritatingly cheerful.

The other detective spoke up. "She made no calls, guv. She just handed her house keys over to the guy in the wheelchair."

"There's no reason why I shouldn't have done," I said, sharply. "You turned me out of my home, but the farm is not a crime scene. Nor does my presence here inconvenience Harry's widow."

"Calm down," DI Collingwood said, in a tone of voice guaranteed to provoke the opposite reaction. "You can give your keys to whoever you please. Now call your lawyer, then we can go."

I did as I was told and Suhad agreed to be at the police station within the hour.

"Ready now?" DI Collingwood asked.

"I want to see my mother out first," I said.

My mother came forward as if to hug me, but I flinched and she backed off. She stalked out to her car without another word to anyone. I was more cordial with Claire, out of sheer self-interest, and promised that I would get in touch with her if I was released from police custody.

"If I'm charged, I won't have much say, but I'm sure DI Collingwood will promise to keep you informed."

He looked away, refusing to catch my eye.

I followed the detectives to the police car and got in the back seat. I hadn't had the time or opportunity to talk to Kelly, but she already had a key, and she knew what was needed with Daniel. I couldn't help hoping that he would know something that would help clear me.

From the back of the car, I asked DI Collingwood if he thought it was possible it was the same cat.

"I didn't see it the first time, remember, so I don't even know there was a first cat."

"That's what I told the Professor you'd say," I said. Satisfied. "But you did see the photograph on my phone."

"I know," he said. "In any case, Professor Buckley has agreed to come in and make a statement. He's also going to wait for our scientific support unit to deal with the cat."

"Is that not your job?" I asked.

He turned round and looked at me. Fortunately, we were stuck in traffic. "I've left a police constable with him. I didn't want a moment of this-."

"Haha," I said. "But you were refusing to believe I had a stalker. That cat was staked to the lawn in my garden. The original cat, I mean. And the stake was like the one through Harry's hand..."

He turned and looked at me again. "In the interview room, please," he said. "I don't know why I let you ramble on this way."

I shut up, and kept my face blank, but inside I smiled. I felt sure that in spite of everything he didn't really believe me to be a killer. I was getting through to him.

At the station all my personal belongings were taken by the custody sergeant, again. He gave me a repeat of the lecture on my rights. "You told me all this a couple of weeks ago," I said. "Can't we take it as read?"

"No we can't, Miss Hunter. As you very well know."

He was right. I was taking the piss. It was my way of dealing with my fears. Why on earth had they arrested me again? The longer the investigation had gone on, the more certain I had been that they would find evidence to clear me, not to charge me.

After all, I hadn't done it. I hadn't killed Harry.

DI Collingwood asked me how long it would be until my lawyer arrived, and I said that she'd promised it would be under an hour.

"In that case," he said, "You might as well wait in the interview room. Detective Constable King will bring you a coffee."

"Thanks," I said. I remembered how good the station coffee was.

I sat quietly, going over in my mind the last time I was under arrest, and how I'd found out Harry Rook was my grandfather. I wondered what surprises DI Collingwood had in store for me now.

In less than ten minutes Suhad arrived, and the DI showed her into the interview room to talk to me before we began.

"Okay," she said. "Is there anything else I should know?"

"Yes, probably. I do have something to confess."

"Don't tell me if—"

"Jeez, Suhad, I'm not confessing to murder, for Christ's sake."

She blushed.

"No, it's just, you are bound by client confidentiality, aren't you?"

"Yes," she said. "The usual exceptions. If someone is at risk, especially a child, then I have a duty of care…"

"*At risk* has a broad range of meaning," I said.

It was no use, I would have to keep it to myself then. I couldn't have Suhad deciding that Kelly must go back to hospital for her own good. That wasn't my risk to take – even if it would help me to have someone persuade Daniel to talk to the police. I would have to trust that Kelly and Daniel would overcome their misgivings about the authorities themselves. It was the only way.

"Never mind," I said. "Do you know about the cat?"

She looked bewildered by my sudden change of topic.

"Remember last time we were here, and the police were refusing to believe that I'd found a butchered ginger cat in the garden?"

"The incredible disappearing cat. Yes?"

I explained about the discovery at the dig, and that the Professor was following it up.

"I tried asking DI Collingwood, but he sees it as a diversion. Maybe he even thinks I killed another cat and planted it there for some perverse reason of my own."

"It does seem a bit random, Alice. When a man's been murdered…"

"Not you too!" I said. "The wooden stake is key, don't you see? Putting it in my garden and then moving it to the farm – that's some kind of threat. Someone killed the cat, and it wasn't me. Knowing who and why may help, somehow."

"Do we have any idea why the police have re-arrested you?" Suhad asked.

"I don't. How about you?" I said. Then felt guilty for sniping. She was doing her best, and at least she didn't treat me like I was crazy.

"Not a clue," she said. "Anything else you think I should know?"

"Nothing comes to mind. Some of the archaeology students are camping over at the farm, keeping an eye on things. Someone was seen wandering around with a metal detector, and Professor Buckley wanted some protection for the site."

"Who knew you were surveying the site?"

"A long list of people, I suppose. The Professor and his friend from the British Museum. The archaeology students and anyone they talked to. Mark Stockman. Maybe the people in his office."

Kelly and probably Daniel too, I thought, but didn't say that part aloud.

"Let's get on with it then," Suhad said. "Time to face the music. We can deal with it much better when we aren't in the dark."

"That reminds me," I said. "My mother turned up at the farm earlier, with my case worker. She wanted to have me admitted to the psychiatric unit again. By force if necessary. Sectioned."

"Why?" Suhad looked bewildered.

"For my own good, like last time. Or it's more convenient for her. Perhaps she thought it would stop them arresting me or would protect me if I'm discovered to be guilty of murdering Harry."

"She doesn't really think you did it, does she?"

"Suhad, I don't think anyone has ever been able to fathom what my mother really thinks. Usually it's whatever suits her at the time. Sorry to sound so cynical, but I'm getting tired of pretending."

"No, that's alright. Best to be honest with me – it helps me to help you. Remember, I know from the terms of your Grandma's will and the Trust, that your mother's not very reliable."

I smiled at her politic understatement, and she went and opened the door, informing the police officer in the corridor that we were ready, any time DI Collingwood wanted to begin.

A few minutes passed, and then we went through the whole interview ritual again.

"You understand why you're here, Ms Hunter?" DI Collingwood asked.

"Same as last time," I said. "I understand that I've been arrested for the murder of Harry Rook. I don't understand why you arrested me, and I still didn't kill him."

He looked at me, a long slow look, and I felt uncomfortable. Maybe he really did believe I could be a murderer.

"Okay," he said. Then paused. A long pause.

"In your last interview here, you denied all knowledge that Harry Rook was your grandfather?"

"That is correct. At that time I didn't know he was my grandfather. I subsequently discovered that he was."

"The DNA evidence was compelling," DI Collingwood said.

"You did a follow-up test," I said. "In case there was contamination. However, my grandmother's lawyer confirmed it was true, and I have since discovered that Harry's widow knew."

"Do I understand you correctly, that you still maintain that you did not know of the relationship?"

"You were the one who told me, remember? Did you think I already knew? Do you think I'm a brilliant actress and that I was faking shock and disbelief? I didn't know. Not only didn't I know, I had never even suspected."

"It's impossible to prove a negative, unfortunately Ms Hunter. But there is evidence that leads me to doubt your ignorance."

"What kind of evidence? I know Mr Harvey didn't tell you I knew – he'd been requested to keep it from me. He saw that as his duty. Harry didn't tell me. Julia hadn't spoken to me since I was knee high. Who else? My mother? I don't even know whether she knows herself or not. I suspect not – if Grandma didn't tell me she wouldn't have trusted my mother with her secret."

"Not someone, Miss Rook. Something. You left a path for us to follow."

I looked blank. He opened the folder in front of him and pulled out some printed papers. He pushed all except one sheet across the desk at me and closed the folder.

"Your internet search history. From your laptop."

I looked at it, bemused. Wikipedia articles about DNA. Inheritable traits. And DNA testing services.

"I don't remember looking at this stuff," I said. "But I can't be sure I didn't. You know what it's like, you follow a link, you get interested in something. I don't see what the big deal is."

"Perhaps this will jog your memory."

He gave me the final piece of paper.

I read it, and almost laughed aloud. This was ridiculous.

"This is a bill for DNA testing. In my name. But that doesn't make any sense."

"Look at the date," he prompted.

"A fortnight before Harry's murder," I said. "But I never ordered this. I never paid for it. I never received the results."

"We checked with the company," he said. "The payment was hand posted through their door. An envelope with cash. They said they're used to subterfuge, but it stuck with them because it was so unusual to be paid in cash."

"Subterfuge!" I said. "With my name and address on the order?"

Suhad spoke up.

"This is ridiculous. You know other people had access to the house and to Alice's laptop. There are other keys around. There's the stalker. Are you pursuing other lines of evidence, or just focusing on Alice?"

Collingwood looked at her.

"I can assure you we are taking this investigation seriously, but that doesn't mean updating you on every avenue we are pursuing."

He turned back to me.

"You didn't expect us to trace it, though. And the results were specifically asked for by special delivery. They were signed for at your address."

I snorted. "I certainly didn't expect you to trace it. It wasn't me. I didn't know."

"The results were delivered to your address, Alice. Who else could it be?"

"I don't know. Even if I had found out Harry was my grandfather, I didn't kill him. It wasn't me who killed the rabbit and the cat. I've never killed anything larger than a wasp."

There was a pause.

"Are you a smoker, Ms Hunter?"

I laughed. "I don't need a fag break. No, I'm not a smoker. What is this?"

"A lot of people start smoking when they're in hospital. It's nothing to be ashamed of."

"I'm not ashamed of something I've never done," I said. "My friend Kelly's a smoker. I've bought cigarettes for her, yes. When we were in hospital together, I pretended to smoke, so she could have my cigarette ration."

"She doesn't vape?" DI Collingwood asked.

"No," I said, wondering where this was going.

I sensed Suhad was startled. Perhaps I shouldn't have mentioned Kelly at all.

"You see, Miss Hunter," DI Collingwood said. "It wasn't the stake that killed Mr Rook. We believe that was an attempt to cover up the murder method."

He opened the folder again and selected some more pages.

"More search history?" I said. "Are you building a case against me based on what I've read online?"

I looked down at the sheets of paper and became confused.

"How did Harry die?" I asked.

"It was a heart attack. The pathologist originally thought it might have been brought on by the shock and blood loss, when the stake pierced his hand."

I read more of the pages in front of me. Poisons which killed and left no trace. Insulin. Digitalis. Nicotine.

DI Collingwood explained. "After we found these in the internet history on your laptop, we went back to the forensic scientists and asked them to do more tox screening. They found nicotine. A closer look at the body showed up an injection site, right next to the wound made by the stake. He was injected with a hypodermic needle into the vein in the back of his hand. Perhaps the stake was to hold his hand still."

"I didn't kill Harry."

"You admit you removed the stake. Perhaps you were trying to do more damage so that the puncture wound would be overlooked. And there were unused hypodermic needles in your bathroom cabinet."

"What? They're left over from Grandma. She was diabetic."

I wanted to burst into tears with the sheer frustration of it all. I almost, almost wished I'd let my mother and Claire spirit me away to hospital.

"He was elderly, but he was no weakling. How could I possibly have forcibly injected him with anything? This doesn't make sense at all."

"She's right," Suhad said. "It's implausible for so many reasons."

DI Collingwood sighed, but maybe we'd got through to him. He had no ready comeback.

I looked again at the printout. The date was yesterday's – so that was the date it was printed. Not helpful. It was no wonder I was paranoid, someone was out to get me. As for DI Collingwood, I couldn't work out if he thought I was a stone-cold killer, or if like Claire he assumed I was having some kind of mental meltdown.

Hard though it was, I had to keep my mouth shut for now. No one would believe me anyway, even if they went to look at the laptop and checked everything out, they were as likely to assume I'd somehow set it all up myself. I had to let them find it out for themselves.

"Look," I said. "I don't remember any of this. I didn't order a blood test. I didn't spend hours and hours researching how to poison someone. I really didn't."

"I suppose you will be saying next that you didn't order this liquid nicotine concentrate?"

He passed me another printout.

My laptop had been busy.

"No," I said. "I didn't make that order. I wouldn't know what to do with liquid nicotine."

"The usual practice is to mix it with a carrier, and perhaps a flavouring. Menthol, or something fruity. Pharmaceutical grade concentrated liquid nicotine is not intended to be used alone. So you can see why it's suspicious that it was the only item on this order."

"I can't understand this at all," I said. "I've never seen those DNA results. I've not signed for a parcel containing liquid nicotine. Have you found the packaging, or anything at all, beyond this online trail? Perhaps that was faked, my laptop hacked?"

DI Collingwood looked at me with something that looked like sympathy. "Alice," he said, "Isn't it time to come clean? Might you have had a breakdown? Some kind of repeat of the earlier episode? Perhaps the shock of discovering your grandmother had lied to you for so long, and that Harry was your grandfather?"

"It wasn't like that," I said. "I'm not some Jekyll and Hyde character, and I don't have any kind of split or multiple personality. Check with my psychiatrist, see what he says."

There was a knock on the door, and DI Collingwood went out. After a few minutes talking in hushed tones outside the door, he returned.

"There has been a development with your sacrificial cat," he said. "Professor Buckley completed the excavation, videoed by one of his companions. There was a stake underneath, like the one used on Harry Rook. Our scene of crime guys are over there now, securing the scene and collecting the evidence."

"So now you believe me."

"For all we know you are the person who buried the cat there," DI Collingwood said. "But for now, you are free to go. Until the evidence has been properly assessed. Bail conditions will be as before, so no going back to your home quite yet."

"I can go back to the farm though?"

"Yes, but we would prefer if you stay away from the location where the cat was found."

"Wouldn't it be easier to leave me in a cell?"

"Don't tempt me," he said.

He walked with me and Suhad to the custody area and told the Sergeant to give me my stuff back. As the plastic bag with all my belongings was located, I asked, "Don't you have any other suspects?"

He looked straight ahead and wouldn't catch my eye. Again. "I'm sure you'll understand that it is not appropriate for me to discuss the progress of the case with you, Ms Hunter."

"Okay, I see that. Only please, please would you try thinking about the possibility that I'm innocent? Perhaps your jigsaw pieces will assemble into a different picture, if you give them a chance."

"We are pursuing other lines of enquiry. That's the job," he said. "We look at all the evidence and we follow where it leads. So far it has led us to you."

"Open your mind," I said again.

He stayed silent.

The custody sergeant handed me the plastic bag.

"It might be more convenient for you to keep the bag, Miss," he said, as I started to empty it on the desk.

"What do you mean?" I asked.

Behind me, I heard voices I recognised. My mother, Claire, and Dr Lal.

I looked at DI Collingwood, and said, "You knew about this, didn't you?" I thought his eyes softened a little, and maybe I heard a quiet apology as he turned and walked away.

Claire said, "It's for the best, Alice. It needn't be for long, especially if you consent to a voluntary admission. So that we can keep an eye on you for a few days."

"I don't need to be admitted," I said through clenched teeth. "I'm doing fine."

My mother spoke. "It's hardly fine being arrested for murder, now, is it?" she said. "You need help, Alice. Co-operate, please."

"What exactly is voluntary about this?" I asked. "Here you are mob-handed, and why? I have done everything that was asked of me when we agreed on the outpatient care plan."

Dr Lal spoke up. "The care plan couldn't take murder into account, Alice."

Then Claire spoke. "You didn't make this much fuss when DI Collingwood arrested you. That shows a real lack of proportionality. And another thing, Alice. We know Kelly's been staying with you. It was one of the reasons for my visit. I saw her."

I lost my temper.

"Kelly was a voluntary admission, and she had leave." I said. "There's no reason at all why she shouldn't be staying with me."

"She was advised not to take leave a week ago," Claire reminded me. "She hasn't called in, and she should have come back. You know that's not right."

"I know that's your view," I said. But there was no more fight in me. I was going back to the unit.

I smiled at Suhad and agreed to go with them. "Take me back via the farm, then I can collect a few things and make sure everything is okay."

"I can sort your clothes out," my mother said.

I almost laughed. She hadn't been able to sort my clothes out when I was a toddler. When Grandma had taken over looking after me, she'd had to start from scratch.

"It's not that," I said. 'The Professor may still be there, and the students. I want to make sure that they have keys to get into the house, so they can get water and so on. It's my responsibility."

My mother started objecting to me leaving them with the run of the property. My eyebrows shot upwards and my jaw dropped. "I trust them," I said.

Claire was already shaking her head to say no.

They really do have control freak tendencies.

Dr Lal interrupted. "Alice has made a perfectly reasonable and responsible suggestion. That's very much the kind of behaviour we'd like to encourage, is it not?" He smiled at me. "You don't have to worry, your stay with us is likely to be very brief. We don't have enough beds to satisfy urgent needs, and it seems to me that you're really coping very well."

At that, Suhad visibly relaxed. My mother looked disappointed. Claire offered to drive me back to the farm.

"I'd rather Suhad took me, if that's okay. Still a few legal issues we have to talk over. See you there?"

Dr Lal nodded his agreement and we went outside to the cars. Suhad pulled out first, and I silently willed her to drive faster, but my mother and Claire were close on our tail.

"They're sticking pretty close," Suhad said. "You're not planning anything, are you? Because you haven't really got anything legal to talk to me about, have you?"

"Don't worry, I won't get you into trouble," I said. "I'm merely prolonging my moments of freedom, that's all. And really, would you want to spend more time with them than you had to?"

"Fair point."

"I do wonder if I should have told DI Collingwood about the Roman silver," I said. "I know we talked it through, but he's not going to take it very well that I've hidden something else from him."

"I don't think you have any legal duty to tell him," she said. "If there was a crime committed, it wasn't by you."

"I'd like you to tell him though, if you can. Talk to Professor Buckley and see what he thinks first. And talk to the Arts and Antiques Unit sooner rather than later."

"I'll do that," she said.

She pulled up outside the farmhouse and I was relieved to see the Professor's car was still there. I encouraged Suhad to go home and said I'd be in touch with her soon. As a final thought I suggested she investigate exactly when the internet searches on my laptop were carried out and asked her to follow up with the DNA testing company, in case anything that could clear me had been missed.

"Do you know something that could clear you?" she asked, sharply.

"Not *know*," I was truthful. "I have some suspicions, but you know, they have a point. I may simply be crazy."

She laughed. Then said, more serious. "For what it's worth, I think they're wrong, Alice. I don't know many people who'd have coped as well as you have, under all this pressure, and they don't even know about the Roman silver hoard."

"I won't be telling Claire or my doctors," I said. "On the unit it would be taken as proof of my insanity. Grandiose fantasies."

She laughed again. "Take care," she said. "Dr Lal seemed pretty reasonable. You'll be out soon enough, I'm sure."

"As long as it's not straight into the cosy cell reserved for me by DI Collingwood."

I waved as she drove off and was quickly surrounded by my mother and Claire. Well, one on each side of me, but I felt surrounded.

"Get a move on," my mother said. "You're deliberately delaying things. Wasting our time."

I looked at her. "Really. You are about to make sure my time isn't my own for the foreseeable future, and you complain because I chatted with my lawyer for a few minutes?"

I looked at Claire. "Are you sure you're planning to take away the civil rights of the correct member of the Hunter family? You do realise how self-centred and abhorrent that was, don't you?"

She blushed. "You agreed to a voluntary admission, Alice," she said. "I don't think we gain anything from these delaying tactics.:"

"You don't. I do. Voluntary means I get some say, right? Stop hassling me and this will be faster. Otherwise you'll have to call Doctor Lal."

I didn't wait for an answer. I walked to the farmhouse and went in. I didn't hold the door open either, just let it swing shut.

The Prof and Adam were still there, sitting at the kitchen table.

"Good, they let you out," Professor Buckley said.

"I guess I have you to thank for that," I said. "The evidence you found with the cat helped, I think. But there's bad news as well."

My mother and Claire were standing inside the door, unsure of what to do now they were outnumbered. Claire spoke.

"Ms Hunter is here to collect her things," she said.

"That's a new one, the police letting you out to collect your clothes," Adam said.

"Not the police," I said. "It looks like I'll be spending some time back in the psychiatric unit. Apparently, my mother and my case worker are worried about me."

That stopped the conversation.

"Anyway, I wanted to have a chat with you about what you might need, because I don't know how long I'll be gone. Is there a disclaimer or something I can sign, giving you free rein to protect the site?"

"That's a good idea," the Professor said. "I'll draw something up."

"If necessary, I'll get the lawyer to do it properly," I said. "Suhad would like to talk to you anyway. Something informal will do for now, I think. Mother, Claire, you might as well make yourselves useful. I don't know about you, but I'm starving. Why don't you make us some sandwiches while I go get my stuff together?"

I picked up my rucksack from the heap by the front door and carried it into the living room. I unplugged the laptop and carefully put it in its case. Upstairs, I opened a few drawers, grabbed some underwear, socks, a couple of spare T-shirts and a fleece. In the bathroom, I locked the door before ransacking the bathroom cabinet. Wash bag with nail scissors. I stuffed the lot into the rucksack.

What else did I need?

Chocolate, muesli bars, and a bottle of water were already packed. That would have to do.

I opened the window and breathed in deeply.

Which was I more afraid of? Going back to hospital won by a whisker.

I gathered up all my courage, and I slipped through and onto the roof of the back porch, which was well out of sight from the windows of the living room and the kitchen. My arms ached from clinging on to the windowsill as I edged my way across, until my bottom was lodged firmly on the tiles. I tried to wriggle down slowly, but the damn rucksack held me in place, caught on the window ledge. Very, very slowly I slipped my right arm backwards and out of the strap, and gently swung the bag round. I slipped forwards and only just stopped myself yelling out, but I was soon sitting securely on the edge of the porch, my legs dangling down.

It wasn't that far a drop. I let the rucksack go first, dropping it into the bushes. As it fell, my heart rose up into my throat and I had to remind myself to breathe.

I prepared myself to follow it down.

THIRTY-SEVEN

WHOOSH.

I landed awkwardly, and jarred my ankle, but when I tested my weight on it, it only hurt a little. Part of me wanted to shout it from the rooftops that I'd faced my fears and done it anyway. I hadn't known I could do it, until I had to.

I swung the rucksack over my shoulder, and cautiously crept round to the front of the farmhouse, flinching on each step. Everyone was still inside, distracted by making tea and sandwiches, I hoped. My bike was chained to the downpipe, and very carefully I unlocked it, then stood still, waiting, listening, to make sure no one had heard.

I wheeled it across the yard and into the barn. Even though it was still broad daylight outside, the light in there was dim. I wheeled the bike across and laid it flat on the floor in the far corner where it wouldn't be spotted by a cursory inspection. Taking a deep breath and steeling myself, I walked over to the hay bales and Daniel's hiding place.

I coughed nervously. "Are you in there? Kelly, Daniel?"

I pulled a hay bale aside.

Kelly turned on a torch, and I could see the hidden nest was a little bigger than it had been. Daniel's head poked out of his sleeping bag, and he looked confused and scared. Kelly was huddled up in a pile of blankets from the house. I squeezed in and pulled the blocks of hay back after me.

"No time to explain, but please keep quiet. They'll be looking for me soon."

"Who?" Kelly said. "The cops?"

"No, my mother and my case worker. Please?"

Kelly turned off the torch and we waited. Our breathing seemed scarily loud, and I was worried we wouldn't get away with it.

After fifteen minutes or so – which felt more like fifteen hours – we heard the door of the barn open. A little beam of sunlight shone over the top of the haystack. I heard Claire say, "No, can't see anyone here. Her bike's gone – she could be anywhere."

My mother responded. "DI Collingwood is no help. Why isn't he answering his phone? He could tell us where she is."

"She's probably taken the tag off by now, Helen," Claire said.

I hadn't had time. If only they would go away and let me get on with it. I'd been counting on having more leeway to deal with the tag, but I'd clearly been over optimistic.

The barn door slammed shut. We all stayed absolutely silent as the minutes ticked by incredibly slowly. I was still fretting that Daniel might decide to let them know I was there – if he had a grudge against me, perhaps he'd be willing to risk his own freedom. I knew Kelly didn't want to go back yet.

An engine started up – at least one of the cars left.

I could repress it no longer. One giggle escaped, and then another. Kelly switched on the torch and looked at me.

"You're really losing it now, mate," she said.

"I can't help it," I said, between giggles. "What is wrong with us all, on the run and hiding in this barn? It's an utterly ridiculous situation. We've done nothing wrong."

I paused and looked at Daniel's face. He wasn't smiling, like Kelly was.

"Well we haven't. Why are you hiding out here, Daniel?"

"It's my home," he said. His face sullen.

"I know," I said. "I'm sorry about your father. You shouldn't have been pushed out like that. I don't understand why you were. If anyone had asked me…"

"I'm underage," he said. "I'm fourteen. They want to put me in care – in a home or find foster parents."

My jaw dropped. "Mrs Banerjee told me you were sixteen," I said. "Or else…"

"Or else what?" he asked. "You'd have dobbed me in. You're like the rest. I can take care of myself."

Kelly gently said, "He's tough. Survived for months now. No need to treat him like a kid." She stared at me, willing me to back down.

"I know. I was surprised, that's all. It was stupid and unthinking of me, Daniel."

He grunted.

"Can I have that flashlight on now, Kels?" I asked. "Trained on my ankle, I mean. I need to deal with this damn tag. Before the police do come looking for me."

"Sure," she said. "What are you going to do? Break it?"

"You gave me the idea," I said.

I dug the laptop out of the bottom of the rucksack and took it out of the protective case I'd bought. I found my nail scissors and started to snip a wide band of the metallic fabric.

"Clever," she said. "Will it work?"

I wished I'd brought the kitchen scissors. The nail scissors were making heavy work of the task.

"According to the internet," I said. "Always a reliable source."

Carefully I wrapped the long strip of fabric round and round the bracelet and fixed it in position with a safety pin out of my wash bag.

"Very punk," Kelly said, approving.

"We need to get away from here, before the police come looking for me," I said. "I'm scared to cross the farm yard though. It's so open and exposed."

Kelly stood up. "I'll play scout. Worst case, I'll run up the lane and act as a decoy. You two get away any way you can."

"Let's go, then." I picked up my rucksack, and Kelly pushed the hay bales back in place.

"Where to?" Daniel asked.

"Over the Beacon to Grandma's house," I said. "We can get in the back way and hole up there while making plans. You don't have to come with me," I said, when I decided there was no putting it off any longer.

Kelly said, "All for one, and all that."

Daniel added, "Yeah, well, there's not much happening here." Then he paused. "Hang on," he said. "I'll leave some food for the kitten."

He poured some water into a bowl hidden away in the corner and shook some dried food out of a plastic container onto an old saucer.

Kelly went ahead, as she insisted. There was no one in sight, and all the cars had gone, so we both followed and caught up with her.

The lane up to the main road was clear, so we were safe for the first leg of the journey – we'd hear if a car approached anyway. We decided to go the long way round, across the fields, and catch a bus to the foot of the Beacon.

As we were walking in the field, shielded by the tall hedges, I couldn't wait any longer. I had to know.

"Daniel," I said. "Have you ever done any rabbit hunting, with snares?" I wanted to ask about the stakes too, but couldn't quite find the words.

He flushed. "I know what you're asking for," he said. "Kels told me about the murder. I had nothing to do with that. I wouldn't. Mr Rook was okay. Not like some."

"It wasn't only the murder," I said. "There was a cat, too. Someone's pet. And rabbits."

"A marmalade cat," his voice rose, full of indignation. "My cat? Paddington. She's missing. I wouldn't hurt anyone's pet, but I've hunted wild rabbits. What of it?"

"Did you stake a rabbit out over on the Beacon?" I asked.

"What would be the point?" he asked. "They're good eating."

Kelly nodded. "I had some of his stew earlier."

"A shotgun is easier for rabbiting," he added. "But I couldn't, anymore."

That was awkward. We all went quiet. The next part would be worse.

We'd reached that oddly shaped rock. Rest and be Thankful. There wasn't room for three of us to sit on it. I dug into my pocket for a bar of chocolate, and sat down on the grass, leaning back against the rock. I broke the bar into three pieces, and shared it out, giving Daniel the biggest piece.

Kelly sat down too, and after a minute or two Daniel followed suit.

"That makes sense," I said. "I can understand that. But. You know where we're going, right? The house where I used to live, over by the West Beach. Opposite the Rook House."

"Yes, course I do."

"Have you been in there? In the last few weeks? With flowers, or something?"

He blushed. "No, I've not been inside. Not ever. I walked past, that's all. Once or twice."

I pushed a bit harder. "You've pushed stuff through the letterbox," I said. "Your art work…"

"No," he said. "I walked up the path once. I wanted to talk to you. I lost my nerve."

"Last week? Someone put some roses in my living room. With one of your drawings attached. Are you sure you haven't been inside?"

He laughed. "Roses? I've been scraping by on barely enough to eat. How would I buy roses?"

"Makes sense," I said.

I guess someone could have picked up a card from the hall and put it with the roses to confuse me. I was stumped, now. I'd pushed him enough, I thought. He was only a kid, and I'd more or less accused him of torturing animals and being my stalker.

Kelly spoke next. "Daniel," she said. "You know what we were talking about earlier? I think you should tell Alice."

Thanks Kelly. I don't exactly want a declaration of undying love from a fourteen-year-old right now. There's more important stuff on my mind.

"Are you my sister?" he asked.

"What?" My head was spinning again. Random thoughts rushed by. If only they'd all line up in a row and make some kind of sensible pattern.

Kelly spoke again. "Daniel's mum did a runner when he was tiny," she said. "Leaving him with his dad, who brought him up alone until—"

Daniel interrupted, talking very fast. "Helen, she came round here, just before Dad... I mean, before he died. He was out when she arrived and she sat at the kitchen table, quizzing me, looking through my sketchbook."

"At the farm?" I asked. He nodded.

"She saw the drawings I'd made of you and she said – well, horrible things. She said she was ashamed to be my mother."

He blushed.

Well, that was something we had in common. My heart went out to him, but I still needed some answers.

"Did you give her any of the sketches?"

"She said she'd tell you I had a crush on you if I didn't. Told me you'd both have a good laugh at that. Should I not have given them to her? She said you were her daughter, that it was more appropriate for her to have them. She said it was sick. That I was like a stalker."

"I'm sorry she hurt you," I said. Could this be true? Or was it another of her cruel tricks? I didn't know what to think.

I looked at Daniel, trying to see any family likeness.

He managed a grin, before looking away. "I look like my Dad," he said.

Kelly snorted, but didn't say anything. Daniel's face was still beet red, and he looked anywhere, everywhere rather than risk eye contact. If Daniel was my brother, my half-brother, then Helen—. I counted back. He was fourteen. He would have been born when I was what, eight? I should have noticed if my mother had been pregnant, or Grandma certainly should. Then again, there were so many times we didn't see her for months on end, sometimes longer. There were countless times Grandma would say, "It seems your mother has gone AWOL again."

I thought it through. If Grandma had known, she would surely have provided for Daniel. There was nothing, not a penny, in the will. She would at least have left them the farm. I was sure of it. Family mattered to Grandma.

"Daniel," I said. "I don't think it can be true. My grandmother—" I paused, cross with myself about the possessive, as if I was refusing to share. "She would have loved to have a grandson, I'm sure of it. She wouldn't have left you penniless."

"My father did," he said. "He didn't care what happened to me."

I shuffled on the grass so that I was close enough, then I put my arm around his shoulders. He pulled away. Who could blame him? I wanted to tell him his father did care, but I didn't know that for sure. If anyone knew what it was like to have a parent who didn't care, it was me.

"Look," I said. "We can find out for sure. One thing I've found out in the last few days – it's really easy to get a DNA test done. Not even that expensive. We'll find out, I promise. As soon as we can."

"Do you mean that?" he asked.

I managed a smile. "Kelly's my adopted big sister, and whatever happens, you can be our adopted little brother. We have so much in common. All of us on the run. All of us have hay in our hair. There's more important things than genes."

I pulled a piece of straw from Kelly's hair and tickled her with it.

"I think we're all on the same side," Kelly said. "Aren't we, Daniel?"

"I guess so," he said.

"Thanks," I said. I didn't really believe it, deep down I didn't really believe anyone could be trusted. But it felt good to imagine us all in this together. My kind of trust was more of a decision than a conviction. I'd seen how it affected Grandma – how isolated she'd become, not even able to trust me at the end. She'd talked so little of her family, of her parents. I didn't know a thing about them. It was possible when she fell so deeply in love with Harry, she was running from something, not running to something.

We got to the bus stop in the nick of time. Fortunately for my nerves, we didn't have to wait fifteen minutes in the open and as planned we got off at the foot of Beacon Hill. Walking across the cliffs to the back of Grandma's house, at most we ran the risk of meeting an odd dog walker. Much more sensible than walking past the police station and Julia's house.

We walked up the hill, talking quietly still, as if someone might overhear us. We passed the turnoff to the clearing where the altar was, where I'd found the sacrificial rabbit. He denied all knowledge. He didn't look guilty, I decided, more bemused.

"Weird," he said. "I haven't seen anyone snaring rabbits around here. Not that I'd know. That's sort of the point, with snares."

We walked on in silence, until we came to the fork in the path where we could choose to go down to the beach, or down past the back of Grandma's house to Beacon Road.

"I want to take a look down here and see what's happened to the old cafe and the amusement arcade," I said.

They followed me. A short way from the bottom of the path I stopped, shocked. Overnight a tall wooden fence had been erected. And a sign. "No entrance during the demolition. Limited public access will be restored as quickly as possible."

"Wow," I said. "Mark Stockman is moving fast on this. Can you see over the fence, Kelly?" She was the tallest of us.

"Not a thing," she said. "We might be able to see from the cliffs up there." She pointed to the Coastguard station.

We all turned round and retraced our steps.

THIRTY-EIGHT

FROM THE TOP of the cliff we could see down to the beach and promenade. Where the cafe and the amusement arcade used to be, there was now nothing. Not quite nothing. There were a couple of portacabin style huts, and a few half-filled skips, but it looked surprisingly bare for a demolition site.

In the distance I could see that the entrance from Beacon Road was also blocked by a tall wooden fence – but this one had a gate, heavy with black ironmongery.

"Why all the fences?" Daniel asked.

"Health and Safety, innit," Kelly answered.

I looked at them, one eyebrow raised. "It doesn't look like there's anyone around. Are we up for a spot of trespassing?"

"How can we get in?" Daniel asked. "Those fences don't look easy to climb."

"There's a path that comes out at the back of the cafe, or rather, the ex-cafe. It will be a bit of a scramble in places, where the chalk of the cliffs has crumbled away, but there's nothing dangerously steep. The fence doesn't seem to go that far."

"So long as we don't get stuck down there," Kelly said.

"Clambering back up will be the easy bit," I said.

"Come on then," she said. "I'm curious enough to risk it. While it's still light."

Good point. Not much longer before dusk made it impossible.

I went first, on the grounds that I knew the route. Or maybe they thought I'd break their fall. The path was more uneven than I remembered, and on one part I gave in to the inevitable and sat and slid down a very steep part. Daniel followed suit, but Kelly stayed upright. She had something of a wobble at the last moment, but we both caught her, one on either side.

We reached the bottom of the hill in no time, and at first we stood looking around in shock. For me and Daniel, it was a childhood landscape completely transformed. Even Kelly had first seen it with the buildings all intact.

It was desolate. Usually there was someone around no matter what the time of day, or what season. Dogs always needed to be walked. Fishermen would clamber up the top of the breakwater in all weathers, ignoring whatever blocked their way – from warning signs to padlocked metal gates. Some of them brought ladders expressly for that purpose.

"There's definitely no one here," I said.

"It's a post-apocalyptic wasteland," Daniel said.

I could see what he meant. It really did feel desolate. "I'm going to take a closer look," I said.

I approached the first portacabin; the smaller of the two. There was a small window at one end, next to the door. Fortunately there were steps up to the door, or I'd never have been able to peer in. I climbed up, leaned over, and took a look. It was dark, and I couldn't see anything clearly. But it looked like it was a place where they stored tools – spades and forks and pick axes.

The other portacabin was bigger and more interesting. For one thing, the windows were shuttered over, and even though there were narrow slats I couldn't see anything at all. On the door there was yet another large sign. Private. Do Not Enter.

I'd had enough with doing what I was told.

I looked at the padlock on the door. It didn't look terribly secure – all I needed was a little leverage. A screwdriver, maybe.

Daniel piped up, "You're not going to break in, are you?"

"I thought I might," I said. "Aren't you curious?"

Silently, he pulled a multi-tool out of his pocket and handed it to me. When he saw me try to use the penknife part to lever the padlock off, he grabbed it back.

"Here, let me."

He unscrewed the plate, and the door swung open. Ah. I followed him inside, and Kelly followed me.

"Don't touch anything," I said, belatedly searching in my pockets for my black cashmere gloves. The police already had my fingerprints on file.

Daniel said, "Hang on a minute, I'll go and wipe around the plate on the door. And on the other cabin before we forget."

I looked at Kelly, shaking my head.

"I was worried I was leading him into a life of crime, but it looks like he's ahead of me."

"You're the one arrested for murder, mate. If it's a competition."

I shook my head in despair, then started to look around. This looked more like it. A table and a couple of office chairs. A filing cabinet, blue painted with two drawers. Right next to it, a pair of muddy boots, which looked familiar, and a metal detector.

"So he's on a treasure hunt here as well."

It was all beginning to make a kind of sense. Mark Stockman had the photograph of our grandparents. He had a reason for wanting to buy Grandma's house. He thought this was where the skyphos had been found. Here, somewhere on Beacon Hill. He assumed that was why Grandma had bought her home and the farm and chosen to settle nearby. He didn't know the real reason – that she was still in love with Harry or punishing him for deserting her.

I pulled open the filing cabinet drawers. The bottom one first. A few books. A Treasure Hunting Guide. The Care and Feeding of Metal Detectors. Roman Artefacts for Beginners.

In the top drawer I found a plastic bag. I tipped it out on the desk and had a closer look. A few coins. A pile of old copper pennies. A few threepenny bits and sixpences. All the kinds of coins that you would expect to find on the site of an old amusement arcade. He must be so disappointed.

"We know Mark Stockman is looking for treasure," I said. "But I wonder if that means he's my stalker? Perhaps he even broke into the house."

"I don't know," Kelly sounded doubtful. "Okay, we've seen him around with his metal detector, but he's been trying to buy the house and the farm, and he bought this land too. That's not the same as breaking in, is it?"

"Yes, but Harry didn't want to sell up, remember," I pointed out. "His death changed everything."

Daniel was back and heard the last part. "What treasure?" he asked.

"It's a long story," I said. "But we think Grandma might have found some Roman silver, years ago."

"Oh," he said. "The archaeology stuff." He lost interest and left the cabin again, prowling around outside. Perhaps he wasn't so blasé about breaking in as I'd thought.

"I think we'd best go," I said, beginning to feel a little on edge myself.

I called Daniel back, and he fixed the padlock and fittings back to the portacabin. If you looked closely, you might be able to see it had been tampered with, but it passed a cursory inspection. We'd not taken anything, not even a threepenny bit for luck. There was still no one around, although we might have been spotted from the coastguard station – if not on the site, then certainly on the path.

Climbing back up the hill was easier than coming down had been, although there was a bit of scrabbling. I wiped my dirty hands on my jeans and checked the electronic tag. The fabric strip was still securely in place, so if luck was with me I wouldn't be broadcasting our location to the police. I wondered if my mother had wormed anything out of DI Collingwood about the signal from my tag yet. By now someone must be at the farm, checking out my last transmitted location. Perhaps they'd have found Daniel's hiding place in the barn.

Soon we reached the slope behind Grandma's house. I paused at the spot where my stalker must have watched me.

"I can't see anyone," I said. "The house looks deserted. Let's go."

This path was less steep, and there was no slipping and sliding. The back gate was locked, but I had the key. Daniel was over the fence before I had it out of my pocket.

I opened the gate, and he came back. "Not yet," he whispered, "Let me have a closer look first. If anyone sees me, I'm a random kid chancing it. If they see you…"

"Thanks. Be careful, anyway."

I kept the gate open a crack and watched him saunter up to the back door and peer through the pane of glass. Then to the kitchen window. He pulled himself up a bit with the window ledge and jumped. Then he went to the library window.

I panicked, and ran into the garden and across the grass, and just in time I grabbed his arm and pulled him away from the metal shutters.

"There's an alarm," I said, after catching my breath.

I heard the gate click shut and turned to see Kelly ambling towards us.

"Shall we go inside or make a lot of noise arguing out here?" she asked.

It was a fair point. I unlocked the back door and quickly deactivated the alarm.

The house had that empty feel, but all the same I decided I'd better check.

I drew the kitchen curtains and left them sitting in the half light of dusk in the kitchen.

Upstairs, I checked the bathroom first and used the facilities. I checked the back bedrooms next. They were not overlooked, except from the hill, but still I didn't turn the light on. I peered out of the window, but there was still no one in sight. In the front bedroom, I was even more careful. There was the possibility of being seen from the road or from Julia's place, so I crawled around the bed, keeping my head well below the level of the window sill. I didn't even attempt to peek out of the window.

Again, there was no one there. From the floor, I could even see under the bed. There was something I wanted. I crawled over to the bedside cabinet, and pulled it away from the wall, revealing the small safe hidden in the wall behind it. I extracted Grandma's jewellery box. I soon discovered how difficult it was to carry a heavy wooden box whilst crawling, so I pushed it in front of me, making quite a racket. Daniel ran upstairs to see what was going on, and carried it down to the kitchen for me, and put it on the table. Kelly was pacing up and down the kitchen and the hallway.

"We were getting worried," Kelly said.

"I'll check the living room, and then we can go into the library – where we can put the light on and talk."

I ducked, and crept into the living room, again careful to keep myself low, even though someone would have to be looking directly down from Julia's bedroom window to see me.

The curtains were drawn.

It was safe to turn the light on and let my mother know I was here. Somehow I was sure she'd be close by, watching and waiting.

THIRTY-NINE

KELLY RUSHED IN and turned the light off and dragged me out of the room, down the hall and into the kitchen, slamming the door behind us.

"What are you thinking?" she said. "You're not supposed to be here, remember."

I needed to get a move on, to get them away before mother arrived. There wasn't much time.

"I need you and Daniel to go out the back," I said. "Take the phone and keep an eye out. When mother arrives you must call Collingwood, and 999 if he doesn't answer."

"We can't leave you here to face her alone," she said.

There were footsteps in the hall, approaching the kitchen door.

"It's too late," Daniel said.

The door opened.

"Tamsin. How the fuck did you get in here?" I asked, looking at the key in her hand.

Kelly said, sardonic as ever. "Hello Tamsin, pleased to meet you. I've heard so much about you."

Daniel had a good long look at Tamsin but stayed silent. He wasn't stupid, that boy. All at once I realised, if he was my brother then he was related to Tamsin too. I felt a pang of guilt – I'd thoughtlessly risked his safety – emotional as well as physical.

"How did you get in?" I asked again.

"I knew Harry had a key. He kept an eye on the place when you were in hospital, right?"

"How many times have you used that key?"

"I came to say I'm sorry," she said.

I started to doubt myself. I'd been so sure my mother was the persistent intruder. I sat down. I'd told the police that the only keys were held by me, the lawyer, Mrs Banerjee and my mother, but obviously Harry had one too. Julia and Tamsin could now be added to the long list of people who had access to the house. I really should have changed the locks.

"How long have you had the key?" I asked again.

"I found it this afternoon. After Helen came to me, looking for you. I knew you'd come here eventually."

Kelly piped up, "I wonder why your mum isn't here."

I wondered too. She was the one I'd been expecting. She'd known about the exclusion zone, but not, as far as I knew, that I'd blocked the electronic tag signal. Perhaps she'd found it impossible to escape Claire's clutches. I found that idea bitterly amusing.

Tamsin said, "They came to see me because we're friends. Cousins. Whatever. I said I didn't know where you would go, but it wouldn't be here, because you aren't that stupid."

"Except you think I am that stupid," I said. "Thanks."

"I wasn't sure. Not until I saw the light."

She grinned, and for a moment looked like my oldest friend again. I almost softened.

"Look," she said. "I really am sorry. I didn't handle it very well when you were ill, and that was bad enough. But this thing about Harry. It wasn't all my fault. I might be a bit slow, but I worked it out in the end."

"Go on," I said.

"I thought you knew he was your grandfather," Tamsin said. "I should have known better, but I believed her."

"Her?" Like I didn't know.

"Your mother. She came to see me the day before Harry's death. Before his murder. She showed me the test results from the lab. The results that proved Harry was your grandfather."

"How did she get Harry's DNA sample?"

"She didn't," Tamsin said. "She asked me to get it. I stole his toothbrush for her. She was really upset. She told me that you'd been keeping it from her, and that Grandma had messed up her life. She'd never known who her father was. She'd been pushed out of the family and left out of the will."

"Why didn't you talk to me, Tamsin? I don't understand."

"I don't know," she said. "I believed her. I suppose I felt the same way she did. Harry was spending so much time with you, and I felt pushed out. She made me believe that you and your grandmother had made fools of us all. Harry and Auntie Julia too. I was so angry with you. I wasn't thinking straight."

"What made you change your mind?"

I wasn't sure I believed she had.

"When Helen came to see me a couple of hours ago. She told me you should be in hospital for your own good. I almost believed that, but she slipped up. She asked me not to tell anyone I'd stolen Harry's toothbrush for her. That set me to wondering about why she'd needed the DNA results. Harry had told her he was her father."

"But you thought I might have killed him?"

"Only if you were out of your mind, Alice. We can all snap."

I looked at her, steadily, and she faltered.

"She played me," Tamsin said. "She used my jealousy. And I resisted seeing the truth because it made me guilty. Complicit. I am sorry."

"Thank you for that much."

"I talked to Aunt Julia. She said that it was important I put things right. She was sure you hadn't known, that your grandmother hadn't told anyone. Not even Harry knew for sure until Grandma was dying. She said I had to go and see the police, to tell them Helen had sent off for the DNA tests. Not you."

"Have you told them?" Kelly asked. "The police, I mean."

"Not yet. I wanted to let you know about Helen first, and to put things right with you."

"Oh, I knew about Helen," I said. "My lovely mother. I simply couldn't prove it. Because I'm paranoid, don't ya know? You might have a word with my psychiatrist while you're straightening everyone else out."

"Just because you're paranoid doesn't mean they aren't out to get you," said Kelly.

"What must it be like?" I said. "To tell the truth and have people actually believe you?"

"Okay," said Tamsin. "I don't expect you to forgive me, I mean, I know how stupid it was of me. I wanted to put it right."

Her family called this The Bitch House.

I could carry it on, or I could let it go. It was time to let it go.

I hugged her.

"Don't be silly. You're my oldest friend. You were played by my mother. We've all been there."

"Not me," Kelly said. "She never took me in."

"That's because you're paranoid," I said.

Kelly laughed.

It still hurt, but at least I could understand how it had happened. I was also intensely aware that Daniel had been soaking everything up. I had to behave well, if only to prove I was nothing, nothing like my mother.

"What shall I do now?" Tamsin said. "I think I should go straight to the police, don't you?"

"I'll come too," Kelly said. "I can back up your story, and I can talk to the social worker and the hospital."

"Are you sure, Kelly?" I asked. "You know what it will mean for you?"

"I'd have gone back earlier, but you needed me," she said. "But this is the answer, right? Now we can prove your mum was setting you up—"

"It doesn't clear me of murder," I said. "None of this shows I didn't kill Harry. But it's a good start."

FORTY

I SUGGESTED DANIEL go with them, but he wasn't ready. I couldn't blame him, knowing it would mean that social workers would descend and he'd be whisked off into foster care. I didn't want to risk losing him though. I asked Kelly to give him the spare mobile phone, so that we'd have a way of keeping in touch. I told Daniel it was so he could call the police if I needed help.

"I'll be in the kitchen with the lights on," I said. "You'll have a good view from the Beacon. If I turn the light off, call the police."

Not that my signalling was terribly effective. Where was she? Why wasn't she here yet?

"999?" he asked, seemingly pleased to be given the responsibility.

I showed him DI Collingwood's number in the contacts. "If he doesn't answer, then call 999," I said.

I couldn't resist giving him another hug before chivvying him out of the back door. He submitted to it with a little more grace than the last time.

Kelly was fretting. "Come with us?" she asked. "I don't like leaving you here."

"I'd rather not," I said. "I want to check on some of Grandma's stuff, first. I'll come down to the police station soon, if DI Collingwood hasn't collected me first."

Kelly and Tammy left by the front door. I stood and watched them, no longer worried that I would be seen. I wanted to be seen.

As soon as they'd gone, I closed the front door, and went back to the kitchen table and sat down. I reached down to my ankle, unpinned the cloth wrapped about the electronic tag, and carefully unwound it. I put the fabric and safety pin in the oddments drawer next to the sink unit. I wasn't expecting to need it again, but you never know.

I was glad I'd left the landline connected. I would have to phone my mother after all, as she'd still not turned up.

Her phone rang and rang, but there was no answer. I paced the kitchen, feeling stupid. My plan was falling apart. The light didn't work, and now she wasn't answering the damn phone.

Then my mobile rang.

"Is that you, Alice?" My mother's voice.

"Yes," I said. "I'm at Grandma's. Time we had a talk, don't you think?"

"What is there to talk about?" she said. "I'm calling the police."

"Don't do that," I said. "I thought we could do a deal."

"What kind of deal?"

"I don't want to go back in hospital, and you need money. You call the psychiatrist off, and perhaps agree to stay with me for a couple of days, to make sure I'm stable. Whatever it takes. I'll be very generous."

"Generous like your Grandma, with strings?" she laughed. "You can't, anyway. You don't have access to the Trust."

"I don't need the Trust," I said. "There are plenty of valuables in the personal bequest Grandma left to me. More than enough to tide you over."

"Like what? A few Roman coins and the odd Egyptian bauble?"

"That odd Egyptian bauble is valued at over three hundred thousand," I said. "Much more valuable than the other Egyptian necklace. You know. The one you took."

She laughed. "You're pulling my leg. The ugly one is worth more?"

"I have the documentation here. The valuation. The provenance. All you need to be able to sell it legally."

"Why would you do that for me?" she asked.

"Mother," I said, "I don't want to go to hospital again. I don't care about the necklace, and I never wanted you to be cut out of the will. You know that it wasn't my idea."

That part was all true. I've never really understood why mother didn't realise the truth was a much easier way of scamming someone.

"I'm on my way, sweetie," she said.

Sweetie? Oh my God. Was Claire still with her? This could still go horribly wrong.

Settling down at the kitchen table, I opened the jewellery box to distract myself. I pulled out the layers carefully, placing them on the table. I selected the few valuable pieces, including the ugly Egyptian one, and wrapped them in velvet from the box, and put them in the cutlery drawer. I left all the cheap trinkets in the trays. I lifted out the last layer to check underneath. All I should have seen was the red silk lining, but it was obscured by the missing book. Roald Dahl's book. *The Wonderful Story of Henry Sugar and Six More*. That was what it was called! The Mildenhall Treasure was one of the Six More.

On the verge of tears, when I could least afford them, I lifted it out. I'd been so afraid it had gone missing with the other things. That somehow mother had known how much it mattered to me. I had a flashback to the bonfire, sitting half-asleep in the garden chair, watching the flames.

It was the copy Grandma used to read to me. Never mind that it was signed, a first edition – that wasn't why I valued it. I opened it, and the dust jacket slipped off and revealed a folded-up sheaf of beautifully heavy, cream vellum pages. Grandma's writing paper.

Putting the book to one side, I smoothed the folded papers open.

'My dearest granddaughter,' it began. 'By now, I am sure you have discovered that I'm not the person I pretended to be. I've let you down, and I am sorry for that. I made some mistakes when I was a young woman – not much older than you are now, as I'm writing this. I spent my life covering them up. Perhaps, this letter won't be needed. Perhaps, I'll have found the courage to talk to you in person, and not take this easy way out. But I am a coward, and I know I am writing this so I don't have to make that choice. I don't have to see the look of disappointment in your eyes when you find out.

Oh, Grandma. She never really knew me, I realised.

It's a sad story, but not a new one. I fell in love with a man, and I thought he loved me. He seemed to, anyway. We made plans, we were going to get married. I was pregnant. But he never took me to his home, never introduced me to his parents. I guess you know who he is now. Harry Rook. He agreed to be trustee for you, when I explained why I needed to have someone to keep you safe.

He is your grandfather. He never knew, but always suspected. That was my revenge, feeble as it was. It hurt me more than anyone else. That's the way with revenge, they say.

There's no need to dwell on what happened. If you need to know more Harry will tell you. In spite of it all, he is a good man, and you can trust him.

I'm the only one who can tell you about the silver. No one else knows the whole story — I made sure of that.

This is how it happened.

I was pregnant with Harry's child, and I was sitting all alone at the back of the church watching him get married. He had never even broken our relationship, or told me he was engaged to someone else. His mother knew though. She recognised me and chivvied me away from the church, out of sight. She reached into her handbag and pulled out her purse. Took a few notes, and counted them, and put them in my hand.

I dropped them, unable to believe what was happening. She carried on speaking, but it washed over me, and I didn't hear a word. I walked away. I walked and walked until I was completely exhausted. I went into The Harbour View and sat on my own, drinking. I bought a bottle of gin from the bar and put it in my bag.

How hurt she must have been.

Where was my mother? She should be here by now, surely.

I pondered phoning DI Collingwood. What if the tag wasn't working after being tampered with? What if it took the agency too long to let the police know where I was? All I'd be left to rely on would be Daniel.

I rang Collingwood's mobile number and it went to voicemail.

"It's Alice Hunter," I said. "I'm back at Grandma's house, I'm expecting a visitor. I'm not the murderer, and you know it. Get here. And don't spook her. LISTEN."

I had to know what came next, so I carried on reading.

It was dusk when I went back outside. I walked up on to Beacon Hill, and sat at the top, near where the Coastguard Station is now. I sat there as it got dark, looking out to sea, and drinking gin from the bottle. It was cold, and I thought that would be enough. I'd lose the baby, or even better, die of hypothermia. That was my grand plan.

You know that didn't happen. Maybe I had more of a drive to live than I realised. It was late and dark, and I was only half way through the bottle and instead of staying put, I got up, and walked and walked.

I reached the place where the Cuckmere Coven used to gather for rituals. Gabriel Stockman was the High Priest back then. I'd attended sabbats. I'd played my allotted part in rituals. But back then I thought it was nonsense – just playacting.

I stood in that sacred place before the stone altar, half-empty bottle of gin in one hand, and I called on the Goddess. I pledged my life to her path if only she would show me the answer. A way to win back Harry's love. Or a way to have the perfect revenge. I didn't much care which.

I felt something. I wrote it off as an effect of the gin, but I felt something. I half-ran from the clearing in terror – seized by something not unlike the original meaning of Panic.

Then I fell. My foot slipped into a rabbit hole, and I twisted my ankle and I fell.

I thought it was a rabbit hole, but my foot hit something hard. I sat down, and pushed deep into the dirt with my fingers, and touched metal. I found the skyphos, that night, although I didn't know what it was then. Later, I came back in the twilight, and dug some more. I found a hoard of Roman silver, Alice.

I heard the key in the front door. There were still pages more to read, so I quickly got up, and stuffed them into the kitchen drawer, and sat back down, playing with Grandma's jewellery box. I put the layers back in and closed the box.

I looked up as she paused in the doorway. Mother. I was relieved Collingwood hadn't got here first, and that I didn't have to persuade him to hide somewhere and listen, but I hoped he wouldn't be too far behind.

"What took you so long?" I asked.

"I was waiting for Tamsin to leave. The others were a bonus. I needed you alone."

"How did you know they were here?"

"I've been renting the penthouse at the marina from Mark Stockman. Didn't you know, sweetie? He was very sympathetic, knowing you needed someone to watch over you."

Who the fuck had known and not told me? Collingwood? Suhad? Mr Harvey? Had they all known?

I forced myself to calm down. I didn't want to lose my temper – I needed to be in control. I poked back.

"Where's Claire then?"

"Professionals get to clock off."

I snorted. "Like that's something you'd know about."

She walked across the room, and before I could react, slapped me across my face.

"I've been longing to do that for such a long time," she said. Then she sat down. "Where's the jewellery then, and the rest?"

I pushed the box towards her and she opened it. She lifted out the top tray, and then the bottom tray. "I don't understand," she said. "Where is it?"

"I lied," I said.

Her lips thinned. I could see she was getting dangerously angry.

"You stupid, stupid child." She stood up, pushed the chair back and started to move towards me.

I flinched.

She didn't slap me this time but put her face close to mine. Her eyes flashed rage, her tongue dripped venom.

"You think you've had a hard time," she said. "You have no idea. You're a spoilt brat, who's always had everything handed to her on a plate. Your life has been easy, and you dare to sit there, passing judgement on me? You've never worked a day in your life."

She backed off a little, started to pace.

"You're wrong," I said. "I worked for Mrs B in the school holidays. I collected the rent. I cleaned the rental properties – the communal areas, corridors, bathrooms, the lot."

"A summer job for pocket money, while all the time knowing Grandma was there with a safety net. That's not something I ever had."

"I know better," I said. "You might have been able to fool me when I was a child, weaving tales of hardship and deprivation, and trying to make out Grandma was a monster. I'm an adult now. I've seen the finances. I know she paid you a generous allowance, and that she still does, through the Trust. How many businesses did she finance for you? I lost count."

"An allowance! A pittance, that only started when you were a baby. She bought you."

I hadn't been sure, but that confirmed what I suspected. If Grandma had bought me, my mother had sold me – for what she now called a pittance.

"Then there was the lump sum she gave you, just before you disappeared out of our lives for two, was it three years? Daniel's fourteen – the timing fits, I reckon. Was it something to do with him, by any chance?"

"My, you have been a busy little bee, haven't you? Pity no one will believe you."

She loved to twist the knife, but she wasn't denying Daniel was hers. We would have to have those DNA tests done.

"Why did you keep him a secret? You knew Grandma would have loved a grandson."

"He'd have loved her more than he ever loved me," she said. "Just like you did. Or perhaps just her money."

"You had a son to punish her, and she never knew. Not a very effective revenge, was it?"

"Oh, she knew. As she was dying, I told her. That she'd made sure I didn't know my father, and that in return I'd made sure she never knew her grandson. There's an almost perfect symmetry to it, don't you think?"

"As she was dying?"

"She clung on to life. I had to give her a little help at the end. I didn't want her hanging on for months, ruining my plans."

Was that true? I didn't have time to be distracted by that. I hardened my heart and carried on as I'd planned.

"When you killed him, how long had you known Harry was your father?" I asked.

"You're the one they arrested," she said, leaning back and smiling.

"I know I didn't kill him," I pointed out. "So, you see, I had a very strong motive to work out who did. Especially when one piece of evidence after another pointed directly at me."

She smiled again. Had her smiles really never reached her eyes? Looking back, I thought they probably never had. It had only ever been my hope I'd seen reflected there.

'I would have shared it all with you," I said. "When I could. You know I would. I don't need all that money."

"It should have all been mine," she said. "Don't you see that? I spent all that time crawling to my mother – I'm not spending another day beholden to my daughter."

"What about the boutique, and the flat?" I asked. "Don't pretend you're penniless. Grandma left you well provided for."

"You think you know everything, don't you?" she sneered at me.

I kept my powder dry.

She stood up. "It would never have come to this. Why was Harry a trustee, and a director, and not me? He said I'd never get any more money if he had any say. That Grandma had warned him what I was like, but he hadn't believed her until he saw for himself. That was when I realised I had to get him out of the way."

"How did you find out he was your father, my grandfather?"

"He told me. He lost his temper. He said Grandma was sure, that he was her only lover. He hadn't wanted to believe it, and still didn't. He wouldn't have chosen to be my father."

"That hurt," I said. "Didn't it?"

I knew how much it must have hurt her, not to be wanted. I knew. In spite of everything, I felt a tug of pity for her.

She shrugged a denial but continued in full flow. "You're as bad as he was. He blocked the sale of the house, and now you're doing it again. You went to Mark Stockman behind my back, cutting me out."

She didn't seem to see the irony in that accusation.

"I need a drink," she said.

"There's tea or coffee. Or your favourite whisky. Unless you drank it all, on one of your clandestine visits."

"You worked that out then. Took you long enough."

She stood up and gestured me towards the library. I shrugged. On the way out of the kitchen I turned off the light, hoping that Daniel was paying attention. Perhaps he would get through to DI Collingwood, if the tag had stopped working.

I opened the library door, turned off the alarm, and sat down on my favourite chair, in the corner, watching her. I was pretending to be calm and relaxed, but on the inside I was shaking. This is how it feels to be frightened for your life, I thought.

She went over to the drinks cupboard, got out a bottle of whisky and two glasses, and put them on the coffee table in front of me. She reached into her handbag and produced a bottle of pills and placed them next to the glass.

"Enough talk. Time to get on with it."

"It's easier to swallow pills with water than with whisky," I said. "Didn't you learn anything from your own suicide attempt? You couldn't even do that properly."

It was like poking a tiger with a sharp stick. Or perhaps more like climbing into the big cats' enclosure at the zoo. Perhaps I was crazy, after all.

"Did you kill the cat?" I asked, suddenly wondering if I'd been wrong. I knew she was capable of fraud, but was she really capable of killing?

"Naturally, it was my idea. I had to persuade the boy to co-operate. He's a more agreeable child than you ever were."

"Daniel? You made him kill his own cat?" I didn't believe her. I'd seen Daniel with the kitten. Even now she was lying. She couldn't help herself.

"Taking off with it and burying it on the farm – that was all him. I was livid – until I realised it was even more effective. Poor, mad Alice."

She went over to Grandma's escritoire and pulled the leaf down. She pulled out a sheet of paper and a pen.

"Here you go," she said. "Start writing."

"What do you want me to say?"

"You know the kind of thing. You can't face a future in hospital or prison. You're sorry you snapped and murdered your grandfather. Blah, blah, blah."

She opened the whiskey, poured me a glass full, poured the tablets out on to the table, and reached into her handbag. She extracted a small gun with a silver inscribed grip. A lady's weapon. Grandma's Tiffany revolver, in fact.

"Write and then drink," she said. "Or I shoot."

I laughed. "Shoot then," I said. "They're good at forensics. They'll be able to reconstruct exactly what you've done."

"Just as well you have a history of arson, then, isn't it?" she said. "Don't think I haven't come prepared."

"I had the smoke detector fixed. That was you, wasn't it?"

"You win some, you lose some," she shrugged. "Now start drinking – there's mummy's good little girl."

"You drugged me too, didn't you? The night of the bonfire." Perhaps she was right. I was slow.

She laughed. "Only just worked it out? It was much easier. You ate and drank whatever I put in front of you. It would have been so much less trouble if I'd finished the job properly then, but I was too soft-hearted."

"You lit the bonfire," I said. "No wonder I couldn't remember any of it."

"That's your illness talking, sweetie," she said.

That last flicker of pity for her disappeared.

"Well hello, DI Collingwood," I said. "You took your time."

"You think I'm going to fall for that one?"

"It was worth a try," I said. "But it's not impossible, is it?"

I pulled my jeans leg up, showed her my tag.

"They could be here at any minute. Do you really expect to get away with this?"

"Why not?" she shrugged. "I have before. More than once. And he's easily charmed, Collingwood. I worked my magic on him. I can always tell."

I'd been working mine too. I wasn't quite so sure of myself as she was, but I hoped...

I looked at the gun and wondered if she would really shoot me. My own mother. And they all thought I was the one who was crazy.

Why did they think that? Mostly because of what she'd said. After Grandma died, she'd been here. Pushing all my buttons. She even made me believe I'd started that bonfire. I could hardly blame everyone else for believing it too. Although I had been drugged. And she'd spent years conditioning me and learning which of my buttons to press. What was their excuse?

"Was it all about the money?" I had to know. "Because the joke really is on you. Take a look at Grandma's silver cabinet." This was the way to hurt her, to get under her skin, to push her over the edge.

"That old junk," she scoffed. But she looked, all the same. "It's empty."

"Yup," I said. "It's in the conservator's room, at the British Museum. The skyphos—" she looked blank, she'd always brushed it aside, dry and dusty history. "The Roman drinking vessel – it's real. It's worth a cool million. A very conservative valuation. The silver platters, the spoons, the whole collection. Well, really, it's priceless."

"Don't be ridiculous. It's all fake."

"No," I said. "The replica skyphos is in America. Grandma found a hoard of Roman silver. She didn't hand it over to the coroner as a treasure trove. She sold it, on the black market. Mark Stockman's father helped her. That's how she built the business."

"You're lying," she said. Her hand was shaking slightly, the hand holding the gun. Time to press the point.

"Mr Stockman couldn't resist it," I said. "She offered the High Priest of the Cuckmere Coven authentic Roman silver ritual ware. He would do anything for her. He made her High Priestess. Wicca was such a middle-class game in those days, and yet a working-class young woman, a nanny no less, became High Priestess of the most important coven in the South Downs."

"You're as addled as I said you were," she said. "I convinced them you were part of it all, but I never really knew you were."

"You had access to a small fortune, and you overlooked it. Who's the stupid one, really? Who's the loser?"

"I found her poppet, you know," Helen said. "The night I set the bonfire alight. Grandma thought she could hex me, that she could control me with magic. I burned it. It's gone, and since then all my plans have worked out fine."

Where was DI Collingwood?

I steadied myself, holding on to the chair, and kept on talking. Now I'd started, I couldn't stop. It held the fear at bay, a little. She wouldn't really shoot me, would she?

"How much time did you spend ransacking the house while I was in hospital? You sold off all Grandma's vintage clothes. The reproduction jewellery. Everything that wasn't locked away. You'd have sold the house, if Harry hadn't stopped you."

She took a swig of the whisky from the bottle.

"You did sell the boutique and the flat. Mrs Papasavas says hello, by the way."

"You are such a fantasist," she said, her voice wavering a little.

"Harry found out, didn't he? He knew about the fraud. It wasn't only that he stopped you selling the house, was it?"

I knew I was provoking her beyond endurance, but somehow now I'd started, I couldn't stop. I'd been holding it all in for too long.

"Sit down. Start writing your confession." She pointed the gun at me, then swung, and shot at the empty cabinet. The glass shattered. "Harry was a fool," she said. "He gave me a chance. A week to start putting things right, or he'd turn me over to the authorities. As if I would be prepared to go to jail over a technical detail. It was mine to sell, morally if not legally."

"Like this house should have been yours, right?"

"It had worked once, why couldn't it work again? It would have done, if it wasn't for that nosey old man, and that blabbermouth Stockman."

"It would have been found out eventually," I said. "Next April at the latest, when the accounts were done."

"I'd have been well away from here by then," she said. "I wasn't planning on wasting my life in a prison cell."

"But you were happy enough to have me sent back to hospital."

"I was, but you forced my hand," she said. "There was a struggle, officer. My daughter had the gun, it was my mother's you know, the child must have found it. She pointed it at her temple, she wanted to kill herself. Anything rather than hospital or prison. I tried to wrestle it from her—" all in some mock theatrical voice.

DI Collingwood walked into the room.

At last.

I breathed a sigh of relief.

"Put the gun down, Ms Hunter," he said.

She pointed it at him, and then at me, wildly swinging her outstretched arm. As she dithered, I threw myself on to the floor behind the armchair wondering exactly how bulletproof it might be, and she laughed.

I said the words I'd been rehearsing in my head for the last twenty-four hours. She was standing on the rug which lay directly over Grandma's pentagram which was painted on the floor beneath. In my mind's eye I saw Grandma in her full regalia, athame gleaming above her head. I saw her take a poppet dressed in green, one which resembled my mother, and wrap it in red cord. Yes, everything came together – the pattern was set.

"Whatever you do now, everyone will know you fucked up. Again." I said. "You'll spend the rest of your life in prison."

My carefully chosen words echoed the ones I'd heard Grandma wield against her daughter, and which my mother had in her turn used on me.

I paused, listening to her silence. One more twist of the knife.

"Grandma was right. You are a disappointment."

In my mind's eye I saw the poppet burn. My mother had put it on the bonfire herself – had used it against me as part of her plan to get me sectioned.

It was as if time stopped for a moment. Surely I should be feeling something? Fear, anger, despair? Instead, nothing. I was numb.

I was watching from a safe distance, as if through glass.

"You win again, Alice," my mother said. "I only wish your Grandma could have been here, to see me desecrate her precious library. Remember, you pulled the trigger."

There was no more wavering. She pointed the gun to her temple and blew her brains out.

FORTY-ONE

I STOOD UP, my knees wobbly. I moved towards my mother. DI Collingwood crossed the room and put an arm around me, and turned me away, so I couldn't see her. I wished I could cry, but my eyes were dry. I blinked.

"Why didn't you trust me, Alice?" he asked. "I was so relieved when Dr Lal showed up at the police station. I thought you'd be safe in hospital. When I heard the electronic signal had been blocked, I panicked."

"Why didn't you trust me?" I asked, angered by the injustice of his accusation.

"I couldn't compromise the investigation," he said. "It will all be someone else's responsibility now."

"Why?"

"Oh, nothing much," he said. "Tailing your mother without following regulations. Not waiting for back up. A few minor details."

"When did you get here?" I asked.

"I was a few minutes behind her," he said. "I heard it all. She's a piece of work, your mother."

"Was," I said. "She's dead. I shouldn't have pushed her like that."

"It wasn't your fault, Alice," he said, looking down at me, his grey eyes softening.

Wasn't it? I'd chosen my words carefully. I knew how my mother would react to them. It wasn't as if there was any need for hexing.

I could have sworn he landed a kiss on the top of my head, then he led me out of the room, past DC King, and into the kitchen. He sat me down at the kitchen table.

Looking down the hallway, I saw DC King opening the front door. A steady stream of uniformed police officers I didn't recognise came in.

"The back-up team are here, guv," DC King said, pointedly.

"Yes, DC King. I know I should have waited," DI Collingwood said. "In my professional judgement, Alice was in immediate danger. Best get the Scientific Support team here, quick as you can, please."

The next couple of hours rushed by as the house was filled with a horde of people all suited up and in paper shoes. I knew what it was for, but it felt strange, as if I was contaminated. Perhaps I did need to go back to Brookfields after all.

My hands were swabbed for gunshot residue, and then the same was done to DI Collingwood. He looked uncomfortable. Not easy to be on the other side, with the suspects. I wondered if breaking the rules, walking into an armed hostage scenario without backup, would harm his career.

I said something about it. His smile was a little crooked. "Do you think they can find some place worse than Cuckmere to send me?"

"The only place worse would be Brookfields," I said.

"For what it's worth, I never thought you were crazy," Collingwood said. "At first I thought you might have killed Mr Rook, but I didn't think you were crazy."

Inexplicably, that cheered me immensely. I managed a small smile and said, "Perhaps you could have a word with Dr Lal and my case worker," I said. "A testimonial like that might help."

"About Daniel," he said. "I'd have the DNA test done if I were you. To have one secret blood relative is unusual enough…"

I managed half a laugh. "I could believe anything of my mother, right now. A secret child. Lying about having a secret child. Trying to kill me. Maybe she did kill Grandma. Daniel's father, too."

He started to say something about me being in shock, but DC King came and whispered something to him.

"Gotta go," he said, placing his hand on my arm for a moment. "Hang in there, it won't be long now. You'll probably be questioned by one of my colleagues, but it should all be plain sailing now."

He was right. It wasn't long. A uniformed policeman brought a paramedic into the kitchen, who looked me over and asked me a few questions.

I told him I was fine and played down how jittery I was feeling. I hadn't had my meds in days, and for the first time I wondered if that was wise. I'd been so sure Grandma had been present in the library. I didn't want to end up in any hospital, if I could help it. I did want the questioning over and done with.

DC King came back and asked me if I was ready to be interviewed. When I said yes, she said, "Best get you down to the station. It will be a lot quieter there."

I asked if I could put away my Grandma's jewellery box, back upstairs in the safe, and she said, "It will be fine where it is, really," as if I was fretting about the trivia of tidying up. Which was true, I suppose.

But she didn't object when I asked if I could take Grandma's letter with me, from the kitchen drawer. I wanted to read the rest of it as soon as possible — but I let her think it was the equivalent of a security blanket. She glanced over it, decided it was nothing much, and let me put it back into the book. I slipped them into my bag.

As she drove me the few hundred yards down the road, I asked her where Tamsin and Kelly were. I'd worry about Daniel later. He'd coped for months on his own, after all. She promised to find out for me.

"DI Collingwood put his career on the line for you," she said. "Not easy, considering…" Her voice trailed off, as if she realised she'd said too much.

"Considering what?" I said. "Come on, you can't leave it at that."

"I suppose you ought to know. Don't let on it was me told you."

I promised.

"Before he transferred to Cuckmere, he was on a murder team in Crawley. A member of the team had a sexual relationship with a female suspect, which compromised the investigation."

She saw my shocked expression.

"No, it wasn't Jon," she said, slipping up and using his first name. "But the team all knew. They all ended up in the shit. He couldn't tell you that we were investigating your mother. She, well, she tried everything to get him on side."

I could imagine.

She pulled up and parked outside the police station.

"So if you thought he was too hard on you…" she continued.

"I didn't, really," I lied, cogs whirring. "Why are you telling me all this?"

She turned to face me and grinned. "I think you know," she said.

I blushed.

She showed me into the same interview room, but this time I was allowed to keep my possessions.

After a few minutes DC King came and replaced the young constable who'd been left to keep an eye on me and sat down at the table.

"DCI James will be along in a few minutes," she said. "DI Collingwood has been sent home on leave. It's a good sign they finished interviewing him so quickly. He'll be interviewed again by Internal Investigations, but he's sure to be back at work soon."

"Did you find out about my friends?"

"Tamsin is in the lobby waiting for you, but I'm afraid Kelly has already gone back to Brookfields. There's a boy there too, Daniel? He was worried about you and wanted to know what was happening. He's waiting on the arrival of a social worker, to find him a temporary placement. Did you know he's only fourteen?"

"I only spoke to him for the first time today," I said.

I didn't muddy the waters by saying he might be my secret half-brother. There was plenty of time for that after a DNA test had proved it one way or the other. I still couldn't help wondering about his father's suicide, though. Not that there was any point in raising it officially. I really didn't want them suspecting me of being paranoid again, and Collingwood's reaction had made it clear that was likely. DCI James arrived at that point, along with Suhad, who had only just arrived back from London.

"Are you sure you don't need some time alone with me first?" she asked, glaring at DCI James and DC King, as though they had bullied me into agreeing to be questioned.

"No," I said, "Let's get it over with, shall we? It's been a long day."

DCI James, a tall and elegant man with short-cropped grey hair, smiled reassuringly.

"If it makes you feel better, Ms Khalifeh, I would like to start the interview by releasing Ms Hunter from police bail. She is no longer a suspect in the death of Mr Harry Rook. She is not a suspect in the death of Ms Helen Hunter, merely a witness."

Suhad sat down and relaxed. "On the record?" she asked.

"Certainly."

Painstakingly we went through what had happened at Grandma's house. The most difficult question was at the beginning.

"Why did you go to the house, Ms Hunter? You know you were supposed to keep away from the place, as a condition of your police bail."

"My mother and my case worker, Claire, were at the farm," I said. "My mother had convinced Claire I was in the middle of a breakdown, and that she suspected I'd killed Harry. It was for my own safety, they said. I didn't want to go back to hospital. I needed somewhere to go."

I didn't say that I specifically needed somewhere my mother would find me.

"I see," he said. "So you all went straight from the farm to your Grandma's house."

I paused for thought. Would Daniel and Kelly have mentioned our breaking into the portacabin?

"We took the bus from the end of the lane," I said. "Then we walked across Beacon Hill, and we got into the house through the back door."

"What happened next?"

"Tamsin was there, waiting for me. She knew I was on the run. She'd heard from my mother, who was looking for me."

"So it was luck Tamsin Rook was there?" he asked, sounding suspicious.

"It was my home," I said. "Where else would I go?"

"Pretty much anywhere else would have been more sensible," DC King said.

We all looked at her.

"Sorry," she mumbled. "Just—"

"No, you're right," I said. "I wasn't thinking straight."

DCI James flicked through his folder and scanned a couple of sheets.

"What did Tamsin Rook tell you?" he asked.

"She explained that she knew we were cousins, because my mother had asked her for help with the DNA analysis. Harry was her great uncle. A couple of weeks before Harry's murder, soon after I was released from hospital. She took his toothbrush, she said."

Poor Tammy. She must feel responsible for Harry's death. No wonder she'd been so angry with me.

"Can you explain your suspicions?"

"I knew I hadn't killed Harry," I said. I'd had my doubts, but it wouldn't help to mention that now. "But at first I had no idea who had. When DI Collingwood questioned me earlier, he told me about the computer searches. How they'd revealed someone had used my laptop to research methods of murdering someone with nicotine. My mother is a smoker, and she's been trying to give up. I knew she'd been trying out vaping. My mother had access to the house – she'd been living there when I was in hospital. She still had a key."

"As your trustee, Harry Rook prevented her from selling the house while you were in hospital?" he asked.

I nodded. "He discovered she'd committed a previous fraud too, in selling the flat in London and the boutique. They weren't hers to sell. They belonged to the Trust."

"That all ties in with the evidence DI Collingwood and his team had gathered," DCI James said. "Knowing all this, why did you call her? Why didn't you wait for the investigation to conclude?"

Because I wanted it over, once and for all?

This was not a time for the truth, the whole truth. This was a time to lie.

"I wasn't thinking straight. I thought if I gave her some of Grandma's valuables, she'd take them and leave me alone. Everyone seemed to believe my mother. The psychiatrist, the police. Last time I ended up in hospital. This time…"

"You took a terrible risk, Ms Hunter. Did you know she had possession of the firearm? Your grandmother's, I believe."

I shook my head. Well, I might have guessed, but I didn't know. It could have gone the way of the Balenciaga coat, and been sold on, after all.

"No doubt we will need to go over it again, but for now let's go through what happened when your mother arrived at the house tonight. While it's still fresh in your memory."

I ran through it all, as it had happened.

He brought up one other outstanding issue. "Could you tell us a bit more about the Roman silver? Everything seems to point to the house being the motive for the murder, but you were remiss not to tell us about the silver."

Suhad spoke up in my defence.

"It's all being handled by the specialist Arts police," she said. "Ms Hunter only discovered the artefacts were real this week. Straight away she came to us, and we arranged through Professor Buckley to have them taken to the British Museum. The proper legal procedures are all in hand. That's where I was today."

"This is a murder investigation, and as such takes priority. It might have been relevant, and we should have been informed," he said.

Suhad blushed. "You are quite correct. The possibility of a connection was overlooked."

I spoke up. "It was my fault," I said. "I still don't understand what it's all about, but I was concerned for Grandma's reputation. I thought it wasn't related…" I paused.

"Although it might be," I added. "Mark Stockman wanted to buy Grandma's house. He bought Harry's property, too, and he's been digging there, I think."

Should I tell about the portacabin? No – let them find it themselves.

"Daniel and Kelly saw him up by the farm with a metal detector, and he offered to buy the farm too."

"So your mother didn't know about the silver, but you think Mark Stockman did? Member of Parliament Mark Stockman?"

I could see the doubts flitting across his face.

"Ask Professor Buckley," I said, my voice steady. "There's a photo of Grandma with Mark Stockman's grandfather in an American museum with a silver skyphos. The Professor is busy tracking down the location of the replica Grandma had made."

"So you think your mother may not have been acting alone?"

"I don't think my mother would have known how to snare a rabbit. Mark Stockman hunts, I believe."

He wrote a few notes, then looked up and nodded at DC King, who dealt with the recording equipment.

"That will be all, for now. Thank you for your help, Ms Hunter. We will be in touch, should we need to ask more questions."

"Thank you," I said, and stood up.

I wobbled alarmingly, my knees almost giving out. Suhad grabbed me and stopped me from falling.

"I'm okay," I said quickly, "Only tired."

The custody sergeant completed the paperwork to release me from bail, and returned all my possessions, as Suhad chivvied him to hurry up.

She walked me to the lobby. Tamsin was still waiting for me, and next to her, Julia.

Suhad said, "Can I take you somewhere? Mrs B's perhaps?"

Julia stood up. "No," she said. "She's coming home with us. It's what Harry would have wanted."

She patted me on the shoulder, and I managed a nod of acceptance. I couldn't face being alone, and who else did I have? Tammy was less restrained, and hugged me, which almost, almost set me off, but I couldn't cry yet. Not until I was alone, in Julia's guest room, at the back of the house, and with a view over the river to the sea and the white cliffs beyond.

FORTY-TWO

THE FOLLOWING DAY, I really didn't want to face the world. Waking up in Julia's guest bedroom was surreal. I wasn't sure how I was going to gather the courage to get up and go down and face her. My mother had, after all, killed Harry. She'd then planned to kill me. In my mind the image replayed again, of the moment she pulled the trigger. And the words I'd said the moment before.

There was a knock on the door.

"Come in," I said.

Julia brought in a tray with orange juice, and two boiled eggs with toast soldiers.

"I feel like an invalid. Well and truly spoiled."

"You must be exhausted," she said. "You don't have to do anything but laze around all day, if that's what you want. There's plenty of time to sort everything else out."

"I didn't say thank you properly, last night," I said. "It really is kind of you, after everything."

"You don't have to say thank you," she said. "I was glad to do something, after I heard what happened, and Tamsin told me... It's time to let the past go, don't you think?"

"I do," I said. "For what it's worth, I'm sure Grandma was full of regrets in the end. She just didn't know how to mend things, and she wanted me to do it."

"That was what Harry told me, and I wouldn't listen. He was starting to love you, I know, and he said one day I would too. Maybe that's not quite the impossibility I thought."

I smiled at her. "I wondered about selling the house," I said. "I've enjoyed living at the farm. I thought it might be a fresh start. And after mother.... I don't know. I still feel that Grandma's there in a way. I don't want to leave."

Julia left me to my own devices.

After eating my breakfast, I got up, showered, and dressed, then settled in the window seat to read the rest of Grandma's letter, hoping to find the answers I needed.

I left most of it where it was, covered it up. I took the silver jar home with me. I felt terrible, still drunk, and very cold, and clutching on to my treasure for dear life. I had discovered something more important than the silver. Life was dear to me, even without love, and I knew now I wanted to live. The next few days I worried. There was some blood spotting, and I thought I was going to lose the baby. I hung on. I didn't dare go to the doctor, as I was unmarried, and didn't even have a boyfriend any more. I was worried about how I would manage, but I knew I wanted the baby too.

I never told you about my parents, and you never asked. I went to see them and told them what had happened and they disowned me. I was a sinner. A whore. I swore I would never be so cruel to my own child, and I tried so hard with Helen, but she was always impossible. Now I wonder if that was my fault too. Perhaps the gin – we didn't know much about it then, only that old wives' tale about a bottle of gin and a hot bath to get rid of a baby. But foetal alcohol syndrome exists; it could have been that. Or I read that prolonged exposure to stress hormones affects the child in the womb. I never wanted her and she knew it, perhaps even before she was born. I once asked my doctor, if perhaps it could have influenced how Helen turned out, but he brushed it off. He was embarrassed, or thought it was the ramblings of an old woman, or he didn't want to tell me the truth.

I tried to tell you when I was alive, Alice, but you didn't want to hear it. There was always something not quite right about Helen. I saw you growing up, and all the time you tried to reach out to her and didn't connect. That was never you, it was her. I tried when she was young, I really did. But I never did connect with her. And that was my fault more than hers.

So that's why I left everything so carefully tied up. Not because I didn't trust you, but to protect you. I know you will do the right thing. I didn't want to leave her destitute, but you mustn't let her have all her own way. Harry will look out for you. I want you to get to know your grandfather. I couldn't bear to leave you all alone, without family. Life's better when you aren't alone.

My eyes filled with tears. There was no holding them back any more. Grandma had spent most of her life never sharing the burden with anyone until right at the end. If only she had trusted me.

It wasn't her way.

No matter what, I would take responsibility for Daniel. If he was my half-brother, then he was family. If he wasn't, then he had no family, so we would have that in common.

The rest of the letter was about the silver. Reading about the Mildenhall treasure had inspired her to keep it for herself. After confiding in Mark Stockman's grandfather, she had discovered a way to have her silver, and sell it. He'd helped her find a ready market amongst his American business contacts. She didn't understand the details, but they were willing to accept dodgy provenance and benefited from some kind of scam in tax avoidance by donating them to public museums. Grandma hadn't been able to bear the thought of the skyphos leaving the country, so she had commissioned the replicas for herself and for the use of the pagan group. When she'd realised Mr Rushton's work was good enough to fool the experts, she hadn't been able to resist temptation.

The skyphos though – we couldn't part with that. It belonged on the land, on the Cuckmere altar. My vision confirmed what the coven had long suspected. People have been worshipping the goddess on that spot for centuries.

We both shared in the profits, she wrote. *Mr Stockman took a generous commission, but he was fair to me. The goddess had chosen me, he said. I became High Priestess of the group, and the path of High Magic became my life. The Goddess had saved me, after all.*

Although I searched Beacon Hill high and low, I never found anything else. But my interest in history, in the past, grew ever deeper. I became certain there was evidence of Roman occupation over by the river, and that was why I bought the farm, even though it wasn't financially viable with a sitting tenant. Perhaps it's the site of a villa like Fishbourne. Who knows?

I'm sure you must have guessed by now that I planted the Roman coin for you to find in the garden. It was from my Cuckmere Hoard. I wanted you to have some sense of the excitement that I felt, having uncovered a hoard of Roman silver.

I have long regretted the disservice I did to archaeologists and historians. Please set the record straight, and make sure the artefacts find a good home. I'm sorry to leave you with such a difficult task. Harry will help you, I'm sure of that. Despite all that went wrong between us so long ago, he is a man who can be trusted. These last few months have proved that.

There's one last thing I need you to do for me, if you can. I'm sure that you know where my regalia is, and my book of shadows. There has been a witch on Beacon hill forever, and it is my duty to pass that on to a woman who willingly chooses that path for herself. Daughter of my daughter, I hope you may find your own blessings in the service of the Goddess. Love is the law, love under will. Do as you will.

Please don't think too badly of me. You were always the best part of my life,
All my love, Grandma.

At that the tears really did start to flow, and I lay on the bed, sobbing, until I was all cried out and fell asleep.

I woke to the sound of a gentle knock on the door.

"Come in," I said, rubbing my eyes and sitting up.

Julia.

"I'm sorry to disturb you," she said. "Only I thought you'd prefer to get this over. Your case worker is here, downstairs."

My panic must have shown.

"Don't worry, she has no intention of having you admitted to hospital. I told her there was no need for that, and that she would have to come back with reinforcements if that was what she wanted."

Julia was quite formidable. It was good to have her on my side.

In the living room, Claire was perched on the edge of the easy chair in front of the fire.

"Hello, Claire," I said, sitting down opposite her.

Julia said, "I'm in the kitchen, if I'm needed," and then closed the door on us.

"I don't know quite what to say," Claire started. "I am so sorry about your mother. How are you coping?"

"I'm okay, I suppose. I'm very tired."

"I'm sorry," she said, again. "DI Collingwood came to see me this morning. He also went to see Dr Lal."

"Oh?"

"He explained about your mother. I'm afraid she had us all fooled. I really believed her – that she was worried about you."

"She had me fooled for most of my life," I said.

"We're supposed to be professionals."

I remembered the story Dr Lal had told me about the Rosenhan experiment, *On Being Sane in Insane Places*. The psychologist had recruited volunteers who had checked themselves into mental hospitals across America. Getting released had proved more difficult, however. The doctors had interpreted every activity as a symptom, every protestation of sanity too.

"There's no question of persuading you to come back to Brookfields," Claire said. "Dr Lal and I are in agreement that the best outcome for all of us is if we continue with your care plan, as agreed when you were discharged."

I thought about fighting it for a moment, insisting that I didn't need mental health support, but common sense won.

"I'll see you next week then," I said. "Same time, same place."

"Thank you," she said, as if I was doing her a favour. "But any time you think you need any extra help, you call, right? No need to worry it will be used against you. We're on your side, remember."

I felt a surge of rage but pushed it back down. Except when you were on my mother's. I nodded, not trusting myself with words.

She stood up and moved to hug me, but I simply couldn't. I stepped back, and shook her hand instead, for the sake of politeness, then showed her out.

I found Julia and Tamsin in the kitchen.

As we sat at the table drinking coffee, we watched the television news. They checked with me first, as if I might be too fragile to watch TV. I appreciated their kindness, but I wanted to know what was happening.

The reporter was standing outside Grandma's house, talking about the death of an as yet unnamed woman, and how the incident was presumed to be connected with the murder of Harry Rook.

Next up came footage of Mark Stockman being led into the police station. I didn't recognise the senior detective, but DC King was there too.

The reporter spoke to camera. "Mr Stockman is being questioned about the incident at the house yesterday. We have as yet had no indication as to whether he has been arrested or not. DCI James has made a public statement that Ms Alice Hunter, who was arrested for the murder of Harry Rook and then released on police bail, is no longer a suspect in the case."

"I unplugged the phone," Julia said, "and there's a policeman standing by the front gate keeping the hordes at bay. I suppose they'll get bored, eventually."

FORTY-THREE

THE NEWS CYCLE moved on, and my life continued.

I went back to the farm after a couple of days, glad I'd established a better relationship with Julia and Tamsin, but desperate for some time on my own. Not that I got a great deal of that.

I continued to work part time for Mrs B, and all that physical labour worked better than meditation and breathing exercises to keep my feet on the ground and to stop my mind from going round in circles.

I went to my regular meetings with Claire, although I no longer felt they were necessary. Once there's no one trying to set you up for murder or trying to kill you, it's amazing how paranoia starts to disappear and panic fade. I wasn't taking my meds any more – not that I told Claire, who believed I was still on the full dose. But I hadn't filled the gap with alcohol, once I realised it wasn't necessary. Not that I'd gone teetotal or anything.

DI Collingwood had taken to dropping in on me from time to time to see how I was doing. I'd assumed at first it was part of his job, but eventually he confessed he came because he wanted to. "Call me Jon," he said.

I didn't drop DC King in it, though I longed to ask him to tell me more of the story about that previous case. He was at a bit of a loose end while he was on gardening leave, but he was being kept in the loop on the investigation.

My mother's schemes were gradually unravelling. Mobile phone evidence had placed her firmly in Cuckmere at the time of Harry's murder. She certainly wasn't on the train at Victoria that morning when she'd phoned me – more likely she was on the hill at the back of

Grandma's house. That extra piece of circumstantial evidence that convinced me, at least, that she was responsible for the rabbit.

They'd also tracked down all the details about the DNA testing. There was even more evidence that Helen had planned to frame me. She'd arranged for special delivery of the DNA results to the house at a time when she knew I'd be at my hospital appointment.

"If only we'd followed up on all those details sooner," he said, shaking his head.

He'd also confessed to knowing she'd been living in Mark Stockman's penthouse apartment at the Marina development. She'd made a big deal of asking the police not to mention it to me, because knowing she was nearby would trigger my paranoia. Jon was apologetic. "She said she needed to keep an eye on you without your knowledge."

"Refreshingly honest of her,' I said.

He winced.

I visited Kelly, who was still in Brookfields. I confided in her my plans for Daniel, and she thought they made sense – although she added that I should check with someone who wasn't currently resident in a mental health unit to be on the safe side. "An actual sanity check," she said, and laughed. She was following all the rules, and complying with her treatment, which they thought was a good sign – and they even let her out for weekend leave a couple of times.

Still, from time to time I found myself hanging somewhere between rage and despair. I couldn't forgive my mother for what she'd done, and I couldn't forgive myself for what amounted to wilful blindness. How could I have conned myself over all that time? All because I wanted to believe that she loved me, when clearly she'd never been capable of loving anybody.

It wasn't only me she'd abandoned.

She'd found it all too easy to abandon Daniel too, until he was old enough to be useful. The DNA tests came back and confirmed what I had already known in my heart – he was my half-brother. I'd visited him at his foster parents' house and we'd talked and talked, but never could work out the whole story.

He still wanted to come home to the farm, and we'd begun to try to make that happen. I'd also started legal proceedings to get him included in the Trust. I didn't tell him, because I had no idea what the chances were, although Mr Harvey was quietly confident.

In any case, I didn't think it would necessarily help him to have dreams of future wealth. He had a lot of schooling to catch up with. More than once I heard Grandma's words coming out of my mouth when I was talking to him.

Our preliminary meeting with his social worker didn't go too well.

"Keeping family together is a priority," the woman said. "But although there's a blood relationship established, you didn't grow up together. You hardly know each other."

"I don't expect it to be automatic or immediate," I said. "But Daniel is fourteen. He's old enough to know his own mind. We'd welcome a plan that gave us a chance to establish a family life."

Daniel spoke up. "I hardly know Mr and Mrs Robertson, either."

She rustled through the pile of papers in front of her. "According to the report, you're settling in very well there. And at the local school. I can see no good reason to disrupt an arrangement that seems to be working."

I tried again. "Daniel's only been with the Robertsons for a couple of months – that's hardly time to settle in to a new life. What you're saying is the longer he stays there, the harder it will be for me to get permission to foster him."

Her lips pursed, and she was silent for a moment or two. "Ms Hunter, the chances of you ever being approved to foster Daniel are extremely slim. Your age counts against you – at twenty-two you have little experience that would qualify you to act in loco parentis to a teenage boy. Then there's your medical history to consider."

That shut me up.

Afterwards I reassured Daniel as best I could – even if we couldn't live together, we would still be brother and sister. And her decision was only temporary – the first stage in a long process. We would take it to the Family Court.

I MOVED BACK to the house. Mrs B's team had cleaned up Grandma's library and once the physical cleansing was done, I performed the spiritual cleansing.

Professor Buckley used his influence to get official permission from the local council for an exploratory survey of the Nature Reserve.

More or less everyone showed up on the day.

Kelly and I were there first, soon followed by the archaeology course contingent. Suhad was with Professor Buckley, who had his arm draped around her shoulder, so I guessed the medic boyfriend was now an ex. I knew they'd been spending time together sorting out the legal ramifications of the hoard discovery. The Professor was wearing his Indiana Jones hat, which made me smile. Adam and a couple of the other students were there too, with cameras and notebooks and electronic equipment.

Julia and Tammy turned up too, and then DI Collingwood. Jon.

The only one who was missing was Daniel. He wasn't answering his mobile, so in the end I reluctantly agreed we should start without him.

Perhaps it was best he hadn't shown up, as it wasn't very exciting. Just a walk, spoiled by constant photography and electronic readings of some kind.

"It's a pity Grandma didn't describe where she found the silver," I said, as we tramped all over the hill.

Professor Buckley laughed at me. "This is what it's like, Alice," he said. "It's not an exciting life."

"I think I've had enough of excitement," I said.

After we'd completed the initial survey, the students took the gear back to the University, and the rest of us trooped down to the Harbour View pub for a well-earned drink, and some food.

The Prof cleared his throat, and all the chatter stopped.

"I have some good news," he said. "First of all, the funding for a major excavation at the farm site has come through. We'll be starting work early next year."

We all cheered.

"Secondly, it turns out the museum in America has no interest in pursuing repossession of the original of the skyphos. They were approached formally by the Arts and Antiques squad, and after some delicate negotiations, it turned out that they were on very shaky ground. The original donor died many years ago, and his heirs were embarrassed at the prospect of publicity over his tax affairs. The solution is straight forward. The museum is announcing that they have agreed to our repatriation request, as the skyphos is an important part of the British-Romano heritage, and they will admit some formalities were skipped. In return they will be accepting our generous offer of an excellent quality replica for their collection. The fact that there doesn't actually need to be a physical exchange is a technicality."

I spontaneously hugged him – the feeling of relief overcame my usual shyness.

"Thank you," I said. "That's the most difficult part of the promise I made to Grandma sorted."

"Does anyone know what's happening with Mark Stockman?" Julia asked.

"He's withdrawn his offer to buy Grandma's house," I said. "I'm not entirely sure why. But as I wasn't planning to sell, it doesn't much matter."

Professor Buckley spoke. "I had a word with him. I explained about the hoard and how it had been declared treasure trove retrospectively. The coroner was happy with the solution we came up with – that the, ahem, irregularities of the past would be forgotten and the artefacts donated to the British Museum. Any new finds would naturally belong with the originals. I also told him that hoards were often buried away from settlements, because the point was to keep them safe and where they could be retrieved. Once Stockman realised that it was unlikely in the extreme that there was any more treasure on Beacon Hill and that the value of the farm site was purely historical, he lost interest."

"Clever," I said. "It was all about the money, then." It hadn't entirely escaped my notice that Stockman was only interested in appearing pleasant when I had something he wanted.

"I didn't mention the possibility that the hoard had been uncovered on the Beacon. On a site like this, so close to a river, and on the top of a hill. They could well have been ritual offerings. It may be worth exploring a larger area."

Archaeology backing up what the Cuckmere Coven had always known. How satisfying.

"Is Stockman in the clear then?" I asked.

DI Collingwood, Jon as I still occasionally forgot to call him, spoke then. "We couldn't find anything that linked him to the rabbit or the crime scene. Mr Stockman's involvement is all circumstantial. DC King told me they passed the files on to the CPS, but we don't expect them to go ahead with a prosecution.'

"What about the cafe, and the amusement arcade? I thought he was planning some big development there?" Tamsin asked him.

"He was mostly interested in treasure, we think. We searched the portacabins on the site that day. There was a bag of coins, and a metal detector, and a few books. Nothing else. Except the padlock had been removed and put back in place very badly," he said, looking at me with an eyebrow raised.

I blushed and became intensely aware that everyone was looking at me.

While their attention was diverted, Jon smiled at me, making me blush even more.

Julia spoke up. "I'm afraid Stockman's development plans won't be going ahead. He thought he had the council all sewn up for change of use so that private dwellings could be built on a commercial site, but I still have a little influence, and I used it. The land's on the market again. Knock down price, as it's a protected site."

Everyone was tired, and soon they started to leave. First Julia and Tamsin, then Kelly made her apologies as she had to get back to Brookfields. In the end, there was only me and Jon, still sipping our drinks.

"I'm back at work Monday," he said. "I've been cleared on all charges of unprofessional conduct. And I'm still a DI."

"That is good news," I said. Then added, teasing, "You'll be glad to get back to arresting innocent citizens then."

He bristled a little, "I do my job, and I do it well."

But he knew I was teasing and laughed a little too.

"What about you?" he asked. "Are you off to Oxford next year?"

"I don't think so," I said. "Now the dig at the farm is going ahead, I'd rather be around for that. I've applied to go full time on Professor Buckley's course."

"So long as it's what's best for you," he said. "But I am pleased. I would have missed you."

I blushed again and pretended I hadn't heard him.

"I know you won't like this," he said, "but I have to ask. You've not talked to your case worker about your mother's suicide, have you?"

"I don't need to talk to anyone," I said. "It's over."

He looked at me and shook his head.

"It's never over, not something like that. Look, it wasn't my first time witnessing a suicide, but I went to counselling. They wouldn't let me back on the job if I hadn't."

"I've had enough counselling to last me a lifetime."

"I understand," he said. "Really, I do."

"I don't think I can take any more, Jon," I said. "I want to forget it."

He promised to drop the subject if I agreed to let him drive me home.

"If we can check the farm out first," I said. I had an uneasy feeling Daniel might be there, even if he didn't turn up for the dig.

"When are you going to learn to drive?" he asked.

"Soon," I said. I didn't tell him I needed to complete my withdrawal from my medication first. I was further along that path that anyone knew, officially, but I wasn't in any rush now. "Are you offering to teach me?"

"I'm not crazy," he said, and I laughed. I was really beginning to like him.

The farm back door was on the latch. It swung open at my touch. I stepped inside.

"Daniel, is that you?" I called.

There was no answer, and the house felt empty.

Jon put his hand on my arm.

"Oh damn it, Alice, I am so sorry," he said.

What had he seen?

On the kitchen table. The kitten. She would never become a fully-grown cat. There was a plastic bag containing a couple of syringes lying next to her, and next to that, a small bottle with a white plastic cap, labelled Nicotine Concentrate with a warning. The evidence must have been in the barn all this time At least he hadn't attempted to stake her to the kitchen table.

It must have been Daniel, all along. All those tortured animals.

There was a postcard next to the kitten. Another sketch of me, this time with Daniel by my side.

Jon pulled a glove out of his pocket and picked up the card. Turned it over.

On the other side, a scrawled note.

'Sorry, sis,' it said. *'I can't take any more of the Robertsons. I'm sorry about Harry. I shouldn't have held him down for her, and I didn't know how to tell you. Her fingerprints might be on the syringe. Mine too, I guess. She said the police would*

believe it was all my idea, so I kept the evidence. In case. She said it was all your fault there was no money for dad, or for her. I guess I'm a dumb kid like she said. I couldn't leave Princess to manage without me. Daniel.'

"He must have been helping her from the start," I said. "How could I be so stupid? As if Helen would get herself messy with dead rabbits and digging graves for cats."

Helen had played him, I thought, sadly. She was charming when she wanted to be, and she'd made him feel special.

Jon had his phone out.

"What are you doing?" I asked.

"I have to call it in, Alice," he said. "He's fourteen. The sooner it's reported, the better a chance of finding him and bringing him home."

"He hasn't got a home. That's the problem," I said. "Please, don't. Harry's dead. Nothing's going to bring him back."

"Alice, think of the risk he poses. To himself, too."

The look on his face was devastating. I couldn't bear to have him so disappointed with me. In my heart, I knew he was right.

"Do it," I said. "Call them."

While he made the call, I turned away, so he didn't see my tears, but he could sense my mood, that I was full of doubt and remorse. Very gently he touched me on the arm and turned me round. He wiped away my tears.

"There'll be a team here to search the farm soon," he said. "He helped Helen murder your grandfather. He killed the kitten, Alice. You know animal cruelty is a serious issue. Perhaps—"

He paused, but I knew what he was thinking. It was the first thing I'd thought of. Perhaps Daniel was like my mother. They'd made a good team, it seemed. Too good.

And I was responding like my Grandma, whose first instinct had been to cover up and protect.

"You're right," I said. "The truth matters."

I'd lost touch with that lately. I'd had to, in order to survive.

I sat down and waited. Jon went out to his car to fetch evidence bags. I watched as he bagged up the postcard and the kitten and wrote on the labels.

I could hear the sound of another car pulling up into the farm yard. The police had arrived. Jon went out to meet them and pointed them at the barn.

An hour later, they'd taken statements from us both and collected the evidence. There'd been no sign of Daniel in the barn or anywhere on the farm. I wasn't surprised. He wasn't a stupid boy.

Then Jon drove me back to The Witch House and he and I were alone together.

I made coffee and took it into the living room.

We sat opposite each other, the tray on the coffee table between us. Apparently he'd forgotten his promise to leave it alone.

"Why haven't you talked to anyone?" he said. "You could have talked to Claire, or Dr Lal, surely."

Maybe he was right. Maybe I needed to let it out.

"I suppose it's fear," I said. "That something I let slip will prove that I'm still disturbed. That something will prove I'm my mother's daughter. There must be something wrong with me, after all. My family – it doesn't look good, does it?"

"Don't talk to them," he said. "Find a private therapist. You have to let it out for the healing to begin."

I didn't say anything.

"You can talk to me," he said, after too long a silence.

"Thinking of moving into social work, Jon?" I teased. But I started to talk. I told him how Julia had named the house, and all that led up to it.

"I thought I'd come to terms with the fact that my mother didn't care enough to bring me up herself. That I'd been an inconvenience she'd shrugged off the moment she could. But underneath, I still hoped. I still kept making excuses for her, trying to understand, trying to put things right between us. I turned a blind eye to all the selfish things she did – to the point where it could have cost my life. Grandma was right – that was why she left everything tied up the way she did. She knew I couldn't be trusted."

"Oh Alice," he said. "I found it hard to believe what your mother was like, the things she did, and I came to it as a detective with years of experience of seeing the worst people can do to each other. There was no excuse for her behaviour – she wasn't overwhelmed by poverty, there's no suggestion she had an especially difficult childhood. She made those choices of her own free will."

I still felt guilty. No one had known Helen better than I had, after all. Even while I carefully kept my eyes averted. I knew she was full of self-hatred. I knew she was essentially self-destructive. I was probably the only person alive who knew about her suicide attempt.

"Grandma wondered if she'd been damaged in the womb – the stress hormones from an unwanted pregnancy, then the excess of gin. Or if it was some genetic flaw. I suppose I can't help wondering if there's something wrong with me. Nature and nurture. Genes and environment. Maybe I'm like them. I push people away, I know I do. Usually with a smart quip – anything to avoid real connection. Because I'm afraid that I don't know how to love anyone properly. It's not something I learned."

"I can think of a long list of people who would dispute that," he said.

I thought of Daniel. How he had turned out to be so like Helen. I wondered about myself too. I couldn't tell Jon how deep that fear ran. I didn't want to risk that look in his eyes changing, as he realised I was exactly like them. If there's one thing you learn when you grow up with a manipulator, it's how to manipulate. Helen wasn't the only one responsible for pulling that trigger.

He reached out and put his hand on mine. I didn't pull away. The world is full of people who can only love people who love them back. Then there are those like me, who find it easier to love those who don't.

Gently, I lifted his hand off mine and I stood. He flinched. He was expecting me to walk away – I could read it in his eyes. He shrugged and stood up, ready to say goodbye and leave.

Instead, I moved towards him, and reached up a hand to his cheek.

"You turned out okay," he said. "For a girl who grew up in The Witch House. You escaped the family curse."

Wilful blindness isn't rare. All I wanted was to be known and loved anyway. Looked like it was one, or the other.

FORTY-FOUR

WHEN GRANDMA WAS alive, there were never any trick-or-treaters on 31st October at The Witch House. Somehow, I didn't think the events of the past couple of years would have eased their superstitious fear of tricking or treating an actual witch, but I had a large bowl of chocolate treats at the ready, in case.

I sat at the kitchen table with the basket I'd collected when I was shopping for treats. I'd been touched when the florist had said she'd included Grandma's favourite anemones, the first of the season. I put together a floral chaplet as I'd seen Grandma do, so many times. In between the foliage, I placed the flowers, red, blue, white. The anemone was specifically a protection from evil, I remembered her saying. I sensed there was something missing, and went out into the garden and saw the pink wild roses, still flowering in the shelter of the wall. I cut a single perfect bloom and added it to the chaplet.

No one came to the door while I was working.

I prepared the ritual equipment and packed my rucksack carefully and dressed in the long white robes for the first time, and hitched them up with a red cord belt, so I wouldn't trip. Over that I wore Grandma's black velvet hooded cape, embroidered with silver twigs and branches around the hem, and silver stars embellished with seed pearls on the hood.

At ten-thirty, I carefully placed the flowers on my head, and gently pulled the hood over. I ventured out of the back door. There had been several fireworks go off earlier in anticipation of Bonfire Night, but now all was quiet. I unlocked the padlock on the back gate and it swung open silently – I'd had the forethought to oil it a few days earlier.

It wasn't as dark as I'd anticipated, with the street lights along the river, and every so often the moon escaped the shrouding clouds, lighting up the Beacon, but mostly it was quiet and dark.

I knew the path well and walked up sure-footed, although I had my phone torch at the ready in one hand. I was prepared in other ways too.

The clearing was empty. I'd been afraid there'd be a dead rabbit or worse defiling the altar, or that there'd be kids messing about with some satanic nonsense, or, worse, a revival of the Cuckmere Coven with Mark Stockman as High Priest and his snooty receptionist as High Priestess.

I breathed a huge sigh of relief and unloaded my rucksack under a stunted apple tree.

I placed my candles on the altar and lit them, muttering blessings under my breath. I unzipped Grandma's leather case containing her ritual silver. In front of the candles, I laid out the silver goblet, and I poured wine into it from my water bottle. I put the silver pot of salt in place, and I took my athame out of my pocket and placed that on the altar too. Finally, the square wooden box with a lock.

I went back to my rucksack to collect the urn with Grandma's ashes, which I also set on the altar.

It was slightly before eleven thirty. Perfect timing.

I looked around once more, to check I was alone, then I picked up the salt and walked all around the clearing sprinkling as I went, creating a barrier with my mind to keep the world out.

At the Western point of the circle, facing the sea, I placed a candle and lit it, then did the same at the other three quarters, South and East and North.

Returning to the altar, I raised the athame over my head and spoke out loud.

My first sabbat. I had memorised the words from Grandma's Book of Shadows and adapted them to my purpose.

"Gabriel before me, Raphael behind me, Uriel on my right, Michael on my left. I call upon of the archangels, guardians of the watchtowers, to protect this circle, by water, by fire, by earth and by air. This is the night when the veil which separates the dead from the living is thin, permeable.

"I call upon my grandmother Frances. She was High Priestess in this sacred place until her passing this year. I honour her and invite her to join me as I take her place on this night and ask her to watch over me always.

"As my grandmother, your blood runs through my veins. As my High Priestess, your spirit guides my heart and soul. I carry you with me always as you live on in my memory."

I shivered, sensing a comforting presence behind me, and I knew, I knew that she was with me.

Sure now of her blessing, I unlocked the wooden box and took out the silver twig and leaf headdress and lifted it up on to my head.

For a moment I closed my eyes and visualised my Grandma anointing me, as she had wanted to do so many years before. Then I had refused. Now I was ready to do as she had wished.

"I, Alice Hunter, granddaughter of Frances Hunter, accept the duties and responsibilities of the High Priestess of Cuckmere. Here I stand and here I will serve the Goddess in all her phases for all the days of my life."

As if with a sigh, the presence was gone. I picked up the casket, and opened it, and I walked again around the circle, scattering my Grandma's ashes as I went, snuffing the candles at each quarter and banishing the Guardians.

Once the circle was closed, I returned to the altar and carefully packed everything away, only keeping my razor sharp athame to hand.

I placed the chaplet of flowers on the flat stone in memory of my grandmother, my High Priestess.

As I walked down the path between the trees, I heard something and started. A broken twig. There was someone there. As I had expected.

"Daniel?" I said, in a loud voice. I was drunk on the ceremony. I had no fear. I was still under the protection of the Goddess.

He stepped out of the trees on to the path.

"I know what you did," he said. "I thought Helen was wrong, but she was right all along."

"Were you watching?"

"I'm an initiate. I'm a member of the Cuckmere Coven. I too can pierce the veil. You left Helen outside the circle. Our mother. On the night of the ancestors."

"She tried to kill me, Daniel."

"Yet she's the one who's dead. You didn't call on her. You didn't even name her in your lineage."

"You're too young to be an initiate, no matter what Helen told you. What you did had nothing to do with the Goddess. It was cruelty and anger and sickness. She manipulated you."

"I'm not a kid. I knew what I was doing. I hoped we belonged together."

"You helped her kill Harry, didn't you? You know what she's like. You're afraid you're like her. Come back to the house, Daniel. We'll talk. Let's sort this out."

He looked at me with such depths of hatred in his eyes. I couldn't reach him. I'd never had a chance because she got to him first.

One last try. I was willing to plead with him.

"You're my brother."

"No. I'm not. This isn't over," he said, and disappeared into the night.

I walked back home, carefully locking the gate behind me.

There's always a witch in the Witch House and now it's me.

So mote it be.

ACKNOWLEDGEMENTS

Writing, they say, is a lonely business. Yet, there have been a great many people who have helped me in a variety of ways throughout the writing of The Witch House.

First, I'd like to thank my good friend Angie, who shared some of her experiences in the mental health system with me and gave me permission to transform them into fiction.

Suhad Khalifeh generously allowed me to use her name, as well as her love of bacon sandwiches and champagne. I hope she enjoys her imaginary dalliance with a charming TV archaeologist.

Thanks are due to all the people who read the novel drafts, sometimes several times over. Pity my husband Ryan, who suffered the most when it came to re-reading. Paul Walsh, Nicky Johnston, Pamela Lee, Riff Phoenix, Alastair McCapra, Babs Saul, Tone Hitchcock, Nicola Gaughan, and David Hickling also read and made useful suggestions.

Mark Bailey consulted on the murder method. William Vine, Elaine LaFrance and Lisa D'Amico provided me with advice on botany. Mistakes are all my own.

So many online friends have supported me in this mad adventure in writing, and have cheered me on when I've been stuck or when I've lost heart. Marion Barnett, Fran Martel and Graham Pugh deserve special mention for the precision of their virtual kicks up the arse.

I owe every single one of you more than I can say. And I can say a lot! Finally I'd like to thank everyone at Red Dog Press. Their professionalism is exceeded only by their enthusiastic support. From the design of the most gorgeous cover, through the sensitive editing which helped me make my novel even more itself, every step on the way has been a delight.

It's also been a joy to virtually meet the other authors in the Red Dog Kennel, and to find more brilliant books to add to my ever-increasing reading list.

ABOUT THE AUTHOR

Ann Rawson has long been addicted to story. As a child she longed to learn to read because she knew there was magic in those pages, the inky squiggles that turned into words and became images in her head – the stories that could transport her away from the everyday. As she grew older, she divined there was truth in books too. They were a glimpse into other minds. Her reading became the foundation of a deep and abiding interest in what makes people tick – and so she soon became hooked on crime fiction.

Age ten, she wrote to Malcolm Saville, author of the Lone Pine Series, enclosing her first short story. He wrote back and encouraged her to continue writing – and she is heartbroken that the letter is long lost. His book, Lone Pine Five, sparked a lifelong interest in archaeology, as it mentions the Mildenhall Treasure which makes an appearance in *The Witch House*.

A lapsed witch with enduring pagan tendencies, she lives on the south coast. She still thinks of herself as a Northerner, although she's been in exile for many years. Almost every day she walks on the Downs or the white cliffs with her husband, plotting her next novel while he designs computer systems.

Ann's debut novel, A Savage Art was published by Fahrenheit Press in 2016. She has published some short fiction, and in 2019 her memoir piece If… was shortlisted for the Fish Short Memoir Prize.

She is currently completing a memoir and working on her third novel.

You can follow her on Twitter @AE_Rawson (where she doesn't go far, to be honest), find her Facebook page at www.facebook.com/aerawson, and her blog is at www.strawintogold.co.uk

Lightning Source UK Ltd.
Milton Keynes UK
UKHW011027090820
367876UK00004B/38/J